So where the devil was Rockhurst?

Even as she was about to give up, a tall figure swept past.

Hermione's stomach turned with that all-too-familiar queasy tilt. The one that always overcame her every time the earl came into view.

She spun round to find the Earl of Rockhurst standing not ten feet from her. He'd paused in a doorway, and Hermione swore his gaze bore directly into her.

Of course that was foolish. He couldn't see her.

Not that he ever had before, she thought wryly.

Still, it was all she could do to breathe, for she'd never been able to just stare at him thusly.

His tawny hair, like burnished gold, was combed back. Her fingers curled into her palm, as she gazed at the strong line of his jaw. How she'd always wanted to trace over his jaw, run her fingers over the stone cut of his lips. Then there were his eyes. How she'd longed for that cool blue gaze to cast its magic in her direction, to shine for her and her only.

By Elizabeth Boyle

Elizabeth Boyle

Tempted By The Night

AVON

An Imprint of HarperCollinsPublishers

AVON BOOKS
An Imprint of HarperCollins*Publishers*
10 East 53rd Street
New York, New York 10022-5299

Copyright © 2008 by Elizabeth Boyle
Excerpts from *Tempted By the Night* copyright © 2008 by Elizabeth Boyle; *Secret Desires of a Gentleman* copyright © 2008 by Laura Lee Guhrke; *All I Want for Christmas Is a Vampire* copyright © 2008 by Kerrelyn Sparks; *To Sin With a Stranger* copyright © 2008 by Kathryn Caskie
ISBN: 978-0-06-137322-0
www.avonromance.com

First Avon Books paperback printing: September 2008

Avon Trademark Reg. U.S. Pat. Off. and in Other Countries, Marca Registrada, Hecho en U.S.A.
HarperCollins® is a registered trademark of HarperCollins Publishers.

Printed in the U.S.A.

10 9 8 7 6 5 4 3 2 1

To Anne Ricci,
whose support over the last few years
has been unfailing.
You dare to live your dreams
and thus inspire me.
My heartfelt appreciation and thanks.

Prologue

May 29, 1810
Mayfair, London

"To the happy couple," declared Thomas, the Earl of Rockhurst, raising his glass to bride and groom.

"To the happy couple," the assembled guests cheered.

As the earl's gaze swept the room, Lady Hermione Marlowe struck what she was positive was the perfect pose that would surely catch the earl's eye. Never mind the fact that she'd spent all morning choosing precisely which gown to wear, because it wasn't every day that your brother got married and asked the Earl of Rockhurst to stand up with him.

Confident the bright capucine color of her silk gown would stop his gaze, Hermione tipped her head just so, put her hand on her chin, glass raised in the other, and a come-hither light in her eyes. Exactly as she'd practiced in the mirror for most of the night.

Truly, how could he miss her?

"Minny, are you unwell?" Lady Viola Marlowe, her twelve-year-old sister asked, looking her sister up and down. "Oh, 'tis the color of that dress. You really shouldn't wear nasturtium."

"It isn't nasturtium, it's capucine."

Vi shrugged. "Capucine, nasturtium. They are both orange, and they make you look very ill."

Hermione cringed. What did a schoolgirl know of fashion? Orange, indeed! Besides, it was horribly difficult to affect just the right stance when one's sister persisted in being a distraction. "This color is my signature."

"Or your social ruin." Vi glanced at the dress again and shuddered. "You said the same thing last Season about that dreadful shade of green. It made you look like you had the plague. No wonder you had only one offer."

"It wasn't green," Hermione corrected, "but pistachio. And I had two offers."

Vi shook her head, a mischievous grin on her face as she rose up on her toes and let her gaze follow Hermione's until it fell on the Earl of Rockhurst. "Now I understand. It isn't your orange dress that has you looking so ill, but *him*."

Hermione flinched. It was true. Whenever she found herself in the earl's vicinity, her stomach had the nasty habit of turning in knots.

Not that Viola was about to help matters. "Oh, by the way, did you know that when you pose like that your eyes are crossed."

Crossed? Hermione wavered. Her eyes certainly were not crossed.

Viola grinned. "You might as well relax, he isn't looking over here."

Hermione glanced in the man's direction and found him engaged in conversation with Lord Boxley. "Oh, jiminy!" she cursed softly, and dropping her hand down to cover her stomach, hoping that would settle the butterflies there.

"I don't see why you are so violently in love with Rockhurst—he doesn't even know you exist," Viola said, settling in to make her unwanted presence permanent. "And he won't ever know it if you keep back here like some awkward wallflower."

Doing her best to ignore her, Hermione struck a new pose. It was more daring than her last, but since her previous one had failed . . .

"Do you want me to fetch him over? I could do that for you." Viola's bright eyes sparkled with mischief as she cleared her throat and shook her hair back from her face. "My dear Lord Rockhurst, may I introduce my sister, Lady Hermione Marlowe, who happens to be so terribly and violently in love with you, I daresay she'd quite happily throw herself in front of a mail coach to gain your favor." Viola paused, her fingers tapping against her quaking lips. "But then she'd be quite flat and rather unattractive, don't you think?"

What had their mother been thinking allowing

Viola downstairs for the wedding, letting her mix about in company where she could say something or do something that would embarrass the entire family?

Just like she was doing this very minute.

But much to Hermione's growing chagrin, Vi's opinions didn't stop there. "I find the earl rather dreadful—like one of those moping fellows in those French novels Mother adores, but I do like his dog." Her sister glanced up at her. "What is its name?"

"Rowan," Hermione supplied. She was, by all accounts, an expert on every matter concerning the Earl of Rockhurst.

"Rowan," Vi repeated. "I thought I might go down and see if cook has an extra bone for the dear thing. Now *he* has a noble look about him, more so than the earl. And far more handsome."

Hermione slanted a glance at her sister. "You're comparing the Earl of Rockhurst to his wolfhound?" Oh, it was almost too much to bear. Really, what did a child still in the schoolroom know of such things? "The Earl of Rockhurst is the most handsome man in London, I'll have you know." Gritting her teeth together, she vowed to keep her pose despite Viola's annoying presence, which her sister maintained with the same steely determination of a Beefeater at the Tower.

Yet, Hermione could grit her teeth together for only so long. "Vi, isn't your governess looking for you? Or should I tell Mother that you are annoying the guests and see you sent back upstairs *where you belong*?"

Viola sighed, unperturbed by her sister's threats. "I

don't see why you just don't marry Hustings and be done with all this."

Marry Hustings? Not that her mother hadn't been saying the very same thing just this morning, but Lord Hustings? There wasn't anything wrong with the young baron, it was just that he wasn't . . . *him*.

Hermione slanted a glance over at Viola that she hoped would quell her little sister. "Leave me be."

"Can't." She nodded toward the punch table. "Mother sent me over here. She wants you to make sure that Cousin Florinda doesn't drink any more champagne. She's quite squiffed as it is, and much more and she'll be singing 'Shule Aroon' from the tabletops."

"Squiffed? I shudder to think what Mother would say if she heard you use such a word. Wherever did you hear it?"

"From you," Vi said oh-so-smugly. "You were telling India Buxton just the other afternoon that Griffin is forever coming home quite *squiffed* and that—"

"Yes, yes, fine," Hermione said.

"That is squiffed, isn't it?" Viola asked, nodding her head toward Cousin Florinda, who was holding court at the punch table, a half-filled glass in each hand and her hat precariously tipped to one side, as she sloshed back and forth like the sherry in her cups.

"Unfortunately, yes," Hermione agreed, wishing Cousin Florinda wasn't *their* cousin.

Sometimes being a Marlowe was a dreadful trial.

As if on cue, their mother, the Countess of Walbrook, came blowing across the room in her usual blowsy and dramatic way, bowling over those in her path and tossing kisses to those she noticed.

She might be a Marlowe only by marriage, but there were days when she was the most Marlowest of all.

"Dears! Oh, there you are!" Lady Walbrook called out as she came careening toward her daughters. The countess was in a capital mood—and why shouldn't she? Her house was overflowing with guests, her son married, and only four more children to match. "Such a triumphant day. Though I wish your father was here. I daresay he'd approve of Charlotte wholeheartedly."

Lord Walbrook had left the family ten years earlier on a scientific study to the South Seas. Periodically they received letters and crates of treasures from him, but he was more stranger than family member now, though to his countess it was as if he'd merely gone around the corner to the tobacconist.

Lady Walbrook fluttered her hands at a passing baroness, then glanced over at her daughters. "Whatever is wrong with you, Hermione? You look positively yellow!"

"Capucine," Vi corrected.

Hermione ignored her sister, who she knew was most likely tossing one of her infamous, "I-told-you-so" looks in her direction. "I am well, *Maman*," she said, using the French designation her mother preferred.

The countess glanced about. "Of course, 'tis the light back here. Why it makes you look positively ancient. Now come out here where you can be seen. And you as well, Viola. Mingle, girls. Meet our guests. And don't worry about Cousin Florinda, she's moved on to the sherry and we all know she never sings when she drinks sherry."

"No, she just starts flirting with men half her age," Hermione muttered under her breath.

"Whatever did you say, Minny?" her mother asked in her usual distracted flutter. "I fear I was trying to decide if that is Uncle Howel over at the sideboard filling his pockets with ham or the silver."

"I believe it is a combination of both," Vi offered.

Lady Walbrook shrugged her shoulders and turned back toward her daughters. "What a perfect crush when one can't even distinguish the full extent of Uncle Howel's sins from across the room! And so auspicious for Sebastian and dear, dear Charlotte to have so many people come to wish them merry."

Viola nodded in agreement. "But really, Mother, shouldn't you be concerned about the silver? There are so many strange people here. Why just a few minutes ago I saw the oddest pair—"

"Dearest child," her mother said, drawing them both close and propping them up to their best advantage as Lord Hustings and his mother strolled past. "We don't call our guests 'odd'—for indeed most of them are family. Though how it is your father's relations always seem to know when the larder is opened up and the sherry casks tapped, I'll never know. Brings them out in hordes, but we must be accommodating." She gave Viola and Hermione a none-so-subtle shove into the crush. "Smile girls, 'tis a happy day." She bustled off, greeting one and all with her bright countenance and affectionate manners.

"Rockhurst is that way and Lord Hustings is over there," Viola whispered, nudging Hermione in the earl's direction. "I'm off to the kitchen to find a bone for Rowan."

That is, Hermione mused, *if Uncle Howel hasn't gotten there first and pocketed them all.* Though she took another furtive glance in the earl's direction, she turned instead toward her friends, Miss India Buxton and Lady Thomasin Winsley. At least there she would find an appreciative and sympathetic audience for her capucine gown and new pose. But on her first step, her slipper nudged something on the floor, and glancing down, she spied a ring there and knelt to pick it up.

I've seen this before, she realized as she stood up, trying to remember where it was she'd seen it. Then it occurred to her. Why, it was Charlotte's ring! The one her friend had inherited from her great-aunt not a fortnight earlier.

Well, Charlotte wouldn't want to lose this, Hermione thought as she slid the ring on her finger for safekeeping.

Immediately it grew warm, and she considered pulling it off, for the uncanny heat made her dizzy. Oh, she was being foolish, she realized, for it was simply this dreadful crush making her unsteady. Taking a deep breath, she smoothed her hands over her gown, but still her hand, her entire body trembled.

And she knew the real reason why. If she went to return the ring to Charlotte, it would bring her right into Rockhurst's company, for he was even now chatting with the bridal pair.

Hermione watched him offering yet another toast to Sebastian and Charlotte's happiness, and Hermione couldn't help herself. A bolt of desire sent her heart beating wildly.

How she longed for him. Dreamed of him in ways that no proper miss should. But she did. And she didn't care if Viola teased her over her infatuation.

Taking another glance at the Earl of Rockhurst, Hermione took a deep breath and started walking toward him.

Oh, if only . . . Oh, how I wish . . .

But then in the middle of her starry-eyed dream came a bolt of reality that stopped her wish in its tracks.

"I wish I were on yonder hill . . . " sang the bright Irish lilt of Cousin Florinda.

"Oh, botheration!" Hermione cursed softly. *She's gotten into the champagne again.* If she didn't hurry, Florinda would be done with *"Shule Aroon"* and move on to her favorite ditty about the drunken Scot and his kilt.

Flitting one last glance at the earl's Roman features and broad shoulders, she sighed and started toward her cousin.

Meanwhile, her unfinished wish hung in the air, trembling and waiting to be completed, but it wasn't to be.

Not yet.

If she had known the power hovering just overhead, Hermione might not have cared a whit what Cousin Florinda was about to sing next. She would have stood stock-still and carefully constructed a wish that would bring her heart's desire as readily as Cousin Florinda could be counted on to make a cake of herself.

But Hermione was a Marlowe. And her wish would come from the same unbidden passionate nature that had Cousin Florinda downing champagne and regaling the crowd with another verse.

> *"I wish, I wish, I wish in vain*
> *I wish I had my heart again . . ."*

One

The arrival of the Earl of Rockhurst at Almack's the next night caused a near panic amongst the other guests. Of course he had the necessary voucher. He'd *always* had a voucher at his disposal. And why wouldn't he? He possessed the fortune of Midas, and if that wasn't enough to pass muster with the patronesses, his handsome visage and hawkish looks were admired wherever he went.

But most importantly, he was single. More than one mother had lamented that an unwed earl without an heir was truly a sin against nature.

Though they hadn't necessarily been talking about Lord Rockhurst. For there was the small matter of his reputation—a man whose tastes favored expensive courtesans and high-stakes gaming, as well as an unsavory penchant for frequenting some of the most dangerous hells and darkest brothels.

To bring him to heel, one matron had declared, *would take a lady of some consequence. A lady who could touch his black, unfeeling heart.*

Yet here he was, at Almack's, all but declaring his intention to find a bride. For what other reason was there for a rich, unmarried nobleman to attend the Wednesday night balls?

Accustomed as he was to the controversy, Rockhurst gave little regard to the stir his arrival caused, for there, to his amazement, was his cousin, Miss Mary Kendell.

He held out his arm to her, and she settled her hand atop it automatically. Taking a glance around them, then back at her, he asked, "Cousin, whatever are *you* doing here?"

"I would ask the same of you," she replied. "Really, Rockhurst! Send around a note of warning before you decide to arrive at Almack's."

He glanced around the room and blinked several times. "Almack's? Is that what this is called?" He patted the front of his jacket. "And here I thought I had tickets to the ballet this evening. Remind me to sack Tunstall tomorrow for driving me to the wrong address."

"The sun hasn't even set yet," Mary pointed out. "I'm sure when you arrived, you might have noticed the difference."

The earl grinned, completely unrepentant. "I will maintain to my dying day this was all Tunstall's doing. Or until his."

"Poor Tunstall," Mary said. "I'm surprised he didn't

fall over with apoplexy when you directed him here rather than your usual haunts."

"Ah, Mary," Rockhurst replied. "As forthright as ever. 'Tis why I adore you above all my other relations."

"Since your only other choice is Aunt Routledge, I can't say I am impressed with your singular favor."

Rockhurst laughed. His cousin was one of the few people who was neither awed nor impressed by his title and rank.

"You still haven't answered my question. Whatever possessed you to come here?" She waved her hand at the ballroom, where a good portion of the *ton* was staring back at the pair of them as if they had arrived dressed for a masquerade.

"I lost a wager." He winked at her and led her toward the punch table.

"You never lose wagers."

Right she was, but he wasn't about to explain himself to anyone. Hell, how could he explain it to her when he wasn't quite sure of the reasons himself. "I will tell you if you can tell me what you are doing here amongst all these dullards, Mary?"

"If you kept to proper society, you would know I am out this Season."

She couldn't have said anything that would have shocked him more. "Out?"

"Rockhurst, I would like to get married. Before it is too late even to consider the possibility."

Quite frankly, he didn't know what to say. He'd never considered that his bluestocking cousin would even want a husband.

She continued on, "And I would appreciate it if you wouldn't point out the impracticality of such a notion like Father or . . . or others have."

Yet there was one point he could argue, glancing around the room one more time and suppressing the shudder that threatened to run up his spine. "Why here?"

"Aunt Routledge," she confessed.

"Bullied you into it, didn't she?"

Mary cringed, then nodded.

He leaned over. "You need to spend more of your days away from your library and out in the world—where our aunt can't find you."

"I haven't the Dials to hide in, as you do," she commented. Then she glanced over at him, taking a measuring glance if ever there was one.

A skill she'd no doubt inherited from their aforementioned aunt.

"You've looked drawn of late," she said. "I take that to mean that your other responsibilities have become more pressing than usual."

"In a manner of speaking."

She lowered her voice, and asked, "You haven't found the hole yet?"

He shook his head, but said nothing more given the curious and close company surrounding them. Mary wouldn't pry further—at least not until she had him alone where she could pepper him with questions. Nothing like a true bluestocking to want every detail of a matter.

If anything, perhaps his troubles of late were exactly the reason he was here. At Almack's.

He glanced around at the bevy of young beauties and heiresses and those who'd just arrived in the world with all the necessary pedigree and nothing else to recommend them, and he shuddered.

No, for a brief second of late, he thought he'd found a lady who was different. Miss Charlotte Wilmont. But it hadn't taken him long to realize the lady had eyes only for another.

But in those few hours in her company, he'd discovered something he hadn't thought possible. A spark of something that he'd never found before. Perhaps it had only been a brief enigma. A happenstance of fate.

Yet here he was, at Almack's, surveying the ladies of the *ton,* in search of . . . someone.

His musings were interrupted by a sharp fan into his ribs, and his cousin saying, "Rockhurst, stop measuring the guests as if they were horses at Tatt's. It is unbecoming."

"Would you prefer this?" he asked, then feigned a loud laugh as if she'd just said something terribly witty, then winked at a passing matron, finishing off his performance with an elegant bow to a knot of giggling debutantes, whose mirth disappeared almost immediately as their mouths fell open at such a favor.

Mary groaned and tugged him past the foolish nits. It wasn't long before they'd arrived at the punch table, and Rockhurst surveyed the tepid lemonade and poor fare with a skeptical tip of his brows. "Whyever does one come here?"

"Because it is entirely respectable."

He shuddered. "Now I know why my Wednesday nights have been occupied elsewhere all these years."

"Which is well and good, for you've got every matron in the room speculating that you've come here seeking a bride."

He glanced around the room. "I hardly think one night under this hallowed, sacred roof—"

"Harrumph!" Mary blustered, sounding exactly like their Aunt Routledge.

But being a gentleman, Rockhurst decided not to point out the obvious.

"You haven't been subjected to enough afternoon teas and card parties to know better," she chided. "You have no idea what you've gone and done."

"Then I will in all haste do something quite despicable to put an end to such nonsense."

She laughed. "There, now that's the cousin I know. Please do, for it gives me such pleasure to listen to all your faults and follies discussed for weeks on end, and all I can do is nod and sympathize over your wasted existence, when I would love nothing more than to tell them all that you are—"

He came to a blinding halt. "You wouldn't dare—"

"You are in a state if you can't see that I'm teasing," she said, turning back and catching hold of his arm again. "Really, cousin, there was a time when you weren't so beetle-headed."

"Beetle-headed?" he asked, his brow cocking upward.

Mary couldn't help herself, she laughed. "Yes, beetle-headed." She shook her head and glanced at him. "Whatever is the matter with you? You used to be so dependable. Flirtations with married women, the finest Incomparables, and now you've gone quite respectable."

"Respectable?" He shook his head. "I think I prefer beetle-headed."

"Then you shouldn't have taken Miss Wilmont to the opera the other week," she chided. "Really, Rockhurst, whatever possessed you to pluck Charlotte Wilmont out of obscurity?"

"I don't know. I'd probably driven past her a hundred times and never noticed her, and then one day, there she was. I couldn't help myself. Not that she had eyes for me, mind you. Lucky devil, that Trent."

"They do suit, don't they?" Mary sighed, twisting her fan about. "However, the point is that if you insist on escorting proper young ladies to the opera, not to mention arriving here at Almack's, then you are going to be seen as respectable."

He rubbed his chin. "What a devilish trap."

"Exactly. I'm still inclined to believe that Trent's wedding has you thinking of setting up your own nursery. Perhaps that is what I will tell Aunt Routledge when she corners me tomorrow," she said, her lips twitching.

"You are an incorrigible chit, Mary. You will do no such thing."

His cousin made a very unladylike snort. "Then what do you suggest I say when she calls on me and demands an explanation as to why you were here? For you know she will. She'll be on my doorstep at some ungodly hour, determined to ferret out the matter so she has the first word on the subject wherever she goes." When he said nothing, Mary groaned. "You've put me in a terrible spot," she complained. "Whatever *are* you doing here, Rockhurst?"

"I wish I knew, Mary," he said, scanning the crowd around them again. "I wish I knew."

"This has gone on long enough, Quince."

The lady in question flinched even as the man she least wanted to discover stepped from the shadows of a curtained alcove. She didn't need to turn around to see him, she could feel his presence.

Knew every curve and line on his handsome face.

And wished she didn't.

"Go away, Milton," she told him. "I've got to time this just right if I am too succeed."

"If," he repeated. "Now isn't that an interesting turn of phrase. *If.* Why not say, '*When* I get your ring.'"

She turned and glanced at his rich attire—tonight it was a bottle green jacket and tight breeches. The gold trim on his coat glistened in the candlelight. Then again, Milton always chose his clothing to dazzle and disarm.

And it worked, even on her, even after all these years. Her heart wavered for a second as she marveled at the breadth of his chest, his jewel green eyes, and his long limbs. All of them.

Until she remembered how and why they were here. That they'd once been happily married, bound together by a ring, until Milton had broken her trust and her faith in him.

Harrumph. "Don't you have some young, foolish

nymph to seduce?" she asked. "Or have you run through all the willing candidates?"

"My, my," he said, tipping his head as he studied her. "Sharp-tongued as always. And not concentrating on the task at hand." He nodded toward the trio of young debutantes gathered in the outskirts of Almack's fashionable set. "Shouldn't be all that hard for someone of your talents to go over there and steal it off her hand. You got it off mine quite handily."

"You were drunk and in the arms of your mistress," she pointed out, her gaze not leaving the object of her quest. Lady Hermione Marlowe. As long as the lady was encircled by her friends, it wouldn't be as easy to steal the ring as Milton liked to think.

"Such a quibbling point," he replied, glancing down at his hand—the one that had worn the ring during their short-lived marriage. "I daresay you were lucky yesterday that her wish was interrupted and that she wasn't able to finish it. Now go get my ring."

"And how do you propose I do that? Go up and ask her for it? Excuse me, Lady Hermione, but do you mind returning that ring to me? You see, it possesses more power than you could suppose, and if you were to make a wish, I would have to grant it."

Milton made a rude noise and took to studying their prey. "She might make it easy and wish for a cup of lemonade and be done with it."

"You obviously haven't had any of the lemonade," Quince remarked, then shook her head, studying their quarry for a moment. "No, I fear if Lady Hermione wishes for anything tonight, it will have to do with—"

"Wha-a-at the devil is *he* doing here?" Milton said, his words coming out in choked panic.

Quince glanced up to the entrance and gaped as the Earl of Rockhurst came striding into the grand room.

"This is your doing, isn't it?" Milton turned to her. "Some jest on my behalf?"

But she wasn't listening. Ring or not, she wasn't about to cross paths with the Earl of Rockhurst. She turned to go the other way, any way that would take her well away from *him,* but Milton had caught hold of her arm and held her fast.

"Quince," Milton ground out as he gave her a small shake. "Did you bring him here?"

She glanced first down at his hand on her arm, then up at him. "Whyever would I do that?"

"You tell me," Milton shot back, a light of panic she'd never seen blazing in his eyes. "I don't care what sort of nonsensical plan you've conjured to punish me, but there is one thing for certain: you aren't leaving this room without my ring. Now, I command you to go get it."

"You command me?" She laughed, then slipped out of his grasp and melded into the crowd before he could stop her. If there was one thing Quince knew about Milton, it was that he deplored mingling with people, something she was counting on.

"Quince, return to me at once. This isn't amusing," he whispered in the direction she'd fled. "There will be trouble with this. You mark my words. I'll not be responsible if she—"

Then he felt the beginning of the tremble that boded only one thing.

That it was indeed too late.

For Hermione Marlowe had also seen the Earl of Rockhurst arrive, and with almost her next breath, cast her wish.

Lady Hermione Marlowe stood in the wings and looked around the crowded room. *Almack's. Again.* She heaved a sigh.

"He'll be right back," her friend, Miss India Buxton said, nodding toward the punch table, where a young lordling was securing a cup of tepid lemonade with great flair and chivalry.

"Who?" Hermione asked.

"Lord Hustings," Lady Thomasin Winsley said. "Gracious heavens, Minny, you've forgotten him already, haven't you?"

"I don't see how you could," India declared. "He's all but asked for your hand."

"I don't want him to ask for it," Hermione said. "He's so . . . so . . ."

"Dull," Thomasin said, nodding in agreement.

Oh, ever so dull. Hermione was afraid that was about the kindest thing she could say about the baron. But sadly, the Lord Hustings of the world were usually what was left to ladies like her and Thomasin and India—in their third year of being "out."

This Season could well prove to be their last if they didn't find matches soon. And with it nearing June, there was precious little time left to find the man who could send shivers down their spines *and* satisfy their parents' desires to see them well matched.

"I do believe Miss Burke is still smarting from how you trounced her in archery this afternoon," Thomasin said, changing the subject, because in truth, none of them wanted to face the future as Lady Hustings.

India tipped her nose in the air. "I thought it was dreadful the way she kept coughing every time you had to shoot."

"A dreadful cheat," Thomasin agreed, nodding in the direction of where the infamous heiress and her friends had established their camp. No wings or alcoves for Miss Lavinia Burke. She and her bosom bows always held center stage at Almack's. "See how the Dewmont sisters are doing their best to rally Lavinia's spirits? Why, she looks as sour as if she'd drunk the entire bowl of lemonade. What a bully afternoon it was, Minny."

India fluttered her fan as she spoke. "When your last shot hit the bull's-eye, you should have seen her face! Oh, the sight of her losing to you was well worth being dragged to that dull party."

"I did like beating her," Hermione confessed. "She is so smug and affected. Why, I heard her telling those dim-witted Dewmonts that she threw Sebastian over and that he married Charlotte in spite!"

"Anyone who sees how your brother looks at Charlotte knows exactly why he married her." Lady Thomasin sighed. "I wish a man would look at me *that* way."

Hermione and India nodded in agreement.

"Oh, dear heavens," Thomasin said, holding her hand up to cover her mouth and keep herself from laughing aloud. "Poor Lord Hustings!"

They looked up to find the man traveling through the crowd in the wrong direction.

"I knew he'd get lost," Hermione said, rising up on her toes and watching the young baron navigate his way through the crowd while cautiously carrying two cups of punch. "Shall we go fetch him before he spills on someone, or just wait for him to realize we are on this side of the room?"

But India's answer was a gasping, strangled sound. Hermione turned to her to find her friend's mouth flapping like a trout.

Thomasin appeared in the same state of shock. "Oh. My. Goodness," she managed to gasp, her eyes wide with amazement as she gazed somewhere over Hermione's shoulder. "You are never going to believe this, Minny."

India blinked and tried again to speak, her mouth wavering open and shut as if she couldn't quite find the words to describe the sight before her.

"What is it?" Hermione asked, glancing over her shoulder and only seeing the narrow, tall figure of Lord Battersby behind her. Certainly his arrival wouldn't have India looking like she'd swallowed her aunt's parrot.

"Oh, let me tell her," Thomasin was saying, rising up on her toes.

"No, let me," India said as she finally found her voice. "I saw *him* first."

Him. Hermione shivered. There was only one *him* in the *ton* as far as she as concerned.

Rockhurst.

Oh, but her friends had to be jesting, for the earl would never make an appearance at Almack's. She glanced at both their faces, fully expecting to find some telltale sign of mirth, some twitch of the lips that would give way to a full-blown giggle.

But there were none. Just the same, wide-eyed gaping expression that she now noticed several other guests wore.

Turning around slowly, Hermione's jaw dropped as well.

Nothing in all her years out could have prepared her for the sight of the Earl of Rockhurst arriving at Almack's.

"Jiminy!" she gasped, her hand going immediately to her quaking stomach. Oh, heavens, she shouldn't have had that extra helping of pudding at supper, for now she feared the worst.

And here she thought she'd be safe at Almack's.

"I didn't believe you," she whispered to India.

"I still don't believe it myself," India shot back. "Whatever is he doing here?"

"I don't know, and I don't care," Thomasin replied, "but I'm just glad Mother insisted we come tonight if only for the crowing rights we will have tomorrow over everyone who isn't here."

"Oh, this is hardly the gown to catch his eye," Hermione groaned. "It is entirely the wrong shade of capucine," she declared, running her hands over the perfectly fashionable, perfectly pretty gown she'd chosen.

Thomasin laughed. "Minny, stop fussing. The three of us could be stark naked and posed like a trio of wood nymphs, and he wouldn't notice us."

"True enough," India agreed. "You have to see that you are too respectable to garner his fancy."

"He fancied Charlotte," Hermione shot back, trying to ignore the little bit of jealousy that niggled in her heart as she said it.

"Oh, I suppose he did for about an hour," India conceded, "but you have to admit, Charlotte was a bit odd the last few weeks. Not herself at all."

Hermione nodded in agreement. There had been something different about Charlotte. Ever since . . . ever since her great-aunt Ursula had died and she'd inherited . . . Hermione glanced down at her gloved hand. Inherited the very ring she'd found yesterday . . .

Beneath her glove, she swore the ring warmed, even quivered on her finger, like a trembling bell that foretold of something ominous just out of reach.

"Did you hear of his latest escapade?" Lady Thomasin was whispering. There was no one around them to hear, but some things just couldn't be spoken in anything less than the awed tone of a conspiratorial hush.

India nodded. "About his wager with Lord Kramer—"

"Oh, hardly that," Thomasin scoffed. "Everyone has heard about that. No, I am speaking of his renewed interest in Mrs. Fornett. Apparently she was seen with him at Tattersall's when everyone knows she is under

Lord Saunderton's protection." The girl paused, then heaved a sigh. "Of course there will be a duel. There always is in these cases." Lady Thomasin's cousin had once fought a duel, and so she considered herself quite the expert on the subject.

"Pish posh," Hermione declared. "He isn't interested in her."

"I heard Mother telling Lady Gidding, that she'd heard it from Lady Owston who'd had it directly from Lord Filton that he was at Tatt's with Mrs. Fornett." Thomasin rocked back on her heels, her brows arched and her mouth set as if that was the final word on the subject.

"That may be so, but I heard Lord Delamere tell my brother that he'd seen Rockhurst going into a truly dreadful house in Seven Dials. The sort of place no gentleman would even frequent. With truly awful women inside."

Hermione wrinkled her nose. "And what was Lord Delamere doing outside this sinful den?"

"I daresay driving past it to get to the nearest gaming hell. He's gone quite dice mad and nearly run through his inheritance. Or so my brother likes to say."

"And probably squiffed, I'd wager," Hermione declared, forgetting her admonishment to Viola about using such phrases. "I don't believe any of it. Whatever is the matter with Society these days when all they can get on with is making up gossip about a man who doesn't deserve it?"

"Not deserve it?" Lady Thomasin gaped. "The Earl of Rockhurst is a terrible bounder. Everyone knows it."

"Well, I think differently." Hermione crossed her arms over her chest and stood firm, even as her stomach continued to twist and turn.

"Why you continue to defend him, I know not," India said, glancing over where the earl stood with his cousin, Miss Mary Kendell. "He's wicked and unrepentant."

"I disagree." Hermione straightened and took a measured glance at the man. "I don't believe a word of any of it. The Earl of Rockhurst is a man of honor."

Lady Thomasin snorted. "Oh, next you'll be telling us he spends his night spooning broth to sickly orphans and bestowing food baskets to poor war widows."

India laughed. "Oh, no, I think he's like the mad earl in that book your mother told us not to read." She shivered and leaned in closer to whisper. "You know the one . . . about the dreadful man who kidnapped all sorts of ladies and kept them in his attic? I'd wager if you were to venture into the earl's attics, you'd find an entire harem!"

"Oh, of all the utter nonsense! How can you say such dreadful things about a man's reputation?" Hermione argued. "The earl is a decent man, I just know it. And I'll not let the Lord Delameres and the Lord Filtons of the world tell me differently."

"Well, the only way to prove such a thing would be to follow him around all night—for apparently only seeing the truth with your own eyes will end this infatuation of yours, Hermione."

She crossed her arms over her chest and set her shoulders. "I just might."

"Yes, and you'd be ruined in the process," Thomasin pointed out. "And don't think he'll marry you to save your reputation, when he cares nothing of his own."

India snapped her fingers, her eyes alight with inspiration. "Too bad you aren't cursed like the poor heroine in that book we borrowed from my cousin. Remember it? *Zoe's Dilemma* . . . No, that's not it. *Zoe's Awful* . . . Oh, I don't remember the rest of the title."

"I do," Lady Thomasin jumped in. "*Zoe or the Moral Loss of a Soul Cursed.*"

India sighed. "Yes, yes, that was it."

Hermione gazed up at the ceiling. Only Thomasin and India would recall such a tale at a time like this. She glanced over at the earl, and then down at her gown. Oh, she should never have settled on this dress. It was too pumpkin and not enough capucine. How would he ever discover her now?

Thomasin continued, "You remember the story, Minny. At sunset, Zoe faded from sight so no one could see her. What I would give to have a night thusly."

"Whatever for?" India asked. "You already know the earl is a bounder."

Their friend got a devilish twinkle in her eye. "If I were unseen for a night, I'd make sure that Miss Lavinia Burke had the worst evening of her life. Why the next day, every gossip in London would be discussing what a bad case of wind she had, not to mention how clumsy she's become, for I fear I'd be standing on her train every time she took a step."

Hermione chuckled, while India burst out laughing.

"I do think you've considered this before," Hermione said.

Thomasin grinned. "I might have." Then she laughed as well. "If you were so cursed, Hermione, you could follow Rockhurst from sunset to sunrise, and then you'd see everyone is right about him."

India made a more relevant point. "Then you could end this disastrous *tendré* you have for him and discover a more eligible *parti* before the Season ends."

And your chances of a good marriage with them, her statement implied, but being the bosom bow that India was, she wouldn't say such a thing.

Still, Hermione wasn't about to concede so easily. "More likely you would both have to take back every terrible thing you've ever said about him."

"Or listen to your sorry laments over how wretchedly you've been deceived," Thomasin shot back.

Hermione turned toward the earl. Truly no man could be so terribly wicked or so awful.

Oh, if only . . .

And then something odd happened. The ring warmed again on her finger . . . and quivered. Trembled on her hand as if nudging her, nay urging her, to continue.

"I wish . . ." Hermione said aloud, as if testing the words. "I wish I were a phantom from sunset to sunrise just like Lady Zoe so I could discover all of Lord Rockhurst's secrets."

Then she finished her wish with three silent words.

And he, mine.

Yet even as her wish tumbled from her lips and heart, the room around her spun, like London itself was tipping into the Thames.

Her hand fluttered to her brow, and Hermione closed her eyes. Whatever was wrong with her?

Her friends noticed her distress as well.

Thomasin caught her by the elbow and steadied her. "Minny! Are you ill?" She glanced around, most likely for Hermione's mother, but then she gasped. "No! Miss Kendell and Lord Rockhurst are coming over here."

Hermione swayed again, the room going from tipped to upside down.

"This isn't another of your poses, is it?" India asked. "Because I wouldn't recommend it right now. It makes you look positively bilious—"

"I think I'm going to be ill," Hermione gasped, before covering her mouth with her hand.

"Not again!" Thomasin exclaimed. "Whatever is wrong with you that every time that man comes near, you toss up your accounts?"

India nodded. "Not in front of him. Not *here*." What she meant was Almack's.

Hermione swayed again, and a mighty buzzing filled her ears. Try as she might to regain her senses, she couldn't. And her stomach . . . She should have known better than to have kippers *and* an extra helping of pudding. Now she was about to cast up her accounts. In Almack's. Oh, she would be ruined!

"Whatever is wrong, Minny?" India asked. "Did you have more than one helping of pudding tonight?"

"Yes," Hermione said, clutching her stomach, opening her eyes just enough to see that indeed, Thomasin was right. The earl was coming toward them.

Jiminy! He is so handsome, and so tall, and so . . .

Her stomach rebelled, and she covered her mouth again to keep from embarrassing herself.

"Too much pudding," India declared.

No, it was something else, she realized as her hand trembled anew. It was this demmed ring of Charlotte's. There was something wrong with it. An edge of panic raced through her, and she tore off her glove and tugged at it.

But to no avail. Where before it had been loose on her finger, now it was stuck tight. No matter how hard she pulled.

She glanced up and found her friends staring at her. Gaping really, and immediately Hermione realized she was making a terrible cake of herself.

More so than usual, she was loathe to admit. "I think I need to go to the necessary."

Thomasin nodded, and with India on the other side, her friends guided her toward the room set aside for ladies. "You might have taken too much sun this afternoon during the archery contest."

"Or too much pudding," India asserted.

Thomasin then laughed. "How unfortunate you can't become invisible right now."

India glanced over at her. "You aren't helping."

"No, think of it. We could blame your disgrace on Miss Burke and claim she's had too much to drink."

Hermione groaned. "Thomasin, you've spent far too much time thinking on this, haven't you?"

Two

The ladies' retiring room had already cleared by the near-hysterical announcement that, "Lord Rockhurst. He's here. At Almack's," so Hermione's less-than-noble entrance and subsequent disgrace was only witnessed by India and Thomasin. And after her initial exchange with a chamber pot, they, too, left her alone to regain her composure.

Hermione glanced at a mirror, then closed her eyes at the pale image staring back at her. Oh, what was it about the man that whenever he came near her had her sick as a cat?

Minny, how do you think you could ever marry the man, her sister Viola liked to tease, *if the very mention of him, let alone the sight of him, has you casting up your accounts?*

And if she wasn't certain her sister wouldn't just tease her further, Hermione would have told Viola why.

And it wasn't because Lord Rockhurst was so handsome. No, somehow, some way she knew there was a secret mystery about him that she, and she alone, was destined to share with him.

With one hand on her stomach and the other waving in her face, she took a few deep breaths.

Yes, that helps, she thought as she opened her eyes and glanced over at the mirror. Her color was a trifle pale, but not so noticeable as to make her look sickly.

She glanced down at her gown and with a critical eye gauged it. Dear heavens, perhaps capucine wasn't her signature color.

Oh, that was even more vexing, for now she would have to spend the next week searching for the right color for an entirely new wardrobe, let alone have to find a way to pay for it out of her already overspent allowance.

But surely Sebastian, who controlled the family purse strings in their father's absence, wouldn't be such a pinchpenny in these circumstances? He'd extend her the extra funds for such an emergency. Hadn't he fallen in love with Charlotte the night she'd worn the perfect blue velvet opera dress?

That was all she needed. The right dress.

Glancing at herself again, she felt a fortifying moment of hope. What if the earl actually adored capucine?

You can do this, Minny, she told herself. *If he is here, that means he is going to settle down and find a bride.*

He'll look across the room tonight and fall in love with the very sight of you . . .

"I fear he won't," a voice behind her said.

She spun around, for she had thought the room deserted, but there stood a lady about her mother's age. Hermione didn't recognize her, but her clothes and jewelry marked her as a lady of some worth.

"He won't see you," she repeated.

"I haven't the least notion—"

"Lord Rockhurst. You were just wondering if he would see you tonight. Notice you. And I fear he won't. See you, that is."

Hermione gaped at the woman. She hadn't been talking aloud had she? For how else could this lady know . . .

"Now we haven't much time, so you need to listen very carefully—"

Hermione rose. "I'm sorry. Have we met?"

"Oh, how terribly impertinent of me. I'm Quince. Now as I was saying, we haven't much time—"

"Yes, well, Lady Quince—"

"No, dear, just Quince. Your dear, good friend, Quince." The lady smiled, her features marked only by a few lines around her mouth and bright, sparkling blue eyes, which seemed to glow with some inner light.

And while she might be well dressed and could possibly be related to one of the very best of families, the sister of a duke even, Hermione suspected the woman was mad. "It was lovely to meet you, ah, Quince, but I think my mother will be wondering—"

"Heavens, I don't remember this being so hard. I had hoped, you being a Marlowe and all, you wouldn't be as incredulous and stubborn as Charlotte."

Charlotte? "You know Charlotte?"

"Of course. You are wearing her ring. At least it was hers for as long as she needed it. Then it became yours when you found it."

Ducal sister or not, Hermione started to edge toward the door. This woman was utterly nicked in the nob. But her next words stopped Hermione cold.

"You made a wish, just as she did. Certainly it is problematic that it involves *him,* and I daresay Milton is none-too-pleased over this, but we'll do the best we can to avoid those complications."

Hermione's confidence that she wasn't going to throw up again fled. "You mean Lord Rockhurst?"

Quince flinched. "Please don't say his name aloud."

"Whyever not? What is wrong with the Earl of Rockhurst?"

Now it was the other woman's turn to look positively green, and Hermione thought better of continuing the subject lest the woman react the same way Hermione did at the very mention of the earl.

If there was any comfort in all this, it was that she wasn't the only person in the world who cast up her accounts over Lord Rockhurst.

Quince had turned and was glancing at the door, her fingers twined around her reticule strings as she worried them nearly into a knot. "If only you'd wished for something more sensible. I do believe Milton is right, this has all the potential to go very ill indeed."

Hermione glanced down at her gloved hand, where beneath the gold silk, the odd little bit of jewelry sat tightly around her finger. Perhaps she could just give the lady Charlotte's ring and be done with the matter. She doubted her friend would mind because she'd never been all that attached to it anyway.

But after tugging off her glove, she found the ring was still tight around her finger. Tug as she might, she couldn't get it off. And for a moment, she swore the ring warmed and trembled on her hand, as if mocking her attempts to dislodge it.

"This is ridiculous," Hermione said, pulling her glove back on. "Charlotte never told me of any wish."

The lady let out a huffy little sigh, the feathers tucked into her hair fluttering like a trio of impatient exclamation marks. "Of course she didn't, for you would have thought her as mad as you think me. Now about your wish—"

"I never made any wish," Hermione replied, as certain as she was capucine was her perfect color, that is until her words from a few minutes earlier came whispering back into her thoughts like a spring zephyr.

I wish I were a phantom from sunset to sunrise . . . .

She glanced up at Quince to find the lady nodding encouragingly at her. "Yes, yes, your wish. *To be unseen.* The sun will set any moment now, and you must be prepared for the transformation. There are some rules and things you'll need to consider, especially in light of the other part of your wish—"

Hermione had stopped listening after she'd said "to

be unseen." Glancing at the door, she knew she needed to go find her mother, who would surely be able to place this woman and see that she was returned to her family . . . or Bedlam.

But when she went to take a step, she found herself wavering, trembling with a strange power. And unbidden, her gaze rose to the small window set high in the alcove, where the pink sky gave all the evidence that one needed that the late-spring sun was making its lazy descent into the horizon.

In the pit of her stomach, a slow, tangled coil began to unwind—as if being pulled to awaken by some unseen hand.

"This can't be true—this is utter madness," Hermione said, taking a quick glance at the mirror and trying to appear calm and composed, patting distractedly at the ribbons in her hair, if only to hide her growing panic. "I suppose Thomasin and India put you up to it. The wish was their idea."

"It might have been their idea, but you are the one who gave it life. So you can either listen to me now or in a few moments, when the transformation takes place."

Mad, Hermione decided. Transformation, indeed!

"Oh, if only Charlotte were here," Quince said. "She'd be able to convince you that I am not some mad sister of a duke."

Hermione flinched. *How was it that this woman knows my every thought?*

"Because you are wearing the ring," Quince replied. "My ring, actually. Well, not quite my ring, but it was mine once. Though that's neither here nor there. Truly all that matters is that you made your wish, just as Charlotte did, and now it is about to come true."

"Whatever are you talking about? Charlotte never mentioned this wish nonsense. She inherited this ring from her Great-Aunt Ursula. It is nothing but a poor trinket."

"Poor trinket!" Quince paced in front of her. "You have more power on your finger than a hundred kings. And you scoff."

Hermione stripped her glove off and held her hand out. "If it is yours, then take it back."

"Take it back, she says!" The lady laughed. "As if I could do such a thing. How I wish I could, for this wish of yours is bound to have repercussions." She sighed and patted Hermione's hand, then pushed it away. "It will not come off until your wish is fulfilled. Or you disavow it." She paused for a moment. "Why don't we try that."

"Try what?" Hermione asked.

"Disavow your wish," Quince told her. "All you have to do is say, 'I don't want this wish any longer.' Or something to that effect."

Anything to make this woman happy, Hermione thought. "I no longer want my wish."

Quince looked around the room, as if she expected the walls to open up and some great cacophony from the heavens to fill their ears, but nothing happened except the wheeze of the orchestra's instruments as they started to tune their pieces and begin the evening's entertainment. "Oh, we'll just have to try again once you've changed. Then you'll be more likely to have some conviction to your words."

Conviction to her words? Hermione started toward the door. Her only conviction at the moment was that this woman was in need of help. "Perhaps there is someone I could call for you?" *Like your neglectful caretaker at Bedlam.*

Quince caught her by the arm and held her fast. Her other hand pointed at the window, where the sky was now a deep crimson. "Remember, even though you will be unseen, you can be touched, trampled, and harmed. You must be careful." She paused and tapped her fan to her lips. "Invisible, invisible. 'Tis been a long time since anyone cast such a wish, but I do believe there is more to tell you, but I fear my memory isn't as good as it used to be." After a few more taps to her lips, she added, "Oh, yes. Anything you hold or wear will be just as you are, unseen. And remember, at sunrise, you will find yourself visible again, so I suggest being home well before then."

"This is utter nonsense," Hermione declared, trying to tug herself free. She wasn't going to listen to another moment of this poor lady's ravings. As if a wish could turn a person invisible.

But one thought nagged at Hermione. Gave some credence to her doubts.

Charlotte. Charlotte's wish. Hadn't Charlotte undergone a remarkable transformation, nearly from the moment she'd received this ring? Charlotte's metamorphosis from forgotten spinster to Society's most brilliant Original had been like something out of a fairy tale.

Like a wish come true.

No, it couldn't be. How could a ring have such power? Her panicked gaze flew first to Quince's, and the lady nodded toward the window, where the sun was finally slipping beneath the horizon.

As the last fiery hue fizzled, Hermione swore the fire and heat invaded her soul. Her ears filled with a terrible noise, like a violent fire burning out of control. Her hands flew to her ears to stop it, but the roar only grew louder. She wrenched her gaze from the window to the mirror and saw the final proof of Quince's madness.

For indeed, one moment she stood before the mirror, in all her evening finery, poised and ready for Lord Rockhurst's admiration, and the next, she faded from sight.

"My dearest Lady Walbrook," Quince said, sliding up beside the matron, taking her hand, and giving it a familiar squeeze. "How lovely to see you again. Such a stunning gown. It sets off your coloring perfectly."

As Quince expected, the countess smiled, albeit a bit flustered. "Thank you. Thank you so much," she said. Rather than reveal her dilemma—that she had no idea who Quince was—she continued in a rambling, innocuous fashion. "When I saw the fabric, I knew I couldn't live without it. That, and Madame Claudius's exquisite•skills were sure to make it the perfect gown for such evenings." Lady Walbrook leaned over. "Terribly crowded tonight, don't you think? I do believe the patronesses are trying to wedge in just anyone these days."

"Quite so," Quince agreed. "I actually came over to see you, for I have a message from your daughter."

"Hermione?" Lady Walbrook said, glancing around. "Wherever is she?"

"I fear she became ill in the retiring room."

Lady Walbrook snorted. "She heard Rockhurst was here and tossed up her accounts, I daresay. Well, there's no use standing about, I might as well fetch her home."

She went to step around her, but Quince caught her in time. "There is no need. Your son was kind enough to see to it already. Neither of them wanted your evening ruined."

"Griffin!" Lady Walbrook complained. "That scamp was most likely only too delighted to flee. But poor, poor Hermione! Whatever am I to do with her?" Her lacy fan fluttered in her hand, and she sighed as the music began to play and couples moved toward the dance floor. "Oh, I suppose I must stay now, if only to have a full account of the evening. Oh, there is Lord Hustings's mother. I suppose she'll want to know why Minny isn't here to dance with her son. I'll have to think of something—" She started to flutter off, but then stopped and turned. "I thank you, Lady . . . Lady . . . "

"Just Quince, madame," she told the countess. "Just plain Quince."

Lady Walbrook nodded and continued into the crowd, even as a hand reached out and plucked Quince back into the shadows.

"Nicely done," Milton said.

"Whatever are you still doing here?" she asked.

"I had thought you were off to fetch my ring." His handsome features turned to stone. "That is, until you let her make a wish."

"I let her—" Quince sputtered.

Milton wasn't done, but this time he tugged her deeper into the shadows and lowered his voice. "Do you realize what she has wished? What this could mean?"

Quince heaved a sigh. "Of course I am well aware of what she wished . . . and the implications. What do you suggest we do?"

"We?" Milton shook his head. "I have no intention of taking any part in this. Especially when you were less than convincing when you told her she could disavow her wish."

"How could you have heard that?" Quince asked. "Not unless you were lurking about the ladies' retiring room." She clucked a *tsk, tsk* under her tongue and shook her head. "I would have thought such adolescent tricks beneath you."

"I wasn't 'lurking about' as you so eloquently put it. I was merely waiting to see if you were going to do as you promised and get my ring back before any further mischief happened." He glanced over at the far wall, where Hermione stood—unseen to anyone other than Quince or Milton. "And now this is the consequence." He shuddered and pressed his fingers to his brow.

"'Tis nothing but a minor invisibility spell." Quince flicked her fan back and forth. "She'll tire of it quickly enough, and you'll have your ring back."

"And what if she doesn't? There is the other part of this wish. Dealing with *him*." They both looked across the ballroom to find Lord Rockhurst striding in their direction. Instinctively, they stepped farther back into the shadowed alcove as he passed. "What if she were to follow him. To discover—" Milton turned the same green shade that Quince had in the retiring room. "You must take back this wish."

Quince shook her head. "You know as well as I that I cannot take back a wish."

"Yes, but *she* can. Convince her to disavow her wish before—" His words came to a quick halt, but Quince was too piqued to notice why.

"Must you always quibble over the finer points?" she asked, examining her fan. "If only—"

"Quince—"

"Milton, why is it that you are always convinced that disaster is but a moment away. If you would only allow—"

"Quince! Where is she?"

"Where is who?" Quince said, looking up and around them.

"That chit of yours. Where has she gone?"

Quince gulped.

Rockhurst. Neither of them needed to say it aloud, for they both took a quick survey of the room to find that he too had disappeared from sight.

"She wouldn't have—" Milton choked out.

"Oh, heavens. I daresay she did!" Quince said, taking his arm to steady herself.

This wasn't the impending disaster Milton had foretold.

It *was* a disaster.

* * *

"Jiminy! What am I to do now?" Hermione muttered as she glanced down at her sleeve. Though she could see the capucine silk, she knew from the mirror in the retiring room it was exactly as she wished, exactly as that foolish French novel had described the perpetually cursed Zoe. To everyone around her, there was no sign of her exquisite gown, her perfectly coiffed hair, or even the dainty slippers she'd chosen because the laces wound enticingly up her ankles and calves—and if a lady knew how to turn her hem just so during a dance, they offered a teasing glance at her legs.

Now it was all a complete waste of her pin money!

Just then, Lord Hustings wandered by, punch glasses still in hand, searching the wings for her. Hermione opened her mouth to call to him, then instead, snapped her lips shut.

The poor man could barely find her when she was visible, but in her current state? But as luck would have it, Thomasin and India bumped into him, relieved him of his punch, and gave him the news of her "illness."

Thank goodness for her friends, she thought, as the young baron took the disastrous turn in the evening's events in great stride by asking India to dance.

"Oh, poor India," Hermione whispered as she watched her friend accept and put her hand on the baron's sleeve. Hustings was a terrible bore, and India and Thomasin were forever teasing her about his attentions. "She'll never forgive me for having to stand up with him."

And worse yet, how was *he* going to notice her. Not Hustings.

Him. The only man who truly mattered to her heart.

Rockhurst. She sighed and rose up on her tiptoes to search the room for him. Her gaze lit first on Quince making her excuses to her mother, and true to form, Lady Walbrook believed the story without fail.

There were advantages to having a mother who wasn't . . . well, quite all there.

So where the devil was Rockhurst? It would be just her luck to make such a nonsensical wish only to find the man had already left! But even as she was about to give up, a tall figure swept past her.

Hermione's stomach turned with that all-too-familiar queasy tilt. The one that overcame her every time the earl came into view.

She spun around to find the Earl of Rockhurst standing not ten feet from her. He'd paused in a doorway, one she thought she'd seen a servant using earlier. Hermione swore his gaze bore directly into her.

Of course that was foolish. He couldn't see her.

Not that he ever has before, she thought wryly.

Still, if being ignored by him was so devastating on her nerves, bearing the full light of his towering examination was enough to send her fleeing all the way back to the retiring room.

It was all she could do to breathe, for she'd never been able to just stare at him thusly.

Well, to be honest, gape at him, as she was doing now.

His tawny hair, like burnished gold, was combed back, though the style barely contained the wavy mane.

Her fingers curled into her palm, as she gazed at the strong line of his jaw. How she'd always wanted to trace over his jaw, run her fingers over the stone cut of his lips. Then there were his eyes. How she'd longed for that cool blue gaze to cast its magic in her direction, to shine for her and her only.

For then he'd cross the most crowded ballroom, ignoring one and all as he rushed to be by her side, his gaze burning with desire. And there she would be, surrounded by beaux and would-be suitors, and he'd brush them all aside to take her hand.

But before she could get to her favorite part—where he kissed her and she swooned to a chorus of matronly protests at such rakish behavior—something nudged her awake.

Her eyes sprang open, only to find the earl was gone, having slipped through the door and out of sight. Odder still, she had no idea who had bumped her, for there was no one around her. Then that something nudged her again, pulling her toward the door through which he'd disappeared.

After a few involuntary steps, she stopped, only to find herself being yanked again, but this time she knew why.

She glanced down at her hand, where the culprit sat wound around her finger. Charlotte's ring!

Hermione froze, on the brink of nausea and something else. Curiosity. Undeniable, unbearable curiosity.

Wherever was the Earl of Rockhurst going in such a hurry?

And whether it was the ring nudging her forward, or

her own desire to discover his secrets, she rushed to the door and slipped through it. Pulled along, the ring thrumming happily on her hand, she made her way down a narrow hallway, which she discovered led to the kitchens in the back, where the chaos of the evening was in full swing.

It was one thing to gracefully navigate a crowded assembly room—even when one was visible—but to get through a raft of servants bearing great collections of cups and trays of Almack's infamously stale offerings, when one was unseen, was an entirely different matter.

Yet there was her quarry, dashing out the back door and into the alley, and Hermione could not resist the compelling and undeniable need to follow him.

She dashed and darted and weaved her way through the room and almost made it to the other side when a large man, laden with an enormous tray of cups swung around, another man sidestepped him but in the process bumped into Hermione, sending her skittering into the tray. She caught her balance by catching hold of the tray, tipping it and sending the cups flying in all directions.

"Why you idiot, look what you made me do!"

The accused turned a black-eyed gaze on his fellow server. "I dinna come near ye. Dinna be blamin' me for your clod-handed ways."

"Oh, dear," Hermione whispered, as the two men came close to fisticuffs. She was going to have to learn to be more careful, she realized as she found her way the last few feet through the kitchen and out the back door.

The alley was a far cry from the grand entranceway of Almack's, and in the dim gloom it was nearly impossible to discern a path. She grimaced, that is until she looked ahead and spied at the end of the byway, silhouetted in the streetlamp, the narrow figure of a wolfhound.

"Rowan," she whispered, never so glad to see the earl's grand dog. For if Rowan was there, the earl wasn't far away.

And then, as if on cue, Rockhurst stepped from the shadows, his hand reaching over and giving his constant companion's head a friendly ruffle. The dog gazed up at his master, and the two of them stood there, on the edge of night, not quite stepping into the light beyond, still clinging to the safety of the shadows.

This time her breath froze in her throat for other reasons. She couldn't shake the notion that the two of them had stood thusly many times—countless nights— watching the darkness fall upon the city before they ventured forth.

And she had to imagine it had nothing to do with spooning broth to orphans or aiding war widows. A chill ran down her spine as she crept toward them, drawn by a desire she didn't even understand.

Didn't know if she wanted to . . .

Just then, a curricle pulled up to the curb, the driver hopping down from the high perch. "My lord," the man said, bobbing his head.

"Evening, Tunstall." Rockhurst said.

"Evening, my lord," the driver replied. "I heard a fine one just a bit ago—"

Hermione continued to draw nearer still, for she couldn't make out all of what Lord Rockhurst's driver was saying. That is until her slipper squished into something. In the meager light she couldn't tell how bad it was, but she had to imagine that in the morning, her slipper would be beyond repair.

And she certainly wasn't about to take it off and see the damage for herself, for she'd most likely ruin her gloves, and they were her best pair—why it had taken her weeks to find just the right shade of silk, then another week to find the right embroidery pattern—

Rockhurst's deep laughter drew her attention back to the matters at hand. "You say Trent and his wife were thrown out of the British Museum? Gads, that Miss Wilmont is a remarkable woman to have led Trent so far astray. Who'd have ever thought—" His words ended, and she swore the earl glanced toward Mayfair, toward Berkeley Square, where her brother would eventually bring his bride home.

A niggle of jealousy ran down her spine. So the earl had held a *tendré* for Charlotte!

Still might . . . a little voice whispered in her ear. *And without her ever wearing a hint of capucine.*

Hermione shored up her shoulders. It was that blue opera dress she'd convinced Charlotte to buy. Well, first thing tomorrow she was going to Madame Claudius's shop and engage her to make another gown just like Charlotte's.

And then she'd wear it to Lady Hogshaw's soiree, and the earl would be unable to . . .

She stumbled forward as the ring once again

nudged her. "Yes, yes," she complained, realizing her dreams of new dresses were for naught as long as she remained invisible. So there was nothing for her to do but continue to follow the earl until she could put an end to this wish. Simply discover his secret haunts, then she'd be back to her old self. That sounded sensible enough. But when she glanced up, she found Rockhurst leaping up into the driver's seat of his curricle.

Tossing a coin to his man, Tunstall, he said, "Catch a hackney back home, then seek your bed. I don't think I'll be home before first light." Then he whistled to Rowan, who trotted a few steps back, then turned and loped back toward the carriage, jumping into his place beside his master.

Hermione glanced over her shoulder toward the door to Almack's. She had promised Quince quite faithfully that she would wait for her in the alcove, but how could she when she had this opportunity?

With the ribbons in his hands, Rockhurst whistled to his horses, and the animals' ears flicked and turned at the sound, their hooves dancing.

And like a child called by the sound of a pipe, Hermione moved as well, dashing across the pavement and onto the back of the carriage, the spot usually reserved for the tiger.

Luckily for her, the street wasn't well paved, so when she bounced onto the back, jolting the carriage, the only one to give any note was Rowan, who barked and growled.

Rockhurst shot a glance over his shoulder, and seeing

nothing, gave the dog another scratch. "Settle in, you foolish hound. There's nothing back there. Save yourself for the real fight ahead."

Fight? Whatever could that mean? Hermione wondered, as she scrambled into place. Oh, he must be jesting. Or so she thought. That is, until they left the more civilized part of London behind, at least the London she knew, and very quickly descended into the very depths of hell.

The house on the dark street was only discernable from the other dreary shops and doorways by the grand peacock painted on the double portals.

When Rockhurst had pulled the curricle to a stop before it, Hermione's heart sank. For secretly she had wished, dreamed really, that Rockhurst's nightly ramblings had some grand *raison d'être*— he was gambling to save orphans, or to rescue a distant, yet noble cousin from a French prison.

But whatever he was doing *here* had nothing to do with anything grand, she surmised as he got down, not that she could see. Shadowy people made their way along the dark street, creeping along, giving the earl and his carriage a wide berth, as if he were the one to be feared.

Yet there he stood, casually leaning against the side of his curricle. He struck a match to the heel of his boot and lit a cheroot, paying no heed to anything other than the bright glow of the burning tobacco.

Above them, soft light spilled from the various windows, while laughter, a kind she'd never heard before—

rough and rowdy—echoed out. Some of it masculine, and some, decidedly female.

Hermione had to guess this was just the sort of place she'd heard Sebastian chastising Griffin for frequenting. At least she thought it was—one of London's infamous gaming hells, where fortunes noble and grand and illicit and ill-gotten were won and lost on a nightly basis. Corinthian and bounder, *cit* and duke could be found deep in cards or dice.

Rockhurst continued to wait, but for what, she couldn't imagine.

Rowan, on the other hand, leapt down from his spot and made his determined way straight for her side of the curricle.

"Nice doggy," she whispered down to him. "Nice Rowan."

The earl's dog replied by growling low, then barking as if the world were about to end.

"Rowan!" the earl snapped, dropping his cheroot and crushing it with the heel of his boot. Then he came around the carriage to where Rowan had her cornered in the tiger's seat. "Be still."

Hermione held her breath, for she'd only been this close to Rockhurst a few times, and that odd flip of her stomach was starting to rise again.

Oh, no, I can't, she realized, her hand coming to her mouth. If she tossed up her accounts, he'd discover her for sure. That is, if his demmed dog didn't give her away first.

Just then the door with the peacock opened, light and music and laughter pouring out. Down the steps teetered the largest woman Hermione had ever seen. She wasn't just fat, she was tall, as tall as the earl, and honestly, all the more intimidating in her grand red gown and garish makeup.

Then Hermione took a second glance at both the woman coming down the steps and up at the various windows, her mouth dropping open. This wasn't some gaming hell . . . but a . . . *a brothel*!

He'd brought her to a brothel.

Up until now, Hermione had been quite content in her fantasy that the outrageous rumors about the earl were just that: outrageous and hardly grounded in fact.

But now . . . well, certainly, as she stared up at the woman on the steps, she knew without a doubt she was going to be sick.

This was the sort of woman Rockhurst preferred?

But that was before the proprietress spoke—in a gravelly, rough-hewn voice that drew Hermione's gaze faster than a sale on silks.

"Rockhurst, demmed fuckin' time you got your arse down here. The entire place is going to hell! Literally. And I blame you for this. I won't see a single profit tonight if you don't do something. And do it now."

"Jiminy," Hermione whispered. The woman on the steps was . . . a man.

And now that she took another look, she realized she, or rather he, looked like something out of one of her mother's amateur theatricals. Which didn't give Hermione any sense of comfort.

"I could leave, Cappon," the earl said, whistling to Rowan and climbing back up into his curricle. "Serve you right if I did. Haven't paid me for the last time I got dragged down here." The two men stared at each other for a moment, and then Rockhurst shrugged and started to pick up the reins.

"Don't you dare, Rockhurst!" Cappon called out, coming down the steps, his thick, meaty hands fisted into his red silk skirts to lift them above the filth on the steps and pavement. "You've a duty here."

"And you've a duty to pay me," Rockhurst shot over his shoulder. "That's the way the tribute works."

Again, they stared at each other, the earl calm and easy, while Hermione could see Cappon's rouged jowls and lips working back and forth. After what seemed an eternity, the madame snapped his fingers, and a dwarf of a man dressed in equally bright silks came from within the house and hurried down the steps to the sidewalk.

"Pay his nibs, Tibbets," Cappon ordered. The dwarf tossed up a pouch, and Rockhurst caught it and gave it a simple heft, as if to measure it.

"A bit short," he said, curling the ribbons around his hands, his horses dancing in the traces, as if as anxious as anyone in their right mind would be to leave such a place.

Cappon heaved another aggrieved sigh, and said, "The rest, Tibbets. Give him the rest."

Another pouch flew up from the little man's stubby fingers, and Rockhurst caught this one just as deftly, it landing in his hand with a heavy *thud* and the jangle of coins.

"Now that's more like it," the earl told Cappon, tossing the reins down to Tibbets and climbing back down. He reached under the seat and hauled out a large bag, slinging it over his shoulder, the contents rattling about with the same heavy mystery as the coins in the pouch. "Now who is it you want me to kill this time?"

Three

Kill? Hermione nearly fell out of the carriage. *This time?* What the devil did he mean by that?

And here she'd been worried about him being a rake!

Meanwhile, Rockhurst strode up the steps in his usual easy, confident manner, Rowan trotting along at his side. There was nothing nefarious in his demeanor, nothing that would suggest he was about to commit murder.

The carriage jolted forward, and Hermione caught hold of the sides. She looked up to find Tibbets leading the horses away.

Jiminy! She had few choices—to hide in the earl's carriage and hope he returned before dawn or follow him inside this house of horrors.

Then once again, the ring made the decision for her, and she found herself tumbling over the edge of the carriage, landing with a hard *thump* on the filthy street.

"Oohhh," she complained, knowing for certain she'd ruined her gown.

Then she glanced around and realized she was all but alone, Rockhurst and Cappon almost to the top of the steps.

One thing was for certain, she wasn't going to stay outside on this dreary street. Whether she could be seen or not, the creatures lurking about in the shadows were enough to make the hairs on her arms stand up. After gingerly getting to her feet, she hurried to follow Rockhurst up the steps.

Murder, indeed! she told herself. It had been just a jest. And not a very funny one. She'd merely misunderstood what was being said, though it did her courage little good as the earl's carriage disappeared into the darkness, for with it went the only bit of civilization in sight.

Rowan turned his head and growled at her, but she didn't care. Being mauled by the earl's infamous dog was preferable to remaining outside as the encroaching shadows from the other doorways and alley loomed forth.

Then just as quickly as the darkness outside had surrounded her, she found herself in the brightly lit entryway of Cappon's establishment. While Rockhurst continued through the wide foyer with easy familiarity, Hermione found herself stumbling to a halt once again.

Never had she seen such a place.

Now Hermione wasn't one to shy away from color or colorful combinations, but even she found the array of silks and velvets boggling. And those were just the drapes and wall hangings and not the colorful display worn by the patrons and Cappon's . . . er, employees.

Eyes down, she told herself, feeling suddenly like a girl of Viola's innocent years rather than a miss well out of the schoolroom and in her third Season to boot! Not that such a thing was something bragged about, but Hermione had to imagine that in this situation a few years of Society would be something of an advantage. After all, she'd heard quite a few *on dits* about what went on outside Mayfair.

At least she thought she had. With a rarely mustered bravado buoying her, she took a deep breath and looked up.

Halfway up the stairs, a brightly clad woman in a low-cut gown waved at the earl.

At least Hermione hoped it was a woman—after her mistake with Cappon, she wasn't too sure she should assume anything.

"If it isn't the devil himself! Rockhurst, darling," the lady called out, leaning way over the railing, her enormous breasts threatening to spill from their satin trappings. "When you've finished that nasty business out back, come slay me with that wicked bit of steel you keep beneath your breeches. My thighs are always willing to be your sheath." She winked at him. "And I promise not to fight back . . . overly much."

"I'm still not convinced you're my type, Essie," the earl called back. "You might be hiding the same thing under your skirts that Cappon likes to forget he owns."

"Ah, but Cappon hasn't got these." Not missing a beat, she dropped the front of her gown so her breasts spilled out for all to see.

Laughter filled the foyer, along with whistles and catcalls. Essie shook her breasts back and forth, which only encouraged her audience to greater revelry.

"I'll see how I fare, Essie. But if I die back there, you've given me a fine image to carry with me to hell."

"Heaven these are, Rockhurst," she told him saucily as she tucked her tits back into her gown. "Heaven on earth they are."

More laughter followed, and even the earl laughed.

That certainly isn't something you see at Almack's, Hermione mused as she followed Rockhurst and Cappon through a door on the far side of the foyer.

She hurried to catch up with them, easing past a couple, the man's boots sticking out from where he knelt beneath the woman's skirts.

Hermione had glimpsed such a thing in a book of French prints her mother kept on the upper shelf of her dressing room, but at the time hadn't been able to fathom why such a thing was done.

Given the look of rapture on the woman's face and the way she clung dizzily to her lover, Hermione gave the French their due for being not as ridiculous as she'd first thought.

"Oh, hurry up, lovie," the woman panted. "Oh, yes, there, yes."

Ahead, Cappon and the earl were arguing before a closed door, which she had to imagine led to the alley out back.

Oh, heavens, not another alley. She still clung to the hope she could end this evening without ruining her gloves. Besides, the street in front had been foul enough—whatever would the alley be like?

She edged her way past the amorous couple to get closer to the earl and Cappon but found Rowan blocking her path. The dog eyed her with an unholy and uncanny gaze.

Hermione had no doubt he could see her.

"Go away," she whispered, trying to shoo the large wolfhound out of her path. "Just stop it."

"Stop?" the man behind her said, coming out from beneath his partner's skirts. "What do you mean stop? I thought you liked this."

"I didn't say stop," the woman complained, shoving his head back down under her skirt.

"But I heard you say—" the man insisted.

"Well, I never. Next thing you'll be saying it's that ugly dog talking to you. Now finish me," she complained, "or there will be none of that fancy stuff later."

The man glanced back toward where Hermione stood, then ducked back under the whore's skirts.

Hermione turned her back to them, doing her best to blot out the woman's moans and concentrate on what the earl and Cappon were discussing.

"I've no idea how it got opened," the proprietor

was saying. "But open it is, and bad for business I tell you."

Rockhurst folded his arms over his chest, his jaw set. "Well, someone is opening the doors—this isn't just coincidence that I've been down here three times this month."

The proprietor shrugged. "I'll have Tibbets nose about," he said. "Sometimes I think his mother was a terrier. He's got a way of getting into the worst ratholes. With a bit of inducement, he'll find the truth of it."

Rockhurst laughed. "See that he does. I don't want anyone getting hurt."

"I fear it's too late for that," Cappon said, as he pulled a long chain from around his neck. After a few tugs, a key popped out of his bodice. With the bright brass in his hand, he stopped short of putting it into the lock. "You should know . . . well, that is to say . . . Sally's newest girl is . . . " He crossed himself, then shoved the key in the lock. "She's been done in by one of them."

Rockhurst reached over and stopped him from opening the door. "Are you sure?"

"Oh, aye. They found her . . . that is Sally found her—"

"Don't finish. I know what she found." He turned his face toward the shadows, and Hermione could see he was trembling. The quiet anguish in his words had stopped her, but this . . . this grief was something she hadn't ever thought she'd see in the earl most of the *ton* regarded as a man only bent on pleasure and sport.

"'Tisn't your fault, milord," Cappon muttered. "Never is. This is what happens."

"Not to my people. Not in my realm."

"Oh, aye, and how can just one man be held responsible for watchin' all of London all the time? Ain't possible. You'll drive yourself madder still if you start worrying over every bit of muslin or urchin what gets nabbed."

"They're my responsibility."

"They are that, but they also know better than to lurk about the shadows. We all learn that lesson early on when you grow up in the Dials. But still there's somes that just don't listen . . . or believe."

"Then let's make it so they don't have to," Rockhurst said, rising up, his shoulders squaring.

"God be with you, milord," Cappon said as he turned the key, then used his great girth to shove the thick, heavy door open.

Rockhurst shouldered the large leather bag and whistled to Rowan.

But the dog just sat and stared at her.

"I think your dog likes to watch," Cappon laughed, for all they could see was the couple behind her. "I usually charge two quid for that."

"Take it out of my bill," Rockhurst said with a laugh, whistling again, this time with a sharp urgent note to it.

Rowan turned immediately, but before he loped off, he looked at Hermione once again, and she could have sworn the hound was saying, *I'm not done with you.*

Once again, Hermione found herself caught in a choice, to continue following the earl or keep to the relative safety of Cappon's establishment, but the moans of the whore behind her and her fear of being left stranded urged her forward.

That, and Cappon's haunting revelation.

They found her . . . that is Sally found her . . .

However they found this unfortunate girl, Hermione had no desire to end up in the same circumstances. For whatever reason, her gaze fixed on Rockhurst's wide shoulders.

Keep me safe, she asked in a silent plea as she stared at him. Then Hermione took a deep breath and added one more prayer.

Or at the very least, save my gloves.

Rockhurst stepped out into the alley, his nose sniffing the air. Eyes could be deceived, but the earl had learned early on that the nose was often the most reliable of the senses. Rowan edged past and took up his place in front. They both stood poised and waited for a few moments to let the world settle around them—sifting out the constant hum of London and gauging their surroundings.

Above them, the rooms were lit, the light filtering through the gauzy curtains, giving the alleyway an ethereal glow amidst the shadows.

The hair on the back of his neck rose, and he turned quickly, but there was nothing behind him but the now closed door to Cappon's.

He stared at the space between him and the door and waited—for he'd had the uncanny feeling all night that he was being followed. Rockhurst stilled and waited a few seconds longer, closing his eyes and letting his senses sweep his surroundings, but still there was nothing distinguishable.

Perhaps Cappon was right, he was going mad. No, make that madder, he mused as he stared at the empty space.

Then it hit him. A hint of perfume. Not the cheap and sharp notes of Cappon's favored fragrance, or those of his soiled doves, but the simple, wholesome hint of springtime worn by those wide-eyed does who pranced about Mayfair.

He inhaled again, but this time all he got was a nose full of garbage and the sort of refuse that could turn even the most hardened stomachs.

Oh, yes, he mused. Springtime in Seven Dials. He was mad. Apple blossoms, indeed!

That didn't stop him from looking once more at the steps and, still seeing nothing, got to the task at hand.

No point in spoiling my new Weston, he thought as he shrugged it off. His valet suffered enough over the way he came home most nights, coats stained, cravats lost, breeches torn. Besides, he rather liked the cut of this coat.

Free of the tight wool, he stretched, then knelt beside the large bag at his feet. Reaching inside, he felt around, his eyes never leaving his surroundings. There was no need to look inside; he knew the contents as well as he knew his own hand.

He smiled as his fingers wound around a smooth oaken stock. He pulled out the cross-bow and held it up to check it over.

And the moment he raised it, Rowan's ears twitched, as did Rockhurst's.

"Aye, I heard it, too," he whispered to his hound, turning around.

A gasp. A single, small gasp.

But there was nothing there. No one behind him.

"Come out!" he ordered, pointing the cross-bow in the direction he'd heard the noise. "Come out right now."

Only silence greeted his command. After standing there for what felt like an eternity, Rockhurst issued his order again, "Come out now, before you anger me."

Yet still there was nothing, not even a nervous stir.

Whatever was wrong with him of late? Singling out respectable spinsters for his attentions . . . showing up at Almack's. Smelling apple blossoms in Cappon's alley . . .

Letting holes spring up unaccounted for all over London.

He shook his head and relaxed his stance. This Season had brought a restlessness to his soul that he'd never felt before. For a brief moment, he'd thought Miss Wilmont might have been the answering call to his reckless, dangerous existence.

But her heart had been destined for another. And now he was alone again, and still waiting . . .

But for what, he knew not.

Well, he certainly wasn't going to find whatever it was the Fates had in store for him here in this godforsaken alley. Not until he finished what needed to be done.

Rockhurst reached again into his bag and plucked out Carpio, the short sword that family legend held had saved the first Rockhurst's life more times than could be counted. And had safeguarded every subsequent earl's life. How Rockhurst loved the bejeweled piece, Spanish in origin, and as sharp now as the day it was forged. Testing it for a moment, he nodded in satisfaction at Carpio's perfect balance and fine blade, slipping it carefully into the simple holder he'd had his valet sew inside his belt. Then, to finish his preparations, he tucked two pistols into his waistband.

They weren't going to do what needed to be done, but they could slow things down if anything went . . . went. . .

Wrong.

The word swung through his thoughts like a noose, and he glanced over his shoulder again.

Yet nothing but shadows greeted him.

Perhaps Essie was right. A woman. That's what he needed. That would solve everything.

Then he laughed.

For certainly that was madness in itself. When had a woman ever given a man anything but more trouble?

Hermione struggled to catch her breath, even now that Rockhurst no longer had his cross-bow pointed at her.

She still couldn't quite believe it. *A cross-bow?*

What sort of medieval madness had she stumbled into? Gentlemen didn't jaunt around London armed as if they were readying themselves for some Crusader's tournament.

Yet here was the Earl of Rockhurst pulling all sorts of armaments out of the leather bag at his feet. Wicked-looking knives, a pair of pistols, a short sword.

Right now she wished he was in the arms of Essie the Fallen Dove, and that was the worst of his sins.

Murder? Death? She'd been quite happy to consider all that talk as nothing more than jesting or some mas-culine cant that she hadn't any experience listening to. But this? A cross-bow and a sword?

She sank to her knees and gauged the man she'd thought she knew better than anyone and now discov-ered she knew so little about.

And what had he been going on about? *His people? His realm?* More nonsense.

The real nonsense was that she'd wished herself here. With him. Whatever had she been thinking?

Her fingers fumbled with the buttons on her glove. When that failed, she tugged it off with her teeth.

Well, she was done. No more wishes. From this night forth, just a sensible marriage to someone like Lord Hustings for her. Tugging at Charlotte's ring, she tried with all her might to get it off.

But the ring stubbornly clung to her finger.

I'll get this ring off, and I'll be visible again, she rea-soned. She no longer cared if the earl ever looked at her. She'd seen enough for one night, and it was time to end this charade.

Then what? If she got the ring off and became visible again, what would she do?

Well, demand the earl take her home. Right there and then. He was still a gentleman, a peer of the realm, wasn't he?

She took a quick glance up at him and answered her own question.

Not. For what noblemen carried around cross-bows and swords as a matter of course? She had to imagine Lord Hustings never did.

But the Earl of Rockhurst . . . well, she knew now he was no . . . no . . .

She glanced over at the man, who had now stripped out of his waistcoat and was pulling off his cravat, and all her arguments and discontent fluttered away into the shadows.

His valet would probably weep to see the once–perfectly ironed and starched linen tossed aside—but all Hermione could do was stare—for here he was, nearly undressed. As he rose, the muscles of his back and shoulders were outlined by his tight shirt.

He stretched again, like a great cat, and all she could think was that it was as if one of Townsend's Greek marbles had come to life—specifically the relief of a man trying to calm a horse. Her mother had called it evidence of the Grecian eye for "artistic glory," but Hermione had thought it a perfectly unbelievable example of manhood.

Now she knew how wrong she'd been, for it was all she could do to breathe at the sight of Rockhurst. She rose as well, catching hold of the railing beside her as her breasts grew full, her nipples tightening, tingling as they never had before. She couldn't do anything but stare at the corded muscles in his arms, gape at the sure grasp with which he held that deadly-looking sword. Her knees quaked, but not out of fear, more so from the way her thighs tightened and grew hot.

No, she wasn't afraid any longer. At least not for the same reasons she'd been earlier.

Her unease had to do with the ache that pulled at her, and she had no idea what it meant—only that she couldn't stop looking at him, couldn't help but wonder what it would be like to see him in his altogether, a true embodiment of a Greek relief.

For stripped of all his guises, she had no doubt this man would know how to ease this trembling need inside her, steal away her fears.

Then something else hit her. She was looking at him without getting nauseated.

Perfect! Now that she knew his hobbies consisted of extortion and murder, she could tolerate being in the same vicinity as the man.

She gave the ring one more frustrated tug.

Rowan let loose a loud *woof,* a bark filled with annoyance at her presence and his master's inability to see her.

Rockhurst glanced at his dog and turned toward her. Those blue eyes that more than one debutante had swooned over bored down on the spot where she stood, and for a moment she swore he could see her.

It sent tendrils of desire through her veins as much as it did fear, especially when he stalked toward her, cross-bow in hand.

He stared at the place she was standing for a moment

longer, then glanced over his shoulder. "What has you in knots, boy?" he said to Rowan. "Something amiss?"

Hermione froze since no more than a whisper separated them. She swallowed back the breath caught in her throat, not daring even to exhale, lest she give herself away.

She gazed in fascinated awe at the lines around his eyes, the set of his lips. When he turned again, he was looking right at her—not that he could see her, but she was used to being invisible to his discerning gaze.

But this? This was utterly disarming.

This close, this intimate, she could smell him. She couldn't help herself—she took a slow, silent inhale, letting the masculine scent fill her nostrils—no bay rum for Rockhurst, but a scent that held stark notes and rich tones. The bolt of desire it ignited nearly gave her away, for her knees trembled, and she continued to cling to the railing, feeling that her wish had cast her into something far beyond her ken, well beyond her understanding.

Shopping and silks. Gossip and balls. Promenades and flirtations. That was her realm. Not this dark world into which Rockhurst had unwittingly dragged her.

Perhaps the gossips and tattlers were right, there was a stripe of evil through the earl that no woman would ever tame.

Hermione didn't want to tame such a beast, even try to contain it, for just then she was struck by an unshakable feeling that something was about to go very wrong.

And then it did.

* * *

Rowan's low growl had Rockhurst spinning around even before the telltale tremble in the ground reached his boots.

He looked left, then right, trying to gauge just where the door was about to appear, until a bit of light started to pierce the darkness before him.

He braced himself and raised his cross-bow. He'd seen this hundreds of times before, the blinding light, the shimmer of colors before the door finally opened. And though he never knew what was going to step through, there was one thing that never changed—whatever it was, it was evil.

But never in his life nor in all the legends that his forebears had passed down had one of them ever described the banshee wail that rose up behind him as his two worlds collided.

He reeled around. Christ, there *was* someone there.

The piercing scream put his every nerve at points. A woman? What the devil was some bit of muslin doing out here? And after he'd told Cappon to bar the door.

Yet he stared at the steps, and there was no one there, just agonizing screams of fright coming from the empty space between him and the door back into Cappon's brothel.

This disruption didn't seem to bother Rowan, for the wolfhound stood his ground, barking madly at the more pressing problem opening up in the alley.

What had started as a tiny crack all of a sudden burst open, the illumination more bright than if it had been the midsummer sun. And then came the roar—like that of a thousand cannons—followed by an explosion of power, a jolt not unlike one delivered by those newfangled electric machines that had Trent's brother Griffin all excited.

As the wave washed over him, instead of standing his ground as he'd always done, he found his boots sliding about in the offal beneath him, and he was thrown back, the cross-bow flying out of his hand and landing at the foot of the steps.

Rockhurst cursed roundly, scrambling to get to his feet. He couldn't remember the last time he'd been caught like the worst sort of greenling.

First Almack's. Now he was covered in this wretched muck.

Could his evening get any worse?

A dark and dangerous laughter filled his heart with dread. "Having trouble, my friend?"

Oh, yes, it could. Rockhurst turned, slowly and cautiously. "Melaphor." His hand rose, but he realized he no longer held his cross-bow, so he had to scramble to draw his sword.

So much for his usual self-assurance.

Standing in front of him, Melaphor laughed again. His dark cloak swirled around his tall, regal figure. "Whatever has you so unnerved, my friend? Weren't you expecting me?" He drew closer, the red of his eyes hypnotic.

But Rockhurst knew better than to look the creature in the eyes. At least not directly. "You have no business here, Melaphor," he said. "Go back where you belong." Rowan growled as well, echoing his master's displeasure.

Melaphor cast an uneasy glance at the dog, but only for a moment. Then he grinned, his teeth like those of an animal, sharp and dangerous. "But I've come to help you," he said, his words coming out in a lazy purr, only emphasizing his tawny, leonine features.

"Help me? Help yourself, would be more like it. As you have been for the last few months."

The evil lord before him stilled. "What do you mean? I haven't been—"

Rockhurst waved his hand, dismissing whatever the creature had to say as more lies and deceptions. "Haven't been what? Feeding? Of course you have. What about the girl from the other night. Or have you gotten so corrupt and aged, you can't remember?"

Taking a step back, Melaphor studied him, his fair brows drawn across his pale features in a taut line. It was almost as if he were weighing these accusations for the first time.

The disquiet that had weighed on Rockhurst earlier resurfaced. There was something wrong about all this. But like the scent of apple blossoms, he shook off such deceptively distracting thoughts.

For it had to have been Melaphor—or at the very least, one of his minions. For who else could have wrought such horrors?

The fiend tipped his head and studied him. "How dull of you to natter on about my age. As for a girl . . ." He gave a negligent shrug of his narrow shoulders. "Was she pretty? I tend to remember the pretty ones more readily." He chuckled, but his laughter held no playful humor but a deadly reminder of the horror he was capable of. "And now that you mention it, I am rather hungry. Indulge me, my friend. Look the other way and I shall reward you. Just this once—a small child perhaps, or some bit of gamine untried flesh. A reward for not killing you a few moments ago."

"If you could have killed me, you would have," Rockhurst said, keeping Carpio pointed at the creature's black heart.

"Truly, would you honestly miss one of these insignificant little mice you call your subjects?"

"I have none to spare."

"Such a poor kingdom for a prince, don't you think? I rather pity you—for we are much alike I think. Desirous of a life beyond our own, shall we say, tedious obligations."

"We are nothing alike," Rockhurst replied. He settled into his boots, his footing regained and his confidence coming to the forefront.

If only he could shrug off the notion that there was somebody behind him. Most likely it had been one of Melaphor's tricks, but then again . . .

"Nothing alike? Don't fool yourself, Paratus. I kill for pleasure—as you do."

"I kill to keep my people safe, and I will kill you if you take one more step into *my* realm."

"Kill me?" Melaphor's eyes narrowed and lips drawn into a sneer, "I think not. For if you did, my entire family would follow me here to feast—"

"What? In celebration of your removal from their midst?"

Melaphor shrugged. "Amusing, but crude. Do you

really think you can kill me, Paratus?" He paced a bit to the left and the right, smoothly and sleekly like a tiger in a cage, testing the boundaries of his prison. "Do you know how many of your kind I've killed? Eighteen. I've left them just alive enough to watch me take my pleasures with their wives and daughters before I ended their servitude in this wretched world of yours. Really, I was doing them a service, one that I would be more than happy to offer you."

"You can try," Rockhurst told him, feeling the surge of power that came just before a fight.

"Not yet, youngling. You haven't mated yet, haven't produced an heir."

"Who's to say I haven't?"

"Oh, you've rutted your way through this city of yours, but you haven't mated. Found that one woman to tempt your lily-pure heart. If you had, I would be able to smell it on you—like the scent of fear." Melaphor paused and studied him. "And I will take great pleasure in killing her, if only to see the pain it will cause you for denying me what I want."

This is a nightmare, Hermione told herself, pinching her arms and hoping she would wake up. But instead of rescuing her from the dark, sleepy realm of Queen Mab, she only gained a series of marks up and down her arms.

No, she was awake. And this terrible creature before Rockhurst was real.

But he couldn't be. Why, he was exactly like some terrible, wicked fae devil their Irish nanny had threatened her and her brothers and sisters with when they misbehaved.

Tall and elegantly attired like some great prince of old, Melaphor stood as tall as the earl, if not a little taller. Sleek of build, he moved like one of the large cats she'd seen at the Tower. Why, his golden hair alone, what with the way it fell to his shoulders in angelic waves, would probably have every debutante in London swooning.

But this man was no heavenly guest, for Hermione sensed the evil clinging to him as thickly as the Floris perfume Lord Hustings wore.

"Melaphor," Rockhurst was saying, "I grow tired of your threats and musings." He pointed Carpio at the glowing opening in the opposite wall. "Go back and amuse your companions in hell with your tales of long-ago valor. You haven't killed one of my kin in nearly three hundred years."

"Amusing, Paratus, quite amusing." Melaphor paused and glanced over the earl's shoulder. "How about that one?" he asked, pointing directly at Hermione. "Can I kill her?"

Four

Kill her?

Hermione tried to breathe as Melaphor flicked his red-hued gaze toward her. She would have liked to point out to both this horrible man and the earl that she'd said nothing about dying when she'd made her wish.

Nothing whatsoever.

But she suspected neither of them would be sympathetic to her plight, caught as they were in some sort of Montague and Capulet blood feud.

Well, before there was any killing to be done, she was going to excuse herself.

Wavering in her ruined slippers, her knees knocking together worse than they had the first night she'd set foot in Almack's, she went to flee—well, slink off unnoticed. But at the bottom of the steps, she stumbled over the earl's discarded cross-bow.

Rockhurst turned at the noise, and Hermione stilled. "What the devil sort of trick is this, Melaphor?"

His enemy paused. "What? You don't see her?" A sly smile spread slowly over his lips. "Well, isn't this a pleasant surprise. Come, sweetling," he called to her. "Speak to the Paratus. Show yourself, as it were."

Hermione shook her head, fear running rampant through her every limb. Never had she seen evil personified, but this Melaphor was everything that was foul, and her gaze was now locked to his, a slow, hypnotic lethargy filling her veins, stealing away her fears.

Come to me, his voice whispered in her ear. *I won't harm you, child.*

Her foot rose and wavered, taking a step of its own volition. Hermione tried to glance down at her ruined slipper, but she couldn't tear her eyes from Melaphor's. This creature was controlling her as if she were nothing more than a puppet, his blood red gaze now a cord that bound her to him. And as he held out his hand to her, she was utterly and inexplicably drawn to him.

"Come with me," he said, in tones that dripped with smooth charm. "I'll show you the heights of a realm you could never imagine."

Hermione's foot moved forward clumsily, that is until it stubbed once again against the oak of the cross-bow. And in that instant of brief pain, she found the wherewithal to look away.

"End this game, Melaphor," Rockhurst was saying. "We have a matter to settle, and settle it we will."

"Ah, not until I've discovered your charming companion's secret," Melaphor replied.

A ripple of panic ran down Hermione's spine, but she didn't dare look up. So she fixed her gaze on the crossbow at her feet.

The ring thrummed to life on her finger. *Pick it up. Pick up the cross-bow.*

Not that she wanted to listen to the very same ring that had gotten her in this mess. Not that she was generally accustomed to listening to jewelry.

But if whatever magic filled this ring held an iota of the same panic she felt rippling down her spine, it was probably well and good to listen to it just this once.

She scrambled down and gathered up the cross-bow up in her arms. While proficient in archery, Hermione had never shot anything like this before. Such weapons were usually found only on the wall of some musty old country house, where the family displayed the relics of their former bloody glory in the same manner one might a treasured Holbein or a Rembrandt.

Meant to be viewed, not used.

At least not in this century, she mused.

Glancing down at it, she realized the basic workings weren't that hard to understand. Already loaded and locked, she raised it to take aim—unsteadily—but aimed nonetheless.

"Now, now," Melaphor said. "You could hurt someone with that."

Hermione shivered, but held the cross-bow fast.

"She looks quite capable of putting up a bit of fight—not that I mind that in a woman." Melaphor tipped his pointed chin up a bit, and as his hair fell back, Hermione could see that his ears had an elfin point to them. "Something else we have in common, eh Paratus?"

"What the devil—" Rockhurst sputtered as he looked behind him at the empty space where his cross-bow had lain.

Whatever you hold, whatever you wear, will be as invisible as you are, Quince had said.

And so it was with the earl's cross-bow.

"You truly can't see her, can you?" Melaphor said, easing toward her, his narrow gaze flitting from Rockhurst back to Hermione. "How interesting. Come, kitten, reveal yourself. The Paratus seems unable to feast upon your beauty." He sniffed the air. "He should be able to, for you're human, but what have you discovered that lets you pass through your own kind unseen?"

And then his gaze fell on her hand. More specifically, on Charlotte's ring.

To say the man looked astonished was an understatement. "By all that's holy," he gasped. Then in a shimmer of soft light, his entire demeanor changed, rippling from deadly to suavely handsome.

He held out a single hand. "Come away with me, dear lady. Forget all I said before—I was but teasing our friend here. I would never harm you. No, I think I would make you the queen of my realm. A queen of all the realms, if you but come with me."

Rockhurst didn't turn around, but said, "Don't believe him. Whatever you have that he wants—he'll kill you the moment he has you."

"Don't believe him, sweetling. At least I can see you

and appreciate your rare beauty. Don't you want a man who can look into your eyes and see the very depths of your soul?"

Hermione's resolve wavered as she mistakenly glanced up at Melaphor, into his eyes. Instantly the cross-bow grew heavy, and she found it wandering from its original target.

That is until the power of the ring nudged her, and her gaze was wrenched away. She blinked away her hazy vision until she could finally focus on the one thing that gave her strength.

The earl's wide, strong back. It rose before her like a beacon to her rattled senses, and her strength returned. She raised the stock back up and aimed anew.

"So the kitten has claws," Melaphor purred in sleek tones.

"Demmit, I grow tired of this mischief," Rockhurst said, raising his sword and pointing it at Melaphor, and then at the spot where Hermione stood. "Let us end this one way or the other."

"Ah, what is it with you, my good lord Paratus? Always killing before pleasure. We could share her," he offered. "I'm feeling generous tonight."

"I don't want anything to do with you and your ilk," Rockhurst said, turning slightly and pointing his sword in Hermione's direction.

Whatever did he mean to do? Run her through? Why of all the arrogant . . .

Melaphor shrugged. "Then kill her first."

"I believe I will," Rockhurst said.

Hermione eased back, the cross-bow now wavering

between Melaphor and the earl. Whatever was she to do?

"But what if she isn't of my ilk, as you so eloquently put it? That would be a terrible mistake, wouldn't it? Violate that driveling code of yours. No harm shall fall on one of your kind? Isn't that how it works?"

Now it was the earl who wavered, his eyes narrowing as he stared into the space where Hermione stood.

Melaphor continued on, "I wouldn't be too concerned, Paratus. I do believe she'll decide this matter for us. Care to wager on whom she'll shoot? With each passing moment your cross-bow grows heavier in her arms—and by the way, she's trembling so, she's as likely to kill you as she is me."

And indeed, her aim began to waver dangerously. Egads, this Melaphor was as distracting and annoying as Miss Burke and her coughing!

Yet for some reason, the image of Miss Burke uncoiled a strengthening fire within Hermione. She let out a long, slow breath and stilled her wavering limbs as she'd done at the archery contest.

Shooting a cross-bow couldn't be that much different from archery, she hoped. Besides, all she really needed to do was to get the deadly-looking bolt into the man. Slow him down enough for . . .

Hermione gulped. Gracious heavens, what was she thinking? This wasn't some straw-filled bull's-eye she was aiming at, but flesh and blood.

"Demmit, shoot!" Rockhurst ordered. "Quit toying with me and either shoot that bastard or finish me off."

Oh, jiminy! He was asking her to . . .

Hermione shook her head, unable to speak.

"That's right, kitten. You don't want to kill me," Melaphor said, his voice all too seductive.

"Kill him, you fool," Rockhurst ground out, extending his sword toward her. "By all that's holy, kill him, or give me back my cross-bow, so I can do it."

It was the moment that Melaphor had been waiting for. With Rockhurst distracted, he sprang forward, his teeth elongating like those of a wolf, the glow of his eyes turning as dark as spilled blood.

The alley and everything around her spun into a howling whirlwind.

"No!" she screamed, taking hasty aim even as her finger tugged at the trigger.

The bolt flew through the air, traveling with a deadly *thwang*. But Hermione hadn't taken the time to brace herself and lost her footing as the kick of the shot knocked her off balance.

She heard a shriek—a scream that pierced the night– then a blinding flash of light as it seemed the entire alleyway ignited into a fireball.

Falling back, she struck her head and was carried into the same darkness that claimed the alleyway, and the silence that followed.

"What the hell just happened?" Rockhurst said as he drew Carpio out of the last glowing remnants of what had been Melaphor's illicit door.

The bolt from his cross-bow had come shrieking out of thin air and hit the bastard in the shoulder, carrying him back through the portal.

The earl had had enough wit about him to drive Carpio into the last glimmering vestiges of Melaphor's entrance to close it and lock it, so he could no longer pass through this leak between their realms.

After a few trembling moments of silence, he glanced over at Rowan. "Well, what do you make of all this?"

The dog looked up at him with the eyes of an aggrieved poet.

"Yes, so I thought. I should have listened to you earlier. Someone was following us. A young woman, if Melaphor is to be believed."

He turned and spied his cross-bow, now lying abandoned near the steps.

"So do I take this to mean you have no intention of shooting me?" he asked. When no one answered, he didn't know whether to feel vexed or foolish for talking to shadows.

"So you won't speak to me, but I have to imagine you haven't gone far," he said, looking for any sign that might give her away. All the while he kept a wary watch on his surroundings. Rowan, too, remained alert.

But there was nothing but silence in the alley—only the muffled murky sounds of the Dials drifting in around them like weary bits of wind.

Rockhurst stilled for a moment. Wind. That was it. He sniffed the air, and amongst the stench and other foul odors, a tiny whiff of apple blossoms caught his nose.

Her perfume.

Which meant she was still here. And close at hand.

Nodding to Rowan, he said, "Where is she, boy? Show me."

He swore the dog smiled as it sprang from its place and trotted directly to the stairs. He tipped his head down and nudged at the empty space.

Rockhurst came over and knelt beside him. When he reached out, his hand immediately ran into the soft rounded curves of a woman.

Her breast, to be exact. A perfectly formed, warm, full breast.

He snatched his hand back and shot an accusing glance at Rowan. "Not really sporting, you mutt. You should warn a fellow before he makes a cake of things."

Carefully, he reached out again, cautiously tracing her outline.

His fingers trailed over her silk gown, over a flurry of ribbons and embroidery, along the lines of her fashionable neckline and short sleeves, down her arm where there was a glove on one hand and when he reached across, he found none on the other.

He'd undressed enough women in the dark to know a well-dressed lady when he felt one. And worse yet, she was young—for her skin was delicate and soft, her body ripe, rather than the lush and full figure of a matron or woman of the world. And her hands hadn't a callus or a rough patch to show that she'd ever done anything more strenuous than pull on her gloves.

He stared down at the space before him and could all but imagine the woman before him.

A Mayfair debutante. He sat back on his heels and shook his head. But whatever was she doing here? In the Dials?

Not to mention, invisible!

No, he had it all wrong. She couldn't be some Bath miss. Despite Melaphor's claims to the contrary, he didn't believe for a second this chit was human. But when he touched her again and his hand fell over the fullness of her breasts, a jolt of desire rocked through him.

"Steady, Rockhurst," he whispered. Well, he'd always been a sucker for a fine pair, and this chit definitely had a plentiful and perfect set.

Rowan snorted, with his usual uncanny ability to read his master's thoughts.

" 'Tis necessary," he told the great hound as he continued his search, "if we are to discover who she is."

The dog didn't appear to be as convinced as Rockhurst tried to sound.

At her throat, he checked her pulse, and at her lips, the warmth of her breath, shallow but steady, teased his fingers.

She's alive.

That thought sent an odd shiver of relief down his limbs.

"Are you hurt?" he asked, though to no avail. She remained still and silent. "Foolish little shadow. I'd wager you didn't get your footing before you shot, and now you've gone and knocked yourself cold." He rubbed his jaw and glanced over at Rowan. "What the devil are we supposed to do with her now?"

Rowan glanced toward the other end of the alley, where surely Tibbets had his carriage waiting. Rowan's thoughts were already on the beef bone the cook had tucked away in the pot over the fire for tomorrow's soup.

So there it was, one vote to leave her. And Rockhurst was inclined to do just that, if it hadn't been for the fact that she'd saved his life . . . in a manner of speaking.

Though if she hadn't been here in the first place, he might have been able to finish off Melaphor once and for all without all the distraction.

But she had saved him, or at least he hoped she had meant to, and that it wasn't as that rotter had said, her shot was more mistake than intent.

"Well, mistake or not, I suppose we have to find out who you are," he said, gathering up his belongings and stuffing them in his leather bag. After pulling on his coat, he slung the bag over his shoulder, and then reached down to pick her up.

He grunted at the effort. "She might be a beauty, but she's no lithe miss," he joked to Rowan. Not that Rockhurst had ever liked a woman with no figure to speak of—a woman should be rounded in his estimation, with curves and hips and full breasts.

The image of those breasts teased him anew, and he jostled her so they weren't pressed quite so intimately against him.

He whistled to Rowan, and was about to set off down the alley, when something at his feet caught his eye. Wavering under his burden, he knelt again and picked up a solitary glove—the mate, he supposed, to the one still on her hand. Awkwardly, he tucked it into his coat. "Come along, boy. 'Tis nearly morning, and I've a desire to see what the dawn brings from the comfort of my own bed."

Hermione lurched awake and almost immediately put her hands on the back of her head.

Oh, dear heavens what a megrim! The sort from too much wine . . . or having listened overly long to one of her mother's matrimonial lectures . . .

But then the images of the night before assailed her. And she remembered.

The blinding light in the alley.

Melaphor's uncanny red gaze.

And the earl. Tall and strong, his shirt stretched over his muscled back. Sword in hand, he'd turned to her . . . Hermione flinched as she tried to remember the rest. *He'd turned to her with a sword in hand and murder in his eyes.*

Egads, the Earl of Rockhurst had tried to kill her!

Her eyes sprang open, and she clamored upright, only to find herself in the tiger's seat of a curricle.

Rockhurst's curricle, to be exact. For there the earl sat not a foot in front of her. And beside him, Rowan. Much to her chagrin, the hound stared directly at her like a sentry.

She glanced around and realized they were driving through Berkeley Square, her house just across the park in the middle. He was bringing her home.

But then she glanced at the sky, where the first fingers of dawn were starting to part the curtain of night.

Nearly sunrise. She sighed with relief that this nightmare of an evening was almost over. That is, until the words of her wish echoed like a warning though her thoughts.

From sunset to sunrise . . .

Just then the carriage started up again, and the earl turned, not toward her house but in the opposite direction.

Toward Hanover Square. To his house.

And when the sun rose, as it was wont to do in about an hour or so, she'd be visible. And worst of all, ruined.

What was it India had said? About the earl's attics? Heavens, what if her friend was right, and Rockhurst was taking her there to lock her up in some ungodly harem?

Given all she'd seen in the past few hours, she wouldn't put it past him.

At the next intersection, a heavy wagon was already making its slow crossing, so the earl pulled his set to a stop.

Hermione glanced at the sky and realized this was her chance. Timing her escape just so, as the earl slapped the ribbons over the back of the horses, she made her leap.

Rowan watched her go but did nothing. Thankfully. Perhaps the dog was as glad to be rid of her—as she was to be rid of them.

Without another glance in their direction, Hermione turned and ran back toward Berkeley Square.

Never again, she told herself. Never again would she follow the earl into the night. Why, it had nearly gotten her killed. She made her way to the back of their town house, where luckily, because her brother Griffin kept such irregular hours, he'd made a bargain with their butler, Fenwick, to keep a key to the servant's entrance hanging in the potting shed.

Not that she'd ever had an occasion to use the key, but now, as she let herself in, she was glad Griffin was such a useless scamp.

From there, she made her way upstairs to her own room and slipped into her bed even as the sun rose. Exhausted, she didn't even bother to look to see if she'd regained her old self—for she fell asleep almost instantly, bedraggled and exhausted, with only one thought.

Never again.

"Mary! Mary! Demmit, where are you?" Rockhurst bellowed as he stormed into his cousin's house at the unfashionable hour of eleven in the morning. "Mary, where the devil are you?"

He hadn't bothered to ring the bell or even knock, having barreled in like the hounds of hell were at his heels.

"I'm in here, you beast," she called out from her library. "And do stop shouting or Papa will think the house is on fire and summon the Watch again."

Rockhurst pushed open the double doors and crossed the large room. He slapped the glove, which he'd had clenched in his fist since the moment he'd discovered his Shadow had slipped from his carriage, down on her desk.

Not really his Shadow, he argued with himself. But where the devil had the chit gone? When he'd discovered her missing, he'd driven round and round through Mayfair with Rowan loping alongside the carriage. But there'd been no sign of her whereabouts. What if she'd fainted again? Was more hurt than he'd realized? He glanced down at the only clue he possessed as to her identity.

Her glove. A gaudy piece for certain, but there was something about its strumpet charm that intrigued Rockhurst in ways he'd never thought possible.

Besides, there were other reasons to find her. She'd saved his life, and he felt a sort of responsibility for the little handful.

Yes, that was it, a responsibility . . .

He paused for a second and realized his cousin was staring up at him. No, gaping at him.

"Well, can you tell me or not?" he blustered.

"Tell you what?" Mary took off her spectacles and set them on her desk.

He glanced down and realized he had yet to remove his hand from his prize. Trying to feign a nonchalance he didn't feel, he pushed the glove across Mary's desk. "Can you tell me where *that* came from?"

Sitting up, she put her spectacles back on and peered down at it. "I would have to imagine it came from a woman's hand."

Rockhurst sputtered something unintelligible before he finally ground out, "Who made it?"

Mary took another glance at the bit of feminine finery and quirked a brow. "Lost another wager, Rockhurst?" She sat back in her chair and looked him over with the same scholarly review as she might some old tract. "You haven't been home yet. Why, you look the very devil, cousin."

He rubbed his stubbled jaw. "Of course I haven't been home. I've been trying to find her." He pointed at the glove as if it were the bane of his existence, when quite the opposite. He huffed a sigh and paced about the room.

"Very intriguing," she said, rising from and moving around the desk to block his path. "Who is she?"

"She's the owner of that glove."

She crossed her arms over her chest. "My, my. I would like to meet her. For I've never seen you at sixes and sevens over a woman."

He ruffled and blustered. "I am no such thing. Blast and damnation, Mary, I need to know who that glove belongs to." Gads, even to his own ears the note of desperation in his voice was a completely unfamiliar tune.

Suddenly Mary's face paled. "You didn't? Not one of those little fools at Almack's last night? Is that it? You've gone and ruined some innocent?"

"Demmit, Mary, it isn't anything like that."

"Then why don't you tell me how it was?"

"Well, I would if you would stop peppering me with endless questions." He raked his hand through his hair. "She might be hurt," he confessed.

Mary took a step back from him. "Rockhurst, what are you saying? You didn't . . . ?"

He shook his head vehemently. "No, it wasn't my fault. And even if it was, she's not . . . not . . ."

"Not what?"

"Not one of us."

She glanced back at the glove. "Oh, dear."

"At least I don't think so."

This stopped Mary. "You couldn't tell whether or not she was human?"

He shook his head. "No, I couldn't see her. A spell of some sort. She was invisible. Melaphor could see her, but I—"

"Melaphor?!" Mary burst out. "What has he to do with all this?"

"*She* shot him. The chit who owns that glove." He glanced at it again and tamped down the urge to reclaim it. Tuck it in his pocket and keep it close.

Now there was no doubt about it. He was going mad. He shoved his hands in his pockets and turned his back to the desk.

"Tell me she killed him."

"Unfortunately not. Though she got the bolt pretty close to his heart, and the force of it knocked him back through the opening."

"Did you get it sealed in time?"

He nodded.

Mary sighed and shook her head. "This is very troubling. Not just the girl, but . . . but . . ." She paused and lowered her voice to finish. "So it is as you feared? Melaphor is the one who's been causing all the deaths in the Dials?"

"Apparently so," Rockhurst said.

"Apparently?" Mary's brow wrinkled, then she took him by the arm and led him to the fire. Pushing him down in her father's chair, she turned and added more coal. It was a task for a servant, but Mary was too practical to summon a servant to do something she herself could accomplish in a fraction of the time. Then she pulled an ottoman close and settled herself atop it.

"What happened, cousin?" she asked, her hands primly folded in her lap. "Tell me everything."

"I went to the Dials last night—"

"From Almack's to the rookeries." She smiled slightly. "You do know how to live."

"Very funny," he replied. "Cappon sent a note around that someone was opening doors—"

As he related the rest of the evening's events, the warmth of the fire slowly eased his tired muscles, not that he noticed overly much, for he was as transfixed by the facts he was relating as was his audience. And it helped him to be able to share them with Mary, for she was possibly the only member of the *ton* who knew his secret.

To London society, he was the Earl of Rockhurst. But to the shadowy underworld that clung to the veneer of their modern world, he was the Paratus, a title taken from their ancient family motto.

Semper Paratus. Always prepared.

And it had been thus for thirty some generations of Rockhursts. They had been given London as theirs to guard and rule by a queen so ancient none but a few scholars like Mary had even heard of her. Beyond the title and riches, the wise ruler had also given her loyal subject, the first Earl of Rockhurst, strength of body and spirit, as well as cunning and intelligence that outstripped those of mere men. These gifts had for the most part protected, though not always, the earls from their enemies, Melaphor in particular.

For the realm they'd been charged with guarding stood between a place of light and magic and an old evil, one that was just as devious and just as determined to return to their former garden as the Paratus was resolute to contain them in their dark prison.

But as the centuries passed, London and its inhabitants had changed, and with them, the old magic faded, and what had once been a matter of fact, that evil could live and breathe, was now considered nothing but legend. Even the Paratus had been shelved and catalogued with those ancient stories, another myth that had no place in their jostling and expanding world.

Except to Rockhurst, who bore with all his heart the family obligation to protect London. Would until the day he died.

"And you have no other clues as to who she might be?" Mary was asking. "Other than that glove."

His hand flexed, and then cupped to the shape of the breast he'd unwittingly caught hold of. He doubted he would ever forget the way it fit in his hand, the warmth of her flesh. But he could hardly make the rounds about London society catching hold of every likely bosom.

Even for a man of his unsavory reputation, that would be beyond the pale.

"No," he told her. "Just the glove."

Mary sat back and sighed. "That isn't much. Why seeing you and Melaphor was probably enough to send her scurrying onto the nearest mail coach to Penzance." She leaned forward and studied the glove. "And you say she was invisible?"

"Utterly. Though Rowan could see her, as could Melaphor. He claimed her to be a pretty bit."

"He thought to make her his nuncheon, so of course he thought her pretty." Mary rose and adjusted her spectacles, her gaze scanning the top shelves of her prized library. "Invisibility isn't something that can be conjured by just anyone. It's a dangerous sort of spell."

Rockhurst glanced up from the fire. "Dangerous?"

"Well, dangerous enough that this Shadow of yours is either one of them, or she's come across the ring."

"The ring?"

"You know," she said, glancing around and lowering her voice. "*The ring.*"

"Milton's Ring?" Now it was Rockhurst's turn to scoff. "You must be jesting. That ring is myth, nothing more than an old story meant to keep the foolish full of dreams."

"I wouldn't be so skeptical. Some would say the same of the Paratus. Perhaps you've heard the story? Of a great nobleman who spends his nights scouring the worst corners of London—"

He held up a hand to stave her off. "Point well-taken. Say Milton's Ring isn't a myth, how did it just suddenly turn up? Let alone grant some miss the power to go about unseen?" He shook his head and looked her directly in the eye. "For that matter, what sort of miss would wish to follow me around?"

Mary laughed. "Given your reputation for moonlit scandals, I'm surprised this is only the first one who's followed you into the night."

Rockhurst wasn't amused. "If it is Milton's Ring, then how do I—"

"Oh, good God!" Mary suddenly exclaimed, whirling around from her shelves of books. "You must find this girl!"

Taken a bit aback by his cousin's uncharacteristic outburst, he asked, "Why?"

"If you were to gain Milton's Ring, you could end your charter," she whispered.

He cocked his head, for he swore he hadn't heard her correctly. "I could do what?"

"The charter," she said, turning back to her books. Over her shoulder, she said, "The one that binds you as the Paratus. You could end it with Milton's Ring."

He rose as well. End the charter? Why it was unthinkable. And he told her so. "I couldn't do that. Then there would be no one to—"

When she glanced again at him, he found her eyes alight with an excitement he hadn't seen there since they were children and he'd shown her London from atop St. Paul's. "That's just it," she told him. "You would wish for the doors to be closed. Forever."

Forever? Rockhurst's breath caught in his throat. He'd be free. Suddenly the warmth of the room overwhelmed him, so he walked over to the window and opened it in search of a bit of fresh air. Free? He'd never imagined his life thusly.

And while he tried to, Mary nattered on. ". . . of course, Cricks would have more information on this, but the possibilities are unbelievable."

That, he had to wager, was an understatement.

* * *

"Oh, Minny, there you are," Lady Walbrook called out, as Hermione walked gingerly into the breakfast room. "Feeling better?"

Hermione nodded. "Yes, Mother, quite recovered." She paused, still teetering at the doorjamb, unwilling to cross the threshold just yet. Good thing she did, for her mother immediately launched into her latest campaign.

Getting Hermione married.

Now that Sebastian had wed, the countess was determined to continue her matrimonial streak and see Hermione happily united with an entirely perfect *parti*.

"Lord Hustings sent flowers over. First thing. Such an attentive man. How unfortunate that he is so dull."

A spark of suspicion rose in Hermione's breast. What was this? Her mother was no longer championing Lord Hustings's suit?

Her mother, meanwhile, stirred another lump of sugar into her tea and glanced up at Hermione as if she were surprised to see her still standing at the threshold. "Come along and take your seat. It is terrible for your posture to loiter about like that."

Hermione did as she was bid and took her place, albeit reluctantly, for she wasn't entirely unconvinced that the better part of valor would be to flee. That is, until Fenwick came by with her favorite breakfast, kippers and toast, which she tucked into with her usual gusto.

Her life might be upside down, but her stomach seemed to be in working order. She couldn't say the same of her capucine gown and slippers.

Or her new gloves! Hermione paused between bites for a moment of mourning. At least she'd saved one of them. The other . . . well, it had best enjoy the rest of its life in the Dials, for Hermione wasn't going back to fetch it, no matter that it was her favorite pair.

Perhaps Monsieur Bédard could be enticed to make another one. That is if she could get Sebastian to advance her a portion of her next year's allowance.

"Well, it seems you are feeling better," her mother noted. "You must do your best not to be overset every time the earl is about. It will not do, Minny."

"I can assure you, Mother, it will never happen again," Hermione told her. All she would have to do was remember the earl stripped down to his shirt and breeches. The sight of his magnificent body had been enough to stir a different sort of trouble inside her.

"I should hope not," the countess remarked, waving at Fenwick to bring her another serving of ham. "For I think you should pursue a match with the man."

Unfortunately, Hermione had just filled her mouth with a large gulp of tea, which she nearly sprayed all over the breakfast table. "You-u-u wa-a-ant me to do wha-a-at?"

"Pursue Rockhurst," her mother said with the same detached sort of manner that one might say "sugar or cream?" or "please pass the toast." The countess glanced up at Hermione. "He is far too rich and really quite a fine specimen of a man. If half the rumors about him are true, he'll make you a content wife."

"Mother!" Hermione's face felt as red as the strawberry jam in the pot before her. Never mind the fact that she'd been thinking a very similar thought not a few moments earlier, but really, did her mother have to say it? *Aloud?* Let alone notice such a thing?

"Well, he would. And don't look at me so! I have more experience in these matters than you do, and I can tell you that a man with some prowess makes a better husband."

"You've always declared him the worst sort of rake," Hermione said, hoping to reawaken her mother's former opinion of the man.

"So I did," the lady replied, waving her toast like a scepter. "But since he took us to the opera—"

"He took Charlotte," Hermione corrected. "We were but there to lend some respectability to the entire evening."

"Yes, yes, but Hermione, you aren't looking at this with the right perspective. He was only showering Charlotte with attention to rouse Sebastian. Such a dear man to help those two find each other."

"Harrumph," Hermione sputtered. Her mother had been too busy chatting with her friends that night to notice how the earl had been looking at Charlotte. But that was neither here nor there, since Charlotte was now wed to Sebastian.

As for the earl, now that was an entirely other matter.

Her mother continued on. "What Rockhurst might lack in morals, he more than makes up for in wealth. And now that he is inclined to marry—"

"I don't think the earl has any intention of—"

"Of course he intends to marry. He made his bow at Almack's."

Which of course every matron in London knew was code for: *I wish to marry your daughter immediately.*

"Either the man has finally gone mad, like the rest of his ramshackle relations," the countess declared, "or he intends to wed. I prefer to think him inspired by Sebastian and Charlotte's happiness, rather than to give in to the rather uncharitable alternative."

Hermione wondered if she should enlighten her mother that she was closer to the truth than she knew.

The earl *was* mad.

So as the countess nattered on, having obviously given up most of the night and morning to planning Hermione's future as the Countess of Rockhurst, Hermione did her best to eat her breakfast and plot an escape route. Perhaps she could take up the scholarly life like her sister Cordelia and hide in Bath. Or if her mother was persistent, as she appeared, she might be forced to join her father on some heathen island in the Pacific.

Far from her mother. And *him.*

The Earl of Rockhurst. And his blue eyes. That steely jaw. And the long lean line of his muscled . . .

Viola and Griffin filed in, taking their seats, and as they caught the gist of the conversation—that it had nothing to do with either of them—they grinned at Hermione and betook of their breakfasts with unabashed joy.

Hermione, on the other hand, found that her kippers tasted off, and her toast, well it was like sawdust in her mouth. For resolving to have no interest in the earl and actually doing it was proving more difficult than she would have supposed. Naturally curious, she couldn't help but wonder a thousand different questions . . .

First, why had Melaphor called the earl "the Paratus"?

And why did Lord Rockhurst think it was his duty to rid the Dials of such creatures? Why didn't he just call the Watch and be done with the matter?

Oh heavens, she'd stumbled, quite unwittingly, into something far beyond her ken. If only Cordelia was here instead of off in Bath digging about the old ruins in their aunt's cellar. She'd be able to determine what a "Paratus" was, and for that matter, what sort of creature Melaphor might be.

"I think a minor production of scenes from *The Tempest* would be the perfect setting for a courtship," her mother was saying.

This was followed by a long, pregnant pause as both Griffin and Viola stared at Hermione, as if waiting for her protest.

Oh, good heavens, what had maman *come up with now?*

"Hermione, stop woolgathering," Lady Walbrook scolded. "I think a theatrical evening, with the earl in attendance, will be the most divine way to show you to your best advantage."

Griffin's and Viola's heads turned in unison, as if they were watching their mother's verbal volley lob its way down the table.

It hit with the same deadly precision as the earl's cross-bow. A theatrical evening? With the earl?

Never mind the fact that for the time being, she wouldn't be exactly visible at night, but her mother wanted to enlist the Earl of Rockhurst into one her amateur theatricals?

Hermione bit her trembling lips together. Perhaps she could induce Rockhurst to shoot her the next time she saw him and save them both the misery of such an evening.

Not that she intended to go following him about again . . .

"*The Tempest* is the perfect play," Lady Walbrook continued, completely oblivious to her daughter's horror and her other offsprings' utter delight. "Rockhurst *is* Prospero, don't you think? An anguished soul if ever I saw one."

"Add tortured, once you get done with him," Viola muttered.

Griffin began tucking into his breakfast with the speed of a coachman, and from the looks of it, ready to bolt for the nearest carriage out of town. Or at the very least, next door to the Kendells, where he'd most likely spend the next fortnight hiding in Sir Joshua's laboratory.

Hermione was almost afraid to ask. "And you want me to play Miranda?"

"Heavens no, dear child. You would have utterly no scenes with Rockhurst. I want you to play Caliban."

She shook her head, for she was certain she hadn't heard her mother correctly. "You want me to play the monster?"

"Why of course, my dear. For the earl will be sure to see your beauty shine through even the most hideous of characters."

That is, if he doesn't kill me first.

Five

Rockhurst was in the process of taking his leave, when Mary's butler, Cosgrove, came in to announce more guests.

"Mr. Griffin Marlowe and Lady Hermione Marlowe to see you, miss. Are you at home?"

"Of course I am," Mary replied. She nudged her cousin. "That is how it is done properly. You ring the bell and ask Cosgrove to announce you. Then you wait patiently in the foyer for him to grant you entrance, not barging in and bellowing like the French have taken up position in Hyde Park."

"I'll keep that in mind," he told her, taking up his hat and gloves from where he'd tossed them. "If the French ever invade."

Mary laughed. "You are the very devil, Rockhurst."

"So I've been told." He glanced at the door and frowned. "Demmed luck."

"What is?"

"Marlowe! That scamp has been trying to buttonhole me for a week, and so far I've done a good job avoiding him."

"Griffin doesn't mean any harm," Mary chided.

"No, not to me, just to my pocketbook. Poor Battersby—the lad had him cornered at White's for most of a night listening to him natter on about his electrical theories. Electricity, indeed!"

"Then you'd best go out the back and quickly if you want to avoid him," Mary said, opening the door, only to find Cosgrove's dignified presence blocking his path.

"Lady Hermione Marlowe, miss," Cosgrove intoned as formally as one might announce the Prince Regent.

"Where is Griffin?" Mary asked, as Lady Hermione Marlowe came bustling into the room, leaving Rockhurst wedged behind the door and completely unseen. He smiled over the girl's shoulder, for her enormous feathered bonnet kept him completely out of her line of sight. He winked at Mary and pointed toward the door as he slipped out of the room.

He tried his best to avoid debutantes at all costs, but a Marlowe? Sebastian Marlowe seemed a steady sort, but the rest of the family? Rockhurst shuddered. Ramshackle. The entire lot of them.

The man who married into that family might just as well book a corner room at Bedlam.

He made his smooth escape as he heard this particular Marlowe let out a little puffy sigh, then say, "Griffin took a detour down to see if Mrs. Jacobs has any scones baking. Really, Mary, I am so sorry my brother is such a trial to you. I'd send him packing if I were you—but then again, there'd be nothing left in our larder if he didn't spend most of his days over here."

Feeling overly smug that he was about to escape undetected, Rockhurst made it to the front foyer when all of a sudden he stopped.

And inhaled.

For there it was—a hint of apple blossoms lingering in the hallway.

Her perfume. He sniffed again. Yes, there it was. How was that possible? Unless . . .

Rockhurst turned around slowly and stared down the hallway toward the library door. Lady Hermione Marlowe? *No!*

But then just as quickly, the hallway filled with the tall figure of her brother, Griffin Marlowe. And when the young man spotted him, his face broke out in a wide grin. "Rockhurst! Devil's own luck running into you! I've been meaning to talk to you about my electrical machine. A time carriage if you will—I've but a few more adjustments to make to my calculations and, of course, the blunt to put it all together, but you seem an intelligent sort—" He clapped his hand on the earl's back and all but pushed him out the door and down the steps. "On your way to White's? No? Well, no matter, I'll trail along with you if only to share with you some of my recent scientific findings. I'm on the verge of discovering how to use self-generated electricity to alter—"

Rockhurst was about to shake himself free and go back inside when a gaggle of young ladies scurried past them, their mothers bringing up the rear and hurrying them along so as to be well out of his notice.

Then he caught a whiff of apple blossoms yet again.

Of course Marlowe's sister wore the same innocent fragrance that nearly every other young miss in London preferred.

Which meant it would be impossible to find his Shadow by her perfume alone. Not that he was about to give up so easily. There was still her glove . . . and her perfect breasts . . .

But his musing was interrupted by the nudge of an elbow into his ribs.

"Scone?" Griffin offered, plucking one from out of his coat pocket. "I can highly recommend them."

"Minny, you are just who I wanted to see," Mary declared, after pouring her a cup of tea.

"Then it is fortuitous that I came over," Hermione replied.

"Indeed. I need to know who might have made this glove, or better yet, have you seen it on anyone this Season?"

Hermione glanced up to find Mary holding a piece of gold silk. The tea in her cup sloshed about and she had to use both hands to steady it.

Her glove.

"However did you—" Hermione started to say, but stopped herself. Not that Mary noticed, for she was in the process of turning the poor glove inside out and quite possibly ruining the embroidery. It was all Hermione could do not to reach out and snatch it out of Mary's irreverent grasp.

Didn't she know one didn't crush silk like that? Especially not when . . . Hermione paused in her indignation as she realized a more important point.

Her glove! Rockhurst had saved it. As he'd saved her by bringing her back to Mayfair. She still wasn't all that convinced he'd carried her out of the Dials for anything other than another prize for his harem, but her glove? Now that was heroic.

Mary shook the piece out. "Does it look familiar?"

Hermione steadied her cup again, then shook her head. "No, I've never seen it before. Where did you find it?"

"I didn't, Rockhurst did. He wants to discover the lady who owns it and see it returned."

She might have been pleased if it hadn't been for the fact that now the earl had a clue as to how to find her. And worse yet, had enlisted Mary to help him.

And now her, by default. Oh, Hermione was growing dizzier by the second. *He wants to find me.*

He wants to kill you, a wry voice corrected.

Hmmm. There is that. Oh, this is a terrible muddle. "You say he wants to find the owner but doesn't know who she is?" Mary nodded. "Why, it is just like some Cinderella fairy tale," Hermione said, hoping she sounded lighter than she felt.

Mary smiled. "I suppose it does sound rather like that, doesn't it?" She worried the glove some more until she nearly had Hermione about to leap from her seat and claim it outright. But finally she stopped wrinkling it, and said, "We should probably keep this between us, though. Poor Rockhurst, I fear he'd be pelted with shoes and gloves and fans everywhere he went if it got out that he was trying to find some chit because she lost her glove."

Hermione laughed. *Yes, why hadn't I thought of that before? Before I knew who he was, that is . . .*

Her hostess continued on, "He just wants to return it . . . because it's expensive," she hedged. "It is, isn't it? I fear I'm no expert in matters of fashion. What do you say?" Mary held it out for her.

Hermione didn't want to take it, but then again, it was safer in her grasp than Mary's. She caught hold of her prized glove and nearly sighed with delight.

Expensive? It had taken nearly all her pin money and then a lucky hand of casino against Griffin to raise the coins to pay for the exquisite pair.

Money was always in short supply in the Marlowe household, and even though Sebastian had gained a substantial windfall recently with a lucky investment, knowing her prudent and overly sensible brother, he'd insist on putting it all away for a real need or an emergency.

As if replacing her lost glove wasn't such a necessity.

"Is it?" Mary asked again. "Expensive?"

"It might be," she said, taking one last look of longing at the poor lonely mitt before dropping it down on the curio table beside her. If she held it much longer, she was afraid she wouldn't be able to let it go. "But I've never seen it before."

Mary reached over and caught it up in her mangling grasp much to Hermione's chagrin. "You know all the best glovers. Who might have made it?"

Hermione glanced over at it. *Monsieur Bédard.* And his best work, in her discerning estimation. "There are hundreds of glovers in London," she hedged. "It would be impossible to guess."

"Yes, but only a handful or so who could make such a fine piece. I suppose I could go around to the ones I know and see if anyone recognizes the work."

Gulping back the frisson of panic running down her spine—for Monsieur Bédard would most readily remember that particular pair, she said, "I don't think it is all *that* fine, Mary. Most likely an imitation someone had made up in the country and brought to Town."

Mary's brow wrinkled. "Oh, dear. I hadn't even thought of that. Why, it could have come from anywhere."

"Sadly, yes," Hermione told her, holding her breath. Oh, thank goodness, Mary cared more for her books than fashion and would readily swallow such a large bite of gammon.

"I fear Rockhurst will be sadly disappointed if he's unable to return it," Mary said, catching up the glove and carrying it over to her desk. When it appeared that Mary was just going to drop it in a drawer, Hermione couldn't stand it any longer.

The pair were after all, her best gloves.

"Perhaps, I could help you," she offered, almost biting her tongue in the process. No, she shouldn't do this. *Stay out of it* . . . But, oh, those were her favorite gloves, and she had a chance to . . .

"Yes?" Mary asked, her hand poised over the drawer, which probably had ink and all sorts of other things that could possibly ruin the glove for good.

"I could take it with me. Shopping that is," Hermione said, smiling brightly. "I could help you." Mary's brow furrowed for a moment, so she continued. "Think of the time it would save you, and you know how you detest Bond Street. Especially since it seems you have so much work at hand," she offered, waving her hand at Mary's cluttered desk, awash in books, papers, and journals.

Mary's lips pressed together, and for a moment Hermione held her breath. Then she glanced once more at the glove, then back up at Hermione. "You don't mind?"

"Not in the least. Not for a friend," Hermione said brightly, holding out her hand and counting the moments as Mary returned from her desk and deposited the prized glove back in its rightful place.

In Hermione's delighted grasp.

Mary sighed. "Now, with that settled, what brings you over? I had half expected Griffin to come by—to see Father, that is. Well, I always expect Griffin over—especially when Mrs. Jacobs is baking."

They both laughed.

"Actually, it was my mother who sent me over," Hermione told her. "She is staging another theatrical evening."

Mary's features widened with horror. "Oh, no." She dropped down into her chair.

"Oh, yes."

Her friend reached for her teacup as if she needed the fortification. "What is it this time?"

"*The Tempest*," Hermione told her. "And Mother would like me to fetch a book on monsters."

Now it was Mary's turn to slosh her tea. "Monsters?" she said faintly. "I don't think I have—"

"Griffin said you had an entire shelf on old creatures and such," Hermione interjected. "Mother is quite adamant to ensure that Caliban . . . oh, how did she say it, 'reflects Prospero's tortured soul and the darkest elements of his lost magic.'"

"Yes, well . . ." Mary managed as her lips twitched traitorously. However, she was far too polite to make any comments about Lady Walbrook's notorious re-writing of the Bard. "That sounds—"

"Perfectly monstrous," Hermione finished for her. "In a manner of speaking." Again they both laughed. "Stay clear of her for at least a week, while she's casting about for likely players."

Mary nodded in agreement. "Thank you for the warning. I'll also tell Mrs. Jacobs to lay in extra provisions for Griffin. No doubt you've noticed he tends to move here when your mother is in one of her—" She bit her lips together as she tried to find the right words.

Hermione knew the expression all too well. "Artistic moods?"

"Yes, exactly." Mary sighed with relief. "And whom does she have in mind for Prospero?"

"Oh, this is where it becomes unbearable. She thinks to corner your cousin for the role."

"Rockhurst?" This time Mary's tea spilled over onto the carpet.

Hermione shuddered, then handed her friend a napkin. "Yes. I fear so. Since he was at Almack's last night . . . well, you know what that means."

"I fear I do. My Aunt Routledge was over quite early, ready to launch her own campaign. But, poor Minny. Does your mother think to have you play Miranda?"

"No, even worse." Hermione paused, almost unwilling to admit what would most likely become the most humiliating evening of her life. She heaved a sigh and got it over with. "Caliban."

Mary paused from wiping up her tea, her mouth falling open. Then she began to laugh, heartily and thoroughly and really, Hermione couldn't take offense. One had to have a sense of humor about Lady Walbrook's theatrical endeavors because sooner or later all her acquaintances found themselves cornered into one of her infamous productions.

Hadn't Mary done a turn as Lady Macbeth not two years earlier?

"Mother would like me to capture the 'devilish' qualities of my character, and Griffin assured her you had just the book."

"Actually, I do. Probably several," she confessed, rising and walking over to the far bookshelf. Pulling out a footstool, she got up on it and ran her finger over the spines of the tombs on the top shelf. "Do you read Latin?"

Hermione shook her head. She barely understood French. Unless that is, it was a French fashion magazine.

"Too bad. I have a wonderful treatise on dark creatures that is impossible to put down. Alas, it is in Latin."

"How unfortunate for me," Hermione said, trying to sound disappointed.

"Ah, here is one. And in English. Mostly." She tugged a thick volume free and blew the dust from it. Glancing at the book fondly, she held it out for Hermione. "As long as you don't read it before you go to bed, you shan't have nightmares.

"I'll keep that in mind." Having just survived a very real life nightmare, Hermione managed a wan smile as she took the thick tome in her hands. *Monsters of Olde, A Complete Compendium.* She flipped it open, and the print on the page was of a horrible-looking creature entitled, "A Derga." As she gazed at the monster before her, a shiver of suspicion worked its way down her spine.

Did Mary know about the earl's nightly rambles?

Hermione opened her mouth to ask, but then clamped her lips shut. What was she thinking? And whatever would she say?

Mary, last night I made a scandalous wish that would enable me to follow your cousin about all night on his reckless rambles. As the sun set, I turned invisible and discovered that your cousin, the Earl of Rockhurst, is some . . . some sort of . . .

Oh, bother, she hadn't a clue what Rockhurst was! And didn't care in the least to discover why it was he felt compelled to dash about Seven Dials on some personal crusade.

Not a whit, she told herself.

That is until she remembered his wild-eyed gaze as he'd raged at her. *Quit toying with me and either shoot that bastard or finish me off.*

Hermione shivered and wondered how he could be so cavalier about his own life. Finish him off? Whatever had he been thinking?

The ring on her finger trembled beneath her glove, as if it knew, it understood, and she clasped her other hand over it and tried to ignore the wretched bit. "Haven't you gotten me into enough trouble," she whispered.

"Pardon?" Mary said, turning around from the shelves. "Did you say something?"

Hermione gulped. "Oh, just that you have so many books. I was wondering why you went to the trouble to keep them all."

"I don't think it is any trouble whatsoever," Mary said in true bluestocking fashion, turning back to the volumes, her fingers moving quickly along the spines. "This one is extraordinary," she said, handing another book to Hermione, who already found herself staggering beneath a stack with such illustrious titles as *Chronicles of the Invasions, Tarasque of Noves,* and *Transmigration between Realms both Ancient and Modern.*

Hermione had to imagine she wouldn't be feigning a megrim this evening if Mary thought she was truly going to read all these.

Besides, tonight I'll be more careful, she reasoned.

Tonight? Hermione ground her teeth together. There wasn't going to be any tonight.

Mary tugged one book down, shook her head, and reshelved it in another place. "Father! He is forever tucking his books away without any thought of keeping them in order."

Hermione glanced at all the shelves and couldn't think of how one kept them all in order, much less remembered what one had. But then she really started to look around, and for a moment she felt a tremor of hope.

What if there is a book here about what has happened to me?

She shook her head. She couldn't ask such a thing without revealing her predicament. Pressing her lips together, she glanced around the room again. Well, if she couldn't ask someone she knew, how about someone she didn't? They might think her mad, but then again, she wouldn't care.

But who? She hadn't the least idea how to find that odd Quince. And Charlotte was off with Sebastian on her honeymoon, so whatever was she to do? Hermione glanced up at Mary and wondered how it was that she or Cordelia or Griffin went about finding the odd answers they sought?

Then she looked down at the stack of books in her arms. Perhaps a bookshop? Wasn't Griffin always badgering *Maman* for extra money to pick up some book or another at Hatchard's?

Well, Hatchard's probably wouldn't be the best place to start, Hermione reasoned, since it was entirely respectable, but there were other bookshops in London, weren't there? She tipped open the book Mary had given her and spied a yellowed label inside.

Cricks, A Bookseller
No. 3 Ivy Row
Newmarket

Inspiration sent a thrill of delight down her spine. Perhaps this Cricks might have a book about how to end her wish.

And about the Paratus, as well, a little voice urged her.

She snapped the book shut. The Paratus, indeed! Her infatuation with the earl was over. Hermione had no intention of tangling with him again. What she needed to do was end this wish and get on with her life.

Why even Lord Hustings was starting to look appealing.

If only she could get the image of the earl, stripped to his white shirt and breeches and wielding that sword out of her imagination. Ignore the way her knees wobbled and the silly way her heart tripped about and how her mouth went dry.

What she needed to do was remember that the man had threatened to kill her. Who knew what sort of foul plans he'd had in store for her when he'd been carting her about this morning.

At least he didn't leave you down in the Dials, that annoying little voice reminded her.

Bother that! He probably intended to add her to his attic harem as India had speculated.

No, what she needed to do was to go down to this Cricks's bookshop and do a little bit of investigation.

She hugged the books she held to her chest and felt quite proud of herself. Why, it couldn't be any more difficult than trying to find the right ribbons to match a bonnet . . .

A few hours later, Hermione wasn't as convinced as she had been earlier that Mr. Cricks would be her salvation. Not when she found herself standing before his nondescript little shop on Ivy Row.

"Miss, if you don't mind," her maid Betty said. "I've a cousin who works just around the corner there on Newgate Street. The chandler shop."

"Oh, yes," Hermione told her, relieved to be rid of her companion. "Go on. I'll be right along in no time."

"Are you sure?" Betty asked, glancing at the darkened windows of the bookshop and the neighboring establishments, which, like most of Newgate market, were butcher shops and other less fashionable trades.

"Certainly," Hermione assured her. "Mother would never have sent me on this errand if she didn't think it was safe." That had been the falsehood she'd told her maid to get her to come along.

Her mother, on the other hand, thought her shopping for a new gown for Lady Hurland's ball.

Her head spun with all the lies she was telling, never mind the fact that she wasn't very good at telling falsehoods to begin with.

"Very well," Betty said, taking one more glance at the shop as if suddenly adding up the likelihood of Lady Walbrook having sent her daughter to such an establishment.

Hermione nudged her toward the corner and went boldly inside, looking far more brave than she felt. If this were a ribbon shop or a milliner's, she'd be in her element. But books? This was more Cordelia's domain or Griffin's. Not hers.

Whatever bravado she'd worn in front of her maid failed her completely as she looked around the dimly lit space, with its narrow aisles and dark recesses.

She stumbled to a halt, for there were books everywhere. Stacked on the tables, crowded into the shelves, and overflowing onto the floor. Dust motes danced in the one narrow shaft of light that managed to slant through a clean spot in the otherwise filthy windows.

Wherever would she start when she couldn't read half the titles before her? Latin, French. One in German, or so she thought it was German. Why it could be Hottentot for all she knew.

And the titles she could discern didn't do much to raise her confidence.

The Witch Trials of 1444: Burning and Torture Cures.

Defense and Counterdefenses Against the Western Plight of Evil.

Ancient Myths of the Faeirie and Their Dark Realm.

Executions of the Enchanted.

Hermione flinched as she read the last title, the image of Rockhurst coming clearly into her imagination. Oh, dear no! She didn't want to start thinking about *him*. Instead, she turned to see if she could find something more relevant.

Such as *Keeping One's Wishes To Oneself,* she mused as she ran her finger along a row of spines, which only resulted in raising a cloud of dust.

Heavens, when was the last time this place was cleaned? she thought, as her nose twitched. She pinched it shut to stop the ensuing sneeze, but it was to no avail. She sneezed, breaking the unworldly calm in the shop.

"Who's there?" barked a wheezy old voice.

Hermione jumped. Hardly the friendly sort. Accustomed as she was to shopping in Mayfair, where the clerks rushed to help her, she wasn't too sure what to do or say to such rudeness.

"Well, either you want something, or be gone!" the still-unseen man grumbled.

She had to imagine that the best plan of action was to ease into the subject.

Then ask him about the Paratus. The ring thrummed happily on her finger.

Hermione flinched and shoved her hand inside her pocket. She was not here to find out about *him*. The only thing she wanted to discover was how to make a wishing ring go away.

"Well, do you want something or not?"

"Uh, yes, I believe you sold my friend this book," she said, reaching into the bag she carried and pulling out one of the volumes Mary had given her. "Do you have anything else on the same subject?"

There was the creak of a chair as it slid back across the floor, then from the shadows in the back stirred a small, hunched figure. Slowly, the man came forward, his shuffled steps and the thump of his cane echoing through the still shop.

She hadn't noticed it before, but the noise from the markets and traffic beyond were barely discernable inside Cricks's odd shop, and there was an eerie calm about the place that defied even the ever-present din of London.

Hermione shivered and wrapped her pelisse tighter around her shoulders. Why, one would have thought it was January, not the last day of May, by the sudden chill surrounding her.

The old man stopped before her, pushed his spectacles back up from the tip of his nose, then flicked his watery glance toward the book, which apparently held more interest to the man than the sight of a Mayfair miss in his lonely shop.

"Mr. Cricks?" she asked, since there seemed to be no one else in the place.

"Oh, aye. I'm Cricks. What have we here?" He reached out and snatched the volume from her. His bleary gaze sharpened as he read the title. "Wherever did you get this?"

"A friend. She lent it to me," Hermione said, tugging it back out of his grasp. For an old man, he had quite a grip, and it took a pull or two to retrieve it. "She suggested you might have some similar works."

Now his gaze returned to sweep from the toes of her boots to the top of her bonnet, before he stared for a long moment into her eyes.

It was then that she realized he was waiting for her to ask the other question, the one she'd tamped down so fiercely at Mary's house.

Ask him. Ask him about the Paratus.

Oh, heavens, she wasn't going down that path. It was paved with trouble, as her mother was wont to say. She wanted only to end this curse and get on with her life.

Find a husband. Bear him an heir or two, and then spend her days in a happy and contented search for the perfect bonnet. Something primrose or maybe that new Sardinian blue she'd spotted the other day . . .

Hermione shook her head. Goodness, she needed to pay attention, or she'd never end this wish.

"You aren't another one of those bluestocking poets?" Cricks was asking. He glanced at her again, then snorted and waved toward the door. "Bah! Get out. I've no time for your silly prattle and foolish—"

"A bluestocking? Oh, heavens no," she assured him, feeling the insult of his words all the way down to the heels of her very fashionable boots. "Do I look like a bluestocking? I'll have you know this gown is in the first stare. No miss with her nose pressed in a book would have thought to use this shade of capucine silk with these ribbons. Why, the lace alone took me three weeks to find." She held out her sleeve for him to examine. "Do you see what I mean?" She drew her arm back and readjusted her pelisse. "I can assure you I've no literary leanings."

Mr. Cricks stared up at her in much the same way she'd gaped at Melaphor. "And *you* want a book on *monsters*?"

Hermione felt nudged from behind as she said, "And other things."

Ask him. Ask him about the Paratus.

No. No. No. She didn't care a whit about the earl. He'd pointed a sword at her and threatened to kill her. Hardly a sporting or endearing trait in a gentleman.

You'd never catch Lord Hustings doing such a thing.

Then again, Lord Hustings didn't make her insides twist into knots and her knees wobble.

Cricks glanced at her again. "Other things? Such as?"

Before she could stop the words from blurting out, she said, "I want to know if you have ever heard of or read about a man called the Paratus?"

Six

At first, nothing seemed amiss when Rockhurst entered the bookshop, with Rowan at his heel. The usual shadows, dusty books, and narrow aisles surrounded him, as well as the sense of the calm that came with entering Cricks's realm.

But that didn't last for long.

"I am not mad," came a voice from the back. "I have proof of what I've seen."

Rockhurst glanced down at Rowan, and then back up at the shadowy nether regions of Cricks's shop. The old codger had company?

"Proof? Bah!"

"Why, you should have seen what that alley did to my best pair of slippers! Ruined them, I tell you. Completely and utterly ruined them. An evil place indeed, to do such a thing to an innocent pair of slippers."

Female company? Rockhurst glanced around to make sure he was indeed at Cricks's, for right this moment he was inclined to believe he'd wandered into Gunter's or a modiste shop.

Ruined slippers?

He was about to turn and leave when the chit spoke again.

"And this horrid Melaphor, you say he isn't like us?"

Melaphor? Rockhurst froze in his tracks, a shiver running down his spine.

"Not at all," Cricks warned her. "Why, I think you are the first person who's ever seen him . . . and lived to tell of the experience."

"Well, it isn't an experience one would want to brag about. What with those horrid red eyes and his teeth." She shuddered, and Rockhurst could almost see the shiver that went along with it. "How can such a horrible creature be?"

There was only one person who'd seen Melaphor and lived, other than himself.

His Shadow.

And now here she was in Cricks's shop.

Rockhurst's fist curled again into that now familiar shape. He closed his eyes, retracing the lines of the woman he'd found in the alley. He could almost see her, and now, as luck would have it, he'd found her.

So much for Mary's theory that he had most likely sent the girl scurrying back home for good. For here she was, peppering Cricks with her questions.

His boot rose, for his first instinct was to go barging back there and corner this miss. But years of experience brought his foot ever so gently and quietly back down. He needed to catch her, yes. Yet rushing forth like a madman wouldn't guarantee she'd be as forthright with him as she was being with Cricks. Let her natter on for a few more minutes and see what he could learn of her.

Besides, the only way of leaving was down this aisle.

Right through me, he thought, planting himself with a wide, impassable stance.

And his plan seemed to be working, for even now, the aged bookseller was unwittingly aiding his cause.

"How can such a creature be? He just is," Cricks said, as if she'd questioned the rise and fall of the sun. The man tapped his cane to the floor. "Some can't see through his glamour. But if you can, 'tis better for you, for he's the worst sort of fiend." There was a shuffle of pages. "Here is the section that details how he killed the eighteenth Paratus. But I warn you, miss, it isn't for the faint of heart."

"Oh, heavens. I had hoped none of this was true. He wants to kill Lord Rockhurst just because he's this Paratus?" A teacup rattled in its saucer. "Well, that hardly seems fair."

Cricks was serving her tea? Like some long-lost relative? The same Cricks who liked to use his cane to hurry unwitting customers *out* of his shop?

Rockhurst gave the girl some credit. She could shoot a cross-bow *and* charm an old curmudgeon. And in that realization, he found himself similarly intrigued.

"Sssh," the old man admonished. "You shouldn't say such things aloud."

"Whyever not? For it seems to me that if something were to happen to Lord Rock—"

"Eh, eh, eh," Cricks chastened.

A feminine huff was followed with, "Oh, really, I don't see why I can't . . . Well, if you insist. What I mean to ask is what would happen to all of us if the Paratus were to . . . perish?"

The last word came out in an ominous whisper.

"It would spell the end of all, for certain."

"Truly?" she gasped. "And here I thought, well everyone does, that Lord Ro—" There was another fit of coughing, followed by another missish sigh. "If you insist then. Yes, I can see that you do. Very well. Everyone knows *his lordship* is the worst sort of a rake. He's quite dissolute—why he has legions of mistresses and spends most nights in some debauchery or another."

A true admirer, Rockhurst mused, crossing his arms over his chest.

"All *Maman's* friends claim he is beyond the pale, despite his wealth."

Her *maman*? Rockhurst shuddered as he always did at the mention of society matrons. Then again, he wondered what her *maman* would think about her daughter's nighttime rambles into Seven Dials.

"All the better to lend him the disdain of Society," Cricks was telling her.

"Oh, yes, now I see how it is," she said with an awestruck air of comprehension, her naive viewpoint tumbling to pieces.

Rockhurst held fast despite the growing urge to end this charade, for just her combination of youth and innocence was a dangerous mix in his world. No wonder she'd caught Melaphor's eye.

Then she said the something that only proved his point further. "I've always thought him something of a romantic mystery."

A romantic mystery? Rockhurst nearly groaned aloud. Lord save him from some starry-eyed debutante.

Who can shoot a cross-bow.

"Now you know the truth," the bookseller said.

"Yes, and now I fear for him, Mr. Cricks."

Oh, no, no, no! He didn't need some madcap, Byron-loving miss following him about.

Especially one who could do so unseen!

There was the telltale sound of tea being poured. "Aye, so do all of us who know him. Know of him."

"It isn't right that he should carry such a burden all alone. Don't you think, Mr. Cricks?"

Alone? That was the only way it could be done, he opened his mouth to tell her.

"Been that way for nigh on a thousand years, miss."

And the way it would stay.

"Truly?" she asked.

"Aye. It's all here in this book, *The Legends of the Legion of the Paratus.*"

Rockhurst cringed. Not that wretched book by that idiot Podmore. A scholarly antiquarian whose curiosity into the realm of the Paratus had been his undoing. And here Cricks had promised him—quite faithfully—not five years earlier that all the copies of the man's book had been destroyed.

All save one, it seems. Why that wily old codger. Worse than Mary when it came to collecting and keeping dangerous tracts.

Cricks heaved a wheezy sigh. "Best you stay out of his lordship's way, miss. You seem a bit young for the likes of the Paratus. Besides, there's the curse to consider."

"The curse?" she gasped. "You mean he's cursed as well?"

As if being the Paratus wasn't bad enough for this foolish little miss.

"It's all here in Chapter Four—"

Now he *had* heard enough. It was time to put a stop to all this nonsense before Cricks completely filled her bird-witted head with myths and tales better forgotten.

He went forward, heedless of where he was stepping, only to plant his boot into a wayward stack of books. The dusty volumes scattered before him, and Rowan, who up until now had been silent, started barking.

Rockhurst turned to the hound. "Yes, thank you, that helps immensely."

"Oooh," he heard the young woman gasp.

There was the scrape of chairs, and before the earl could take another step, Cricks came blustering out of the shadows, brandishing his infamous cane.

"Who dares come in my shop?" the old man croaked out, before he came to a wheezing stop and had to catch hold of the counter to catch his breath. His watery gaze blinked again. "Who goes—" The cane clattered to the floor. "My lord! Whatever are you . . . " He glanced over his shoulder at the room behind him.

Rockhurst said nothing. He didn't need to. He raised one elegant brow and stared down at the old man.

After another nervous glance over his shoulder, Cricks managed to ask, "How can I help you, my lord?"

"Introduce me to your guest."

"My wha-a-at?" Cricks might be a great scholar on all things ancient, but he was a terrible liar.

"Your guest. The lady you were serving tea . . . " Rockhurst nodded toward the back room.

Cricks managed a dusty old laugh. "A lady, my lord? I'm a bit on in my years for such—"

"Cricks!"

"There's no one—"

Rockhurst was done listening to him. He pushed past the man and into the back of the shop.

The *empty* back of his shop, where Cricks's chair sat at an odd angle, beside an overturned stool, a table with two cups and saucers, a teapot, and a plate of half-eaten biscuits atop it.

And beyond that, an open door leading into the alley, along with the last lingering trail of her perfume.

Of course Cricks would have more than one way out of his little shop of mysteries and monsters.

Rockhurst whistled to Rowan, and the pair of them were out the door in a flash. But to his dismay, the short alley was also empty, and not a sound revealed her whereabouts. Either she was very still or quite quick on her feet.

"Find her," he ordered Rowan, who just sat and looked up at him with his large hound eyes. "Nothing?"

The dog lay down and put his head on his paws. *Nothing.*

Then there was no choice but to continue after her. Rockhurst ran down toward Newgate Street, Rowan instantly springing up and loping beside him. But when they came to the corner, they were greeted by the chaos of the markets. Maids and housekeepers, footmen and servants of all sorts jostled their way through the streets as they sought out the best picks from Newgate's grocers.

Even if he knew what she looked like, if he could even see her, how would he find her? The myriad of bonnets made it impossible to discern miss from matron.

He glanced down at Rowan to see if his hound was having a better time of it, but Rowan had already sat down and was looking up at him, awaiting their next move. A hound he might be, but wolfhounds hunted by sight, not scent.

Rockhurst ground his teeth together. There was nothing left to do but go back and see what Cricks knew of her. With Rowan at his heel, he marched back into the shop.

Cricks railed against him the moment he crossed the threshold. "You didn't catch her?!" He thumped his cane to the floorboards sending up a cloud of dust. "She stole my only copy!"

A shiver ran down the earl's spine. "Your only copy of what?"

Cricks's jaw worked back and forth before he confessed, "Of Podmore." But his contrite words were quickly replaced with angry ones. "That girl is a thief."

"And you, sir, are a liar. You told me you had accounted for all the copies of that volume."

"I had."

"But apparently you forgot to destroy them all."

"Harrumph! It was my copy. Never intended to see it go walking out the door."

"It was never intended?" Rockhurst exploded. "Who are you to decide?"

Cricks backed up. "My lord, I am so sorry. It's just that she was such a nice, pretty little bit." But he wasn't so contrite that he still didn't mumble. "My only copy. It's thievery it is."

Rockhurst slanted a nod toward the table. "She thought enough to leave you payment."

The man poked at the coins, making a *tsk, tsk* over the paltry amount.

But something else he'd said struck a nerve in Rockhurst. "What do you mean by saying that the girl was a 'pretty little bit'?"

Cricks shrugged, and then colored a bit. "Well, you know, like a little lady. Don't see many of them about my shop. With the exception of your cousin, that is. And Miss Kendell is well and fine, but this one, well she was pretty."

Rockhurst nodded. "Pretty how?"

"I've never been one for those winsome types—too pallid and full of themselves. But this one, she had such fine eyes. Even an old man can fall prey to a pair of green eyes. Why they sparkled, they did!"

Rockhurst's heart tilted slightly, but then he shook his head. Demmit, if he wasn't careful, he'd be as befuddled as Cricks, for suddenly another realization struck him. "You could see her?"

The old man slanted a quick glance at him. "See her, my lord?"

"Yes, see her. See the color of her eyes, of her hair, her face?"

Cricks's shoulders straightened. "I'm not so blind as all that."

Rockhurst shook his head. "No. No. You misunderstand. I met the lady . . . last night. But the woman I encountered was unseen."

"Unseen?"

"As in *invisible*." The earl let that last word fall like an irresistible gem into Cricks's steel-trap mind.

"Invisible?" he wheezed. "No!"

"Most decidedly," Rockhurst assured him. "But you say you could see her."

"Just as plain as I am looking at you." A light of intrigue illuminated his gaze, and catching hold of his cane, he set off at a mad clip down the shop's main aisle. "Oh, that's a fine one. Unseen you say?" he asked again over his shoulder.

Rockhurst nodded.

"And completely corporeal during the day. *Hmmm.* That's rare. Very rare." Cane tapping, Cricks scanned his shop, then turned to the right and headed for an overcrowded shelf. "I do believe I have something on such cases. She's either inherited this ability, or it is a spell of some sort." Cricks paused. "Since you've come here, that means Miss Kendell hasn't anything certain in mind, am I right?" he asked, all too correct in assuming that the earl had already consulted Mary.

"My cousin is of the opinion that our mysterious friend has discovered Milton's Ring."

Cricks stilled. "Let's hope that isn't the case."

"Why not?"

"For if she's made a wish, the only way to end the spell is for her wish to come true." Cricks's bushy brows furrowed into a fat caterpillar of worry. "Or . . . "

"Or?"

He shook his head. "You have to promise me you won't."

"Won't what?"

The old man heaved a sigh.

"Cricks?" Rockhurst used his status as the Paratus to push him into confessing what he appeared reluctant to reveal. "You have a duty and obligation to help me."

"Oh, aye, my lord, I'm not forgetting who you are and what I owe you, but she was such a pretty little thing. And not likely to harm anyone . . . "

"Cricks, if she holds Milton's Ring, we could all be in danger. Now tell me, how else can I end this spell?"

"Kill her," he blurted out. "You would have to kill the miss. 'Tis the only other way to end such a wish."

"Hermione? Hermione, darling? Where are you?"

Hermione sat up in her bed and cringed as she looked around the rumpled sheets. There wasn't time to hide any of this. She glanced at the door to the hall, and then at the one that led to the dressing room she shared with Viola, and considered fleeing for her sister's room.

Not that Viola wouldn't just turn her over to their mother, bothersome little scamp that she was. Still, perhaps Viola could be bribed, Hermione thought as she scrambled out of the bed even as her mother's determined tread rounded the landing.

"Hermione, I hope you are ready, for I would like to arrive a bit—"

Her mother swung into her room, dressed in her evening splendor—a great turban atop her head, feathers dancing every which way, and a morone gown, the bright red color like that of a peony. The grand lady paused, rather posed for a moment, smiling broadly, that is, until the sight before her registered. Her mouth fell open, and she gaped at her daughter as if she had just found her *in flagrante delicto* with a footman.

In her usual dramatic fashion, Lady Walbrook paled, then reached for the doorjamb to steady herself.

"Hermione!! What is the meaning of this?"

"This" being the books she'd borrowed from Mary and the one she'd taken, well, purchased, from Mr. Cricks.

"Are you . . . you cannot be . . . tell me you aren't . . . reading?"

"I'm sorry, Mother," Hermione rushed to explain. "But you do remember you asked me to discover the essence of my character, and I sought out Miss Kendell's assistance—"

"That bluestocking!" Lady Walbrook teetered back and forth like an oak in a fierce gale. "I said to ask her, not carry her library over here."

"I was only—"

"And those?" her mother said, an accusing finger pointed at Hermione's nose.

She put her hand up and found the offending piece. "I couldn't make out all the words, so I thought Cordelia's old spectacles might help."

She'd have been better served having told her mother she would rather marry a pauper than a duke.

"Take them off!" the countess intoned.

Hermione did, whisking them out of sight. "Truly, Mother, there is nothing to be upset about. Most of these are in Greek and Latin, at least I think they are. I thought I'd send them down to Cordelia and see if she could translate—"

Wrong again, Hermione.

"Oh, gracious heavens, why couldn't I have an ordinary daughter? Just one!" her mother wailed, now going from dramatic outrage to outright grief. "One who sneaks French novels and the only study she would ever admit to is memorizing the pages of Debrett's Peerage!"

"I was only doing as you asked," Hermione shot back. "You said I should explore the character more if I was ever going to be convincing as Caliban. Miss Kendell suggested—"

"I meant for you to read the play. Weigh Mr. Shakespeare's words. Not take up this . . . this . . . study." She shuddered, as if even the word was enough to send her into spasms.

"I'll put them away immediately, Mother," Hermione said, scurrying back to her bed. For it hadn't been that many years ago that her older sister Cordelia had declared she preferred her scholarly pursuits to pursuing a husband in London. And off she'd gone to Bath, without any intention of ever getting married. Their mother had been inconsolable for months.

"You will do more than that," Lady Walbrook declared. "Dorcas!" she bellowed, summoning her faithful maid. "Dorcas, take those dreadful volumes and return them to Miss Kendell. Immediately!"

Dorcas hurried forward, her usual patient expression strained by the countess's high dudgeon. Hermione had no choice but to surrender the ones she held.

"All of them," her mother said.

Hermione gathered up the rest of the volumes, and was about to give them over when she spied the Podmore lying at her feet.

Somehow in her haste to get up, it had fallen to the floor unnoticed.

And unnoticed it would remain, Hermione decided.

"*Maman*, is that your new gown? Why, the color is everything you declared it would be!" she said, as she handed the last of Mary's books to a now overladen Dorcas, and at the same time with her foot, slid the Podmore under her bed and safely out of sight.

As a way of ensuring her mother didn't notice her deception, she smiled brightly. "I've always thought you should wear morone."

Lady Walbrook heaved a sigh as Dorcas passed by, but at the mention of her dress, she brightened. "Yes, yes it is. I fear the color will set tongues wagging, especially at my age—"

She left that opening hanging for Hermione, and she latched right on to it. "No, *maman*! Never. The color is divine on you."

Her mother preened, her hands smoothing over the sleeves and the skirt, but her diverted attention didn't last for long. The countess glanced up at Hermione again. This time her eyes narrowed. "Gracious heavens, Minny! You aren't dressed! We are to leave for Lady Thurlow's ball in less than ten minutes. Never mind dressing, your hair alone is utterly unfit to be seen."

Her hair? That was the least of her worries. For she couldn't very well tell her mother that in only a matter of twenty minutes or so, everything about her would be unseen.

"Well, there is nothing left to do but to summon Dorcas back and fetch up that girl in the kitchen. The one who did your hair when Dorcas was sick last month. Perhaps between the two of them—"

There was nothing like her mother now that she was determined to see Hermione placed in the forefront of Society. Still, she must find a way out of the evening's plans. "*Maman*, I would only serve to make you late."

The countess continued on, "But you *must* go, Minny. I have it from Lady Belling, who heard it from Lady Doust, who saw Rockhurst this very afternoon at Gunter's. *Gunter's!* Can you imagine anything more respectable? Well, if that doesn't mean the man isn't seeking a wife—"

Or an invisible debutante . . .

"—I'll give away my pin money to charity." She heaved a sigh. "Now where was I?"

Accustomed as Hermione was to redirecting her mother when she wandered afield, she answered her without thinking. "Lord Rockhurst," she supplied, and then winced.

Her mother sparked back to life. "Rockhurst! Exactly as I was saying. He will be at the Thurlows' tonight."

"Oh, *maman*! You can't believe such a thing." Hermione shook her head. Really! Lord Rockhurst at such a dull event? It was unthinkable. Unimaginable.

"He will be there," her mother insisted. "He told Lady Doust exactly that."

That explained her mother's determination all right. So there was nothing left for her to do but give the finest performance of her life.

Caliban, be damned. Hermione was about to do justice to *Romeo and Juliet*.

She rocked back and forth. "Oh, dear, *maman*," she said faintly, stretching her hand out to her mother before collapsing atop her bed.

"My head! Oh, my head!" Hermione moaned.

"Minny!" her mother called out, rushing forward and taking her hand. "What is the matter?"

"My head, oh, I am so dizzy." She let her eyelashes flutter about. "Oh, I fear I read too much. For now my head aches so terribly. I should never have tried to translate Greek!" Hermione even got a tear or two to well up in her eyes. "Mother, I must be a horrible disappointment to you."

Lady Walbrook was a formidable, bossy lady, but she loved her children unfashionably, and they all knew it. "Oh, there, there, Minny," she said, patting her daughter's hand, before brushing her hair back from her forehead. "I had such high hopes for you tonight. Lady Belling also told Lady Doust that Lady Routledge is determined to see that Lord Rockhurst sets his cap for that dreadful Miss Burke."

"Miss Burke?" Hermione blurted out, forgetting she was in the throes of her final moments.

"Yes, exactly," Lady Walbrook said encouragingly at this first sign of life. "Think of besting her, my dear. Make that your rallying cry, to get you past this desperate megrim. Think of your new gown."

Hermione cringed. For she did have a new gown to wear. A light shade of capucine trimmed in green that was stunning to behold. Sure to catch the eye of . . .

Of no one. Dash it all. This wish was ruining her life.

"Minny, dearest, bravest girl," her mother coaxed. "Just try to get up? For me?"

Oh, gads, this was terrible, Hermione realized as she saw the mountain of expectation in her mother's eyes. She knew that the countess had high hopes of marrying at least one of her children very well, and currently those dreams lay on Hermione's slim shoulders.

Even slimmer chances now.

Leaning heavily on her mother, Hermione did her best to rise, and felt nothing less than crushing guilt when she had to collapse back onto the mattress groaning.

"Well, there is no use!" her mother declared. "Better you stay home tonight and be well rested for tomorrow."

"Tomorrow?" Hermione replied faintly.

"Heavens, you are unwell. We are to go to Lady Belling's garden party." The countess paused. "What is it this Season with all these garden parties and Venetian breakfasts? Doesn't anyone know how tiresome it is to have to arise before two?"

Hermione sighed. At least she could attend those events.

"There, there, dear. You get a good night's rest, and you'll be in fine form for tomorrow's festivities."

Her mother leaned over and placed a kiss on her brow, and never before had Hermione felt more guilty. She had no morals whatsoever about lying to her pinchpenny brother Sebastian about her expenses and shopping forays, but she didn't like deceiving her mother.

Lady Walbrook smiled and waved from the door, before she left her daughter to her rest. Hermione lay still and quiet for the next quarter of an hour, listening to the familiar sounds of the house—her mother calling to Dorcas for her cloak, her chastising Griffin for being so late, and finally bidding Viola a good night.

When the front door shut for the fourth time—for it always took her mother at least three trips back and forth from the carriage before she was assured she had everything she needed for an evening out—did Hermione rise from her bed and slip to the window.

But it wasn't the sight of the hired carriage carrying her mother and brother away that held her attention but the skyline beyond. For there the horizon burned red as the sun set, and Hermione felt herself slip away with it.

So much so, that when she turned to face the mirror, there was no reflection.

She was again unseen.

And left behind, she thought as she took another envious glance at the carriage before it turned the corner. The Thurlow ball. It promised to be a crush, and now the night would belong to Lavinia Burke. Of course.

Hermione let out a breathy sigh. She didn't even dare look in her dressing room, where her new gown hung. The one she'd thought for sure would gain the earl's attentions. Why the ribbons alone had taken her a fortnight of dedicated shopping to choose.

She had envisioned herself wearing it more times than she could count. Pausing at the entrance to the Thurlow ballroom, so all heads could turn at the sight of her in such a ravishing creation.

Now all the attention would be on Lavinia Burke and whatever fabulous gown she'd donned, for there was no expense spared for Miss Burke's gowns and hats and shoes.

Hermione plunked down on her bed and frowned. It wasn't just Miss Burke who had her so crosspatched, but someone else.

The Earl of Rockhurst.

Hermione rolled over and covered her head with a pillow. Bother the man. It gave her no comfort that she'd been right about him all along—he was a tortured soul—and it would be terribly romantic and appealing if he weren't inclined to murder every shadow that wandered into his realm.

Or at least, that was what Mr. Podmore claimed was the duty of the Paratus.

Still . . . she mused, *he had saved her.*

Then, and not for the first time this day, she found herself wondering how it was he'd gotten her to his carriage. Had he carried her all that way? In his arms? Up against his chest, with his lips just mere inches from her own?

She tossed the pillow aside. Oh, why did she miss all the best moments of her life?

And why hadn't he killed her?

Hermione sat up. Perhaps there was some tender aspect of his heart that hadn't been eaten up as yet. So there might even be hope yet for the Earl of Rockhurst.

Not that she was inclined to find out. No, not in the least.

She rose and went to the window, watching the carriages roll by as they carried members of the *ton* to the evening's various entertainments.

Really, what was the point of being invisible if one couldn't make something of it?

She bit her lip and tried to recall what it was that Thomasin had said. Oh, yes, that was it. If she were invisible, *I'd see to it that Lavinia Burke had one of the worst nights of her life.*

Hermione giggled. Thomasin would do such a thing.

A mischievous little light burned to life inside her. So why shouldn't she?

There was no reason she couldn't go to the ball. And if someone just happened to tread upon Lavinia

Burke's hem, well it was nothing more than a horrible, tragic accident . . . that would be the talk of the *ton* by morning.

Hermione got up and rushed to her closet, catching up her old cloak. She turned around and glanced about her room.

Where the devil were her boots?

She got down on her hands and knees and dug around under her bed. She found the volume of Podmore first and cast it up on her bed.

The soft *thud* as it landed on the coverlet gave her pause, and for a moment all she could do was stare at the leather-bound volume.

The Legends of the League of the Paratus.

What if Podmore was correct and "a League" implied more than one? The odd scholar and author asserted there were at least four, maybe five, Paratuses in England.

Hermione shivered. Five men, all like the Earl of Rockhurst?

One was enough for her, as she recalled the earl's well-formed body illuminated by that wayward shaft of light from Cappon's. The way he'd moved as he'd tested his sword, swinging it with an even, familiar rhythm, as if the blade had been cast for his hand, and his hand alone.

And yet, even with all his apparent skills, the powers that were his inheritance, she knew now how truly vulnerable he was.

As mortal as any of us, Podmore had written.

She bit her lip and wondered why he continued on.

Did he ever get lonely? Probably not, given his rakish reputation.

But what if, like Mr. Cricks had told her, the earl's notoriety was just gossip to disguise his real identity?

That would make a person very lonely, indeed. Poor Rockhurst, she thought, pressing her fingers to her lips as she considered this new side of the earl. That would mean that he didn't spend his nights wooing and seducing every Incognita and Cyprean in London.

Leaving him very lonely, indeed. So much so, Hermione mused, he might even welcome . . .

To her shock, her door swung open, and she nearly jumped out of her skin—as much at the interruption as in embarrassment as to the direction of her scandalous thoughts.

"There you are," Quince said, bustling into the room. Making herself right at home, she dropped her gloves on the bureau and glanced around. "Safe and sound. A good thing, that is."

"Mrs. Quince," Hermione gasped. "What are you doing . . . I mean how did you get in?"

"Your dear brother let me in just before he left," she said, pulling off her pelisse and plucking her hat from her head. Without an invitation or any other pleasantry, she dropped them on a nearby chair. "And it is just Quince, dear. I thought I'd keep you company tonight."

Hermione shook her head. "That is very kind, but I already have plans."

Fishing around one more time, she found her boots.

"You're going out?" Quince asked, her brows rising in alarm.

"Well, yes," Hermione said. Really, what did it matter to the lady? She started tugging on her boots, first one, then the other.

Quince fluttered back and forth. "It is just that we never got to finish getting acquainted last night, especially after you left so abruptly . . ." Her words trailed off, full of questions that Hermione had no intention of answering.

Well, there wasn't any harm in telling the lady her intentions for the evening. "I'm going over to Grosvenor Square, to Lady Thurlow's ball."

Quince's brow furrowed as she studied Hermione's ensemble. "A ball?"

Hermione glanced down at her rumpled day dress. "Good thing no one can see me. But it hardly makes sense to put on the gown I intended to wear. What if I were to ruin it?"

Those elegant brows rose higher. "Why would you ruin it?" she asked in perfect imitation of Lady Walbrook when Griffin came in after an all-night bender.

Hermione bit her lip. *Jiminy!* She really needed to learn to mind her tongue. "No reason. But it is rather difficult, you can imagine, getting about when no one can see you. I wouldn't want someone to trample the train."

Quince's jaw set like that of a matron confronted by a willful daughter.

Gads, she's worse than Maman, Hermione thought as she continued getting ready, trying her best to ignore Quince's growing discontent.

"It would be better if you stayed home," Quince said.

"I do know how to play cards. Perhaps a rousing game of casino."

"I gave all my spare coins to Mr. Cricks today, so I haven't anything left to wager with."

"Oh, we don't need to play for coins, for I haven't any—" Quince's light words came to a blinding halt. "To *whom* did you give your money?"

"Mr. Cricks," Hermione said over her shoulder as she glanced about the room looking for her pelisse.

A stony silence fell between them, and Hermione glanced up to see Quince staring down at the volume of Podmore on the bed, her finger pointing at it as if it were a serpent.

"You bought *that*?"

"Yes," Hermione said, catching it up and tucking it into the top drawer of her dressing table.

"And you were reading *it*?"

"Not all of it," she said. Gads, not another lecture on the inappropriateness of reading.

"And you are still going out?"

"Of course." Hermione spotted her pelisse sticking out from beneath her cloak. She caught it up and wrapped it around her shoulders.

"You've been reading *that* book, and you still want to go out?"

"I haven't read all of it," Hermione told her.

"Then you don't realize the danger you are in from . . . from . . . ?"

"The Paratus?" Hermione finished for her.

Quince closed her eyes and shuddered. "Yes."

"He wouldn't harm me," Hermione assured her. "I'm

mortal." She wasn't too sure she could say the same about this Quince, but Mother always said it wasn't polite to pry into someone's breeding. At least not to their face. "He cannot harm me."

Quince snorted. "I wouldn't be so sure."

"It matters not, for I have no intention of ever going near the man again."

"Then you are over your *tendré*?" Quince sounded ever-so-hopeful.

"Yes," Hermione said, trying her best to convince the lady. Convince herself, more like it.

The ring quivered, as if it knew the truth of the matter and wasn't about to let her forget.

Ignoring the obnoxious little bit of metal on her hand, Hermione reached over and gave Quince's hand a squeeze. "I am merely going a few blocks to a ball. I have no intention of drawing the earl's attentions. I just have a small score to settle." She smiled again. "Really, whatever could go wrong when no one can see me but you?"

Seven

Hermione's confidence in her plan remained high, for she was able to slip quite easily into Lord and Lady Thurlow's town house, then make her way to the ballroom without the least slip-up.

Taking up a spot in an alcove, she watched the evening begin with an interest she hadn't felt since her first Season. How fun to be able to watch everyone and not be admonished for staring!

She spied Lord Hustings wandering about, most likely in search of her. He was becoming quite insistent in pursuing his suit for her, but Hermione couldn't bring herself to give in and accept his proposal.

Not yet.

She spied India and Thomasin in another corner, their fans fluttering as they gossiped and commented about the ebb and flow of guests.

Hermione felt a stab of envy, because Thomasin was always a font of gossip, and India, because her love of fashion—which was exceeded only by Hermione's own—made them boon companions. They'd have spent the evening in jovial spirits watching the other guests.

Then there was her quarry, Miss Lavinia Burke. The heiress was holding court in the middle of the room, as usual, and surrounded by likely beaux who sought to catch her eye, and misses who hoped to steal a bit of her limelight.

Now it would only be a matter of working her way around the crowd. . .

Suddenly an anxious sort of hum filled the Thurlow ball, the sort that Hermione knew heralded only one of two things—either the arrival of the Prince Regent or someone so scandalous that their mere appearance would be remarked upon for days to come. She rose up on her toes and craned her neck to spot this unlikely arrival, just as everyone else in the ballroom was doing.

That is until she spied him.

Rockhurst!

"Jiminy," she gasped. She really hadn't believed Lady Doust's gossip about his attending tonight, yet here he was. Whatever was he doing here? Hermione's heart stilled. Unless her mother's assertions *were* true. That he was here looking for someone.

But it wasn't the bride her mother believed him to be seeking, but a lady nonetheless.

Her. A shiver ran down her spine, and her earlier wayward thoughts made a sudden reappearance; but they didn't last long, as they were followed by Quince's warnings—which didn't seem as cork-brained as they had in the safety of her bedchamber. She drew a steadying breath and put her hand over her fluttering stomach. Well, at least he couldn't see her and hadn't a notion who she was.

So there was little chance of his finding her.

Though she still wasn't sure how he'd found her last night after she'd been knocked out. If she'd been invisible, how would he have known where she'd fallen or even that she was still about?

Then she got her answer, for to her shock, and then dismay, the crowd parted to reveal the guest Rockhurst had brought with him.

Rowan.

A wolfhound at a ball? No wonder the crowd was abuzz.

And then Hermione was as well, as she watched Rowan turn his great shaggy head toward the place where she was standing and look directly at her.

"Rockhurst! What are you doing here?" Lady Routledge held up her looking glass and peered first at her nephew, and then at the giant hound sitting beside him. "This is a ball, not a hunt."

He cupped his hand next to his mouth, leaned over, and whispered to his aunt, "I daresay, Rowan doesn't know the difference."

She groaned loudly. "Rockhurst, don't take this unkindly, for I am beside myself with joy that you've started making the rounds to find yourself a bride, but this . . . this . . ."

"Dog," the earl supplied.

"Beast," his aunt corrected, "does not belong here. No one brings a dog to a ball."

"I do," he told her in a tone that would have brooked no opposition. In anyone other than Aunt Routledge.

"Take him out," she said, pointing toward the door.

"Lady Thurlow didn't seem to mind," he replied, holding his ground. His aunt could be the most pestering, nagging bit of muslin in all of London, but he was awfully fond of her.

Well, that and she was so easy to tease.

"Of course not," Lady Routledge said, snapping open her fan and fluttering it about. "Lady Thurlow is in such a state of alt over your arrival that she probably didn't notice. *But others are.* Never mind that you'll hardly find yourself a proper bride with that hound at your elbow."

He grinned, then gave her a peck on the cheek. "Whoever said, Aunt, that I am seeking a 'proper' bride?"

"Rockhurst!" she blustered as he slipped into the crowd, the *ton* giving him and Rowan a wide berth. "You will rue the day—"

But he was no longer listening, for he hadn't come here to find some proper little miss to marry, as his aunt wanted to believe.

He'd come to find *her*.

For what if Cricks and Mary were right, and this chit had found Milton's Ring, and say for even a second the demmed myth was true, and it could grant its wearer one wish?

A wish to break the Covenant, which had bound his

family for generations to a long-ago queen. Without the pact, he could live his life however he chose.

He could even consider . . . no, that was too much to hope.

Yet ever since his flirtation with Miss Wilmont, he couldn't help wondering what it would be like to love a woman and not fear for her safety every moment of the day.

For that alone, he'd find this chit and hazard anything to get his hands on that ring.

He glanced around the crowded room and wondered if she was even here. Being invisible hadn't stopped her from going to Almack's. And certainly a good portion of the *ton* hadn't been able to resist the Thurlows' invitation, so why should she?

For the thousandth time, his fingers flexed, as if revisiting the curve of her cheek, the hollow of her throat, the swell of her breasts . . . mostly it was the breast part that he relived the most, but he was trying to be a gentleman about that portion of her anatomy.

Then again . . . he surveyed the room with renewed interest. He'd spent most of the day letting his imagination run rampant, but still he had nothing more than the softness of her skin and the shape of her breast to soothe his musings . . .

Beside him, Rowan nudged his hand, and absently he scratched the dog's silky ears. "That's why I've brought you," he told his constant companion.

For if Rockhurst couldn't discern where this Shadow lurked, Rowan would have no trouble finding her.

"Eh, boy," he said, ruffling the dog's soft head. "You'll find her, won't you."

And when he did, he wouldn't kill her, for he'd reminded Cricks it was against the Covenant to harm humans.

If she was human.

No, there were other ways to bring a woman to heel. Seduction came to mind.

"Ah, Rockhurst, is that you? I daresay, I thought it was!" a familiar voice called out.

Battersby. The earl groaned inwardly as the man clapped him on the shoulder. There was no escape now.

"Thought that was you!" the baron said, sidling up to the earl and taking his place as if they were the closest of chums. He even had the nerve to reach over and give Rowan an awkward pat. "Glad to see you, Rockhurst. Thought I was going to have to wade through this sea alone." He rocked on his heels, his thumbs tucked into his waistcoat, a shocking combination of pea green and lilac trim. "Met my good friend, Lord Hustings?" he asked, nodding to the pale man beside him.

Rockhurst bowed slightly at the young lord.

Battersby continued on, "Hustings has his eye set on Lady Hermione Marlowe."

"Really?" Rockhurst couldn't help himself from asking.

Hustings blushed a bit. "I know, I know. One of those Marlowes," he said, shaking his head a bit as if he was indeed nicked in the nob.

"Determined to have her," Battersby added. "Even over his mother's objections."

Rockhurst couldn't help but think of a few objections himself—like having Griffin Marlowe for a brother-in-law, or Lady Walbrook as a mother-in-law. But as to the lady in question, he tried to remember what the chit looked like, but for the life of him he couldn't.

Meanwhile, Battersby was nattering on. "Some company, eh? Hear you're thinking of getting married, eh, Rockhurst? The parson's mousetrap. Leg-shackled. A tenant for life. Hustings to Lady Hermione, me to my angel, and you to . . . who is it that you said you're planning on making your countess?" This came with another clap on the back that set the earl's teeth rattling.

"I didn't," Rockhurst told him.

Battersby nudged him in the ribs. "Coy, eh? I understand. Keeping your plans close to the chest. Good idea." The man paused only to take a breath. "All us Dashers out of circulation and gone from the Marriage Mart. That will be a day mothers across London will mourn for certain." He rocked again, then nodded toward a cluster of young ladies. "Thinking of that one. Might make a proper baroness."

Rockhurst didn't know if he wanted to look upon the poor miss whom Battersby had set his sights on. But then again, that was one less debutante for his aunt to push in his direction, so he might as well encourage the man. "One of the Dewmonts?"

"Heavens no," Battersby said, looking horror-struck. "Can you imagine not being able to tell your wife from her sister. Could be terribly awkward."

Rockhurst chuckled. Personally, he hadn't looked at it that way, but then again, he wasn't all that proper.

Hustings, for his part, continued to scan the room in his own befuddled way.

"With Trent having fled the field, as it were," Battersby said in a confidential manner, "I think I'll take my turn at Miss Burke."

"Miss Who-o-o?" Rockhurst sputtered.

Battersby puffed up a bit, if a man that skinny could do such a thing. "Yes, you heard me. Miss Burke. Might not have an earldom behind me like Trent, but I've got assets enough."

Rockhurst didn't know what was more devilish. Battersby—for the drubbing he was going to take for even thinking of going after the Season's most coveted Original, or worse, if the man managed to snare Miss Burke, he'd find himself saddled to the nasty chit for the rest of his life.

"Look at her, my good man, she's a veritable angel," Battersby was saying. "But I daresay I'll have to get over there and do my best to edge aside that annoying pup, Heriot. Mushroom of a fellow, don't you think? And about to ask her to dance! Well, we'll see about that, if my name isn't Battersby."

The earl murmured some answer, for his gaze hadn't landed on Miss Burke, but rather on the space between the Season's reigning Original and her mother.

For a strange, odd moment, he swore he saw a glimmer between them—the outline of a young woman. Yet in the blink of an eye, the vision was gone.

But then again, there really wasn't time to take another glance, for in that instant, Miss Lavinia Burke had started to step forward to accept Heriot's outstretched arm, but instead of placing her hand on his sleeve with her usual grace and poise, the proper, perfect miss tumbled forward in a tipsy fashion right into the young man's arms.

If that wasn't enough scandal, her fall was accompanied by a loud *ri-i-ip,* as the back of her gown gave way and tore.

And that might have only caught the attention of a few nearby witnesses, but Lavinia let loose a shriek that, as Lady Routledge told an entire salon full of eminent ladies the next day, "gave proof that the Burkes aren't as far removed from their fishwife and shopkeeping forebears as they like to believe."

"Heavens!" Battersby squeaked. "How could such a thing happen? My poor, dear angel!"

And he was off in a flash to save his Miss Burke from her rather improper entanglement with Harvey Heriot and didn't hear Rockhurst's chuckling reply, "Shadow, shame on you."

While the rest of the company surged forward to witness tomorrow's *on dit,* Rockhurst turned just in time to see the garden door open and close—all by itself.

Obviously, his little Shadow thought to slip out the back gate.

"I have you now," he whispered as he waded through the crowd that was still pushing their way toward Miss Burke.

Yet all of a sudden, he found a matron in a bright red gown blocking his path. "Lord Rockhurst!" the lady said, beaming a wide, coquettish smile at him as she caught him by the elbow and anchored him in place. "Or should I say, my next Prospero!"

Hermione stumbled into the Thurlows' garden and then doubled over with laughter. Oh, such a sight.

Miss Lavinia Burke toppling from her pedestal in front of nearly every member of the *ton*. Just as Thomasin had wished.

Hermione had to admit, seeing the smug girl humiliated took some of the sting off all the nasty things Lavinia had said or implied about Charlotte and Sebastian in the past few weeks.

And Hermione had escaped the earl, to boot. Oh, and Quince had said she was courting disaster. Disaster indeed! She danced down the path toward the back gate, that is until in one twirling little step, she found her skirt caught on an overgrown rose-bush. She tugged at it until the telltale creak of the French doors brought her head up.

"Jiminy!" she cursed under her breath, and frantically tried to wrench her gown free. There was no mistaking the man's outline in the doorway.

Rockhurst.

Her gloating was lost in the face of this impending disaster, and she knew she needed to make her escape. Now.

But that proved impossible, as one of the rose-bushes had her caught well and good, so she froze instead, holding as still as she dared and hoped he wouldn't be able to discern where she stood.

Perhaps he'd only come out to catch a breath of fresh air. Or even to escape the party.

"I know you are out here," he said, planting himself in front of the door, his arms folded over his broad chest.

Hermione bit her lips together, afraid even to breathe. *He knew?*

Then he stepped aside slightly, and Rowan wiggled past. "Find her, fellow. Find our friend."

The loathsome beast trotted down the path, as easily as if she'd a beefsteak tied around her neck, and settled happily in front of her.

"Now that wasn't so hard, was it?" Rockhurst said as he came walking down the gravel path, stalking toward her with a grin on his face.

Dear heavens, if he didn't mean to kill her, whatever could he mean to do to her?

Oh, why hadn't she just stayed home and played cards with Quince? Where it was safe . . . and dull.

She took a tiny whisper of a breath as he came to a stop right beside Rowan. Glancing up into his sharp blue eyes, she spied a devilish light there that sent a shiver down her spine.

Oh, she was in trouble.

Slowly, Hermione reached for her dress and tried to get it free.

That was her first mistake.

For the rose canes rattled loudly, and it made him grin all that much more.

She closed her eyes. Oh, heavens he was going to kill her.

Instead, she felt the heat of his breath on her neck.

"Caught?"

Cautiously she opened her lashes and found him but a whisper away.

He spoke again, his words brushing up against her so intimately, she couldn't help but shiver, rattling the rose-bush yet again. "Why is it that I must constantly come to your rescue?" And to prove his point, his hand found her shoulder, his fingers caressing her arm, exploring her.

Hermione sucked in a deep breath. No man had ever touched her thusly. His fingers curled around the edge of her bodice, over her shoulder, and along the front of her gown, leaving her a wavering bundle of nerves.

Either her knees where about to give way, or she was about to throw up. She only hoped he'd forgive her for the latter.

"Why haven't you?" she managed to whisper.

"So you do speak," he said, as he finally freed her dress from the bush.

But he didn't release her.

"Of course I speak, I'm not—"

His hand traced a lazy path along her arm, sending tendrils of awakening desire in its wake. His fingers twined with hers, stroking her palm, pulling at each finger playfully, as if he were counting them.

"Why haven't I what?" he asked.

"Par-don," she stammered.

"You asked why I hadn't done something? Am I missing anything?" Just then his hand trailed over her hip and curled around her backside.

Her insides trembled and quaked. "Why haven't you killed me?" she managed, for his touch was a different sort of torture.

"Who says I won't?" he teased back, his hand pulling her closer.

"Please—"

"Please you?" He hauled her right up against him.

"Oh, no!" she managed, trying to wiggle free, but he'd effortlessly trapped her in his arms. "Please let me go."

"Now why would I want to do that? I may not be able to find you again."

He came to find me.

Just as you came here to let him, a warning voice echoed.

"I did not," she muttered aloud.

"Excuse me?"

"Nothing," she shot back. "Please let me go."

"I don't think so," he said, as if it were his right just to haul any miss he chose into his arms and . . . and . . . wreak havoc on her senses. All of them. For with him holding her thusly, she could feel *him.* The man was lean and hard, all angles and masculine lines. And his hands weren't just tracing her outline, they were exploring her, stroking her, pulling from her desires she'd never known she possessed.

In places she'd never imagined.

Now she understood only too well why most of the mothers in the *ton* steered their daughters well out of the earl's path.

"Who are you?" he asked softly, teasing her ear with his breath and, for the briefest second, his lips.

She shivered again. "The better question, my lord, is who are you?"

"Ah, a barrister's daughter."

"Hardly," she told him, trying to sound bored. "Just immune to your charms."

"Really?" His lips found her earlobe and nibbled at the space right behind her ear.

Hermione clapped her mouth shut to keep a very improper moan from escaping her lips.

Oh, Jiminy! The man wasn't just the Protector of London, but the despoiler as well, for not even being invisible was enough to stop the man.

"You have an unfair advantage," Hermione sputtered.

"One might say the same of you," he said. "Your little trick on Miss Burke could hardly be called sporting."

Hermione bit back the grin that rose on her lips. "I thought only of her character."

"Her character?"

"Yes. It was about time it had a fair and open airing."

Then he surprised her. He laughed. "Now I know who you are."

"You do?"

"Yes, you're an unrepentant minx."

A minx? "Hardly so—"

"Exactly so." His hand reached up and cupped her chin. "So who are you, minx?"

"Don't call me that!" She tried to squirm out of his grasp but to no avail. "I'm no one."

"I doubt Miss Burke would have inspired such a nasty turn if you were no one. So tell me who you are, or I will have to resort to guessing again."

Harrumph. He could spend all night guessing, and he'd never manage it. Why, they'd been introduced half a dozen times, and he never remembered her.

"Silence, eh minx? Or better still, Shadow," he christened her. "Is your invisibility to hide a terrible case of spots?"

"I haven't spots!" she sputtered.

"The last lady I knew who was thusly concealed was covered in them."

This took Hermione aback. "There are others like me?"

"Well—" he hedged.

"Oh, you're teasing me. I can see it in your eyes."

"I wish I could see yours," he whispered back. His hand curved around her cheek. "No, you haven't any blemishes. In fact, your skin feels like rose petals." He paused for a second, his thumb tracing a sensual path along the edge of her mouth. "And I have to imagine your lips would taste the same."

And before she could even wonder what he was about to do—so utterly mesmerized was she by his touch—that she never thought he'd do the unthinkable.

His head dipped down and his lips expertly claimed hers.

Not even a "mew" of surprise could escape his trap.

Hermione had never been kissed, and she'd imagined her first kiss exactly like this—alone in a garden with a man of some experience.

But innocently, the rest of the matter had been nothing but dreamy speculation and left her unprepared for the very real sensation of having a man haul her up against him, into his arms, his lips covering hers and demanding . . . yes, demanding she submit to his will.

She didn't know whether to be furious or thrilled.

And while the first few stormy moments of his assault had taken her unaware, she felt the shift in his tactics almost immediately. Far from insisting upon her submission, his lips, his tongue now urged her to open up to him, tempting her with languid caresses and the promise of passions to come.

Passion his hands were awakening as they roamed shamelessly over her body.

He had no concerns about modesty, exploring the curve of her hips, up over her stomach, and curling around her breast.

She sucked in a deep breath at the sensation, for he was unfurling ribbons of pure pleasure through her. She felt wanton and reckless, and quite ruined all at the same time. And thankfully he couldn't see the blush that rose from her toes all the way to the tip of her nose.

He was ruining her, here in the Thurlows' garden. Why if anyone came out and saw them, she'd be . . .

She'd be . . . she'd be . . .

Well, she'd be nothing, she realized. For no one could see her.

And therefore no one would spend the next day reporting to one and all that Hermione Marlowe had been ravished by Lord Rockhurst.

A thrill ran down her spine, or it could have been the earl's hand at the small of her back pulling her closer still.

No one could see her. She was utterly and completely free to . . .

Indulge herself. For this bliss . . . this passion was hers. Hers to have without any recrimination, and she had no doubts she'd never taste such freedom again.

So when his kiss deepened, and Hermione tentatively opened up to him, let his tongue sweep over hers, answered him with her own explorations, minor and inexperienced as they were, they seemed to work, for Rockhurst groaned, and his hold on her tightened.

In that moment, Hermione came alive, lost some part of her innocence, forgot every warning that mothers drilled into their daughters from the time they showed the first whispers of womanhood.

She gasped for air as he wrenched his mouth from hers, his lips seeking a new torture, kissing her neck, her ears.

"Temptress," he whispered in a voice so masculine, so guttural. "Who are you?"

"I don't know," she said back. For honestly she had no idea.

His mouth sought hers once again, and this time the kiss was deep and searching, as demanding as he'd been when he'd ensnared her in this prison.

All this time she'd stood still and powerless beneath him, but now she reached out and touched him, one hand clinging to the lapel of his coat, the other tracing the lines of his jaw, then reaching up to rake through his tawny mane.

The earl groaned. No, he growled. Something so raw and untamed, her breath caught in her throat. Then the entire moment ended, for he tore himself away from her.

Hermione staggered on her own two feet, surprised to find how much she'd been clinging to him for support.

"Now we shall see who you are," he told her.

With her blood racing through her limbs, her body trembling with passion and her head spinning, she was feeling far too saucy, far too sure of herself, and so she said, "And how do you propose to do that?"

"Like this," he whispered into her ear.

Then his hands caught her by her hips and he slung her, like a sack of oats, over his shoulder.

"Put me down!" she protested, hammering his back with her fists. "If you think you can haul me through that ballroom, and I'll cooperate, you are mad."

He laughed. "Hardly mad, my little Shadow. Just resourceful."

And with that, he strode to the back of the garden and kicked open the door to the mews and hauled her, kicking and protesting, down the alley.

Eight

"I won't tell anyone," the woman on his shoulder said, as Rockhurst hauled her up the stairs of his town house and carried her into his bedroom, where he dumped her rather unceremoniously on his bed.

"Excuse me?" he asked, having not really heard what she'd said. He'd all but plugged his ears to her caterwauling about halfway down the alley.

Too bad he couldn't as easily stop the arousal she'd sparked inside him.

"I won't tell anyone," she repeated. "I mean to say, I won't tell them who you are if you'll just let me go."

He shrugged. "Go ahead."

The bed shifted. "You mean I can leave?"

"No." He turned around, went back to the door, and locked them both inside. "But go ahead and tell whomever you see fit."

While his original intent had been to kidnap her and keep her until she appeared, which Cricks had suggested might be at dawn, he hadn't given a bit of thought to the long hours ahead . . . not before this impertinent bit of muslin had nearly unmanned him with her kiss in the garden.

Perhaps she wasn't all that innocent after all.

He took a furtive glance at the bed, and in his imagination he saw a lush, full beauty sprawled out on his bed, furious and impassioned.

His blood rang with a heady rush in his ears. And other places. Rockhurst glanced back at the door. Perhaps, he shouldn't have brought her *here*.

"Here" being his bedchamber.

You should have locked her in the wine cellar and been done with the matter until first light.

No, he knew exactly what he was doing. He would stick with his original plan. A little seduction until he discovered her wish, or keep her until first light or however long it took to gain the ring or discover her identity.

He did his best, however, to forget the moment when she'd finally surrendered to him in the garden, her mouth opening to him, her body arching up against his. It had been all he could do not to toss her down on the small patch of grass and take her right there.

Oh, that would have been a sight. Him with his breeches down, fucking the bare grass for all anyone else could see.

No, much better to bring her to your bedroom. Rockhurst raked his hand through his hair while his reason waged a war with his rampant passions.

And how do you even know the ring on her hand is the ring?

Because she has a ring on her hand and she's invisible, he argued with himself.

Like a ring on a lady's hand was an improbable occurrence. Many young ladies wore simple rings—gifts from godmothers, family relics handed down from mother to daughter, or even a token from an admirer. Well, whatever it was, it was impossible to discover as long as she remained invisible.

Of course there were two possibilities he hadn't considered.

What if it is an engagement ring? *Or a wedding ring?*

He stopped himself and glanced again at the bed. He wasn't used to meddling with married women.

Oh, what sort of tangle have you gotten yourself into now, Rockhurst?

He winced. Perhaps he needed some reinforcements. Or brandy.

Brandy sounded good.

He strode over to the cabinet in the corner and pulled out the bottle and glass he kept tucked away there. For emergencies. He glanced back at his empty bed and saw in his mind's eye her lush body naked and writhing beneath him.

Yes, this qualified as an emergency. He poured himself a healthy measure.

She'd been silent and still all this time, so when she spoke, it startled him slightly. "You don't care if people know you are the Paratus?"

"That's not the point," he replied, before taking a hasty gulp. "Tell whomever you like. No one will believe you. They'll think you're mad." He tipped the glass toward her. "Care for some?"

"No, thank you," she said primly. "*Maman* says spirits make a lady vulgar."

"Wise woman, your *maman*," he agreed. "Do I know her?"

She blithely ignored his prying attempt. "I wouldn't have told anyone, but not because it would make me appear nicked in the nob—" she paused for a moment, "—rather, what I was saying is that I'm not prone to prattle on."

"*Harrumph,*" he snorted, before he took another drink.

The bed shifted again. "I'll have you know that I'm no widgeon."

He had yet to meet a Mayfair debutante who wasn't. Then again, his Shadow was hardly some Bath miss—for he doubted those illustrious schools of ladylike virtues taught young debutantes to kiss as she'd done.

That, or she was a very quick study—a notion that lent him all kinds of erotic visions, of a night spent tutoring her on the subject. All too quickly, the room grew stifling. He shoved his glass aside and yanked at his cravat.

"Why did you bring me here?" she asked, panic in her words as she mistook his actions. "Because if you think to seduce me again—"

He continued to tug at his cravat, now sending a leering wink toward the bed. "If you wish—"

There was a hasty scramble atop the coverlet. "I do not!"

"Are you sure?"

"Yes."

He stalked toward the bed, her innocent perfume tickling his senses. "Liar."

She had no answer for him, remaining stubbornly silent.

And that was more answer for him than if she'd continued her protests. For a moment they stayed there, just a few feet apart, and he felt the tension between them as if *it* were visible. A cord binding them together that acted like an odd game of tug-o-war, his desire prodding him toward the bed, and if he wasn't mistaken, hers pulling him closer.

He wasn't mistaken.

Hermione couldn't breathe with him this close. This was the kiss in the garden all over . . . but more dangerous. For here she was perched on his bed, and her body, oh, her rebellious body, wanted him to kiss her again.

To pull her gown off and cover her with his magnificent body. To touch her . . . all over. To kiss her . . . everywhere. And she'd open her legs and wrap them around his hips as he . . .

She shuttered her lashes, closed her eyes. What was she thinking? She'd never had such erotic thoughts before. Wherever were these images coming from?

The ring trembled, sending ripples of anticipation down her limbs.

Wretched bit, she chided silently, but she didn't mean

it. For hadn't she, even in her innocence, wished for this?

"Shadow?" he whispered, his hand reaching out for her.

She leaned into it like a cat, letting him stroke her hair. It was all she could do not to purr as his fingers plied the strands and expertly plucked out her pins. "Yes, my lord?" she managed to reply, as her chignon tumbled down around her shoulders.

"What are you thinking?" His fingers followed the line of her jaw and traced an almost kiss over her lips.

She pressed them together, her cheeks flaming with a blush she swore went all the way down past her garters.

Tell him. Tell him of your wish . . .

"I was . . . that is, I was thinking of . . . back in the garden when you . . . " The words stalled in her throat, for it had suddenly gone dry.

Jiminy! She couldn't do it.

"Strange coincidence that," he murmured, as he climbed onto the bed beside her, his fingers now trailing over her shoulder and down her hand. She hadn't bothered tonight to wear gloves, so her hands were bare, and she shivered as his fingers twined with hers, as he pulled her hand to his lips and began to kiss them.

"How so?" she gasped, as he took one of her fingers in his mouth and suckled it.

Rockhurst glanced up at her, as if he could see her eyes. "I was thinking the exact same thing."

He was? She looked again into his eyes and saw there a man's desires and needs and drew in an unsteady breath. He wanted her?

He couldn't. It was impossible. This man, who'd never even glanced at her in passing, wanted her?

This is what you wanted. What you wished for . . .

But I don't know what to do, she wanted to rail back.

Luckily for Hermione, the earl did. He pulled her up against him, and kissed her anew, as he had in the garden, plying her lips apart with his strong pair. His breath, warm and vibrant, washed over her, and she felt drawn toward him, to him.

His tongue brushed over hers, so intimately, coaxing her to try this playful diversion.

She couldn't resist. The temptation of being his swept aside any bit of caution she still claimed. She tasted him, letting her tongue tangle with his, then discovered the first thrill of passion as he groaned and pulled her ever closer.

Nor did the fact that he couldn't see her clothes stop him from opening her gown, plucking her laces open, and easing it off her shoulders. Then the laces of her corset met the same fate, opening up beneath his expert and nimble fingers.

Before she knew it, her gown and corset were nearly off, and she clung to Rockhurst, wondering how she would ever hazard such a feat if he could see her? Why she'd die of mortification to be so exposed.

He leaned her back atop the coverlet, but not before he shrugged off his jacket, his cravat, and his waistcoat in such a haphazard fashion, she had to imagine his valet would be in high dudgeon for a sennight.

For a moment, they stilled, half-dressed, both trembling, and Hermione realized being like this, unseen, gave her a courage, a bravado that made her feel like the most experienced courtesan.

That is, until his fingers curled around her breast, his thumb rubbing over her nipple until it tightened and swelled into a ripe bud.

"Oooh, Rockhurst," she gasped in surprise as desire, hot and thrilling, coursed through her veins. She'd never felt anything so wonderful. She sighed anew, and to her delight, he did it again.

If that was all the encouragement he needed, she'd cry his name all night long.

When he had both nipples taut and thick, he leaned down and took one in his mouth and sucked on it until she thought she'd die from the pleasure of it.

His hand reached down and plucked off her boot. As it came free of her foot, it became visible and he eyed the sensible bit of footwear with a wry expression. "Hardly what I expected," he said as he tossed it aside. "But then so are you." The second boot quickly followed the first. Her stockings were tugged off, and from there he traced lazy, haphazard kisses up her bare legs.

As he climbed higher and higher, his lips hot and eager, his tongue laving over her skin with teasing swipes, Hermione's gut tightened, even as that place between her thighs started to throb.

He wasn't going to . . . he wouldn't think to . . .

Rockhurst rose from his ministrations for a moment, then tugged her gown completely off, as well as her corset. She was bare beneath him, except for her garters, which he was now playfully tugging with his teeth.

"Do you know what you are doing?" she gasped, as his lips went higher, to her thighs, his hands catching hold of her hips.

"I damn well hope so," he said rakishly. "But do tell me if I'm getting it wrong."

Wrong? Was he mad? Hermione groaned again, this time as his fingers brushed over the curls of hair, stroking her thighs as if he knew the secret to open them.

Oh, he knew it. His breath blew hot upon her core, and her legs parted before his impatient course.

Then it wasn't just his breath upon her, but his lips, his tongue, and Hermione's hips rose and bucked as he kissed her there.

Her fingers twisted into the coverlet, while her heels dug in as well. She'd never been touched, let alone kissed thusly, and his tongue teased her softly and gently, just as it had when he'd first kissed her. Yet as her body began to rock, he seemed to sense the growing urgency inside her and pressed further, suckling her, exploring her.

Hermione moaned loudly, and the earl chuckled. "Not yet," he told her. "There's still more to come."

More?

Then gently he slid a finger inside her. It was tight at first, but when he went to withdraw it, she felt the first inklings of what "more" meant. She rocked back against his hand, and this time he eased two fingers inside.

It was like something she'd seen in those illicit

French prints of her mother's. And while the title had baffled her, *Un goût de ciel*, she knew now she wouldn't so much call it a *Taste of Heaven*, but the kiss *from* heaven, for she felt herself being pulled upward, drawn ever quicker toward an end that promised nothing but bliss.

Her hips rocked, his lips continued their sweet torment, and all of a sudden, she was crying out his name as she discovered exactly what heaven was. . .better than a volley of colorful Chinese rockets or a sale on silks. Oh, she tried to breathe, tried to make sense of what was happening.

His rumbling chuckle told her he knew. Of course he did! He'd done this magic thing to her. Hermione sighed and looked up at him and saw in his eyes a glint that told her this was just the beginning.

Oh, was it possible? She hazarded a glance at him again. Specifically at his breeches, which bulged from the hardness there.

A longing like one she'd never felt before filled her with curiosity . . . and desire.

And being the curious minx that she was, she reached for him and pulled him closer.

Rockhurst felt her hands tug beneath his arms, drawing him up toward her. He climbed up, kissing her belly, kissing her breasts, and finally, capturing her lips in a deep kiss that brought more moans from her and the tease of her hips as they rocked up to meet his.

He found he didn't need to "see" her. He closed his eyes and let his imagination take over, for she was a sensuous little puss, his hands exploring her body, his blood running hot with desire as he memorized every curve, every ripe contour.

Here he'd thought to seduce her, and now she was tempting him. This Mayfair miss. This mysterious little hoyden.

She kissed him thoroughly, her tongue swiping over his. Gone was the reluctant lady in the garden, and in her place, a flirtatious bit of muslin.

Her hands ran down his back and came to his breeches and there they stopped as if unsure what to do next.

Undo them, his red-hot passions clamored. *Demmit, take them off.*

And as if she heard him, she did so, her fingers trembling as she undid the buttons, and then tentatively pushed them down over his hips.

Her fingers were warm on his skin and only drove him further into madness. Having listened to her moans and soft gasps, then that final breathless moment when she'd given in to her crisis and come, he'd nearly been swept along with her.

With a hasty shrug and quick tug, he tossed his pants aside. He was rock hard, and it was all he could do not to bury himself inside her.

Madness, he told himself. This was utter madness, but he wanted her like he'd never wanted any woman before. Forgotten was his plan to seduce, long tossed aside was any sense of reason and his usual calculated reserve.

That is, until his hands slid up her arms, his fingers twining with hers, and he remembered exactly why he was here.

The ring.

Even as he touched it, it seemed to tremble on her hand.

And it called to him.

Take me, it seemed to whisper. *Take me any way you can.*

His eyes glazed over with a blackness, and his passions turned to a lust of another kind.

A blood-lust.

How easy would it be to kill her now. . . a niggle of voice whispered to him. *Kill her, and it will be yours.*

Beneath him, her hips rose up to meet him, to tease his erect manhood. "What do you want?" she whispered.

The ring. I want that bloody ring, he nearly shouted.

And then his eyes wrenched open, and he knew how close he was to just taking it. Taking everything that could save his soul. Save his life.

But it would mean taking more than just her innocence. It would mean taking her life.

Yet even that horrific thought didn't stay his hand from moving up toward her throat.

It would be such a simple thing . . .

Rockhurst wrenched himself up from the bed. He fled to the farthest reach of the room and shuddered, his breath coming in unsteady, ragged heaves.

What had he been about to do? He'd been about to . . .

There was a rustle on the sheets. "What's wrong?" she whispered.

"Everything," he told her, trying to shake the wayward and dangerous darkness from his very soul. "Everything about this is wrong."

* * *

It took some time for Rockhurst to regain his senses. He'd taken refuge by the window and put his back to her.

There was no doubt that the ring on her finger was Milton's Ring. It had to be.

He'd listened to her gathering up her clothes, quietly straightening the room, as if she too had heard and seen the darkness that had passed through his heart.

After what felt like an eternity, she broke the uneasy silence between them by saying, "I suppose you are right—no one would believe me. About who you are and all of this."

He cocked a brow but didn't turn around. "Quite so."

"It wasn't always so, was it?" she whispered. "There was a time when the citizens of London would pay you tribute. Well, not you exactly. But your ancestors."

Rockhurst glanced over at where he thought she was standing. She'd been reading Podmore.

Here was a first. He'd brought a bluestocking to his bed. Then again, the sensible boots and dull gown should have been his first warning.

Well, he'd indulged her passions, why not indulge her mind a little. "There was an age when everyone understood the balance of light and dark in our world," he told her. "Now . . . well, we live in enlightened times." At least so he'd thought up until a few minutes ago.

Just before he'd been seized by an unholy desire to commit murder.

Suddenly uncomfortable with the entire subject, he

parted the curtain to look out into the darkness of his realm, trying as he could to make sense of this implausible night.

"You make it sound as if it is wrong to be modern," she said, following him. She'd brought his wrapper with her and eased it over his bare shoulders.

He glanced over at the hook where it had come from, about to offer her his other one, but saw that it was missing. Then he heard the telltale rustle of silk, and knew she'd pulled it on. Good, better to have clothes on, something separating them.

"Modern?" he mused, wrapping the robe on tight. "No, not in the least. It just makes my work more difficult."

"Because you have so much to conceal."

Astute, he realized glancing over his shoulder at her, though to him it was only an empty space. But what if it wasn't? What if he could see her?

"What do you look like?" he asked. He had a fair idea of her height, and her proportions, but what color was her hair? Did she have freckles?

"Nothing very special," she demurred.

"Modest?"

"Hardly. Just used to being compared to the Miss Burkes of the world and coming up lacking. Not all of us are Originals, my lord."

"An honest woman. And that, my little Shadow, makes you a novelty and an Original—whether you want the title or not."

There was a huffy sigh right near his elbow, so he had to surmise she didn't want the crown he'd offered.

Oh, yes, she was an Original, invisibility aside.

She shivered, and, without a word, he reached awkwardly for her, and when he found her, he swept her into his arms and glanced over at his bed—where he could lay her down, his hands could touch her, his lips could explore hers . . . so he could finally take . . .

A dark veil began to cloud his vision, and it was all he could do to shake free of it. What was he thinking? Hadn't he learned his lesson earlier?

And yet, he kept finding himself drawn to her.

Or was it the power of the ring?

Absently, he caught up her hand and kissed her fingers, until he came to the one with the ring. The ring tightly affixed to her finger.

Cricks had said the ring could come off one of two ways. By her wish coming to fruition, or . . .

By her death.

He let go of her hand.

Get the ring, his reason urged. *How hard would it be?*

He released her and turned back to the window.

You've killed before.

Only that once, he argued back. And he'd had no choice. Not that it had made the act any less chilling . . . or less haunting.

But then again, he'd never once considered having the chance to break the Covenant. To live a normal life. To love a woman and raise children without always being shadowed by the dark forces he was bound to stop.

His thoughts ran wild, dark and tangled by the possibilities, all hinged on one thing.

This woman's life.

The silence in the room grew disconcerting, so he asked, "What else did you learn about me today?"

She shifted behind him. "Pardon?"

"Podmore," he supplied. "You must recall it. The volume you stole from Cricks—"

"I haven't the vaguest notion what you—"

"You were at Cricks's this afternoon." He turned to face her.

For a moment she remained silent, and he had to wonder if she was actually considering denying it.

Well, she didn't quite deny it, rather argued around the point. "*If* I was at this Mr. Cricks's shop this afternoon, I'd like to see you prove it."

He went back to his original theory that she was the daughter of a barrister. "In a few hours I'll prove it by escorting you back to Cricks's, where you can return the book you stole from him."

She ruffled up, the sheets moving. "I didn't steal it. I bought it. I left every coin I had to pay for it."

"I think he would have rather preferred to keep his book."

"He can have it back when I am done reading it."

"I wouldn't bother. 'Tis nothing but lies and fabrication."

Now it was her turn to make a very unladylike snort. "So says you. I rather like it."

"Bluestocking!"

The floorboards creaked violently as she stomped toward him. "Oh, now that is beyond the pale," she snapped. "I am no bluestocking."

He could almost see her hands fisted to her hips. "Demmit it, minx, don't get your garters in a knot. I know you aren't a bluestocking."

"Well, that's better." Then she paused, before she sat back down, the mattress dipping where she'd planted herself. "How do you know I'm not a bluestocking? You've never seen me."

"Well, having seen your boots and gown it would be easy to see why I would think such a thing," he teased. "Hardly the first stare of fashion."

There was a sputtered sort of reply before she managed to get out her defense. "I wore those on purpose. And it is entirely your fault."

"My fault you chose that hideous gown and fishwife boots?"

"I wasn't about to let you ruin another pair of my slippers! And you should see the gown I did have on last night. Beyond repair. Not to mention my . . ."

Rockhurst crossed his arms over his chest and realized he was quite enjoying this verbal joust. "You need not have followed me."

"It wasn't as if I had a choice. If I hadn't wished—"

Wished? Rockhurst straightened. Had he heard her correctly? Ever so carefully, he stilled his racing heart, then asked as nonchalantly as he could muster, "You wished this?"

She sighed. "You wouldn't believe me if I . . ."

He shook his head and waved his hands at her. "I think of anyone in London, I'd be the one you could explain this to." He tapped his chest. "The Paratus? Remember?"

"Oh, yes, I suppose so," she conceded. "Well, you see

I made this wish, a rather imprudent one," she began to say. "And now here I am."

"Until sunrise?" he prompted.

The bed shifted as she got back up, obviously having forgotten her ire. "Yes . . . Oh, how did you know?"

"Cricks surmised as much—since he could see you during the day, and I'd been unable to at night."

"Hmm," she murmured as if weighing what to say next.

Sunrise! Now he knew the parameters of her wish. So there was nothing left to do but wait for the morning to answer the rest of his questions. Starting with her identity. Still, he couldn't stop himself from asking another question. "Does anyone else know about this wish?"

Now here would be the real test as to whether or not she did "prattle on."

The bed shook as she answered. "Oh, no! Who'd believe me?"

Who, indeed! He was in the same room as her and still found it rather unbelievable.

"Let me see," she began. "You and Mr. Cricks, obviously."

"Yes."

"And Quince, of course."

"Quince?" This was a bit of a wrinkle. "Who is Quince?"

"I don't really know who Quince is," she told him. "She has this rather disconcerting ability to appear when I least need her, and she's rather high-handed about its being her ring. Oh, and she mentioned someone else—Milton."

Milton's ring.

Rockhurst closed his gaping mouth.

No wonder Melaphor had tried so hard to coax this chit into his realm.

For with Milton's Ring . . .

Rockhurst shuddered. He didn't even want to consider what could happen if this ring fell into the wrong hands.

Meanwhile, his little Shadow was prattling on. ". . . I've tried and tried to take it off. Soap. Lard. Why I've pulled on it until I thought my finger would come off—"

"That won't work," he told her, knowing that more than her finger would have to be removed to gain the ring.

"I know, or so Quince says. I thought it might come off after you . . . well if we . . ."

The blush in her words caught his attention. If they did what? Then it struck him. "If we made love?"

"Yes, that. But it didn't, then again I don't think we entirely—"

"No, we didn't," he told her, only half-listening to her, but suddenly her confession tumbled together. "You wished for me to make love to you?"

"No-oo-oo. Not exactly. Oh, heavens, this is so mortifying." She paced about, and he had no idea where she was other than by the soft tread of her feet as she padded along.

"You and I are well past mortifying," he advised.

"Yes, I suppose so," she agreed, coming to a stop, he guessed, near the fire.

"What exactly did you wish for?" Given what he already knew of her, he was almost afraid to ask. He got up and walked toward her, until she reached out and stopped him before he ran her over.

"You'll think I'm foolish."

"Hardly that," he said. His blood began to race anew, for this close he could smell her, could almost see her outline.

"You'll think I'm such a bluestocking."

"I thought we already settled that," he teased. "Besides, I know you aren't a bluestocking from kissing you."

"You do?"

"Most decidedly. That and Cricks told me you weren't exactly . . . How did he put it? Oh, yes. He claimed to have old coppers with more sense than you."

"Why, of all the—" She sucked in a deep breath, indignation in every bit of it, and he laughed.

"Don't be insulted," Rockhurst told her. "He also said you had a bonny pair of green eyes that made him wish himself a much younger man." He winked in her direction.

She muttered something about "keeping Cricks's smelly old book" before she finally settled down.

"Now about your wish . . ." he began. For if it was nothing more than making love to her, she could have her boon in a trice. Then he'd have the ring, and this Mayfair miss could toddle back to her *maman* with a knowing little smile on her lips.

"Must I?"

"How am I to help you solve this . . . this . . . nightly

dilemma of yours if I don't know what it is you wished for?" *For if I can grant her wish, then I can set aside this dark temptation of what I'd have to do if I cannot...*

After a few moments of silence and one large sigh, she whispered the words that changed his life.

"I wished to know all your secrets."

Hermione's words hit like a cannon ball, and the earl reacted as if it had landed at his feet.

He backed away from her. "You wished for what?!"

"To know all your secrets," she repeated. That wasn't the entire truth, but given the outraged look on his face, and the frisson of fear running down her spine, she stilled her tongue from telling him the rest.

Besides, she wasn't ready to reveal hers. Not anytime soon.

"How could you wish for that sort of thing? Why, discovering a man's secrets could take a lifetime."

A lifetime? "Oh, dear," she whispered. "I hadn't thought of that."

"Apparently not," he shot back, his hand swiping through his hair. He paced back and forth in front of her.

Hermione drew back her toes for fear of having them trod on. "In my defense, I believe I only meant to learn the important ones."

"Such as?"

"Well, I would have thought discovering who you are, or rather what you are, and well . . ." Her cheeks grew hot again and she tripped over her tongue as she tried to say it. "Being with you . . . in your. . ."

"If you are going to make these wishes, you better damned well be able to say it. Sex. We were having a tumble, a bit of fun."

"Yes, that," she replied, the sting of his blunt words leaving her tiffed. *A tumble?* Of all the cheek! She'd have this wretched ring on her hand for the rest of her life if that was all she garnered. "I would have thought that would have done the trick, but it is still on tight." She held out her hand to him, but then remembered he couldn't see it.

Meanwhile, the earl paced about the room.

Hermione retreated behind the chair. "I don't understand what has you in this state."

Rockhurst whirled around, finger wagging anew. "You wished yourself into my life. Without my permission."

"You didn't seem to mind a little while ago," she shot back, her temper getting the better of her, "when you were *tumbling* me." Hermione tried to stop herself, but she was in a pique now. "And if you would but look at it from my point of view, this is entirely your fault—"

"Is this about your demmed slippers again—"

"Oh, bother my slippers—"

"I'll buy you an entire shopful," he finished, his hands waving in the air.

Hermione eased around him and gathered up her gown and boots. "Perhaps it would be better if I left," she offered. Then she made the mistake of brushing past him.

"Oh, no," he said, catching hold of her. "No, you aren't going anywhere. Not until sunrise. Until I know all your secrets, my little mistress of the shadows."

All her secrets? That would never do. For then he'd

discover who she was, and Hermione couldn't bear that. To see the disappointment on his face? To no longer be his "Shadow"? His minx. But merely Lady Hermione Marlowe, and one of *those* Marlowes to boot.

No. She wasn't about to reveal anything. Not yet. So she tried to shake herself free, but he wasn't letting go.

Rather, he towed her over to a chair, where he dropped down into it, and then pulled her into his lap. Up against his chest, right there where she would have to spend the rest of the night looking directly at his lips—knowing full well what they were capable of doing to a woman.

And when the sun came up, she could only guess his reaction.

Lady Hermione Marlowe? I beg your pardon for ruining you. How will you ever forgive me? Perhaps by doing me the honor of becoming my wife?

That was about as likely as her becoming a scholar.

Biting her lips together, she thought as hard as she could to come up with some way to escape him. If only he would fall asleep . . . she stole a furtive glance up at him and found him staring moodily into the fire. And, unfortunately, wide-awake.

If I could slip away and steal the key from his jacket.

She glanced around the shadowy room but couldn't spy where his jacket had landed when he'd flung it off. Just before . . .

He'd kissed her so ruthlessly . . . teased her until she'd . . .

Hermione's face flamed to life. Gads, she needed to concentrate on the problem at hand, not continue woolgathering about the earl's prowess . . . in other matters. But it was rather hard to think of anything else when he persisted on holding her bundled up against his hard chest . . . perched atop his lap and his hard . . .

She shuddered again.

"Cold?" he asked.

"No," she told him. Quite the contrary. *Oh, why didn't I listen to Quince and just stay home and play casino.* That's it. Cards. They always made her mother sleepy. "You wouldn't happen to have a deck of cards, do you?"

"No."

"Any books?"

"I would have thought you were tired of reading."

"Well, I cannot sit here all night atop you like this," she blustered, wiggling in his lap to emphasize her point.

"I should have killed you when I had the chance last night," he muttered.

"Excuse me?" she said, a ripple of outrage running down her spine.

He turned to face her. "I said, 'I should have killed—'"

"Yes, yes, I heard you the first time. But you can't kill me." She crossed her arms over her chest and wished he could see the self-assurance she'd pasted on her face. "Need I remind you what the Covenant says?"

"Not more Podmore!" He shook his head. "Utter fabrication!"

"Thou shalt not use your power to harm your fellow kith and kin," she quoted.

"None of my 'kith or kin' turn up invisible," he

pointed out. His sarcasm landed as sure as the arrow she'd shot at Melaphor.

"Podmore says that in the Legend of the Paratus—"

He got up and dumped her quite unceremoniously on the floor. "One more word about that idiot, and I *will* kill you."

She crossed her arms over her chest. "This bickering is getting us no closer to solving my problem. If you are such an expert on these matters, why don't *you* tell me the Legend of the Paratus?"

"Tell you—"

"Yes, why not? Perhaps if you tell me the tale, it will give me enough information to end my wish." Hermione pressed her lips together, knowing full well that her wish would only come true once he knew all her secrets, but what she really needed to do was find some way to end all this talk of killing.

Especially killing her.

"If I knew everything about the Paratus, at the very least it might loosen the ring up a bit."

"Yes, perhaps," he growled, pacing about in front of her. "But you sit there," he said pointing at the ottoman beside the chair.

Nine

"In the darkest days of England's history, there was a champion who rose above all others," he began.

"The first Earl of Rockhurst?"

"Yes," he said.

"The first Paratus?" she asked, her hand coming to rest on his sleeve.

The moment her fingers touched him, a spark ignited inside him.

What was it about this prattling little minx that had his blood racing every time she touched him . . . or he touched her?

Rockhurst paused and slanted a long glance at the ottoman where she sat. "Do you want me to tell the story, or do you want to?"

"Oh, so sorry," she said, pulling her hand back. "Please, continue."

He regretted the loss of her touch, but continued anyway. "Thomas of Hurst was his name—"

"As in Rockhurst," she said.

"Yes, well, the 'Rock' part came later."

"And Thomas, which is your given name, is it not?"

"Yes."

"But no one calls you Thomas."

This stopped him, for it was true. No one had. Not even his Aunt Routledge, not even Mary. It had been so long since he'd heard his Christian name, he'd nearly forgotten he possessed one. "No. No one does."

"Oh," she whispered.

And then she was silent, as if pondering this point, so he continued, "As I was saying, Thomas gained vast lands and wealth with his skill at the blade and jousting."

Even before he took a breath, she was embellishing the tale anew. "And he ruled over the people in his domain with great care and honesty. A nobleman and a hero in every sense of the word."

He glanced over at her, quirking a brow.

"Oh dear! I did it again." Her hand returned to his sleeve and squeezed his forearm. "I'm afraid I have a fondness for French novels. And the hero is always just and honest, and so I assumed . . ." her dithering stopped, and there was a moment of silence before she said, "I won't do it again. I promise."

He didn't believe a word of it. "Do you talk through the opera as well?"

"Never," she said. "Well, not unless there is someone there worth mentioning. Or some really truly odious gown. Or someone has a lady of questionable virtue in his box, or just the other night when Lord Boxley brought Miss Uppington to meet—"

Rockhurst closed his eyes. This could take all night.

"Heavens, I'm prattling. I think it is because I am so nervous."

"Nervous? About what?"

"Because I've never been alone with a man before," she admitted.

There it was. The truth if he'd ever heard it. "I've never spent the night with an innocent before," he replied.

"I'm not completely innocent," she pointed out. "We did do that bit in the bed . . . and then you did that . . ."

He could hear the blush in her words that betrayed her as the innocent she was. And a little part of his anger with her melted, for he'd loved hearing the surprised gasp when she'd reached her pinnacle.

His hand twitched to touch her again, and he wondered if she'd cry out with the same delight a second time . . . or a third . . .

Oh, what the devil was he thinking? He tugged his wrapper on tighter and wished he had his trousers on as well. And his short sword and cross-bow.

God save him from innocents! Wasn't that his mantra and always had been. This was exactly why he'd always avoided the London Marriage Mart. For fear of being entangled in some scandal with one of them.

Mayfair misses were possibly more dangerous than derga. With their wide eyes and fluffy lashes and come-hither glances.

And this one, oh, she was really dangerous. She'd done it all with nary a glance.

Yes, a lot of good his lifelong avoidance of such creatures had done him. Now that he was so completely entangled, he hadn't the least idea how to get rid of her . . . other than the obvious one.

"Yes, I recall what happened," he said, doing his best not to. He waited for a moment to see if there were going to be any more interruptions, but when there was still only silence, he continued.

"Then one year whispers reached Thomas's ears that there was a rival who claimed he was the greatest warrior in the kingdom. These tales continued to flow into the valley where Thomas lived, and every troubadour and traveler who passed through told of a man whose unholy power in battle could not be beaten."

Her hand eased back over to his sleeve, and he paused. For a moment he recalled as a child climbing into his mother's lap at precisely the same moment in the story. Then he shook off that long-lost memory and continued.

"And as this terrible fiend swept through England, he killed many good men, ravaged their lands and . . . and . . ." Rockhurst faltered to a stop. Should he give her the version his mother told him or the one his father had shared when Rockhurst had been old enough to understand?

"And?" she prompted.

No reason she didn't deserve the truth. Might even bring her to her senses.

Or scare the ring off her finger.

"If there were no women and children in the room, the troubadours would tell the rest of the story. That this foul beast would beget the daughters and servants of their victims with children too vile to be allowed to live past their first breath."

Her fingers tightened around his arm. "Melaphor," she gasped.

"No, it wasn't Melaphor. But a derga," he said without thinking.

"Not a derga!"

He glanced over at her. "You know what a derga is?"

"Well, I've seen a picture of one. But I hardly know what one is besides being terribly ugly."

"You were close when you thought it might be Melaphor. A derga is a cousin of Melaphor's, if you will. They are ancient messengers from Hell."

"I take it their messages aren't always good."

"A derga's message is never good. They are portents of death."

"Jiminy!"

Rockhurst resisted the urge to smile at this mild oath. There was one more clue she hadn't had a Bath education.

Thank God, he mused, having no doubts that such an upbringing would have ruined her quirky views and spontaneous outbursts.

"And these derga are worse than Melaphor?" she was asking.

He shook his head. "Not worse, just different. A derga lives to kill and bring destruction. Melaphor wants that and power. The power to rule."

She shivered. "Who would have ever thought such a thing possible?" Then a few moments later, she urged him to continue, "Please go on."

"So Thomas—"

"Being a good and just hero—"

"Who's telling this story?"

She shifted atop the ottoman. "You are."

"Yes, I am." He slanted a slight smile at her. Demmed chit. She was getting under his skin. He furrowed his brow and got back to the tale at hand, "So Thomas . . . being a good and just hero—" he couldn't help but add for her benefit, "—knew he must defeat this villain, so he sent out a challenge and journeyed to meet his enemy."

"That was terribly foolish."

Rockhurst shook his head, for he swore he hadn't heard her correctly. "Foolish? If you haven't forgotten, there was a monster terrorizing the countryside. Thomas would have had to fight him eventually."

"Well, yes. But wasn't Thomas worried about his wife and children and all that begetting?"

"I don't think he had any children at that point. Or a wife."

"No wonder he was less than sensible," she told him. "*Maman* says men have no sense until they have a wife to guide them."

He really needed to make sure he avoided her "*maman*." She sounded like a twin of his Aunt Routledge. Rockhurst closed his eyes and shuddered at such a possibility. "Where were we?"

"Thomas was being less than sensible."

"Yes, lucky fellow without a wife to guide him."

"Is that why you've never married?"

This time Rockhurst pulled his arm free from her grasp and turned completely to face her. It was a little disconcerting to talk to someone who was invisible, but then again, most of his life was a series of disconcerting events, so it wasn't all that out of the ordinary to him. "Do you want to hear this story or not?"

"Of course," she told him. "But I also want to know why you've never married. Is it because you don't want to be sensible, or are there other reasons, like the ones Melaphor said."

You haven't mated yet . . . And I will take great pleasure in killing her, if only to see the pain it will cause you for denying me what I want.

Rockhurst glanced at the fire, trying to force out the words of denial.

I don't care a whit what Melaphor says. I'll marry when I damn well want to.

But there was too much truth in that sly, evil creature's threats for Rockhurst to ignore them. For them not to have haunted his dreams since the first time he'd taken a woman to his bed and realized the risk he'd placed her in.

How many of his ancestors had died thusly? At Melaphor's hands or at the hands of the derga, with the last thing they heard being the cries of their doomed wives and children?

No, all the riches and lands and power that were the Paratus's by right came at a very high price.

"Are you afraid if you marry," she whispered, "that Melaphor might—"

Rockhurst swung around. "He'll never!"

"Of course not," she gasped. "I didn't mean to imply—"

They sat for a moment in that strained silence. Melaphor would never harm the wife or child of another Paratus because Rockhurst had no intention of ever marrying.

Not that he could easily do so even if he were so inclined.

The Paratus didn't just dance about Society and choose his bride from the most comely or the richest of offerings. He made his decision slowly, deliberately, looking for a woman from one of the ancient lineages, the old families, who with every passing century were growing smaller and fewer in numbers.

But there was something about that shared heritage that carried with it an innate understanding of duty and obligation that went well beyond one's own life.

The various Countesses of Rockhurst had carried the fierceness of warriors in their blood, that, if need be, gave them the strength to fight when necessary.

Ruthlessly and without hesitation.

The image of the bolt from his cross-bow flying out of nowhere jolted him back to the present.

Lucky shot, that, he told himself. But still, he glanced anew at the ottoman.

"Where did you learn to shoot a cross-bow?"

"Me? I don't know how to shoot a cross-bow."

"Then why did you pick mine up last night?"

"I don't know," she said, faltering a bit. "I was so scared, I just did. I suppose I thought it might be like archery."

"You shoot?"

"A little," she demurred. And, as she had when describing how she looked, he knew she wasn't telling the entire truth.

He leaned back in his chair. "Miss Burke has quite a reputation for having a deft hand at archery."

"She cheats," the woman beside him huffed.

"You've shot against her?" Nothing but silence greeted his question, and he smiled slightly. Another clue, another chink into her mysterious identity. One he'd uncover the moment the sun rose over the horizon.

Her slight hand and warm fingers returned to his sleeve and pulled him out of his solitary musings. "You don't have to tell me why you haven't married," she was saying. "I think I understand."

And God help him, he knew she did. That in itself sent a shiver through him, as if awakening some long-dormant place in his heart. Hadn't his own father's last advice been to find a woman who understood?

A woman pure of heart with the fire of passion in her eyes.

And he didn't need to see *this* woman's eyes to know they could burn with desire.

"Where was I before you interrupted me?" he asked hastily.

"I didn't—"

Cocking a brow at her, Rockhurst didn't need to utter another word.

"Well, perhaps I did. Yes, yes, I suppose so. Now where were we? Oh, yes, Thomas was traveling to meet his certain death."

Because he hadn't a wife . . . he could almost hear her adding.

"Yes, poor Thomas," he agreed. "He arrived outside the gates of London and pitched his camp near a stream."

"A stream?" she asked, sitting up. "Which stream?"

He shook his head. It was the sort of detail his cousin Mary would find compelling and necessary. A bluestocking would declare imperative. "How could that be important?"

"I think it is very important," she said with a huffy little breath.

"Are you sure you aren't a bluestocking?"

"I thought we agreed—"

"But I still don't see how the name of the stream is important," he said, folding his arms over his chest.

"It is important to me."

Nonsensical chit! But nonetheless, he told her, "Walbrook," just to avoid another roundabout argument. "They were to fight near Walbrook." He waited for her to answer, but only silence greeted him. So he took this opening as a gift and continued on in good haste.

"Word of the impending battle had drawn so many spectators that the field looked more like a summer fair than the life-or-death struggle that would settle the fate of England."

"Wouldn't they be worried that they may be eaten or begotten if Thomas lost?"

He had to imagine she hadn't been to a cock-fight or bear-baiting matches. "I believe the spectacle of it all outweighed their common sense."

"*Harrumph.* I wouldn't have gone," she told him.

"You followed me into the night," he pointed out.

"I hardly knew what to expect."

"I suppose it was the same for the people who came to see Thomas fight. Besides, I believe their faith in him outweighed their fears."

"I hadn't considered that. Then again, I knew you would win last night," she told him.

He sat back. "You knew?"

"Of course," she said.

"However would you *know* such a thing?"

"I just did," she told him. "I cannot explain it. I just knew." She nudged him with her elbow. "Do go on. I believe you are getting to the good part."

I just knew. She couldn't have just known, not unless . . .

He ignored the shiver that ran down his spine and went on with his story. "On the eve of the battle, Thomas knelt in his tent to pray, for he had seen his enemy and knew in his heart his fate was dire. But rather than flee as his vassals urged him to do, he vowed to stand and fight and prayed that Carpio would be true."

"Carpio?" she asked.

"His sword. The sword that every Paratus has carried since." Rockhurst took a breath and waited for an interruption, but this time there was none, so he continued, "And after he prayed, he feel instantly asleep and found himself in a deep slumber. There in his dreams, a lady in white came to him. She knelt by his bed and soothed his worried brow."

"The good part," she whispered.

"Depends on your point of view," Rockhurst said wryly.

"This is where it becomes a romance," she said with such assurance he wanted to laugh.

"No, this is the part where a man is once again tricked by a woman's wiles."

"That is a rather cynical way of looking at things."

"It is my story," he told her.

"It would be better as a romance," she replied. "But go on and let us see where you can improve upon it."

Rockhurst opened his mouth to point out that this wasn't a French novel or a serial in some ladies' magazine, but his family's history.

A romance, indeed!

He took a deep breath and launched back into his tale. "The lady in white begged Thomas to help her, saying, "My good lord, you must defeat this foul murderer. For if you do not stop him, he will come for my kingdom next."

"Poor woman," she said.

Rockhurst snorted. "Wily wench, is what she was."

"How so?"

"If you would but let me finish—"

"Then finish!" she huffed. "I hardly see how I am stopping you."

Rockhurst closed his eyes and counted to three, then began again. "Thomas could only bow his head and concede his fears to the lady in white. 'I do not think I can stop him,' he told her. 'Have you not seen him, my lady? For he has powers of another world.'"

There was a shift of movement on the ottoman. "But she did help him."

"In a manner of speaking," Rockhurst told her. "She offered him equal if not greater powers if he would but swear allegiance to her. And so he did. And the next day, he defeated the derga."

"I think you are leaving out the romance."

"There is no romance," he told her.

"She came to his bedside and just took his vow? It never works that way in French novels. Usually such a gift is sealed with a kiss or . . . or . . ."

Rockhurst turned so he faced the ottoman and crossed his arms over his chest. Now it was his turn to put her on the spot. "Or what?"

"You know," his guest whispered. "The rest. After the kissing . . . She and Thomas . . . well, they . . . well, she is kneeling beside his bed, need I say more?"

No, she didn't. The mix of innocence and curiosity to her words teased him. Tempted him in ways he couldn't explain.

His control, his resolve began to slip away as he remembered how she'd felt in his arms, naked and moving beneath him, holding him and pulling him closer.

No more than Thomas could resist, Rockhurst found himself entwined by his own mysterious lady.

Ever so slowly, he reached out for her, his hand brushing off her shoulder. From there, his fingers caught hold of her and traced their way up to the curve of her cheek.

He heard himself whispering the rest of the tale, but at the same time, he felt himself transported as if he'd been in that tent, been himself entwined by the lady's offer.

She leaned over Thomas and soothed him with honeyed words. "Your enemy's powers are great, but you could possess the same strength." Her words held all the enticement of rich wine. Her hand stroked his forehead, and she leaned closer and kissed him, the taste of her lips like rose water.

Rockhurst drew the woman he held closer, catching hold of her and pulling her into his lap.

She came willingly, lured by what he didn't know. Her curiosity, the warmth of his touch, the promise of passions as yet unexplored. He didn't hesitate to use his own strength, and tugged her closer so he could taste her lips again.

The moment they touched his, he was lost.

Thomas's resolve wavered. What the lady offered was immoral, but then again, his death on the morrow was all but assured. And it was as if she knew his fears, for she said, "You will defeat him. You will."

The wrapper she wore slipped from her shoulders, and she was bare to her waist. His hands cradled those perfect breasts, and when he kissed her anew, his body sprang to life, hard and clamoring for the release he'd denied himself earlier.

"Love me, Rockhurst," she whispered. "Please love me."

He rose from the chair with her in his arms and carried her to his bed.

"All you must do is to promise that you and your sons and their sons after them, will protect this realm from my enemies. And I will see to it that you and your

descendants are blessed forever with wealth and power in repayment for your service."

As he climbed into his bed, the dressing gown fell from her, and she lay before him, entirely naked. He didn't need to see her to know she was splendidly perfect—from her long limbs to her full breasts.

She reached for him and pulled him down atop her, and all too quickly they were entwined. They kissed and touched and explored each other until they were both in a state of ragged need.

The white lady took his hand and placed it on her breast, over her heart. "Swear to me your allegiance, and we will seal your troth this very night."

Now whether it was the temptation of her body, or visions of gold and power, or even the very thought of defeating his enemy and living through the next day, Thomas swore his allegiance and spent the rest of the night indulging in passions unimagined.

"Oh, please, Rockhurst," she pleaded, her body slick and hot, her cleft already trembling. He'd brought her right back up to the brink, and awakened a delicious hunger in her that he knew just how to sate. Rockhurst wound his arm around her waist and raised her hips as he poised himself to enter her. Her legs wound around him.

"I want you," he whispered into her ear, nibbling at her earlobe, leaving a trail of hot kisses over her neck. He'd never felt so hard, so in need, that he couldn't think of anything but filling her, giving himself completely over to the warm cleft between her thighs.

Madness, his reason clamored. *This is utter madness.*

But the Paratus disagreed, and drove himself into her, finding only heaven.

Whether it was all part of the magic of her wish or the power of the ring, Hermione had discovered in the last few hours that she possessed a wanton nature. Freed from being the proper daughter of an earl, hidden behind this veil of invisibility, she gave herself up to the passion Rockhurst awakened.

She arched up as Rockhurst entered her. Her channel stretched to accommodate him, but once he filled her, once he'd pierced her maidenhead, she discovered what he'd meant about more.

Oh, he'd given her a taste of what a man and woman could share together, but this joining was something altogether different.

Magical, really.

If he'd paused as he'd breached her innocence, he hadn't stopped for long. He was as lost in the passion as she was. He began to stroke her, and her hips met his dizzy cadence, rising up and seeking every bit of him.

Magic, pure magic, she thought, as she swore she was no longer in his bedchamber, but a tent, and the scent of spring surrounded them. The wind whispered over their heated naked bodies, weaving the spell tighter and tighter around them.

And Hermione's desires pushed her past reason, with only one thought, finding her release. And then, as Rockhurst buried himself in her, deeply, and let out a thick moan, her body exploded with passion, for in his release, she found hers.

"Thomas," she cried out. "Thomas!"

"I'm here, Shadow," he whispered huskily in her ear. "I'm here."

Hermione wanted this moment, this entire night to last forever, so she closed her eyes and reveled in it all . . . the strength of his arms around her. The way her body continued to quake and tremble from her release.

She shivered, not from cold, but from the mystery of it all.

He gathered her closer, and holding her tight, still inside her, still bound together, each unwilling to break the spell that held them together.

Rockhurst finished his story, whispering it into her ear and brushing her tangled curls from her face.

"And the next morning Thomas rose from his bed, more powerful than he could have imagined. He defeated his enemy to the acclaim and joy of the people."

"They cheered," Hermione told him. She rather felt like cheering herself.

"Aye, they did," he told her. "They cheered and chanted, and christened Thomas of Hurst with a new name."

"Paratus," Hermione said, ignoring the way he smiled at her interruption. "And the wealth and titles the white lady promised came to him in overflowing abundance."

Rockhurst nodded. "But so did the duties of protecting her realm, and he soon discovered that he had given more than his allegiance that night. He'd given up his life as he knew it to battle the unholy spirits who continuously sought to dethrone this wily queen."

Hermione had the sense that he was about to roll from her, break the connection between them, but she wasn't ready for that yet, and so she wound her arms around his neck and pulled him closer.

"And his descendants?" she asked.

"They knew no other life," he told her.

"I suppose it wasn't a romance then," she conceded.

"No," Rockhurst said softly. "Not in the least."

Not until now, he would have told her.

If he'd dared.

Outside the earl's town house, Quince paced back and forth in the shadows as she awaited Milton. She'd summoned him, the first time she'd actually sought his company in so long, and she was starting to wonder if she still had the power to do so since there was, as yet, no sign of him.

Glancing at the sky, where it still held the inky cast of night, she sighed. There were, thankfully, a few hours left to fix all this.

At least, she hoped there was.

She pulled her pelisse tighter around her neck to ward off the damp dew growing with the coming morning. Yet, she still found herself shivering.

And it wasn't from the chill.

"Quince, what the devil do you want?"

She flinched, for there was no mistaking the annoyance in her husband's voice. Still, he'd come. Though when she glanced over her shoulder at him, she found his brow furrowed in a deep line and his sky-blue eyes hard and unforgiving. Mayhap, she shouldn't have summoned him.

Milton wasn't known for a generous spirit or a forgiving heart. At least not in the last eight hundred years, give or take a century.

Still, he'd arrived, and that perhaps was better than nothing. For frankly she was out of ideas as to how to solve her current problem.

Their problem, she corrected silently. *For if he hadn't . . .*

Oh, heavens, it wasn't time to reiterate their fractured marriage. She had a problem, and he was going to help her.

"Unless you've summoned me here to tell me that you have my ring back—" His words came to a staggering halt as he took a glance at his surroundings and recognized where they stood. "Are you mad to summon me *here*?"

She could see that he was about to flee, so she caught his arm and held on. "He has her."

"Has whom?" Milton asked as he tried to shake her off. Milton was afraid of few things in this realm, but standing nearly on the doorstep of the Paratus was not something anyone of their ilk did willingly. For even though the man was the duly appointed champion of their Queen, that didn't mean he wouldn't kill first and ask questions later of any creature not entirely mortal.

And if one really wanted to quibble the point, Quince and Milton weren't really supposed to be loitering about this human realm as it was.

"Let me go. If this is some trick, some trap to get me to—"

"Oh, do be still, Milton," Quince snapped, tightening her grasp. Really, sometimes he could be quite tiresome. "She is inside with him. Hermione. The one who made the wish."

Milton's struggles ceased. "Tell me you are joking."

She shook her head. "I wish I was."

"How could you—"

"I would never have—"

"Quince!"

"This isn't my fault."

"You let my ring fall into that girl's hands, and now . . . now . . . look at where it has landed you."

"Me?" Quince bristled. "This is *our* problem."

"I hardly see—"

Quince caught him by the lapel of his jacket and pulled him close, whispering furiously. "Do you really think the Queen will be so pleased with you if you just leave me to solve this by myself when that girl is wearing *your* ring, as you like to call it."

Milton's jaw worked back and forth. "It isn't like he can get it off her hand."

"Don't be a fool. He has only to kill her to gain it."

"He can't do that," he scoffed. "She's mortal."

"Not with that ring on her hand. She carries a piece of both of us with her."

Milton groaned and in his anger found the wherewithal to shake off Quince's hold on him. Now it was his turn to pace about.

"Does she know the danger she is in?"

·

Quince bit her lip. Botheration! She'd hoped he wouldn't pry too deeply into this predicament, rather have some handy solution and be gone.

Without all the fuss and worry of pestering questions.

"Quince?"

She shook her head, then waited for the explosion.

It came. "By all that's holy, Quince! How could you let it come to this? Why didn't you summon me immediately?"

Other than for the obvious reasons? she wanted to shoot back, but chose to refrain from escalating this into a fight that went beyond their current, more pressing problem.

"None of this bickering is helping," Quince said, after they had both taken a few deep breaths. "We have to find a way to get Hermione out of there."

Milton glanced over at the house. "Does he still have that beast of a dog?"

"Yes, but I hardly see—"

He shrugged off his great-coat, then his jacket, and ended by loosening his cravat. "I can't believe I am about to do this."

"You don't mean to—"

"Yes, I suppose I must."

She couldn't believe it. He was going to help her? Of course that had been the reason she'd summoned him, but she hadn't thought he'd actually roll up his sleeves and do something.

For the first time since they'd gone their separate ways, Quince looked anew at her husband and found him studying her as well. She swallowed back the spark of passion that seemed to come to life in that glance.

"You'll do a splendid job," Quince encouraged, giving him a little nudge toward the curb and away from her before things got any more confusing. "As long as you keep ahead of that foul beast . . . and stay out of range of the earl's cross-bow."

"And here I've always enjoyed hunting," he muttered as he went to cross the street. "Never thought I'd find myself in the role of the fox."

"Just make it to the park," Quince offered. "That'll give me enough time to get her out."

"Get her out, then get my ring," Milton ordered.

"Yes, yes," Quince said, shaking off her own pelisse and eyeing the earl's house for the best spot to slip inside.

Get his ring, indeed! she thought as she made her way down the block to the mews that ran behind the houses. So much for her foolish thoughts that he still had any feelings for her.

She only hoped that after a night with a devil like Rockhurst, Hermione's innocent *tendré* for the man had lost its luster as well.

"So what is your name, Shadow? Tell me, and I will open that door," he waved at the locked entrance behind them, "and drive you home myself."

"I can't tell you that," she protested. *I won't tell you.* Tell you and watch you be utterly disappointed that the woman you seduced is nothing more than that odd little Hermione Marlowe.

"Perhaps I can persuade you another way," he said, dipping his head down and covering her lips with his.

Well beneath them, Hermione heard Rowan's deep, booming *woof*. And then it grew louder. When it had become nearly a continuous howl, there was an urgent knock at the door that pulled them both apart.

"My lord, Rowan is—"

"Yes, Stogdon, I can hear him—"

"Do you want us to let him out?"

Rockhurst cocked his head and listened to the barking that was approaching madness. He heaved a sigh and put a kiss on her brow. "I must go see to this," he whispered. Then he rose from the bed. "I'll be right down, Stogdon."

A relieved sigh echoed from the butler.

"I am going to lock you in for the time being," Rockhurst told her, almost apologetically. "But it is for the best."

"The best for whom?" she asked. "Let me go, Rockhurst—"

"Why? I thought you were enjoying yourself."

I am, she wanted to tell him.

"I'll be back, and we'll see how you feel then," he said, going out the door. A key turned in the lock, and then he was gone, his determined step moving down the hall.

Oh, bother. If only she had one more wish. She'd wish the sun would never rise again, and this night . . . would never end.

But the sun would come up, and she knew she needed to be well away before this magic wore off.

There had to be another way out.

She got up from the bed and tried to still her racing heart. No easier, she discovered, than trying to stand on her shaky legs.

"Jiminy! What has he done to me?" she whispered, her fingers trying to tuck her tangled hair back into some semblance of order.

Oh heavens! What had he done to her? Everything, she had to imagine, drawing a long, slow breath, and then hastily getting dressed.

He'd certainly ruined her, she thought as she pulled on her stockings, then her boots. Ruined her for any other man as well. For she couldn't help but think there wasn't another man alive as skilled in pleasure as Rockhurst.

Rowan's barking grew louder, and she heard the front door open. Hermione raced to the window and spied Rowan take off after a man in a white shirt and black breeches. Tall and elegant, the stranger moved like a great buck long used to eluding predators.

And a few seconds later, the earl was dashing after the pair, shouting at Rowan to come to heel.

And the moment Rockhurst rounded the corner, the bedroom door rattled. She turned toward it. He was back? But it couldn't be, for she'd seen him—

"Hermione?" came a whispered voice.

"Quince?" She rushed across the room and knelt before the keyhole. "What are you doing here?"

The lock rattled, then, to her surprise, the door opened.

Quince bustled in and sighed in relief as her eyes lit

on Hermione. "The better question is, what are you doing here?" Then once she'd had a moment to take in Hermione's state of *déshabillé*, her eyes widened in alarm.

"Oh, Quince, I had no intention of drawing the earl's attentions when I went to the Thurlow ball," she rushed to explain.

"Seems as if you've failed in that. Rather miserably, I'd say." Quince caught her by the hand and dragged her from the room. "Come along. We haven't much time."

"I didn't mean for any of this to happen," Hermione told her as they dashed down the back stairs.

"Harrumph."

Well, she hadn't. Hermione stole one last glance back up the stairs. Certainly not all this. "It happened so fast. He found me in the garden, and then he caught me and carried me off. I couldn't get away."

Not that you truly wanted to . . .

"You're lucky I came along when I did," Quince scolded. They paused at the bottom of the steps, then dashed out a servants' door that turned out to lead into the mews. "I only hope this incident has cured you of your *tendré* for the man."

"It has," Hermione told her. For that was the truth.

For now she feared she was completely in love with him.

Ten

Rockhurst arrived at Lady Belling's garden party later that day, a man determined.

He'd been tricked and deceived, and he was in a foul humor. For now he'd have to take desperate measures to find his Shadow.

"I assure you, nephew," Lady Routledge said from his side, "every respectable and eligible young lady will be here this afternoon." She looked like an old cat with a bowl full of cream before her.

Yes, it had come to this. Aunt Routledge. He'd enlisted her aid in sorting through the mountain of invitations that usually sat unnoticed in his salver. Why she'd actually grinned from ear to ear when he asked her, nay, begged her to determine which ones were appropriate for finding a young lady—specifying he only wanted the events that occurred during daylight hours.

His aunt, delirious with joy at the prospect of matching her sister's only child, hadn't even protested his unusual strictures.

If Rockhurst was of a mind to marry, she'd hire the carriage to drive him and his bride-to-be to Gretna Green.

Even if he insisted on bringing his wretched hound along.

Though Rowan, turncoat that he was, feeling no responsibility in the deception that had let his Shadow slip from his fingers, was even now contentedly lying down on the edge of the grass gnawing at a large soup bone he'd found near the gate.

Of course, Rockhurst hadn't told his aunt the real reasons for his search, for being related through his mother's side, she knew nothing of his other life. Of the other world he inhabited.

He glanced over at her, with a bemused smile on his lips as she nattered on about the glowing attributes and noteworthy accomplishments of one debutante after another and wondered what she'd say if he asked if any of the young ladies in attendance had a propensity toward invisibility?

Or bringing soup bones to garden parties. For he had no doubt where that bone had come from.

Smart minx. Charming his hound, as she had him last night.

"Heaven forbid. There's no avoiding her now," his aunt muttered. "Completely beyond the pale, but there's nothing left to do but smile."

Rockhurst glanced up and found Lady Walbrook bearing down on him. Smile? How about run for his life.

"She's casting another of her theatricals," Aunt Routledge complained.

"Weren't you once—"

"Do not remind me," she complained.

He did any way. "Othello?"

Lady Routledge groaned, then swatted him with her fan. "Mark my words, your day will come."

"It already has," he admitted.

His aunt swiveled around. "You?!"

"Yes. You are looking at Lady Walbrook's next Prospero."

Then Aunt Routledge did something he'd never seen happen before. She laughed. "You?"

He nodded.

"Oh, poor Rockhurst." His aunt continued to chuckle as Lady Walbrook drew nearer. "However did that happen?"

"She cornered me last night at Thurlow's and would not let me pass until I promised to take the role."

His aunt was one of the most formidable ladies in Society, but nothing compared to the fear struck in the hearts of one and all when Lady Walbrook was casting about for players for one of her reenactments of Shakespeare.

"I have no intention of doing it," he informed his aunt. Which only made the old girl laugh harder.

"Rockhurst, you haven't been out enough in Society. Once you agreed to Lady Walbrook's request, nothing

short of an early death will save you from the role."
She glanced over at him, as if envisioning him in a costume, and began to chuckle anew.

"Don't laugh too hard, my dear aunt," he said. "Or I shall inform the countess you would like to redeem your poor performance as Othello by undertaking a new role. Say Hamlet?"

Lady Routledge's humor disappeared immediately. "You wouldn't dare."

"Care to wager on it?"

Lady Walbrook drew closer, and Rockhurst realized she was towing along one of her daughters. The one who was friends with Miss Wilmont and his cousin Mary. The chit Hustings had been going on about.

"What the devil is her daughter's name?" he asked in an aside to his aunt.

Lady Routledge barely spared a glance. "Lady Hermione."

"Are you certain?"

"Of course. She's wearing that wretched shade of orange. She's worn it all Season. I haven't the vaguest notion why, for it is a horrible color, but one can never tell with those Marlowes. Mad—all of them."

Rockhurst smiled. "Are you warning me away from poor Lady Hermione then?"

"I don't have to. The girl is all but engaged to Lord Hustings."

"Ah! How fortuitous," Lady Walbrook said, as she arrived in a flurry of ribbons and feathers. "Lord Rockhurst—or should I say, my dear Lord Prospero!"

"Yes, well, Lady Walbrook, about this theatrical, I fear I—"

"You haven't the experience necessary!" she finished for him.

"Exactly!"

"Of course you don't," the lady agreed. "That is why you'll have to come to the afternoon practices I've arranged for the next three Tuesday and Thursday afternoons. Light refreshments will be served, of course." She patted his arm. "Never fear, my lord. By your debut, you shall be as famous as Kemble."

"I believe you've made an excellent choice," Lady Routledge added.

Rockhurst shot her a withering look, but apparently not even the threat of a new role could suppress his aunt.

"And do meet your Caliban," Lady Walbrook said, sweeping her hand back to reveal her daughter, who'd been, up until now, hiding behind her mother. "My dearest daughter, Lady Hermione."

"Caliban?" Rockhurst said, slanting a glance at Lady Hermione and feeling a bit of pity for the poor chit—for it was apparent she was ill at ease in society.

"Um, yes," she muttered, then began coughing. She appeared so mortified, she couldn't even look him in the eye.

Then an unlikely rescue arrived.

"Lady Hermione!" a man called out. "There you are!"

Rockhurst glanced up to find Lord Hustings joining their party. The man took the girl's hand. "I've been quite beset of late by your ill health."

She only smiled at the man, and then mumbled some shy platitudes.

Lord Hustings bowed to the two matrons. "Lady Walbrook, may I borrow your daughter for a stroll about the grounds? I believe the fresh air will put some color back in her cheeks."

"How kind you are," Lady Walbrook said, not sounding the least happy to have the man taking her daughter away. "Yes, of course you may, but please bring her back as soon as possible, because Minny and Lord Rockhurst were just getting acquainted for their roles in my new production of *The Tempest*."

"Roles? You're casting again? I would be so honored to play even the smallest role, if only to see Lady Hermione as Cordelia."

"Cordelia is from *King Lear*," Lady Hermione corrected.

"Oh, yes. How right you are!" Lord Hustings exclaimed. "But a bright star you shall be, whatever mantle you don."

"I fear there aren't any roles left," Lady Walbrook told the baron. "Perhaps next year, Lord Hustings. Lord Rockhurst is going to be our shining lead." The lady beamed at him and at the same time nudged Lady Hermione forward.

Rockhurst saw all too clearly what was happening. His aunt had been right. Lady Walbrook was trying to match him to her colorless daughter. Horror filled his chest.

Mary's warning from the other night at Almack's rang in his head.

You have no idea what you've done. . .

With Lady Walbrook now bearing down on him like a Spanish armada, he had a very clear idea what she'd been nattering on about.

And a means of escape.

"Perhaps here is your true Prospero, Lady Walbrook," he suggested hastily, gesturing to Lord Hustings, offering the man up, a willing sacrifice if ever there was one.

The younger fellow brightened and blushed. "I would be honored beyond my expectations, my dearest countess. While I haven't an artistic nature, I am sure I would be able to stand in the shoes of Prospero."

Lady Walbrook's lips pursed into a tight line. "Lord Hustings, that would never do. But if you are determined, perhaps you might be our Ferdinand—the light of Miranda's heart. I had thought to cast my son, Griffin, but he's been most unreliable of late."

Hustings beamed at Lady Hermione, who appeared to have turned the same shade as her gown.

"Yes, you would make an excellent Ferdinand," Lady Walbrook said, tapping her fan against her lips.

The baron bowed and stammered some more nonsense about "living out his dream of tripping about the boards," before Lady Hermione all but towed him away.

And if Rockhurst had been looking, he would have seen her take a last furtive glance over her shoulder at him. With green eyes that held nothing but longing for the man who didn't recognize her.

Instead, he bowed to his aunt and the countess and made his excuses, then waded into the crowd looking for a saucy minx in sensible shoes.

"Lavinia, dear, whatever did happen to you last night?" Miss Patience Dewmont asked when she found her friend at Lady Belling's garden party. "Perpetua heard Lady Routledge telling Lady Boxley that she thought you might have been . . . well," she lowered her voice to a loud whisper, "drinking too much wine beforehand."

Miss Lavinia cringed, for she hardly wanted to discuss the events of last night, let alone recall the horror of finding herself in the arms of Mr. Harvey Heriot.

A third son, no less!

"Do you think your gown beyond repair?" Patience persisted. Obviously, the drinking portion of the gossip was of no consequence to the dim-witted twin. "You left so suddenly afterward, and then when we got home, neither of us could remember if it was the green satin or the blue crepe, and all I could do was pray it wasn't the green satin since we had a hand in helping you shop for the right shade of—"

"Please! Miss Dewmont! I beg of you, please do not speak another word of last night!" Lavinia said, her voice rising from its characteristically smooth and polished tones. As quickly as she lost her temper, Lavinia did her best to calm her ruffled composure. It wouldn't do to have yet another scene. Her mother had been of the opinion that she shouldn't even attend a party so soon after her debacle at the Thurlow ball. But Lavinia, holding a fair share of her father's mercantile genius, had averred that she wasn't going to hide from Society, instead rising like a lady who stood head and shoulders above petty gossip. Though that didn't mean she wouldn't need loyal allies to regain her lofty position. She took a deep breath, and said in the most confidential of tones, "It was the worst evening of my life. So very lowering."

Having never been any higher on the social rungs than the shadows of Lavinia's skirts would allow, the twins nodded with understanding, and their eyes lit with pleasure at being admitted to Lavinia's confidence.

"But what happened?" Perpetua asked. "How could you have stumbled? Why, you are the most graceful creature in all the *ton*. Everyone says so."

"I never stumbled," Lavinia told them. She tucked her nose in the air and gave them the bit of gossip the two sisters would be best suited to spread from one side of Mayfair to another. "I was pushed."

"Pushed?" they both gasped.

"Yes, indeed." Lavinia leaned closer. "I cannot prove it, but I felt a hand on my back, and then I fell most violently."

"Who could ever hold such an ill-will toward you, Lavinia?" Patience asked. "Why, it is a wonder you are even up and about today."

But Lavinia wasn't one to wallow in self-pity for long. "I quite felt like Lady Hermione," she said with a little laugh. "Now I know what it is like to spend an evening tripping about in her unfashionable slippers."

The Dewmont sisters laughed, as Lavinia knew they would.

Then Lavinia did the one thing that changed her

fortunes—at least raised them up from the ashes of the previous night's disgrace. She smirked at the Dewmont sisters. "Jiminy! I don't know how that happened," she exclaimed, doing a perfect imitation of Hermione and giving them all a good laugh.

Then when she glanced up, she found to her surprise the Earl of Rockhurst looking at her.

No, gaping at her, as if he had suddenly and violently fallen in love with her.

She smiled back, and then raised her fan to hide her face ever so slightly. She was, she would remind one and all, no flirt.

But then again, she was no fool.

"Try again," Quince urged her.

Hermione tugged and pulled at the ring, but it remained fast on her hand.

They were standing in a secluded spot of Lord Belling's prized rose garden, a spot usually reserved for a different sort of tryst.

"It should just fall off," Quince told her, "but you must truly want this wish to end."

"I do," Hermione told her. "I do want this to end."

For she had spent a good part of the afternoon watching Rockhurst follow Miss Burke about like an infatuated puppy.

Deplorable man, she cursed under her breath as she tugged anew at the ring, which held stubbornly fast to her hand.

Worse yet, the entire party was agog at the sight of the Earl of Rockhurst dangling after a lady.

A respectable one, at that.

"Respectable!" she muttered. *Tug, tug.* "A regular angel." *Yank, pull.* "Oh, jiminy, Quince. I fear it won't come off. What am I to do?"

Quince heaved a sigh. "I don't know what is wrong. It's always worked before. As long as you are sure you want your wish to end."

"I do," she said vehemently. She'd even gone so far as to bring a soup bone with her and left it near the garden gate just in case Rockhurst arrived with Rowan in tow. Luckily for her, the contented hound had spent the better part of the afternoon lounging on the grass with his prize.

"I cannot continue to rescue you," Quince complained. "Concentrate, Hermione. Think of what you have to gain if this wish is ended."

And how much shall I lose, she almost said. Hadn't last night proved that quite eloquently? And to her chagrin, her body trembled in agreement.

Rockhurst kissing her, undressing her, claiming her body.

He'd ruined her. She should hate him for it.

Wish him to perdition.

Well, she did now. Now that he was dangling after Lavinia Burke like Rowan with his soup bone.

A sour pit turned in Hermione's stomach. Lavinia Burke with her perfect blond hair, her sumptuous gowns and elegant Bath manners. He couldn't think Lavinia was her . . . was his Shadow, so why this great show of showering her with his attentions?

Of course, what had she done when her mother had

dragged her up to see Rockhurst earlier? She'd turned three shades of red.

And she hadn't dared look him in the eye, for fear he'd notice the color of her own.

For as much as she wanted to declare herself, and in her imagination saw him falling down on bended knee and begging for her hand, she knew the more likely outcome was his rejection.

His attention this morning had been cutting, for he'd barely spared her a glance. Then again, as she looked down at her own gown, a bright capucine and covered in ribbons and froufrou, one she had thought quite perfect when she'd had the modiste sew it up . . . but now it seemed so impossibly foolish. She glanced through the rose-bushes toward where the party had gathered to begin choosing partners for the archery contest, and in the middle of it all stood Lavinia, elegant and cool in her plain white muslin—so self-composed, never posing, never trying to be anything she wasn't.

That was the sort of woman the Earl of Rockhurst favored. Not bumbling, foolish, tongue-tied Lady Hermione. Not one of those "odd Marlowes."

"Perhaps it is because of the time element to your wish," Quince was saying. "Mayhap we need to wait until sunset."

"I hope so, for I am running out of excuses for why I suddenly turn ill each evening. My mother is threatening to call the surgeon to have me bled if I do not 'perk up' as she calls it."

"Then we have no choice but to wait," Quince declared. "But do your best to avoid him until then. It will do you no favors if he learns of your identity."

Hermione stole a glance over at the archery field, where the earl was bending over Miss Burke's out-stretched hand. Oh, what she'd give for her bow and one arrow. She'd prove her skill by sending a shot directly into his well-sculpted—

And as if on cue, Lord Hustings came blundering down the path. "Lady Hermione! There you are. I've been looking for you everywhere."

Hermione smiled at the man and then turned to Quince, but the lady had disappeared. Hermione thought if she was ever to get another wish, she might ask for such a power—for it would be demmed convenient to be able to slip off every time Lord Hustings came searching for her.

"It seems you've found me," she said as she pulled her glove back on.

"Yes, indeed, and just in time," he said.

"In time for what?" she asked.

"The archery competition," Lord Hustings declared, taking her hand and settling it on his sleeve, then towing her toward the field. "We are set to shoot against Lord Rockhurst and Miss Burke. Devil's own luck, wouldn't you say?"

"A fine shot, Miss Burke! Most excellent," Lord Rockhurst declared. "You have quite a natural flair for archery."

Hermione's fingers tightened around the bow she held. *A natural flair for archery.* Indeed!

The archery contest was proving to be more than a competition of sport, but rather a competition to keep Hermione's temper in check.

She nearly snapped her arrow in half as she glanced over her shoulder and found the earl bent over the infamous heiress, dangling after her like the worst sort of Lothario, all under the guise of "helping her."

Hadn't those same strong masculine hands been roaming over her just last night? The one now cupping Miss Burke's elbow, the other resting so nonchalantly on her hip? Had he forgotten about *their* interlude so easily that he could spend this afternoon dallying with some other woman?

And not just dallying, helping her!

Hermione's blood boiled.

"Helping himself," she muttered as she raised her bow and took her shot. It went wide of the target, sailing into the rose-bushes beyond. Pressing her lips together, she bit back the curse that rose almost immediately.

"Tough shot that," Hustings said as he strode forward. He leaned over her shoulder and gauged the target. "You were aiming for that one, weren't you?" he asked, as if she didn't know where to shoot the arrow.

"I do believe Lady Hermione was aiming for France," Miss Burke chirped. "Perhaps she meant to stop Bonaparte."

There was a general bit of laughter, for nearly everyone at the party had gathered to watch the archery contest. And Hermione knew it wasn't from a keen interest in sport but rather the fact that Lord Rockhurst had spent the entire afternoon at Miss Burke's side, when, that is, he wasn't fetching punch or her parasol for her.

So as the crowd enjoyed Miss Burke's jest, Hermione had no choice but to force a smile on her lips to avoid being seen as a bad sport.

I know exactly where my next one could go. Accidentally, of course, she thought as she turned and yielded the field to her partner.

"Never mind, Lady Hermione," Lord Hustings was saying. "'Tis a difficult sport, archery. Let me rectify our standings." He squinted at the target and let go the bowstring, and Hermione cringed as his shot barely made the target, hitting in the far outside ring. "Hmm," he said, looking down at his bow. "Usually don't shoot this badly."

From out of the crowd, Thomasin and India came forward.

"Whatever is wrong with you?" whispered Thomasin over Hermione's shoulder. "I've never seen you do so poorly. This is your chance to show the earl your superior skills."

"If he wasn't so distracted," India said, nudging Hermione in the back and nodding toward the earl, who at the moment was bent on one knee to take a rock out of Miss Burke's slipper.

At least that was his excuse, Hermione thought as she watched his hand slide over the girl's ankle, just as he had done to hers the night before.

How he'd pulled her stockings from her legs, and then traced lazy, haphazard kisses up her bare skin.

As he climbed higher and higher, his lips hot and

eager, his tongue laving over her skin with teasing swipes . . .

"Is that better, Miss Burke?" he was asking Lavinia.

Why that wretched bounder, Hermione thought. *Whatever is he doing?*

"Oh, yes. Thank you, my lord," Miss Burke was saying in her polished, I-went-to-finishing-school-in-Bath manner of speaking. "I am quite indebted to you for rescuing me from that horrid pebble." Miss Burke took her place and shot. A perfect hit in the bull's-eye. She turned and smiled gracefully, one might even say, gratefully, at the enthusiastic applause and more than a few masculine cheers from the onlookers.

"Come now, come now," Hustings called out. "Let us get on with this, or we'll never finish before the sun sets."

"Sunset?" Hermione gasped, looking to the west and seeing for herself the sun lolling low in the sky. How had it gotten so late this quickly?

"Yes, quite my favorite time of day," Rockhurst declared, before he made a perfect shot, and now it was Hermione's turn.

"You can do it," Thomasin whispered at her. "You are the finest shot around. When the earl sees how well you shoot, he may not be so enamored with Miss Burke."

True enough, Hermione realized. She'd best Miss Burke with this arrow and win the prize. She'd show the earl how well a lady could shoot.

But when she took her stance and aimed, she glanced back where Thomasin and India stood with fingers crossed, and Lord Hustings offered an encouraging smile.

But it was the earl who stopped her. For he was watching her. Not Miss Burke. But her. Hermione.

And now was her chance to catch his eye.

But if she did, then he would know her secret. And surely then the ring would fall from her hand, and her wish would be over.

She glanced at the target and took aim.

Her wish would end. No more nights spent in his bed. No more evenings spent being *his* Shadow.

Over. Ended. Finished. With one shot. She could do it. She must. Her hands trembled, and she did her best to still them.

And then she glanced back at him and saw what so few others did. The tired resignation behind his charm.

The loneliness. For being the Paratus was a solitary occupation. Rowan, notwithstanding.

He hadn't looked so last night. Not when he'd told the legend, as they'd made love.

The bow slumped in her hands, and she bit her lip and considered what she must do.

She *must*. She *should*. She *would*.

And so she raised her bow and took her shot. As the arrow sailed well over the target and into Lord Belling's prized rose-bushes once again, all Hermione could do was bow her head. She couldn't even look at the man, let alone see the disappointment and amazement that would surely be on her friends' faces.

How could she explain her decision to them when she barely understood it herself?

*   *   *

Rockhurst had tried all afternoon to discover who Miss Burke had been mocking when he'd heard her say "jiminy" to her friends.

It had been a perfect imitation of his Shadow, and since he was well aware of the animosity between the two, he thought perhaps to use that to his advantage.

But to his chagrin, Miss Burke had strung him along, being coy with her answers and giving him hints, and before long he knew she was using his attentions to shore up her suddenly flagging reputation. Wily chit. No wonder she was so loathed by every other miss in London.

Still, he remained at her side, for he couldn't shake his suspicion that his Shadow was here. At this party. In full view, no less. And while he'd spent a good part of last night memorizing her every curve, her every line, he had no more clue of what she looked like than what the back of his own head did.

"And the archery purse goes to Lord Rockhurst and his delightful partner, Miss Burke," Lord Belling was saying. "And thank you, Miss Burke for not deflowering my rose-bushes as Lady Hermione did."

There was general laughter at the marquess's jest, but instead of laughing, Rockhurst glanced around. Where was Lady Hermione? He had a moment of pity for the poor, awkward chit. No wonder she'd fled more of Lavinia's nasty taunting.

"I do believe," Miss Burke said. "Lady Hermione has gone to fetch her arrow . . . all the way in Paris."

There was general laughter from the crowd and much jostling, as everyone drew near to offer their congratulations—and most likely get a closer look to see if Rockhurst was truly in love with the legendary Original.

But the earl was paying them all little heed. Because he couldn't shake the image of Lady Hermione out of his thoughts. For an odd moment, as she'd drawn up her bow and poised to shoot, Rockhurst had stilled. There it was, the curve of her cheek, the line of her brow, the full thrust of her breasts. And something else, something else about her features that had struck him—but what it was he couldn't remember.

And even as he went over the moment again, he found his breath catching in his throat as it had until she shot. Then her arrow had gone wide for the second time in a row and he knew he'd been mistaken.

He glanced back down at the archery field and what he saw there stopped him cold—a lone figure standing in the last bright rays of light. From this distance, it was impossible to discern who she was, for the sun left her in a stark silhouette, but he could see she held a bow.

And when she raised it to shoot, it was like watching Diana, goddess of the hunt. For the lady shot, true and perfectly, the arrow zinging through the air and landing with a strident "*thump*" square into the bull's-eye.

A more perfect shot could not have been imagined.

But when he trained his eyes back at the lady, he saw her only for a second, and then she shimmered like the last bit of the day's determined light and vanished, just as the sun dipped below the horizon.

Eleven

Rockhurst took off across the lawn in a flash, leaving a gaping Miss Burke behind him.

Not that he would have cared, for the chit was utterly, and completely, forgotten.

Not when *she* was close at hand. Something pulled at his heart, drew him as if he were being tugged along by a set of chains.

Was it the ring? Was he as bound to the ring as she was now?

He whistled to Rowan, who came loping along. "She's got you charmed as well, I see," he said to his hound, reaching out to ruffle the dog's head.

Rowan, bone still clenched in his giant mouth, looked like he was grinning. Rockhurst knew in an instant his dog was as much a milksop as he himself was in danger of becoming.

He turned the corner on the path and came to a stop where the garden gave way to the marquess's prized rose garden, a twisted and twined arrangement of paths and thorny bushes, now cast in growing shadows.

But he was only interested in a certain shadow.

"Where have you gone," he said aloud. "I know you are about." He glanced down at Rowan to see if the dog had caught sight of her, but his turncoat hound had eyes only for his prized bone. "So you've gained Rowan's attention, wouldn't you like a little bit of mine?"

"What? So you can kidnap me again?" came a voice so clear and familiar, it sent shivers down his spine.

Spinning toward an arbor, he swore he'd heard that voice today. But where and when, and more importantly, from whose lips, he couldn't place. "From all accounts, you didn't seem to mind."

There was an indignant gasp, then a shuffle of stones on a path as she moved. "Why don't you go back to your new paramour. You looked quite content simpering over her."

He resisted the urge to smile.

Having been with enough women in his time, he knew the way to raise the ire (and ardor) of one lady was to pay attention to her rival. Obviously his pained afternoon of listening to Miss Burke lord her position over one and all hadn't been ill-spent.

Not in the least.

"She has her charms," he teased. "And to her advantage, I know her name."

"Harrumph!"

Jealous little puss. But if she was jealous, that also meant she . . .

He shook off that thought. He didn't want to know that she cared for him. That could be dangerous. For her. For him.

He should walk away. Leave her to her mischief, her wish. Whatever magic it was that had left her a creature of the night.

But he couldn't do that. Not as long as she wore that ring on her hand.

The ring . . . that was the reason he was pursuing her. Or so he told himself.

"Go back to Miss Burke," she told him.

And now he couldn't resist. He laughed. "She doesn't compare to you."

"How so?"

"Her breasts are too small." He turned toward where he thought she stood. "Yours, on the other hand, are more of a devilish handful, as is the lady attached to them."

There was another sputtered snort, but this one wasn't quite as indignant. "Then why . . . why would you—"

Oh, the jealousy in her voice teased at him. *Tempted him.*

"Spend the day with her?" he offered.

"Well, yes." He could almost see her lips pressed in a firm line, a furrow across her silken brow. "She's really quite odious."

"True."

"Then why would you spend the day—"

"Letting everyone think I admired her?"

"Yes, exactly. You've quite given her another reason to prance about Town, preening and placing herself well above—" There was that sputtering sound again.

"Her situation?"

"Precisely," she told him. "There are any number of ladies who are—"

"Of better lineages? Older families?" She was thinning the herd for him as if she were a sheep-dog.

"Why of course," she said.

"Like you?"

A shocked silence filled the space between them. He wished he could see the furious glint to her eyes as she realized she'd been tricked. Led down the path by the piper's tune.

"You are a wretched devil, Rockhurst."

"I am, aren't I?" He grinned toward where he thought she stood.

"That still doesn't explain why you were dangling after her like one of those . . . those . . ." A stone skipped forward on the path where her toe had kicked it up.

There. Now he knew where she stood. "Other fools?" he supplied.

"Yes."

"Jealous?"

"Oh, I would never be—"

He cocked a brow and stepped toward her, watching the gravel to see if she moved. It didn't, and his heart quickened. "Now, now, it is unbecoming of a lady—and you are a lady, we've established—to lie."

"I'm not—" The gravel creaked beneath her unseen slippers as he grew closer, but she didn't give ground.

It was something he liked about her. Nonsensical as she was, she was a stubborn chit.

"A lady?"

"*Rockhurst*," she warned.

"No, my dear little Shadow, I spent the day dangling after Miss Burke for your pleasure."

"Mine?" Disbelief and skepticism coated her response.

"Yes," he confirmed. "Yours. For I can see my attentions quite raised your passions."

"My wha-a-at?"

"Passions. Ardor. You proved it so last night," he said, reaching out and catching nothing but air.

Damn. He thought he'd cornered her.

But his attempt made her laugh, and then it was a simple matter to catch hold of her. With a tug, he had her right where he wanted her. Against his better judgment, against anything that made sense. He had this mercurial little mystery right up against his chest, trapped in his arms. "You are a creature of your passions."

"I am no such—" she argued, twisting a bit in protest, but, he noted, more because that was what a lady was supposed to do.

Then again, she wasn't your usual lady.

"I rather like your passionate side." He nuzzled her neck, inhaled her perfume.

"Rockhurst, let me go," she ordered.

He nuzzled her neck. "You left me."

"I escaped you," she pointed out. "You were holding me against my will."

"I hardly think—"

"You kidnapped me, carried me off to your bed-chamber, and ruined me."

"Ruined?" Now it was his turn to sound offended. "You make me sound like some calf-handed fellow. *Ruined*. That implies that I didn't know what I was doing."

"I hardly found it to my liking." There was a pained little sniff added to her words that only seemed to add credence to her lack of enthusiasm.

Oh, the little minx. She was good. For now she had his blood boiling.

"Is that so," he said, before he swooped down and kissed her fiercely, sweeping his tongue past her lips.

But the spell he hoped to cast over her turned on him, for her lips were sweet, her eager response taking him by surprise. Her tongue tangled with his, her body pressed closer.

Those breasts, the ones he'd called devilish, were full and lush, rubbing against his chest, her tight nipples teasing him through her thin silk gown. He reached down and cupped one, pulling the edge of her bodice down, freeing it to his touch.

There was an advantage to ravishing a woman who was invisible—no one could see her state of *déshabillé*—but he could. Even as he felt the silk of her skin, traced the curves and lines of her body, he could *see* her.

He dipped his head lower and took a nipple into his mouth, sucking deeply, until she gasped, rising up on her toes as if offering him even more of her bounty. And so he took it, plucking up her gown, so he could delve beneath her skirts, his fingers tracing a line up her legs, over her thighs, then teasing the soft curls at her apex.

She shuddered again, her legs opening at his touch. There wasn't a man alive who didn't know *that* invitation, and he continued to seduce her, teasing her nether lips apart, so he could touch her, stroke her, until she was trembling and rocking against him.

"Rockhurst," she gasped. "I don't want to stop."

"Neither do I," he said, considering taking her right here and now, but he wanted more. He didn't want to just tumble her and have her slip back into the shadows.

He wanted to make love to her for the entire night.

And for that, he needed a bed.

"Will you come with me?" he whispered.

"Yes," she gasped.

"To an inn?" he offered, realizing she might not trust him enough to come willingly to his bed. An inn would seem safe, when in truth, he intended to make love to her all night, keep her so occupied that she'd never notice the dawn. Not until it was too late. "Will you go with me?"

"Please," she said, her voice quaking with need.

Catching hold of her hand, he tugged her down the path to a door that appeared carved into the wall. Like so many of the old houses in this part of London, Lord Belling's garden gave way to his neighbor's, the Earl of Brichet. Rockhurst towed her past the man's collection of classical statues and prized camellias.

Ducking through yet another garden door, he led her down a long alley to the street, where he had left his carriage in Tunstall's able care.

Up until now, Rowan had been ambling along behind them, his bone held tightly in his huge jaw. But the sound of it hitting the pavement, and the low growl out of his lips was enough to bring the earl to a sudden stop.

"Ooof," she gasped as she skidded into his back, her hands clutching at his hips. "Whatever is . . . "

. . . wrong?

Her unfinished question was answered by the sight of two creatures blocking their way.

"Bron," Rockhurst said, nodding to the first. "Ah, and Dubhglas, of course."

Not both of them. No, this didn't bode well. Not in the least.

"We have a message for you, Paratus," Bron said, as he rubbed his large hands together.

Dubhglas laughed. "That is, if you live long enough to hear it."

One moment Hermione had been lost in a haze of passion, dashing along with Rockhurst toward . . .

Another night of complete ruin, most certainly.

And she hadn't cared. For she knew he wanted her. Not Miss Burke. Not any other woman. *Her.*

But the visions of a night spent in his arms, of hours of feeling nothing but him, were dashed away in a moment at the sight of the two horrific creatures blocking their path.

She peered around the earl's back, clutching his coat like a wayward child, afraid to move.

"Derga," she whispered, remembering the drawing

she'd spied in one of Mary's books. If the rendering in the book had sent a chill down her spine, the living breathing examples were enough to send a shock of cold fright down her limbs.

Oh, jiminy! What had Rockhurst said last night about these creatures? *Portents of death.*

Death? Oh, that wasn't going to bode well for the passionate evening the earl had just promised her. Not if he was dead.

Hermione let out an aggrieved little *"harrumph."* Well, this wasn't going to do at all.

Rowan, in the meantime, had moved between his master and their foes, planting himself like a great stone edifice. The dog stood so erect, so still, that one might have thought him as harmless as a garden statue.

But there was no mistaking Rowan's intent as he growled low and menacingly: To get to his master, they would have to come through him.

"Paratus, it is a great honor to be chosen to kill you," the larger one was saying. Bron, she thought Rockhurst had called him. His red eyes glittered ominously in the growing darkness.

Kill him? Hermione glanced from the earl back at the boastful, scaly-looking fiend. They couldn't kill Rockhurst. Not when he hadn't finished what they'd started.

Indignation ran down her spine. Rather like the time Miss Burke had purchased an entire bolt of a blue silk that she knew Hermione had wanted, and then given it to her maid to have made up into curtains for the poor woman's attic room.

" 'Tis a great honor to kill the Paratus," the other one repeated.

"And to die trying, so I have heard, Dubhglas," Rockhurst tossed back, throwing down his challenge as casually as if he'd just added a paltry sum at an evening's card party.

Hermione poked him in the back. "Rockhurst," she whispered furiously. "Whatever are you thinking? There are two of them."

"It isn't the first time this has happened," he whispered back.

She glanced up the alley, where at the end sat the earl's carriage. "But you don't have anything to defend yourself with."

"That does give them a bit of an advantage," he said under his breath, his gaze never leaving the pair before them.

"What are you muttering about?" Bron called out, his red eyes squinting.

Dubhglas nudged his brother. "He's praying we make a quick end to him."

"I don't think they can see me," Hermione said. Gingerly, she stepped out to test her theory. She wiggled her fingers at the brothers, but neither of them paid her the least bit of heed. "They don't see me at all."

"Just stay behind me," the earl told her, trying to wave her back.

"Hey, what are you doing?" Bron said, rising to his full height, which made him at least a head taller than Rockhurst. "If you think to distract us, so you can run away, it won't work."

"Did the last time," Rockhurst said. "And then I killed your brother, as I recall. *For he dared to follow.*" He lowered his head and whispered to her, "When they charge, you are to run back into the garden and hide."

"I have a better idea," Hermione said, convinced she could help. That was, until they did charge.

Bron and Dubhglas launched themselves forward, and happily so, Rockhurst noted. Perfect. He had two idiot derga coming at him, most likely having been filled by Melaphor with promises of riches and glory if they killed him.

And if they managed to do so, he knew what would follow. The two would be filled with a blood-lust that they would let loose for the night on any poor mortal who unwittingly fell into their path.

There would be more murder and mayhem than his untimely end tonight if he didn't stop them.

He only hoped his little Shadow was well away.

Rowan caught Bron by the leg and chomped down hard, growling in triumph. The derga howled, not that he was going to get any help from his brother. Dubhglas was completely intent on gaining eternal glory all for himself.

The mighty demon swung hard, his long arm and huge fist hitting Rockhurst with a blinding punch. He heard the crunch of bone as his nose broke, and blood sprayed everywhere as he went flying through the air and hit the wall behind them.

His head cracked against the bricks, and he slid down into the refuse, stars and the red haze of blood obliterating his vision.

Dubhglas screamed in triumph, but it was the other scream that Rockhurst heard through the howl of pain that was piercing his head.

Shadow.

Demmit, she was supposed to be fleeing for her life, not watching him get pummeled.

Just the thought of her nearby, the possibility of one of them even coming near her, filled him with a rage he'd never known.

Shaking off his pain, he rose, reaching into his coat as he staggered to his feet. From within, he pulled out the long-bladed knife he kept inside. While the wicked steel would have been enough to deter a thief or ruffian on the street, to a hulking derga the sting would seem more of a mosquito bite than anything fatal.

But it was better than nothing, he told himself. He tipped his head and cracked his neck, settling all the bones back into place, feeling the great strength that was the legacy of the Paratus fill him.

Heal him.

"Beast, unhand me," Bron growled down at Rowan, who tenaciously clung to the giant's leg. The derga swung his meaty fist at the hound, but Rowan was too smart for him, dodging out of the way, and then barking once before he caught hold of the man's other leg, digging in, and growling as if he hadn't had so much fun in ages.

But Dubhglas had no such hindrance, and he towered before Rockhurst and smiled. "Melaphor will be so surprised to find that we've finished you off. He's claimed you were too dangerous, but I can see now you aren't so fierce."

"You've come without permission?" Rockhurst asked, setting his feet and trying to come up with a plan. Anything.

"So? What business is it of yours?"

"It's just that I believe your master intended to kill me himself."

Dubhglas leaned forward, his foul breath washing over Rockhurst as he said, "I haven't permission. With you dead and by my hand, then Melaphor will have no hold, and *I* shall rule."

"But how the devil—"

"Did we escape?" Dubhglas grinned. "There's a new hole not even he knows about. Been having a grand time in that slum of yours, but tonight we feast on your heart."

So this was who'd been killing in the Dials. Not Melaphor, but Bron and Dubhglas.

But who had opened a hole for them? And how would it get closed if he died this night?

Rockhurst swung back his arm and drove the dagger toward the derga's heart, but it was a feeble attempt, for Dubhglas brushed it aside, and swept him off his feet.

He hit with a heavy thud on the cobbles. Winded, he struggled to catch his breath, to rise anew and fight, but once again all he could see were stars. Dubhglas was proving formidable, and he couldn't recall any derga being this strong. Obviously the weeks of feeding had given him greater strength.

"Now you die, Paratus," the beast said as he moved in for the kill.

Rockhurst knew there was only one thing that would bring this monster down. If only he had his—

Thwack!

Bron rose up to his full height, howling. His pained cries tore Dubhglas's attention away from killing Rockhurst.

At least for the moment.

And as Dubhglas turned, Rockhurst could see what was causing Bron so much pain.

A bolt from his cross-bow stuck out of his shoulder, having come through his back and out the front. The derga clawed at it, crying and cursing in pain.

Thwack! Came a second, this one piercing his side. Bron staggered around, looking for his assailant.

"Shadow," Rockhurst whispered. The little fool. She'd succeeded in getting away, only to come back to the fight.

He should be furious, for he was the Paratus. This was his fight by right and duty. And though he'd fought battles like this countless times, with worse odds, there was a part of him that thrilled at the very notion of having someone, anyone, at his side.

Perhaps he had, as she'd said last night, been alone too long.

"I'll tear you from limb to limb," Bron bellowed, lumbering down the alley toward where the arrows were coming from.

Her third shot hit perfectly, right into the creature's black heart. There was a moment of disbelief on the derga's face as he looked down at his own destiny, and then he was gone, bursting into a cloud of dust, as old as the thousand or more years he'd been terrorizing humanity.

"Come out where I can see you," Dubhglas growled, striding down the alley. "Cowards only fight from the shadows."

Her reply was a bolt that appeared out of nowhere, flew furiously through the alley, grazing the giant derga in the shoulder, and sticking in the wall behind him.

Dubhglas whirled around, from the force of the shot or in disbelief, which it was Rockhurst couldn't tell. "What is this sorcery, Paratus?"

"The kind that will see you finished," he said, having risen to his feet.

"Not if I kill you first," the derga growled, his long teeth glittering in the night.

The earl braced himself, fists balled, ready for the fight, when he heard her call to him.

"Rockhurst!"

And then there it was. What he'd longed for just moments earlier.

Carpio.

The ancient sword appeared out of the night, flying through the air, arcing slowly around, almost hypnotically.

Dubhglas gaped at it, as if he couldn't believe his eyes.

Nor could Rockhurst, but he had more wits than a derga and snatched the blade out of the air and drove it into his enemy's chest.

For a moment, they stared at each other, with only

the hilt separating them. But the gulf between them was now far wider, as death closed in on the ancient creature.

With his last words, Dubhglas said, "Now he has no choice but to come for you. I've killed you as surely as if I—"

Then it was his turn to share his brother's fate, and he burst into dust.

Yet it seemed as if his last words still clung in the air, like unholy dust motes.

. . . as surely as if I'd done it myself.

A clank at the end of the alley drew his attention, the cross-bow having appeared where she'd dropped it.

"Jiminy! You're bleeding," she was saying, her footsteps padding toward him. "Oh, bother, where did I tuck my handkerchief?"

There was a rustle of silk, then her hand curled around his, and she guided the linen square up to his nose. "Dear heavens, you are bleeding all over. There are cuts on your hands and a horrible one on your thigh. What did that devil do to you?"

"Tried to kill me, I imagine," he said, glancing over what were ordinary wounds to him. They hurt now, but soon they'd heal over and be gone.

Not so his Shadow. She continued on as if he were on his deathbed.

"And whatever were you thinking?" she whispered. "That you could fight them alone?"

"I've done it before," he said, marveling at the warmth of her hands. They quite stole away every last icy reminder of death that had connected him to Dubhglas.

There was a snort of disbelief, then a *tsk, tsk* as if such a thing was just, well, ridiculous.

"You shouldn't have to. There are others, you know."

Others? He shook his head. Wherever had she gotten such a notion? Then he found out.

"But Mr. Podmore says—"

Podmore! Rockhurst cringed. The man was the bane of his existence. "That fool? Don't believe a word of his. There are no others."

Again with the *tsk, tsk*. But oddly, it wasn't as annoying as when his Aunt Routledge did it.

"There are," she insisted. She pulled his hand back. "You need some sticking paste for this."

"My nose always bleeds like this when it gets broken," he told her. "But it will be healed before long." He pulled the cloth back and showed her. "See, the bleeding has already stopped."

"Jiminy!" she whispered. "You've had this happen before?"

"Many times," he said, shrugging.

"And that is supposed to ease my fears?" She threw her arms around his neck and pressed herself entirely against him, one hand on his shoulder to steady herself, while her breasts and hips rode against him.

He no longer had any thoughts regarding his aching head, rather it was another part of him that was throbbing now.

"You could have been killed," she complained.

"I had the situation well in hand." He caught hold of her hips and pulled her closer, marveling at the way she fit against him.

"Harrumph!"

Well, she needn't sound so skeptical. "I did," he told her. "I've been in tighter spots."

"Again with the reassurances," she chided. "They aren't helping your cause."

"I don't see that it is any of your concern."

"Of course it is," she shot back. "When I have to step in to save you—"

"Save me?" he sputtered.

"You at least have to concede that I saved you," she said. "Therefore, you owe me a boon." She took a little breath. "The Paratus is honor-bound to safeguard his realm and grant boons to those who aid his cause."

Not more Podmore. He ground his teeth together. The insufferable fool was a thorn in his side. More to the point, now this creature was.

"I think you will find my terms quite reasonable," she was saying.

And now she was dictating to him? That part of him, that very Paratus part of him, reared back its talons in anger. He wasn't used to being prodded into doing what was his to grant.

Nor hers to demand.

That is, until he heard her request.

"Grant my wish, my lord," she whispered, her hands tugging at the lapels of his jacket. "Take me this very night and ruin me again."

Twelve

They barely made it to the nearest inn.

Rockhurst had caught hold of her hand the moment she'd made her offer and dragged her down the alley, rife with need. Every few feet, he stopped, hauled her into his arms, and kissed her anew, hungrily, his hands roaming over her body, exploring her, awakening her.

And while every nagging doubt told him this was wrong, he couldn't stop himself.

Ruin me . . .

He knew exactly what that meant, and now because of him, so did she. So why was he pursuing this madness, when he, Thomas, the Earl of Rockhurst, had always made it his rule to avoid innocents?

He, who was known for his mistresses, the high-flying Incomparables whose beauty (and price) put them out of reach of ordinary men, of men with scruples. He adored those women because in their world, the rules were clear.

But this . . . some unknown Mayfair miss, well, this was uncharted territory·for him, and what he should be doing was setting her down in the middle of Berkeley Square and running for his life.

Instead, here he was bursting into a barely fashionable inn and demanding a room like a madman.

The owner, who knew him, the earl having once removed a mert demon from his cellar, was only too glad to repay the Paratus by offering him the best room in the house and offering to send up a full tray for supper, but Rockhurst had waved off such generosity, asking only to be shown to a room, immediately.

The innkeeper nodded and ignored his lordship's current eccentricity by shouting orders to his staff: for a boy with a bucket of coals to kindle his lordship's fire, one of the maids to fetch a basin of hot water, and finally blustering at the cook in the kitchen to, "move your lazy arse and get a tray for his lordship."

Rowan was greeted with the same fanfare, a spot near the fire cleared for the great wolfhound and a large bone plucked from the soup pot for his pleasure.

The last the earl saw of his beast of a dog, he was happily ensconced on the hearth, enjoying his wellearned supper.

"The room, my good man, the room," Rockhurst said, nudging the innkeeper toward the stairs.

"Oh, yes, my lord. Of course, my lord," the man said. "But it will only be half-ready."

"It will be ready enough," he assured the fellow.

Rushing up the stairs with his unseen Shadow at his side, she whispered to him, "They think you are mad."

"I am," he replied.

"Excuse, my lord?" the innkeeper asked. "Is something amiss?"

"Nothing, my good man, I just need a room."

"To see to your injury? Is there someone I can call? A surgeon, perhaps?" he asked as he unlocked the door to a large, clean room that looked down on the stable yard. He hurried about the chamber, lighting candles and ordering the boy with the coals to see to the fire.

Rockhurst shook his head and all but pushed them both out of the room, taking the basin of hot water and cloths from the maid who was about to enter. "I need only some rest. See no one disturbs me," he told them before closing the door in their astonished faces.

Then, with everyone banished, he scanned the room. "Shadow?" He put the basin down on a side table, the water sloshing over the sides.

"Yes," came the seductive little purr as one of the candles snuffed out, then another, casting the room in only the glow from the coals in the grate.

Shadows for his Shadow. He grinned. "I thought I'd lost you in that mob."

"You very nearly did," she said, her voice coming closer. "The boy with the coal bucket came quite close to clouting me, what with the way he was swinging it about."

As her words drew nearer and nearer, his body tensed, waiting for the moment . . . the moment when she would touch him again.

And then she did, her fingers splaying over his chest,

her body sliding up against his like a cat. "I believe you owe me a boon, my lord."

"How much of that demmed Podmore have you read?"

"Not as much as I would like to have," she confessed, her hands winding around the lapels of his coat and pushing the Weston creation over his shoulders. "But much to my annoyance, I was too tired this morning—after such a long night—to read more than a few pages."

"Bluestocking!" he teased.

"You sound like my mother," she shot back.

"And she would be?"

There was a lilting bit of laughter from her. "Someone you generally avoid."

Now it was his turn to laugh. Oh, yes, that narrowed his search down quite a bit—to every mother in London with a marriageable daughter.

She took his hand and led him to the chair near the table. Then the cloth disappeared into her grasp, and she wrung it out in the bowl. Ever so tenderly, she began to clean his face.

"Does it hurt," she asked, her fingers tracing carefully around his jaw.

"Not in the least," he told her. "Not now."

"But how?" she asked. "It looked broken before."

"It was."

"But it couldn't have been. How could it just—"

"It just does," he said, taking the cloth from her hand and wiping his face clean. "Simple things like broken bones, or flesh wounds heal almost immediately."

"I would hardly call those 'simple' injuries."

"I suppose not, but it is how a Paratus survives."

What he didn't say, what he couldn't say, was that he would survive, until something so grievous struck, something so irreparable, that not even the magic that aided him could save his soul from being wrenched from his broken body.

No man, not even a Paratus, liked to think of that inevitable reckoning.

"'Tis all part of the curse," he told her instead.

"If it saves your life, I would call it a gift."

He caught hold of her and pulled her into his lap, kissing her anew. "You are my gift."

"My boon, Rockhurst," she said, having worked his coat off and begun unwinding his neckcloth.

"I don't even know your name," he told her. "I make it a rule always to know a lady's name before . . ."

"Before you make love to her?" She shifted in his lap. "We are well past that, my lord," she whispered as she rose and slipped into the shadows. There was a rustle of her gown as it hit the floor.

He couldn't see the color of it, for she'd cast it into a dark corner. Not that he looked overly much, for just then the bed creaked as she climbed into it.

His body went hard as he imagined her there. Naked and lithe, her lush breasts full and tight, her lips parted and waiting to press them to his, to kiss him wherever he desired.

He rose and crossed the room, undressing as he went, pulled by the very thought of her. When he got to the bed, he leaned over and slid his hand across the top until it nudged into her shoulder, then he leaned over to nuzzle her neck, inhale her perfume. He tugged her closer and kissed her right behind her ear. The little chit shivered and purred in delight.

"Now my boon, my lord Paratus."

It was enough of an invitation for Rockhurst, his blood still boiling from their interlude earlier. He sealed her request with a kiss, one that fused them together.

No longer shy, she responded with enthusiasm, clinging to him, her hips riding up against his erection.

He took one last furtive glance at the corner where her gown lay, hoping he'd recognize it. For he'd also spent a good part of the afternoon memorizing nearly every gown there, and the lady within it.

"Rockhurst," she whispered, pulling his attention back to her. "My boon."

And any thoughts of her gown flitted away. He'd find the demmed thing in the morning. For now, he had a boon to repay.

And so much more.

Hermione's body came alive the moment Rockhurst joined her in the bed. His weight tipped the mattress, and she rolled into his arms.

His mouth found hers, and he kissed her with a desperate hunger. She understood, for she felt the same.

He lived tonight, but what about the next time? Or the time after that. What if his next wound wasn't a "simple" one?

Hermione felt a rare desperation—she wanted him to live forever more. Always. So that every night she could know this bliss of tumbling into a bed with him, of feeling him take such heady possession of her.

His tongue explored her mouth, running over her lips, pressing inside her, and she shivered, for it was like a taste of what was to come . . . when he entered her.

Her hips rose, and he caught hold of them and held them close.

"God, woman, what is it that you do to me?" he gasped, before his head dipped down, and he captured one of her nipples in his mouth and sucked it to a hard peak.

The same thing you do to me. Her fingers raked down his back, over his buttocks, and around to the front of him, where his manhood was hard and erect.

She slid her hand over it, running from the wet tip all the way down to the base.

Now it was his turn to become insensible, as he groaned, his hips moving up to meet her hand as she stroked him again.

Not one to be undone, he reached down and teased her legs open—and open they did, quite willingly. For she knew what his touch could do. Where it could take her.

And it did, his fingers finding first the taut nub there and teasing her into a torrent of desire. With each touch, each slip of the rough pad of his thumb, she moaned and arched.

Wanton with need, she no longer wanted just his touch, she wanted him. Rolling onto him, the mattress creaking as she went, Hermione drove herself down atop his manhood.

"Oooh," she gasped as he filled her, and she rode him all the way down. It was like heaven.

She drew back, slowly, sliding over him and enjoying every bit of his hard length, until just his tip sat at her cleft, then she slid back down, sighing loudly.

Beneath her, Rockhurst chuckled. "Wanton."

"Don't you feel it?" she asked, as she slid over him again, rocking her hips as she went.

This time his body rose up to meet hers, fill her, going farther than she'd thought possible, and he groaned in pleasure.

Oh yes, he felt it.

Back and forth they teased each other, him pulling out slowly until she'd gasp for fear he'd be gone, and her riding him back down, rocking her hips and taking her time, until the heat of their play changed the rules.

Hermione felt the shift as her desire became rife, an aching need to find completion—not just for herself, but for Rockhurst as well. He caught hold of her hips and began to stroke her in earnest, until she was past reason.

"Rockhurst," she gasped. "Oh, please. Now."

And he knew what she meant.

He wound his arms around her and rolled her with him, so he covered her. His body now atop hers, he pushed deeper and harder into her, and Hermione's heels dug into the mattress so she could rise to meet him.

Her world spun round, the shadows and flickering light a blur, and the roar in her ears was her own moans, her desire coming to a fiery head.

He moaned, deeply and passionately as he found his release, and those uninhibited, frantic strokes that followed carried her along as the room disappeared and she melted into his arms, into the only world she ever wanted to know.

* * *

As Hermione drifted back down, Rockhurst rolled to one side, and she made a mew of displeasure at losing the heat of his body. There was something about being inside the circle of his warmth, his strength, that made her feel as if she—no, *they*—were far from the dangers that she now knew lurked in the night.

He laughed and tugged her into his arms, and she nestled into the crook of his shoulder and laid her head down on his chest where, just beneath her ear, his heart still hammered wildly.

She sighed happily. She'd done that. Made his heart beat in this haphazard tremor, made him wild for his release.

His fingers toyed with her hair, wandered over her shoulder, and traced a lazy circle around her nipple.

"I love your breasts," he said, leaning down and nuzzling her there. "I would love them better if I could see them."

His hand trailed down her arm and over her hand, until it came to the ring on her finger. Playfully, he tugged at it, but it held fast to her hand.

"Obviously you weren't trying hard enough to tell me all your secrets," Hermione teased.

"I would rather show you them," he said, kissing her deeply.

And then he did. Show her. Again. And one more time after that, until they both fell into a lover's slumber, spent and happy, and safe in a world all their own.

Some hours later, Hermione stood on a street corner near the inn and wondered how the devil she'd ever be able to hail a hackney when she was still unseen?

It was pure luck that she'd been able to slip out of Rockhurst's arms, don her gown, and escape the inn in the final hour of darkness, but she still needed to get home before dawn.

Bad enough she'd lied to her mother the night before at the Belling garden party, telling her she was going to the opera with India and not to have Dorcas wait up for her. But she needed to be home before their ever-vigilant maid got up.

"Where have you been?" a voice said over her shoulder.

Hermione nearly leapt out of her skin. She whirled around and found Quince, hands fisted on her hips and looking, well, none-too-pleased. At least Quince could see her. Perhaps she could prevail upon this try-as-she-might fairy godmother to help her.

But one glance at the disapproving furrow of Quince's brows suggested that helping Hermione was the last thing she wanted to do.

Strangle her was probably more at the top of the odd lady's list.

Too bad, for Hermione felt glorious. She'd never imagined, never realized that a man could . . . She shivered at the memories of being in bed with Rockhurst.

Of his kisses, his touch, the way he'd stroked her until she'd . . .

She heaved a sigh, which was met by a disgruntled "*harrumph*" from Quince, who took her by the elbow and steered her down the street to the corner, where the early-morning traffic was beginning to pick up.

London, Hermione marveled, never slept, and who

would want to when one could spend the night in such glorious pursuits?

"Did you hear what I said?" Quince was nattering on. "Dear heavens, girl, stop woolgathering and pay heed to what I am trying to tell you. You are in grave danger!"

"Danger?" Hermione shook her head. "I can't see how."

Oh, but she could. Of losing sight of everything she was supposed to hold dear and spending every night she could in his arms. In Rockhurst's bed.

Quince waved at a passing hackney, the sleepy-looking driver appearing none too happy about another fare when all he wanted was to seek his bed, but then again, how could he pass it up when Quince offered him a shining piece of silver for the ride.

Hermione found herself bullied inside and prodded for directions.

"You little fool, do you know the danger you are in?" Quince said, the moment the hackney rolled away from the curb. "This is far worse than I first feared."

"I am in no danger from him," Hermione assured her, patting Quince on the arm. Really, the woman was overreacting. The earl would never harm her. "Just because he is the Paratus—"

"Sssh!" Quince warned. "Don't say such things aloud. You have no idea who he is."

"But I do," she insisted. "I've been reading the book Mr. Cricks gave me, and I know all about the earl." She folded her arms over her chest. "Besides, I think he loves me."

"Loves you!" Quince glanced heavenward, in a gesture similar to what Hermione's mother did when Griffin gambled a little too deep. She lowered her voice to furious whisper. "The Paratus is incapable of love."

Hermione shook her head. "He loves me."

"He does?" Now it was Quince's time to turn the tables. "So why haven't you told him who you are?"

"That is hardly the point," Hermione said, glancing out the window, where the sky was starting to turn pink.

What was it her father had always said? *Red sky in the morning, sailors take warning.*

Well, that didn't apply to this morning, she told herself.

"Why haven't you told him who you are?" Quince persisted. "Why isn't this besotted lover of yours driving you home?"

"That is a rather complicated point," Hermione said. "I can hardly tell him who I am. Then he'd feel compelled to—"

Quince's brows arched, daring her to finish.

Offer for me.

Hermione shifted in her seat, feeling the heat of Quince's probing gaze. Of course he would. It was the honorable thing to do.

But what if he wouldn't?

"Exactly my point," Quince whispered, as if Hermione had said it aloud.

"I don't care if he were to offer for me or not, I love being with him. Why, just last night I saved him. We stopped two derga."

"Yes, I know."

"You do?" Hermione's eyes widened. "You were there?"

Quince shook her head. "Thank heavens, no. But such news travels quickly. That is why I spent the better part of the night looking for you." Quince huffed. "And imagine my surprise when I discovered *where* you were."

Hermione blushed.

"And I wouldn't be so quick to boast about stopping that pair of brutes. Derga usually come in tribes of twelve. There are ten others who will be happy to avenge their brothers' deaths."

"Ten more?" Hermione gulped.

"Good. I am finally getting through to you. This is no simple flirtation, my dear. All of Melaphor's servants most likely know that you are wearing that ring, and any one of them could get it in their head to come seek it."

Hermione glanced down at her hand, the simple band of silver looking quite plain. Hardly something to be sought by the very devil himself.

Quince leaned in and poked Hermione in the arm. "Have you thought that *he* might be using you to gain the ring for himself?"

"No-o-o!" Hermione sputtered, even as she remembered how he had stroked her hand, even pulled at the ring, joking that he would have to try yet again to loosen it.

"You cannot undo what is done," Quince was saying, "but you have the power to stop it all. Before it is too late. You must disavow your wish. Then give me the ring, and I shall hide it where it will never be found again."

"It won't come off," Hermione told her.

Quince took a deep breath. "You have only to disavow your wish. Disavow it, and you will be free."

The carriage turned into Berkeley Square just as the sun arose, and Hermione felt the sunlight fill her, trembling and warm, and in an instant she reappeared.

"I've tried, Quince," she said.

"It only works if it is what you truly want."

And there was the rub. Hermione didn't want to disavow her wish. She wanted to spend every night with the earl, just as she had this one. Entwined in his arms, holding him close, letting him make love to her until she thought she'd weep from the bliss of it.

"Truly, all will be well," Hermione told her. "I think you are making more of this than is necessary. The earl will protect me, and I promise not to take any more chances at night."

"No," Quince admonished. "It must end now, before it is too late."

The carriage stopped, and Hermione bounded down. The driver blinked, trying to figure out how he'd gained another passenger in the course of their travels. He gaped down at her, then, before he could collect his fare, clicked the reins and drove off at a frantic pace.

"Well, of all the cheek," Hermione said, trying to discern whatever had made him look as if he'd seen a ghost. "Whatever was wrong with him?"

Quince nodded toward the front of Hermione's gown.

Then in an instant all of Quince's warnings gained some meaning. As she looked down at herself, a deadly shiver ran down her spine—a premonition of things to come if she'd been inclined to believe such things.

For the entire front was covered with the earl's blood.

Thirteen

"Whatever is wrong with you, Minny?" Lady Walbrook asked for the thousandth time. "You are fidgeting. Try to stand coolly, calmly like a Diana or a Venus. Follow my example." The lady drew herself up and stood as if she were in one of her dramatic productions.

Hermione forced a smile to her lips and did as her mother bid her. Jiminy! How was she supposed to stand still when the sun was about to set, and she was trapped in the middle of a crowded ballroom.

She'd put off her mother with one excuse after another all week, but tonight the countess would have none of Hermione's dithering. She was going to the Abington ball and that was the end of it.

The only thing she could be thankful for was that

they were quickly approaching Midsummer's Eve, and the days were now stretched to their longest hours.

Still, it would be the end of everything if she just vanished into thin air in front of the entire *ton*.

Not that the past week hadn't had its fair share of trials. She'd done as she'd finally promised Quince and stayed well out of Rockhurst's path, but that hadn't stopped the ache in her heart. Especially when her mother had spent every breakfast giving lengthy reports of Rockhurst's odd behavior.

Furtively, she stole a glance at the window. Though she needn't have looked. She could feel the sun creeping down toward the horizon, pulling her along with it. Only a few minutes more, and she'd disappear completely.

"Do you see Rockhurst?" her mother said to the matron next to her, fan fluttering wildly as she pointed across the room, her admonishment about statuelike poise forgotten. "Why, it is almost as if the man has gone mad!"

"I wager he has," the lady said, peering at the earl through her lorgnette. "For I'd bet my best silk gown that he's finally fallen in love."

"The earl is in love?" Hermione's mother pressed her lips together. "Why, this is terrible. I had such high hopes for my dear Minny. Well, I must go speak to him anyway, for my rehearsals are to start next week, and I can't have him forgetting his promise to—"

Hermione stopped her ears to any more talk of the earl.

Rockhurst in her house? Beside her? She wasn't

sure she was going to manage the next few moments of standing in the same ballroom with him—for right now she was a trembling mess of unanswered need.

Her breath caught in her throat as she watched him stalking through the room, scanning the lines of debutantes, waiting for the music to begin. She knew from her mother's gossip that he'd ask as many as he could to dance, beg introductions of every likely and some unlikely misses, and then prowl on to the next Society event.

So while other ladies exhibited faint blushes and tender glances in his direction, all in an attempt to catch his eye, Hermione looked away. She didn't need to see the man.

She'd been in his bed. Held in those long, strong arms. Felt him fill her, cover her, take her both gently and in a rough, hurried way that had left her breathless.

Her knees wobbled, while another, more private part of her tightened and trembled. She ground her teeth together and tried to think of something else.

Like his kiss . . . or his touch.

Oh, jiminy! This would never do. So she watched him as he paced about the ballroom, his wild-eyed gaze scanning the ladies lining the walls as if he were a wolf hunting for a likely lamb.

And when he wasn't measuring each and every chit, he was watching the horizon.

Waiting for the sun to set.

Yes, she'd promised Quince she wouldn't seek the earl out, for the lady's warning had cast a shadow over her heart.

Have you thought that he might be using you to gain the ring for himself?

Oh, those terrible words left her filled with doubts as to why he sought her, but when she looked across the room at him, she had only one thought, and her doubts mattered not.

She wanted him. And for the first time all week, the ring trembled awake.

Soon. Soon we can be together.

But not until I find a way to get away from Maman, she thought, glancing first at the window, and then at her mother.

If only she could disappear unnoticed and slip through the crowd. She would brush past him and whisper a seductive invitation.

Come with me, Rockhurst. Make love to me this night. I love you like no other, I want no other.

And he'd follow her, as sure as the sun was about to set. He'd follow her into the garden, where he'd pull her lustfully into his arms and devour her with his wicked kiss. Give in to her invitation. Spend the entire night making love to her.

To her. His Shadow. The woman he loved.

Yet into her thoughts sprang a voice not unlike that of Miss Burke's. *He might love his Shadow, but you? Lady Hermione Marlowe? Now that's a fine jest.*

Hermione's convictions wavered. Whatever would he do if she were to walk up to Lord Rockhurst and make the same invitation as herself, plain and odd Hermione Marlowe.

She pressed her lips together even as her toes began to

tingle. Oh, heavens, she only had another minute or two!

"Minny?" her mother whispered. "Whatever is wrong with you? You look as pale as a cod!"

"I don't feel so well," Hermione told her quite honestly. She never did as she made the transformation. "I think the room has grown terribly close." She wavered again, her knees now trembling. She didn't even dare look down at her slippers, for fear they were already gone from sight.

"Oh, heavens, girl. Don't faint. You'll make a spectacle of yourself. If you feel unwell, go out into the garden and take a few deep breaths." Her mother prodded her toward the door, and Hermione needed no further urging. She fled through the crowd, weaving her way through the bejeweled matrons, pretty misses, and dazzling gentlemen until she came to the French doors that led to the garden.

They were already cracked open to let in some air, so it was nothing more to slip into the garden and into the growing dusk.

Rockhurst spied the hasty departure of a young lady out the garden doors, and his heart stilled. Then he glanced beyond the lady's shoulder to the garden beyond. Bathed in hues of red and gold, it sang with the coming of night.

Shadow.

It had to be. And though there didn't seem to be anything remarkable about this miss, he knew better.

For in minutes she'd move from being seen to unseen. And still unknown.

Not if he could reach her first.

For the past week he'd done nothing but search for her—through dull musicales, soirees, endless balls, even an entire Wednesday evening at Almack's—all the while waiting for that moment when he'd feel her fingers slide onto his sleeve and hear her whisper an invitation that would take them all night to explore.

He'd ignored his duties, his obligations, and he'd thought he'd go mad with longing, all in search of a single flower amidst a garden of blossoms.

Until now.

Ignoring the scandalous gasps and the scathing glances as he trampled his way through the crowd, he was nearly to the door when a blundering fellow stepped into his path.

"Rockhurst! A-a-a-a word with you, my good man. About your treatment of Miss Burke! I'll have you know—"

Battersby. Rockhurst heaved a sigh and tried to dodge past the fellow, but he was as obstinate as he was foolish.

"Miss who?" he asked, his gaze fixed on the garden. He had minutes, maybe only moments.

"Miss Burke! You were quite attentive to her last week at Lord Belling's garden party, then you left her quite alone for the supper. Why, I'll have you know I had to step forward and escort her myself! Had to play the knight to your rogue."

"And that was a problem? I thought you favored the chit."

"Favor her? I adore her! And to see her left in such embarrassing circumstances—"

"Battersby, I haven't time for this. I left the path wide open for you. Might even have a chance to win her hand now. You should be thanking me instead of annoying me." He leaned down until he was nose to nose with the man. "Because I would hate to have to take affront to the tone you are using and put a bullet through your chest before you even had a chance to propose."

Battersby blinked. Then he blinked again, this time a light dawning in his dim brain. "Oh, well, hadn't thought of it that way. Not at all. How right you are, Rockhurst. Always are." He smiled widely. "Should have known you were there in my camp. Ready to help me along with the chit. I can see it now, you and I, breaking hearts wherever we go."

He took the man by the shoulders and none-too-gently pushed him in the general direction of Miss Burke, not knowing if he was doing the man a favor or he should just challenge the fool and end his life before he did himself in by offering for Lavinia Burke.

A whisper of wind flitted through the room, bringing with it the scent of the garden beyond. Rockhurst needed no further reminders, taking giant, quick strides the rest of the way and sending one and all the haughtiest look of scorn he could muster, if only to save himself any more interruptions. Finally, he made it to the garden unencumbered, but one look over the garden wall showed all too clearly that the sun was down.

That and the fact that the small, narrow garden was entirely empty.

At least of any visible woman.

"Demmit!" he cursed, loudly and roundly. He was too late.

Her laughter did little too soothe his frustration.

"You almost found me out, Rockhurst," she said in that teasing way of hers. "Almost."

"I have another way to determine who you are," he offered, trying to discern just exactly where it was she stood.

"And that would be?"

"I could kidnap you again and keep you in my bed."

"And seduce me into revealing my identity? You are good, my lord. But it hasn't worked so far—"

"I wouldn't need to seduce you."

"You wouldn't?"

Was it he, or did she sound disappointed?

He grinned. "No, I'd keep you well satisfied just long enough for the hue and cry to be raised for a missing young lady. And then I'd know exactly who you are."

"You are a rogue, sir," she replied. "For then I would be ruined."

"More so than you already are?" For she'd certainly ruined him for any other woman.

"Ah yes, but that is our secret."

Secrets . . . there it was, the solicitor in her again, always finding the loophole to wiggle through. "It wouldn't be tomorrow."

"Have you not realized that my ruin could well have me banished to some remote part of Scotland?" She paused, and then he heard her slippers tripping lightly up the gravel. "And were I banished, my lord, with whom would you dally?"

Minx! She knew she had him.

"Do you really think I'd allow you to be banished?"

"Because this is *your* realm?"

"So it is," he said, feeling his heart twist slightly as she drew closer. He'd never felt like this before with a woman. She left him aching like a greenling, acutely aroused and, at the same time, all too unsure of himself.

"And if I were banished, I couldn't go out socially," she whispered as she came right up in front of him. He didn't need to see her to know that she was just a breath away.

He could feel her. Smell her. Nearly taste her.

"You don't really go out socially as it is," he teased. "Given your current predicament."

"I don't consider it a predicament," she said huskily, her hand coming to slide up under his jacket, over his waistcoat and coming to rest over his heart. "I consider it a boon."

"A boon? To be unseen by one and all?"

"I am seen by you, and I consider that the finest boon I could have ever gained with just one wish."

"Then your wish has come true?"

"Not quite yet."

"How so?"

"You haven't made love to me yet this night."

"The sun just went down," he protested.

"Then why are we wasting time standing about here?"

He needed no further invitation, his mouth crashing down on hers in a bruising kiss. The chit had him hard and ready, and there was nowhere to go.

Cheap bastard, Abington. Not even a potting shed to be had.

"Isn't there a gate?" she asked.

"No," he told her. "Only one way in and out." He started toward the French doors, her hand in his, but he stopped abruptly and shook a finger at her. "Leave Miss Burke be."

"Must I?"

"If you want me to . . ." he whispered an erotic promise in her ear, and she teetered against him, her breath coming in quick little gasps.

"But—"

"No buts!" he told her. "You so much as bedevil one hair on her head—"

"I thought you didn't like her."

"I don't," he said. "But as you said before, you'd be wasting precious time."

She laughed. "Devil!"

"Minx!"

They kissed again, her body rocking up against his, urging him to forget the demmed bed and just take her right that moment. He would if he hadn't planned to carry her off. Take her back to his bed and pour champagne over her enticing body, then drink it from her silken skin.

Then he'd . . .

A racket of barking, then a pained "yelp" rose from beyond the house. Rockhurst immediately dropped her hand and stilled.

The sound was so fearsome, so plaintive. So unmistakable.

Rowan. Howling as if the very fiends of hell had him cornered.

For they did.

Hermione raced after Rockhurst as he bolted from the garden, through the crowded ballroom, and out the front of the baron's town house.

She hadn't as easy a time negotiating the thick maze of guests, for he had breadth and height to his advantage, and she could barely stay in his wake before the crowd would swell back together, and she'd be cut off.

Finally, she gained the curb out front and spied him sprinting across the street, toward an alleyway.

"Rockhurst!" she shouted. "Wait for me."

But he was oblivious to her cries, continuing head-long toward the commotion.

Rowan's growls and barks sent an uneasy shiver down her spine, for she'd heard Dubhglas's last words.

Now he has no choice but to come for you. I've killed you as surely as if I . . .

She dodged around the carriages in the street, coming dangerously close to being run down, for the drivers were unable to see her. As she crossed, she spied the earl's carriage, a lad holding the reins. She climbed in and caught hold of the bag stored beneath the seat. Yanking it open, she searched first for Carpio, then the earl's cross-bow. With those secured, she caught up a handful of bolts and ran for the alley.

Hermione only made it a few steps before Quince rushed into her path.

"You cannot follow him." The lady caught her by the arm.

Hermione tried to tug herself free, but to no avail. "Get out of my way," she cried, juggling the weapons in her arms to get a hand free. "He could be killed."

"If he is, then surely you will be as well," Quince said. "And then the ring will fall into *their* hands." Her brows creased into a firm line. "I cannot let that happen—for with that ring, they could do terrible things. Cause tragedies for this world and mine."

Horrible things are happening right now, Hermione wanted to shout at her. Tears stung her eyes, for around the corner Rowan's great growls and barks had faded to pained whimpers and yelps.

Each one tore at her heart. They were hurting Rowan. Terribly. And that could only mean . . .

They had Rockhurst cornered . . . or worse.

That thought, that horrible picture in her mind was enough to give her the strength to shove Quince out of her way.

As she rounded the corner, she searched frantically for any sign of Rockhurst, for in her path stood all ten of the derga Quince had warned her about before. One of them larger than even Dubhglas.

The fearsome creature turned toward her, as if he sensed her arrival, but she didn't think he could see her. That didn't stop a cold chill from running down her spine, for the loathsome fellow held Rowan high in the air, as if the massive wolfhound were a child's plaything.

And beyond him, stood three others with Rockhurst held fast.

He was already bloody, but he fought them nonetheless with a wild, anxious agony.

Hermione tucked Carpio under her arm while she shoved a bolt into the cross-bow, then struggled to pull the lever back and lock the bolt in place.

"Leave him be," the earl was saying, cursing with words she understood and with ones she didn't.

She glanced up and looked with horror at Rowan held so high in the air. Oh, heavens, that monster wasn't going to . . .

Hermione tugged at the lever again. She didn't remember it being this hard, but then Rowan's life hadn't hung in the balance.

Save Rowan, save Rowan, she whispered, her every limb trembling as she took one more deep breath and pulled with all her might. The bridle clicked into place, and she raised the cross-bow to take aim, but it was too late.

The derga threw the faithful, fearless dog across the alley. With a horrible, heart-wrenching *thud,* Rowan hit the wall, then slid down limply to the cobbles at her very feet.

She couldn't even breathe. The shaggy fur, the great paws, the muscled shoulders that had always seemed so full of life were suddenly so very different.

So still.

Hermione scrambled to Rowan's side and knelt before him, wishing with all her heart that she was wrong. But this wish couldn't be granted.

Rowan, the finest wolfhound a Paratus had ever owned, was lost. She knew it with a certainty that cut to her very heart.

And so did Rockhurst. He wrenched himself free and rushed to Rowan's side, close to where she knelt.

He shook, with rage or grief, she knew not. Both, she assumed. And when he looked up, she swore he stared directly into her eyes.

A look that burned with an unearthly hatred. His usually bright blue eyes glowed with a dark light that wasn't natural. Like something out of one of Mary's monster books.

Hermione pulled back, seeing this man she loved anew.

Seeing for the first time the fearsome power of the Paratus.

Yet with all the power in the world, it was still ten against one. So she placed Carpio atop Rowan's body and released the hilt, letting it reappear.

He didn't even blink, didn't look for her, didn't even acknowledge her gift.

The affable Rockhurst she knew and loved was gone, the lover who'd tenderly possessed her body lost, and the Paratus arose, sword in hand, and did what the protector of London had been ordained to do for over eleven hundred years.

He killed them all.

Hermione buried her face in Rowan's still-warm fur and clung to the dog as the Paratus went about his ruthless revenge.

It wasn't until an eerie calm descended over the alleyway that she finally lifted her gaze.

Rockhurst's chest rose and fell in heavy, ragged thuds, Carpio trembling in his tight grasp.

But he wasn't done fighting yet, slashing out and thrusting the sword into the now-empty spaces, as if his lust for blood knew no end.

"One left," he was muttering, his wild gaze sweeping the alley. "I can smell you, I know you are here. Come out and die."

Hermione had heard whispers of such madness, of people driven out of their minds in the face of some horror. And she feared Rowan's death had sent Rockhurst past the point of no return.

Beneath her fingers, the wolfhound's soft fur gave her comfort. She ran her hand over his silky ears, tears streaming down her cheeks.

Whatever would Rockhurst do without Rowan at his side?

Who would protect him, watch over him, as Rowan had?

"I suppose now there is no one else but me," she whispered to the hound.

Slowly she rose, still trembling from what she had just witnessed.

Oh, why hadn't she spent more time learning about the world, instead of wasting most of her life poring over fashion plates and gossip columns? What did she know of these things? Her sister Cordelia was better suited for such a charge, with her vast knowledge of the classics. Or even her friend Charlotte. Practical, sensible Charlotte. She'd know what to do.

But she? Lady Hermione Marlowe? With her horrible taste in fashion and oblivious to anything that wasn't a whispered *on dit*?

Whatever had the Fates been thinking putting her in this fix?

"Come out! I order you to come out!" Rockhurst shouted, as he swung and thrust Carpio at demons only he could see now.

Hermione covered her mouth, quelled the "jiminy" that had been about to slip out. Jiminy, indeed.

"Oh, demmit!" she whispered.

This madman, this grieving aching man that she loved, seemed to have forgotten her, as he continued to slash and curse his enemies. He needed to stop, he needed to give up Carpio before he harmed someone, or worse, himself.

She took a quiet step toward him, and then froze as he sliced into the space before her.

Whatever are you doing, Hermione? she thought in a rare burst of common sense. *He's as likely to kill you . . .*

She glanced back at Rowan and shivered. Oh heavens, for there was no else to help him.

"Rockhurst," she called out in a shaky voice. "'Tis me—" *Lady Hermione.* She bit back that confession.

The poor man was bereft as it was, no need to tell him the truth about her.

"It's me," she called out. "Your Shadow. I'm here. Right here." She bit her lips and considered what she could possibly say to coax him out of the darkness that had stolen his soul. "Rockhurst, come back. Rowan needs you. He must be seen to. Properly. Please, Rockhurst, it's over."

He swung around wildly, but only too late did she see that his eyes were still filled with that horrible, unseeing light, that the one he was searching for, the "one left" was her.

For before she could gather enough wits together to run, he rushed toward her, Carpio raised high in the air, with only murder on his mind.

A woman's scream pierced the blackness that had descended over the Paratus. With it came a blinding flash of light and suddenly, the powers that had held him in their thrall left, rushing back to whatever cubbyhole in hell they'd come from, and leaving Rockhurst wavering and reeling in their wake.

What the devil had just happened? The earl tried to breathe, his lungs burning. Then, ever so slowly, his vision cleared, and he spied Rowan lying before him on the cobbles.

Only then did he remember.

Immediately the blackness threatened to engulf him anew, a hatred and fury like he'd never known, and for the life of him, he welcomed it, wanted it, for it blotted out the horrible grief descending toward him.

But then he looked again at Rowan and sank to his knees, steadying himself with Carpio.

A Paratus shall do no harm.

No harm . . .

Oh, God, what had he done?

His eyes jerked open and looked around. Aside from Rowan, there was nothing but ten piles of dust. And for a moment he gave over to a smug sense of satisfaction.

That is, until he spied a bright red stain of blood amongst them.

Blood? Derga didn't bleed.

But humans did.

His chest clenched, and he clamored to his feet, gasping for air. "Shadow?" he called out, his gaze swinging from one side of the alley to another. He knew he couldn't see her, but that didn't stop him from looking.

Oh, God, I've killed her.

Slain her as surely as he'd laid waste to Dubhglas's clan.

He took a staggering step forward, out toward the street, where a lamp glowed like a beacon. And there beneath it, he spied another bit of blood, and then farther on, more.

She was moving. He hadn't killed her.

And he would have continued after her, but suddenly he heard her voice, as if carried on the wind.

Go back. Rowan needs you. He must be seen to. Properly. Please, Rockhurst, it is over.

She'd been the one calling to him, pulling him out of the darkness. And her only thought had been for Rowan.

He glanced over his shoulder. *Rowan . . . no.* It couldn't be true. He stumbled back to the alley, falling to his knees and burying his face in the familiar soft fur, his hands gathering up his lost friend and holding him close.

And there and then Rockhurst did something he hadn't done in nearly twenty years. Not since the night he'd found his father slain, and he'd had to carry his broken body home to face his mother's grief.

The Paratus wept.

Fourteen

Mary Kendell settled into her favorite chair in the library and let out a contented sigh. She had a newly acquired text Cricks had sent over for her to translate and didn't have any pressing social engagements this evening.

She didn't even feel guilty about not going out. As much as she'd proclaimed to her father that she was going to find a husband this Season, she certainly wasn't making much of a splash.

"It would help, you muttonhead, if you would go out," she chided herself. But why ever would she want to go out when she had this little-known treatise by Cicero to translate? Better the comfortable reliability of a good book over the social maze of disappointment that awaited her outside her own doors.

That is, until the library door opened.

She glanced up, but no one was there. Not Cosgrove or one of the maids or even a footman.

"Hello?" she called out, rising to her feet. She cocked her head and studied the empty space between her and the door.

Empty space or not, she knew without a doubt someone was in the room with her.

"Whoever you are, you had best introduce yourself."

"You already know me, Mary."

Mary stepped back. She knew that voice. "Hermione?"

"Yes, 'tis I. I'm afraid this is going to be hard to believe, but I'm—"

"Invisible," Mary gasped.

"How—" Hermione's voice faltered before she spoke again. "Oh, never mind. I suppose one has only to look at your library to realize you, of all people, wouldn't find this shockingly appalling."

She shook her head. "Hardly." But then it hit her. "You! You're Rockhurst's Shadow!"

"He told you about us—" Hermione's words revealed the blush that must be coloring her cheeks. "Oh, dear, I thought it was all a secret."

"Us?" Mary's hand went to her gaping mouth. The implication was unmistakable. *Us.* Now it was her turn to blush. "You don't mean to say . . . ?" Then she shook her head and waved her hands back and forth. "No. No. He didn't tell me anything personal, just that he was seeking a lady who roamed the night unseen. He had the glove . . . your glove!"

"Yes, that was my glove."

"Oh, heavens," Mary whispered, as it all tumbled together. "And he found you?"

"I'm afraid so" she whispered, a painful note to her words.

That didn't sound good. "Hermione, what has happened?"

"That's why I'm here. I can't find him."

"Rockhurst?"

"Yes. Not since the other night, when Rowan died."

Rowan? Mary's knees rocked beneath her as Hermione's words sank in. She reached for the high-backed chair nearby to steady herself. "Rowan is lost? When? How?"

"Oh, Mary it was awful. Horrible," Hermione said, a ragged sob cutting off her words.

"You poor dear," Mary said. "Sit and tell me what happened." For she needed to sit as well, her legs were about to give way. Rowan lost? A Paratus without his wolfhound? It was unheard of.

And what else had Hermione said?

I can't find him.

A black fear filled her heart. For without a Paratus to safeguard the city, mayhem could ensue.

But it was more than that. Rockhurst was her cousin. Her blood. And without him . . .

Then she became conscious of Hermione's voice coming from the sofa, so Mary sank into her chair and turned her attention to the story Hermione was telling.

"Four nights ago. In an alley near Grosvenor Square—"

As Hermione's story unfolded, Mary's fears grew more piercing.

Rockhurst had never really trusted his heart—perhaps it was the fact that he knew his fate would eventually entwine any woman he married—leaving her a legacy of an early widowhood. Nights spent wondering if he was coming home. Odd callers at all hours. Or worse, living each day with the fear that the man she loved, had promised her heart to, was in mortal danger from his enemies.

Instead, he'd flitted away his years with courtesans and in blithe dalliances with women who could never touch his heart.

And now if what Mary suspected was true, he'd lost his heart and lost Rowan as well. She doubted her proud, stubborn cousin would ever admit to the pain inside him . . . or that the love he'd avoided so studiously could now be the only thing possibly to save him.

And without even being able to see her friend, Mary knew Hermione loved him. Now she only hoped she could help.

And there was only one way to find out. Mary glanced over at the chair where Hermione sat. "I know where to find him."

An hour later, Hermione glanced over her shoulder at Mary's carriage as it pulled away from St. Paul's, thankful for the ride that had brought her here from Mayfair but wishing she possessed more of Mary's certainty that Rockhurst would be here. Especially as she gazed up to the very top of the cathedral, towering like a behemoth into the night sky.

She made her way to the side door Mary had promised

would be open, and it was, and once inside, she walked down the main aisle toward the magnificent center dome.

I can do this. Yes, I can do this, she told herself, even as she glanced at the great stone tombs and soaring ceilings shrouded in darkness.

And what if Mary is wrong? And he isn't here? a little voice, edged in fear, piped up. *Then what will you do?*

"He must be here," she told herself.

"Hello? Is someone there?" One of the young priests held up a candlestick. "Is someone there?"

Hermione stilled, her lips pressed together.

"There is no one there, Simon," an older voice called out. "You are hearing things."

Undeterred, Simon held the candle higher. "I swear, monsignor, I heard steps and a voice."

"You'll hear those all your life in this place," the old man said. He came forward and patted Simon on the shoulder. "'Tis the nature of the Lord's house to welcome all those who come here."

"Even him?" he whispered, nodding to one side of the center dome, where Hermione could see a door cracked open.

Right where Mary said it would be.

"His lordship most especially. He keeps us all safe and from things more unearthly than your phantom footsteps." The man sighed. "We owe him sanctuary when he asks."

She shivered and closed her eyes. Rockhurst. They were talking about him. Hermione didn't know if she was relieved finally to have found him, or terrified at the prospect of what she needed to do next.

Oh, jiminy! she cursed as she glanced again at the

doorway. Why couldn't he have a more sensible place to go soothe his soul, say like Gunter's? Didn't he know a good bowl of ices had remarkable restorative powers?

But this? She shuddered as she slipped quietly through the door and looked up. Candles fluttered in their sconces, twisting up and into the darkness.

All the way to the very top of the cathedral.

"For Rockhurst," she whispered, as she took first one step, then another. Up and into the very sky of London.

Rockhurst sat on his perch and let the rain fall on him. He was damp all the way through already, so what would a few more drops do?

As he stared out over the rooftops of London, he wondered how many times he'd come up here. Most of them he remembered with aching poignancy. When he'd killed for the first time. When his father had died. When he'd found Podmore. . .

There had been so many other times as well, lost in the images of his life, events that he'd rather forget.

But this time, this time was different. Usually after a few hours up here, even through an entire night, the sun would rise, and he'd find himself filled again with purpose, with hope.

A sense that this new day would be different.

Of course, all those other times, he'd descended down the stairs and ladders to find Rowan waiting for him, usually gnawing away at a bone one of the younger vicars had nicked from the rectory kitchen for the friendly hound.

But this time there would be no great tail wagging, no swipe of his rough tongue on the earl's hand to welcome him back to earth, back from his sanctuary in the sky.

This time the only thing different would be the fact that his companion and protector wouldn't be there.

And his days? His sense of hope?

"Demmit," he muttered. What were the sum total of his days and nights? Death and destruction. What sort of existence was that? What kind of legacy to leave?

He stared moodily into the inky darkness. Whatever had Thomas of Hurst been thinking?

Rockhurst made an inelegant snort. He knew exactly what the fellow had been thinking if family legend was true.

The idiot had been seduced by a beautiful woman.

So apparently he wasn't too far removed from the family tree.

He groaned, thinking himself twice the fool Thomas had been.

"Rockhurst?" came a soft voice.

Shadow! He twisted around, without any reserve, without the cool detachment he'd spent the last three days hoping to find when it came to her. He listened to her tentative steps as they drew closer, but she stopped well out of his reach—which was telling in itself.

"Is it *you*?" she whispered.

He knew exactly what she was asking. Had he shaken off the darkness that had consumed him that night?

"I've been worried," she continued. "Terribly so."

But she came no closer, proof she feared him now.

Good. That was how it should be.

"Please say something."

"What the hell are you doing up here?"

There was a small laugh. "I barely know myself. Why couldn't you have found some sensible place to go lick your wounds? Like Almack's or Vauxhall? Did you have to pick some place so high?"

He wanted to smile, for she was still, after all she'd seen the other night, the blithe and light spirit he loved.

He loved?

In a blinding moment of revelation, he nearly toppled from the ledge. He *loved* this woman. Loved her so thoroughly, so terribly.

"Just go away." He waved toward the door behind her. "You don't want to be here."

"You're right about that," she shot back. A feminine little sigh escaped her, and her footsteps came closer to where he sat. "Won't you come down off that ledge and at least face me?"

"What does it matter? I can't very well see you." He turned his head in her direction, and suddenly he longed to. Like nothing he'd ever wanted before.

He wanted to see her. To see that pert nose that he'd covered with kisses, to see the color of her hair—tresses like silk, but ones he wanted to see spread out over his sheets. He wanted to know whether or not she had freckles. He'd wager his house in Cheshire that she did.

And he wanted to see her eyes. The green ones Cricks had called magical. "Green," he muttered like a curse.

"Pardon?" she whispered, closer than he ever suspected she'd venture.

Then he caught a whiff of her perfume on the night wind, and it wound through his senses like a favorite memory. "Your eyes, that's all I know. They're green."

"Just green. Nothing special."

He leaned back and closed his eyes. *Green*. That he could see. And he had to imagine her eyes were as mysterious as quicksilver—as she was to him.

"Will you come down now?" she asked. "Please, Rockhurst."

He shook his head. Stubbornly. For if he came down, he was afraid of her hold over him. She might even be able to make him forget. Or at least ease this pain in his chest.

And he couldn't have that. Not now.

"Whyever not? You look soaked to the bone, and you'll most likely end up with a chill . . . or worse."

He snorted. "I never get sick. I'm the Paratus. Remember?"

She sighed. "How could I forget?"

No, how could she? He'd made damned sure of that the other night when he'd butchered Dubhglas's brothers. Made them pay for their crime like he'd never done before.

The sight of Rowan's limp, lifeless body had ignited a madness inside his heart. The madness she'd kindled the night they'd made love in his bedchamber. But Rowan's death had brought forth a different force. It had unleashed a black, dangerous power that had given him a strength he'd never known he possessed. And without any thought to the consequences, he'd used it.

Used it without remorse, for even now, he wouldn't change a thing. He'd kill them all again just as ruthlessly.

And now he feared not only for himself, but her.

He'd nearly killed her.

His head turned toward her. "You're well? I didn't—"

"I'm unharmed."

He didn't believe her, for he'd heard the catch in her voice as she'd spoke. "You were bleeding."

"It was merely a scratch."

"Carpio never leaves a mere scratch." That thought, above all the others, had been the one that had kept him awake these past few nights.

Killed his Shadow. Caused her harm. He wondered how cursed he'd be then?

"How did you explain it to your mother . . . to your family?" Rockhurst asked.

"I didn't have to. In the morning the cut was healed. There isn't even a scar."

He shook his head, for he'd seen the blood.

"I'd show it to you if I could," she insisted. "Your cousin said it was most likely because of the ring. That the same magic that makes you the Paratus forged this ring, and therefore protects me. Of course, according to Mr. Podmore, there is the argument to be made that—"

Rockhurst spun off his perch and jumped down onto the parapet so he stood right in front of her. "What did you say?"

"Well, if you'd let me finish," she huffed. "According to Podmore—"

He caught hold of her and held her firmly. "No. Not about that idiot. What you said before. *About my cousin.*"

"Oh." There was a moment's pause. "I'd rather hoped you hadn't heard that."

"You know Mary?"

There was another sigh. "Yes."

"How long has she known?"

"About the ring? Well, it seemed to me that she knew—"

"Not about the ring," he ground out. "About you. How long has my cousin known about *you*?"

"Only since tonight," she confessed. "I went to her when I couldn't find you. I just thought, well I hoped that she might . . ."

"Might know where I'd hied myself off to?"

"Yes."

Of course Mary would know. How many times had she come up here herself and fetched him down? Hell, he'd brought her up when they were just children, having sneaked them both away from their governesses and landed themselves in a vast amount of trouble. But he'd never forgotten the light in Mary's eyes as they'd gazed over the city. His domain, he'd boasted to her. And she'd smiled up at him, in that unassuming way of hers, and nodded happily, quite content and willing to let him have it.

He might not have shown this chit the way, but she had followed him as innocently as Mary had all those long years ago. Trusting that he would keep her safe, even despite her fears.

"She said to tell you," his little Shadow was saying, "that she would have come herself had she known . . ." She paused for a moment, then spoke with a catch in her voice. ". . . about Rowan, that is. She's bereft. Everyone is."

"Everyone?"

"Of course." She pulled her arms free of his grasp and laid her hands on his chest, and then tucked her head into the corner of his shoulder. The warmth from her touch caught him off guard, and he shivered. She sighed and nestled closer to him. "Your staff is beside themselves with worry. It is all they speak of. And your Aunt Routledge—she's about to summon Bow Street. She's called three times a day, if not more. She's quite bedeviled Stogdon, for she thinks he knows something of your whereabouts and isn't being forthright with her."

"Then perhaps it is better I've been up here," he said. "I'm safe from her meddling."

"No, I daresay she has more sense than to make such a climb. Even for you."

He laughed as well, though he felt no humor. "How do you know about my aunt, about my staff?"

She didn't answer, but she needn't have, for it occurred to him readily enough. He stepped out of the warmth she offered and held her at arm's length. "You've been prying around my house at night!"

"Well, I would hardly call it prying . . . like your aunt, I've been worried sick over your disappearance." She huffed a sigh and moved right back up against his chest. As if she had every right to be there. "Poor Stogdon looks as if he has aged ten years in the past few days," she chastened, as if she had the right to do that as well.

If the warmth of her body touched him, her concern and meddling did so in other ways. "Stogdon's haggard appearance is probably due to the repeated visits of my aunt."

"You cannot make light of this, Rockhurst. Your staff loves you. And they are just as hurt and grief-stricken as you are."

This time she cut him to the quick.

He shook his head and looked up into the cloud-filled sky. He didn't want to hear about their grief. His own was crushing enough.

Still, she pressed on with her case, like the badgering little solicitor he'd come to know so well. "Your cook, bless her heart, was in the kitchen in tears for she couldn't bring herself to put the entire order of bones that came from the butcher in the soup pot, because it included the extra ones she always ordered for the 'dear wee hound.'"

The gruff and sturdy Mrs. Grant? Buying extra cuts of meat on the sly for Rowan? He didn't know what to think, especially after all the years of listening to her complain about Rowan tracking mud into her kitchen and stealing scraps.

His Shadow sniffed and swiped at her face.

Then he realized her tears weren't the only ones falling.

"And two of the house maids took up a collection from the other servants and bought flowers to make a wreath. It's quite lovely and is hanging in the garden."

He closed his eyes and could see it. Hanging on the wall over the spot where he had . . . His chest tightened until he thought it would crush him.

"You need to go home," she pleaded. "You need to help them grieve."

As they will help you.

"I can't," he told her, forcing the words out. "Not yet."

"Then when?" she persisted, pushing away from him. "How many more must die before you come to your senses?"

"What are you talking about?"

"Cappon has been sending notes every night for you."

"What did the notes say?"

"How would I—"

"Shadow—"

"Well, I might have looked at one of them, but it wasn't meddling, since you weren't there to do anything about it."

"What did they say?" he ground out.

"There have been more killings in the Dials. And the Rookeries as well."

How dare they? his black Paratus heart clamored, as the darkness started to blur his vision. *With the ring you could end this . . .*

He shook that black fury away. "I care not what happens there. It is no longer my concern." He turned his back to her and leaned against the stone railing.

"Not your concern?" She caught hold of his sleeve and spun him around. "Rowan's death should never have happened. But it did. Now you must continue on. There are people who depend upon you." She paused. "People who love you."

"They shouldn't," he said with steely cold.

"But I do," she whispered. "Oh, Rockhurst, please come down from this place. Come with me."

For she has the ring. If you were but to take it . . .

"No," he said, more to the insidious voice inside his head, than to her. "I will not."

"Is this because they killed Rowan?"

How could she ask such a thing? Wasn't the answer obvious?

He turned his back to her again, his gaze flicking

over the city that sprawled out from St. Paul's in all its majesty and glory. In all its sins and failings.

When he didn't answer, she continued, "Oh, Rockhurst. I'll never understand why they had to kill Rowan. Why Rowan?"

Why Rowan? What sort of idiotic question was that? Was this still some sort of madcap game to her? A masquerade meant to entertain? He spun around on her. "They killed Rowan because I couldn't protect him. Because I failed."

He stopped short of the rest of his confession. *Just as one day I would fail you.*

She sucked in a deep breath and stepped back from the fury in his words, the chilled space between them growing wider than the Atlantic.

Good. Why ever had she come here in the first place? Couldn't she see the danger she was in, the little fool? The danger he put her in?

Well, if she couldn't, perhaps he'd make it perfectly clear. He drew out his knife and held it before her. "I killed him as if I'd put this blade to his heart."

"No-o-o," she gasped. "No it wasn't that way. I was there. You hadn't a chance—"

And neither do you. Kill her. Kill her now, and take the ring. The power it holds will change everything. Could save you . . .

"But that's the point," he bellowed. "I hadn't a chance. Not then. Not now. Not as long as that hole is open for those devils to come scurrying through like plague-infested rats." He groaned, raking his hand through his wet hair, his knees sagging beneath him.

She caught hold of him and steadied him. "Then close it," she said, as matter-of-factly as one might decide between one invitation or the next.

"Can't you see? I am only one man. And to stop them, I must . . . I'll have to—"

"Become the Paratus?" she whispered. "As you did when Rowan died."

So she had seen.

A tiny spark of hope blossomed in his chest. *Yet, still she is here. She believes in you.*

But she shouldn't. It was nothing short of suicide. Hadn't she witnessed what they'd done to Rowan?

And what he'd done in return?

What he might do to gain the ring if this dark voice inside his head triumphed?

"Get out of here," he told her, pointing at the door. "Get out of here and go back home. Go back to your *maman* and stay there."

"I will not," she argued, standing her ground. "I'll not be ordered around like Tunstall or Cricks or any of your other loyal subjects. I am not under your rule."

Not under his rule, was she? The darkness crept into his chest, twined around his heart. "Everyone one in this city is subject to my rule, whether they know it or not."

"Jiminy, Rockhurst! I think your aunt is right. You've finally gone mad. If you think I'll—"

Mad? He'd show her exactly how mad he'd been driven.

He caught hold of her, for he seemed to have developed a sense of where she was. One hand curled around an arm, the other her waist. He tugged her into his chest and held her fast, ignoring the surprised "*o-o-ooh*" that escaped her lips as she slammed into him. "Mad, am I? And what of you? What were you thinking, coming here?"

Demmed little fool. A debutante tempted by the secrets of the night.

"I was only thinking of you," she managed to gasp.

His heart contracted, but only momentarily. For he tamped down the warmth her confession brought with it, embraced the cold chill that now seeped into his bones.

To be warmed by her would leave him as distracted and weak as he'd been the other night.

This foolish, irresponsible, distracting Mayfair miss needed to be taught a lesson, and he knew how, letting a bit of that darkness creep back into his soul.

"Let go of me," she said, squirming against his tightening grasp. "Rockhurst, unhand me."

Her struggles only fed the black ether, the dangerous threads now cutting off every bit of reason he possessed.

His lips crashed down on hers, and he kissed her with a burning, brutal need. He forced her lips apart and ravished her mouth, devouring her sweet temptation.

Inside his head, the dark raw power howled, seeking this gratification like a blood-lust. He wanted to touch her, all of her. He wanted to taste her, everywhere.

And mostly, he wanted to forget himself between her thighs.

He caught hold of her gown and pulled it up, his hand catching hold of her round buttocks and hauling her right up against his already hard manhood.

She managed a gasp, before she said, "What the devil are you thinking, Rockhurst?"

"I think I am going to fuck you, right here and now."

There was another gasp, this one a little more outraged than the last. "You are mad. You wouldn't dare."

"Wouldn't I?"

He kissed her again, stifling her protests, kissing her until she gasped for air.

"You came up here," he told her. "I told you to leave. I warned you."

He tugged off her pelisse and threw it over the rail. Then opened her gown by cutting her bodice in two, her breasts spilling out. He tossed his knife aside and caught hold of her, leaning down to take the ripe flesh into his mouth, sucking hard on a nipple. His other hand went farther down, until it came to her sex, stroking her until she moaned in submission.

He kissed her anew, nibbling at her ears, her throat, where her pulse beat wildly beneath his lips.

"I am the Paratus," he told her, barely recognizing his own lust-filled voice. "And you will do as I say."

Part of Hermione wanted to rebel, to argue against his arrogant and overbearing presumption. That she was his, his to order and use at his discretion.

But that was the very heart of it. *She was his.*

From the moment she'd put on the ring and wished to know all his secrets, she'd been bound to him like no woman had ever been bound to a man.

So as he tried to bully her, frighten her, use her body, she'd discovered that she possessed a strength of her own.

One well matched to that of the Paratus. For her body sang with passion and desire as he plundered her lips, tore her gown from her body. For he only left her exposed to his rough and heated exploration, left her trembling with ragged desire.

She was no more Lady Hermione Marlowe tonight than he was the Earl of Rockhurst.

"So then fuck me, my lord Paratus," his Shadow told him, her body arching up to meet his ravaging desires. "Take me if you dare."

Her challenge sent his blood coursing in a roar of fire through his veins. His shaft throbbed, ached to find release. She wanted him? She could have him. Without a moment's hesitation, he took her to the tiles, cold and wet from the chilling rain.

She reached up and caught hold of his breeches, pulling them open and freeing him. She caught hold of him and stroked him, her hips rising, her thighs opening, offering him the solace he was seeking.

And he took it. Took her. Plunging himself into her, all the way in one hard, angry movement. It was wrong, and he knew it, but the madness, his grief were devouring him, and he couldn't stop.

Yet there was still some part of him that knew he couldn't do this to her. Not to this woman, and how he did it, he didn't know, but he found the wherewithal to stop, pausing before he plunged into her again.

And then he saw them. Her eyes. They were bright and full of passion. He could almost see her face, a hint of freckles, a full mouth, lush and swollen from his kiss.

But it was her eyes that saved him—for they were full of passion, and desire, and something else.

Something he couldn't name. Something he feared more than death.

Her love.

And when he blinked, and looked again, they were gone, like a trick of light on a hot summer's day. But he could feel her. Her hips rising to meet him. Hear her, as a hungry moan slipped from her lips. Her hands clung to him, wound into his coat and tugging him closer, deeper into her.

He kissed his way up her neck, where her pulse raced with a wild, tremulous beat, up her throat, and to her mouth.

Her tongue tangled with his, stroking him. Reminding him of what she'd dared him to do. *To take her.* His fury came roaring back to life, and he thrust himself into her, hard and fast. She writhed beneath him, encouraging him, calling his name, tugging at him to go deeper, harder.

With each thrust, the darkness became louder, a roar in his head, a dangerous abyss of passion that he wondered how he would ever free himself of.

"Oh, yes, oh, yes, Thomas," she gasped. "Please, please . . . oh, please," she cried out, as her climax crashed over her, the ripples of her body, the wild cadence of her hips, pulling his release from him.

Oh, he was lost. So very lost.

It wasn't long before the chill of the night curbed the heat rising between them. Rockhurst came to his senses in a blinding bolt.

Christ, what had he done?

I'm going to fuck you.

And he had. Taking her without any regard for anything but pleasure.

He scrambled across the wet tiles of the walkway that encircled the top of the cupola and backed away from her.

As much as he wanted her to hate him, to run from him like a bad case of consumption, a very deep thread inside his chest mourned for something else.

For the woman who loved him. For the woman who understood him. All too well.

"I'm . . . I'm . . ." he stammered.

"Sorry?" she replied. "I hope not." There was a purr to her words. "While it certainly wasn't as comfortable as your bed . . . it was exciting." Her clothes rustled as she gathered them up. "Did you really toss my pelisse over the wall? *Harrumph.* Well, I suppose I never liked that one overmuch, but still, Rockhurst, you've quite run my wardrobe ragged. Now where are my shoes? Oh, yes, there's one of them."

She came closer and tugged the boot out from beneath him. Her fingers cupped his chin, and she laid a gentle kiss on his forehead. "Now that you've gotten done with that, are you coming down? There is much to be done before the sun rises."

He closed his eyes and tried to gain his equilibrium, for inside of him, the darkness of the Paratus struggled to wrench away his weakened control. "What do you mean?"

"The hole. We need to find it and close it."

We?! Was she mad? That very ancient Paratus part of him stirred with renewed anger.

Who was she to order him around? "That is none of your concern."

"Of course it is," she shot back. "Now are you coming or not?"

He rose to his feet, stretching his muscles and feeling his strength returning. "You are not a part of this—"

She began to sputter, but he staved her off with a flash of his eyes. "Besides, what do you think you can do?"

"Help." She had that tone in her voice that Aunt Routledge used when she had a particular debutante in mind for him. Oh, yes, he could almost see the fisted hands on her hips and a determined thrust to her chin.

"You? What do you know of these things?"

She huffed a sigh. "Quite a bit, because while you've been up here, I've been reading the rest of Mr. Podmore, and he is quite clear that to close—"

"Podmore!" he exploded. "Haven't you listened to anything I've said? Have you forgotten what happened to Rowan? You will cease this meddling and go home."

"Oh, really, Rockhurst—"

He stalked right up to her. "Do you know what happened to your precious Mr. Podmore?"

"He perished, but he didn't have you with him, and I will."

Her confidence in him, instead of rallying his spirits, only served to anger him more.

Fool. Little stubborn fool, he wanted to shout. But he had a better way to make his point. "Let me tell you how Podmore died." He caught hold of her by both arms. "His limbs were torn off."

She said nothing.

"His eyes gouged out."

Again, silence.

He leaned over and whispered to her in a dark and threatening voice. "And his ears were removed. Bitten off, from the looks of it." When still she didn't say anything, he finished. "And despite all that, he was still alive when I found him. Before I ended his misery."

She shivered. Good. She was finally seeing the folly of "helping."

There was more, words he'd never told anyone, but suddenly they came tumbling out. "It was all my fault. He'd come to me, asking questions, nosing around. And in my foolish youth, I answered them. Shared my family history. Bragged about our exploits, our role in history. I lent him maps, journals, books so old I know not what is written in them. Everything. But I never thought such a mouse of a man would ever . . ." He let go of her and backed away.

"Seek to see it for himself?" she whispered.

All Rockhurst could do was nod. When he finally spoke, the words choked in his throat. "I found him. I'd never seen anything so horrible, and it was all my fault. He'd never been to London before, had spent most of his life holed up in the libraries of Oxford. What could he have been thinking?"

"I don't know," she whispered, seeking him out, her hands smoothing over his sleeve.

"There was nothing I could do when I found him. Nothing left to do but to draw out Carpio and finish him." He tried to breathe, but his throat constricted at the memory, his heart pounding with the same fear that had gripped him that night.

"You ended his suffering—"

"I took a human life."

"He made his choice, he had to have known—" she argued.

"I should never have let him in. I should have sent him packing back to Oxford the moment he dared knock at my door. And I vowed that night I would never make that mistake again."

But her courage—nay, her stubborn foolishness—astounded him. "Someone must close that hole," she persisted, returning to her original argument. "And we can do it together, if you would but read what Mr. Podmore—"

He shook her. "We? There is no 'we.' You are nothing to me but a hindrance and a distraction. The very reason that—" He stopped, right there and then, catching hold of the darkness threatening him, but it was too late.

For she knew exactly what he meant.

"That Rowan is dead," she whispered. Now it was his turn to stand there in stubborn silence. "Don't you think I know that?"

He took a deep breath. For the wolfhound's death wasn't her fault. It was his.

As her death would be if she continued persisting in following him.

"Go home," he told her. "Go home now."

"I will not. Not until you tell me that we are going to close that hole. Together."

Blinding rage filled his ears, tore his reason in half. "Demmit, woman, I order you to leave this be!" he thundered.

But his outburst was met with only silence.

"Shadow?" he barked out, crossing the distance that had separated them, his hands waving wildly before him, in search of her. "Shadow! Don't be a fool. Leave this be. Do you hear me?"

But she didn't. For she was gone, and he might as well shout his impotent orders into the wind.

His fists crashed down on the ledge and he let loose with a string of curses.

Then, as if to aggravate him just that much more, a hint of her perfume tickled at his nose. His eyes snapped open, and he looked around, half-expecting to see her standing before him.

His wild, mad little Shadow.

But there was nothing before him but the sleeping city of London, spreading out all around him for as far as the eye could see.

His city. His domain. His responsibility.

"Demmit." The little idiot was going to end up as lost as Rowan, or, God help him, Podmore.

He sucked in a deep breath, the images of that horrific night sending a spike of terror through him.

"Shadow," he whispered, taking a step toward the doorway, but found his legs failing him as he wavered back and forth. He turned and looked over the city. He wasn't ready to leave this haven in the sky just yet. But he must.

The shadows in the night demanded it.

Hermione fell to her knees outside the steps of St. Paul's and began to sob. Oh, everything had gone so terribly wrong.

"There now, there now," came Quince's familiar voice. The lady's hand caught hold of hers and pulled her up to her feet.

"Quince, you must end all this. I've made a terrible muddle of all this. I killed Rowan, I've made a mess of everything, and he despises me. He'll never . . . can never . . ."

Forgive me . . . love me.

Quince heaved a sigh and dug a handkerchief out of her reticule. "There now, there now. It cannot be as bad as all that."

"He insists on closing the hole himself. He'll be lost if he tries. Without me, without Rowan at his back, he will be lost."

Quince pressed her lips together and glanced up at the top of St. Paul's. "Then he must have help."

"If only Rowan hadn't died," Hermione sobbed. "It was all my fault."

Leading her away from the great cathedral, Quince handed her a handkerchief. "A Paratus without his wolfhound. I don't think I've ever heard of such a thing. You have every right to be worried."

Hermione glanced up at the towering cathedral. "Then if he won't accept my assistance, I'll find someone's help he will take."

Fifteen

Rockhurst spent the better part of the next week searching for the hole—and tamping down any thought of *her*. Horrible reports reached his ears of killings so foul, they could only be the work of derga. So as each day drew closer and closer to sunset, a deep fear settled into his chest.

Of the night when the horrors of that other realm would overrun his world . . . and he would be helpless to stop it.

Worse yet, each report brought the creeping chill of darkness inside him, its cold fingers threatening to overtake his soul. He could unleash it, and with it, he suspected he'd find the hole and close it, banishing the derga and Melaphor forever.

But however would he find his way back out of that abyss?

He'd be lost forever, and there would be no one else

to battle the evil that constantly threatened London.

For they always found a new way through the fabric that separated them.

Rockhurst paced up and down his armory, Carpio in hand. What the hell was he going to do?

Cappon had Tibbets out searching, but so far the little man had found no clues. Even Mary, who had helped him countless times before with her scholarly prowess, refused him support. Of course, it didn't help that he'd demanded she tell him who his Shadow was and that she'd refused. He'd stormed and raged about her library, threatened to burn every one of her books if she didn't reveal the secret she held fast.

Not that Mary believed a word of his bluster. And when he'd become unreasonable, she'd sent him packing as only she could and told him not to set foot in her house again.

And to add insult to injury, she'd given him a copy of Podmore on his way out the door and advised him to read it.

Read Podmore! As if he had time for such idle pursuits. The man had ended up scattered across the four corners of Seven Dials, and Rockhurst had no intention of sharing his hideous fate.

He'd even sent a note to the man who'd sold him Rowan, looking for another wolfhound, for the dogs were rare and hard to find. But the man had written back that he had no more such hounds.

It seemed the breed was all but lost, and Rockhurst understood their plight, for he felt sure he was about to share it.

And his Shadow? She'd disappeared as well. After his raging behavior atop St. Paul's, he wondered if she'd ever come near him again. Oh, he'd been an idiot. In so many ways.

He paced back and forth through the armory that made up what was once probably intended as a ballroom, eating up the length of the cavernous room in great, impatient strides, racking his brain for any memory or legend of how to defeat this enemy.

Unaided and alone.

"My lord," Stogdon called out from the doorway. "There is someone to see you."

"Is it Cappon?"

Stogdon's nose pinched. Rockhurst's butler had a deep-seated aversion for the flamboyant brothel owner. "No, my lord. It is a young lady."

Without even hesitating, Rockhurst glanced at the window, where the sun was just about to set, the last twinkling of light still holding fast to the day. A shock of disappointment ran though him.

For he still hadn't given up one small bit of hope that she would . . . might . . .

"My lord—" Stogdon nudged ever-so-patiently.

He wrenched his gaze from the window. No, this visitor couldn't be his Shadow, for she'd never come to the door. The wretched minx would come strolling in, bold as brass, and without any invitation.

"Send her away," Rockhurst said. "I'll not be subject to some marriage-mad matron's plan to trap me."

Instead of leaving, Stogdon stood his ground. "My lord, I think you should see *this* young lady."

He was about to argue when a deep "*woof*" rang through the house. A bark as familiar and beloved as the house itself.

Rowan?

Rockhurst stormed past his butler and went tearing down the hall. Even as he skidded to a stop, he found himself being happily mauled by a wolfhound.

At first he thought by some miracle Rowan was alive, but this dog was larger, more muscular, but just as energetic and active as Rowan had ever been.

"Sit," he ordered, and the dog did, looking up at him with those big, brown eyes, eager to please and ready for any command.

A wolfhound! He couldn't believe it. And one, which from the looks of his sharp gaze, held all the intelligence and intuition that Rowan had claimed.

"Teague," a familiar voice said to him.

"What?" he said, glancing up, noticing for the first time the young lady across the way. She stood with her back to him, her lofty bonnet concealing her features.

She might have her back to him, but he knew who she was.

"Shadow?" He rubbed his arms, for they were now covered in goose-flesh. He couldn't quite believe she'd come to him.

"The dog's name is Teague," she repeated, without turning around. She reached out and straightened a bowl on the curio table. "He's Rowan's brother. I apologize for taking so long to bring him here, but it took some work to find him. Mary gave me the name and directions of the man who sold you Rowan, so I sought him out."

"But he has no more dogs," Rockhurst said, staring still at Teague.

"True enough, so I asked him if there were other dogs from the same litter. And with some persuasion, he told me so I could seek those dogs out."

He gaped at her. Why hadn't he thought of that? Of course, he'd only sent a note, an order. His Shadow had made it her mission.

She continued her story. "I believe he'll be perfect for the challenges ahead. The farmer I bought him from was all too glad to be rid of him. Claimed the dog spent most of his nights barking at shadows."

Rockhurst looked down at the dog and grinned. Just like Rowan. "Welcome, Teague, to the League of the Paratus."

The dog wagged its tail and looked as happy and contented as Rowan used to when he would spy a derga on the loose.

Or a good beef bone for the taking.

He glanced up and found Stogdon dashing back tears and furiously wiping his nose lest any of the staff see him in such a state. But no matter, word of the dog's arrival had spread, and from every door and crack peeked members of the earl's household, all there to welcome the newest member.

"Come along with ye, ye bunch of lazy good-for-nothings," Mrs. Grant said, as gruff and formidable as always. She hustled her help back down toward the kitchen, but then stopped and glanced at Teague. "Well, what are you waiting for you mud-dragging, eat-us-clean-from-the-cellar-to-the attic hound! I've got just the bone for you. Come along now," she said, wiping the tears from her eyes with her apron.

Teague took one glance at Rockhurst, who nodded for him to go, and the dog dashed past the cook straight for the kitchen.

"Oh, aye," Mrs. Grant said, shaking her finger at Rockhurst as if he were still a lad in short coats, "this one will make the butcher rich and happy, that he will."

And then she shooed her staff along, while Stogdon, following her lead, sent the footman and maids scattering.

And then he and his Shadow were alone.

"Where have you been?" he asked.

"I thought I explained it. You wouldn't believe the state of my boots from tramping about to one farm after another—"

"I'll buy you a shopful," he offered.

"You shall. I had a devil of a time finding a dog for you." She shifted again, this time turning slightly, but then stopped as she must have realized what she was about to do. "People quite gape at you when you explain you want a mad wolfhound. Rather like mixing capucine silk with primrose ribbons."

He laughed, for she was still his minx. "Shadow, turn around for me." He held his breath, but he might as well have been whistling at the moon.

"Still think you can order me around?" It was her turn to laugh, but worse, she shook her head and refused him.

From his vantage point, he could see her chin, just as he'd imagined it, determined and set.

"When will you learn that you may command London, my lord, but not me?"

The earl took a deep breath. "Please." God, he'd never wanted anything more than to see her face. The night atop St. Paul's, the vision of her that he had seen was like a hazy dream he couldn't quite trust.

"I can't," she said, taking a step toward the door.

He caught her before she could slip through it. He'd nearly lost her the other night, he wasn't about to repeat that mistake.

"Please, let me see you."

She shook her head. "I don't want to see the disappointment in your eyes. The other night . . . well, that was enough. Believe me, you don't want to know who I am."

But he did, and he didn't care what she mistakenly thought or feared. Be disappointed in her? How could he be?

He knew exactly who she was.

The woman who had stolen his heart.

His fingers tightened around her wrist, the warmth of her skin flowing through him, stealing at the chill that had descended over him since the night he'd . . . Rockhurst closed his eyes.

Since the night he'd lost Rowan.

"Let me go," she whispered. "Please. I must—"

She trembled beneath his grasp, and he opened his eyes to find himself looking into an empty space. His gaze shot to the open door, where the deep red fingers of a glorious sunset stretched high in the sky.

He might still be holding her, but she'd disappeared.

"Demmit," he cursed, unwilling to release her, for fear she'd be gone before he could . . .

He could what? Beg her forgiveness? Ask her to stay with him?

Nothing had changed. The hole remained open, and she was still in danger.

Hell, everyone was until he . . . until he did what he'd been ordained to do since birth.

And he was about to tell her so, when a hackney pulled up in front of his house. Cappon climbed out, the carriage swaying back and forth with his great girth. Dressed in a flamboyant bottle green gown and hat, the driver nearly fell out of his perch when Cappon began cursing him like a sailor for taking so long to get to Mayfair.

"Bugger!" the brothel owner muttered as he stalked up the stairs toward the front door. "Oh, there you are, my lord. My apologies for coming directly to you and not sending word, but Tibbets is missing, and I fear the worst."

Rockhurst let go of Hermione the moment Cappon shared his bad news, and she took advantage of his unwitting (or intentional) lapse to shrink away into the corner.

Little Tibbets lost?

Hermione trembled, for she knew what this news meant. She'd lied to Rockhurst before. She hadn't been away the entire time. In fact, she'd spent just last night watching him from the confines of the high-backed armchair in the armory. She was all too aware that Cappon's rattish assistant was their last hope for finding the hole.

Now their talented spy was missing, and there was no one else. No one save . . .

Hermione backed straight into the wall and let out a little, "Oh my."

Both men turned, Cappon staring at the space with a surprised look on his face, but Rockhurst's sharp gaze missed nothing.

"Wait here," he told Cappon. He strode over to the door that led down to the kitchens and whistled loudly. Almost immediately there was a great *woof* and the hard patter of large paws against the wooden steps.

Teague arrived in a flurry of anxious power.

Cappon's jaw dropped. "That ain't—" he gasped, pointing at Teague. "But I thought—"

"This is Teague," Rockhurst told him, giving the big beastie a ruffle on his head. "A gift from a friend."

"And I thought that other wretched beastie of yours was big. That one is a monster."

"Let's hope so," Rockhurst said, glancing down at the dog. "Stogdon!" he bellowed for his butler.

"Yes, my lord?" the good man called out, reappearing, as he always did, with sudden alacrity.

"Tell Tunstall to get off his arse and fetch my carriage. The phaeton! And bring it with the grays." He winked at the corner where she stood, before he strode off toward the armory, most likely to fetch his bag of wares.

The phaeton? Hermione fumed. There would only be room for the earl and Cappon. Then Teague would take up the rest of the space, leaving her . . . well, behind.

Oh, no he wasn't! She went marching after him, but when she turned the corner into the armory, he caught her, his arm snaking around her waist and catching hold of her in his vise-like grasp.

"Let go of me," she sputtered.

"Not until I have you safely locked away," he told her.

Hermione twisted and turned in his grasp, fighting him with every step he took. "You bugger!" she said, having not the least bit of shame quoting Cappon.

"That is exactly why you are not coming with me," he said. "Such language! Such manners you've picked up. Your *maman* would be shocked."

"Ooooh, Thomas, let me go," she said, as she tried to pry his fingers off her as she realized his intent.

He'd opened the hidden closet where he kept his best weapons. Pulling out the great black bag with his free hand, he then shoved her inside.

"Don't do this!" she cried out, rushing toward the door, but it was too late, he slammed it shut in her face. She beat against the door. "You need my help. Without Mr. Tibbets, you cannot think to do this alone. You must take me."

"You are right, Shadow," he said through the keyhole. "I do need you. But I won't release you. Not now. Not until the morning."

"But then it could be too late," she cried, sinking to her knees, the hot sting of tears leaving a trail down her cheeks.

"Have faith, little Shadow," he whispered. "You know who I am."

She did. And how she wished she didn't.

Rockhurst was nearly down the front steps when, to his dismay, he found his cousin Mary and Cricks blocking his path. "Mary, I haven't time for this," he told her as he tossed his bag into the tiger's seat. Teague followed, taking his place, just as Rowan always had, and for a moment, a light of hope warmed in his chest.

Perhaps he could . . .

"Rockhurst, you will listen to me," she managed, after taking an astonished glance at the hound. "I came across something important, and Cricks agrees with me." She leaned closer, and whispered, "Is *she* here?"

"No." He glanced over at Cappon. "Well, what are you waiting for? Get in."

Cappon eyed the dangerously fast phaeton, with its high-sprung wheels and narrow seat, not to mention the pair of horses that pranced and danced in their traces, as if they couldn't wait to take off on a wild ride. "And I thought the Dials would kill me," he muttered as he climbed up and into the seat.

Rockhurst went to sidestep his cousin, but Mary was too fast and was already in front of him. Again.

"You must take her," she insisted. "Find her and bring her along. She's—"

"Been safely seen to," he told her. "I'm not taking some Mayfair miss down into the Dials."

"You did before," Mary argued.

"Unwittingly," he replied. "But this time is different. Mary, I won't have her harmed." He glanced up at the house. "I've seen to that, and I'll brook no argument on the subject."

Not that Mary was opposed to disagreeing with him, order or not. "Rockhurst, don't be an idiot. You *cannot* do this alone."

Cricks added, "My lord, if you would but read Podmore, along with the volume we believe was his source—" The man paused for a moment and glanced over at Mary. "Does he read ancient Gaelic?"

Mary shook her head.

"No matter," Cricks told him. "Miss Kendell can translate. It is imperative—"

"It is imperative I go." The brows rose, and he sent his most imperious glance at the bookseller, who scurried behind Mary.

His cousin stood firm, unscathed. "You cannot go alone."

"I am not," he told her, moving her firmly out of his path. He climbed into the curricle. "I have Teague." A rough cough from beside him prompted him to add, "And Mr. Cappon's able assistance. Now go back to your books, Mary."

She groaned. "Did you at least read the volume of Podmore I gave you?"

"I did not," he replied. "I burned the damned thing." Then he snatched up the reins and gave the grays their freedom, letting the pair take off at a wicked pace.

There was an outraged gasp from Cricks, while Mary growled and stomped her foot in rage. "That idiot!"

"To burn such a rare book—" Cricks agreed.

"No, not about the book, about going alone. Whatever are we to do?"

"There is nothing to do but to find the young lady." Cricks blinked owlishly at the growing night. "But I fear it will be hard to do now."

Mary sighed, trying to think of how they could find Hermione now that the sun had set.

Then she glanced up at her cousin's house. What was it Rockhurst had said about Hermione?

That she'd been "safely seen to."

"She's in the house," she announced, already halfway up the steps.

"But Miss Kendell, how can you be sure?"

"I'm sure," Mary told him, barging in without ringing for Stogdon.

Cricks followed, looking around the well-appointed house with an eye of fear. "Won't we be cast out?"

"Hardly," she told him.

"And how do you propose to find her?"

"Mr. Cricks, I spent a good part of my childhood in this house playing hide-and-seek. There isn't a closet, cubbyhole, or hiding spot I don't know."

"It's a rather large house," he said, following her toward the armory.

"Then best we start quickly," she told him.

Even before Rockhurst came to a stop before the peacock-emblazoned door of Cappon's brothel, he knew something was wrong.

So did Teague, for the dog growled in a deep, menacing rumble.

"I don't like this," Cappon declared, climbing down from his seat. "I don't like this at all."

"Nor do I," Rockhurst agreed, his eyes narrowing as he scanned the empty streets around them. He nodded to Teague, who leapt down from his perch and immediately began circling the phaeton, growling and looking in all directions, as if he couldn't figure out exactly where to go.

Rockhurst felt it also, a sense of being ensnared on all sides. Then he drew a deep breath and got down as well, hauling his bag with him. With haste born from the way the hairs on the back of his neck were standing at attention, he pulled it open and started arming himself—the long knives into his waistband, the pistols beside them. He tucked a garrote into a pocket and an extra knife into the top of his boot. He slung his cross-bow over his shoulder and, finally, rose from the dirty sidewalk with Carpio in hand.

"Christ!" Cappon exclaimed. "What fool would cross your path now?"

Rockhurst grinned. "Remember me thusly when you think to lighten the tribute you owe me."

The faux madame raised his gloved hand, and said, "Never again, my lord. Never again."

Then from around a corner came the patter of feet, and all three of them turned, Teague leaping forward and putting himself in front of his new master.

"Tibbets!" Cappon exclaimed at the sight of his lost servant. "You've come back."

As the little man moved into the light, Teague growled furiously at him—unwilling to let the man close.

And Tibbets froze, having found himself face-to-face with an angry wolfhound. His tiny chest heaved up and down, as if he'd just run across London, while tears ran down his cheeks.

"Tell that idiot dog to leave him be," Cappon shouted. "Can't you see he's been hurt."

True enough, for one of Tibbet's eyes was swollen shut, and a gash on his head was black with dried blood.

"'Tis probably the blood," Rockhurst said, catching hold of Teague and hauling him back.

Cappon shook his head, then rushed to his favorite servant and hugged him close. The giant madame sobbed, as did Tibbets, at this unbelievable homecoming. "Oh, Tibby, I thought I'd lost you for certain."

"Almost I fear," the little man said. "I didn't think I'd get here in time."

"In time?" Rockhurst asked.

"Oh aye, my lord!" Tibbets gasped. "You must come quick, I've found the hole."

"Show me," Rockhurst said, pointing Carpio in the direction the man had come.

And Tibbets would have gone ahead if Cappon hadn't stopped him, catching hold of his "Tibby" and refusing to let go of him. "No he won't," he protested. "He's been hurt. Tibby, you need to be seen to. I won't have you lost again."

Tibbets shrugged himself free and tried to smile for Cappon's benefit. "It ain't so bad as what will happen to all of us if his nibs here don't come right now and close that bugger of a hole."

"Right you are," Rockhurst told him. "Can you show me where it is?"

"Oh, no you won't!" Cappon trilled.

"I gotta," the man said. "I'm the only one what knows where it is."

"Then let's go," Rockhurst said, as Tibbets scurried toward one of the alleys.

"You lose me my Tibby, Rockhurst, and there will be no tribute this month," Cappon told them, completely rooted in place. "Or the next," he added furiously.

"Go on and count it out," Rockhurst told him, locking a bolt into place on the cross-bow. "I'll be back for it soon enough. With Tibbets."

"If you live," Cappon muttered under his breath as he climbed the stairs into his brothel.

Tibbets, after one last look of longing toward the peacock door that Cappon was slamming shut, scurried toward the dark alley, with Teague and Rockhurst bringing up the rear.

They wound through the shadows of the Dials, around corners and down streets that Rockhurst wondered if they ever saw the light of day.

Finally, Tibbets turned a sharp corner and one more before they came to a dead end. There was no way forward and only one way back.

The ill ease that had been nudging Rockhurst's senses came to full alert. Teague didn't even bother to bark, he just laid his ears back and growled quietly—as if the dog feared awakening the unseen evils all around them.

Rockhurst didn't think he'd ever seen this corner of London. "Tibbets, what is this place?"

He glanced over his shoulder at the little man, to find his one good eye now glowed a horrible red.

"The place you'll breathe your last," Tibbets said as he drove a knife into a chink in the bricks.

Rockhurst surged forward to stop him, but it was too late. The rat-faced traitor twisted his knife as one would a key, and with it, opened the flood gates to hell.

"Open this door," Mary yelled out, hammering on Cappon's peacock doors with all her might. When no one answered over the loud music and laughter inside, she turned to Hermione. "Are you sure this is the correct place?"

Having been freed by her friend and Mr. Cricks from Rockhurst's armory, Hermione had insisted they bring her to Cappon's.

"I fear so," Hermione said, adding her own fists to the pounding. "Open up now!" she shouted.

The door opened, but merely a crack, and Cappon himself peered through it. He took one look at Mary in her plain brown gown and ugly bonnet and his eyes grew wide.

"If you are looking for work—I don't think even I could sell you, but if you are looking for something else—"

"I am looking for my cousin—" Mary began.

"Your cousin isn't here," he told her, trying to close the door, but Hermione had the forethought to stick her boot in the crack.

Cappon frowned when the door wouldn't close.

"I need to find my cousin," Mary repeated. "I know he is here."

"But I doubt he wants to be found," Cappon told her. "And not here." The giant man in the green silk dress looked her up and down again. "And not by you." He drew the door back and, this time, slammed it closed.

As it hit Hermione's foot, she yelped in pain and drew it back.

"This will never do," Mary complained, as she retreated down the steps. "Why, of all the inconsiderate—"

Hermione crossed her arms over her chest and stood fast. "Oh, demmit, Mary, this isn't the time to use Mayfair manners."

"Hermione!" Mary gasped at her friend's use of such language. "I fear your association with Rockhurst has tarnished your tongue! What would your mother say if she heard you cursing like a—"

. . . your association with Rockhurst . . .

Hermione turned around and hammered on the door with all her might. "Open this door in the name of the Paratus or so help me—"

When the door swung open this time, it revealed Cappon holding a cudgel.

Hermione yelped and scurried down the steps to Mary's side.

"Who are you?" Cappon asked, shaking the fearsome-looking weapon at Mary. "And how do you know about him?"

Mary's mouth flapped open, and she stammered a bit, that is until Hermione nudged her sharply in the ribs.

"Tell him who you are," she whispered.

"I'm Lord Rockhurst's cousin, and it is imperative that I find him." Hermione nudged Mary again. "Immediately," she hastily added.

Cappon cocked his head. "I do remember you on his steps. And I also remember he didn't seem overly fond of seeing you."

"Tell him about the trap. Tell him Rockhurst is in danger," Hermione whispered.

But she needn't have bothered, for just then the entire night sky lit up as a massive explosion rocked the Dials.

The proprietor crossed himself and muttered some quick prayer. Then he glanced down at Mary, "I think you've found him."

* * *

In the shadows near the explosion, there glowed a pair of red eyes. The creature behind them would have smiled, but there was too much work ahead to celebrate just yet.

Melaphor had been waiting too long for this day— now finally all his plans were coming to fruition. Seeding the traitors who thought to overthrow him, planting his own spies and surprises. Now he had only a little bit longer, and the last Paratus would be dead.

He glanced up as out of the chaos came the patter of feet running from the destruction. With a smooth, quick movement, he caught the fellow by the scruff of his coat and dragged him up into the air, his small feet pedaling in dismay.

"Let me down, let me down," the fellow complained.

"Ah, my good man, Tibbets," he said as he brought the insignificant fellow up to eye level. "What an excellent job you've done for me. Is it all as we have planned?"

Tibbets settled immediately. "Oh, aye, Master Melaphor," he said enthusiastically. "The Paratus is surrounded, and those fiends are a hungry lot. He's in a devil's own trap, if you don't mind me saying."

"Good work," Melaphor said, glancing in that direction.

"About my payment—" Tibbets began.

But the man's request never finished, for Melaphor had snapped his neck and tossed him into the gutter with the rest of the garbage.

Payment indeed! Certainly, the dwarf had done his task admirably, but Melaphor never rewarded traitors.

Sixteen

Hermione dashed toward the bright light and the sounds of battle. From time to time, Teague's sharp bark or the ugly howl of a derga would pierce the night, which only served to hasten her steps.

Even as the Dials had exploded, she'd pushed Mary and Cricks inside Cappon's and ordered the man to keep them safe. While the brothel owner had gaped at the unseen lady barking orders at him, he hadn't lived in the Dials all his life not to know the face of danger— even an invisible one. With the door shut tight, and after Hermione had heard the bar put in place, she'd gone in search of Rockhurst.

"Saol amháin, grá amháin," she whispered to herself as she went along.

Mary and Cricks had come up with a theory that the

doors to that realm could be closed by using the magic inside Milton's Ring. If Hermione could get it off in time, and Rockhurst used it to seal the door, it would be closed forever, ending the need for a Paratus.

She paused at a corner and tried to get her bearings. Seven Dials certainly wasn't Mayfair, for the streets were so narrow and twisted here it was impossible to find one's way easily. But then she caught sight of an unearthly light and continued on, muttering under her breath the Gaelic words Mary had said she must use.

"Saol amháin, grá amháin," she repeated over and over.

One life, one love. It was a pledge of fidelity, the same one with which the ring had reportedly been forged.

One life, one love. Hermione knew exactly what it meant, for she knew without a doubt that Rockhurst was and would always be her one love.

Oh, if only he has a life left. Lost in her own worries, Hermione stumbled over something and landed with a thud on the filthy cobbles.

"Not another ruined gown," she muttered, vexed that she wasn't going to have a single muslin left before this was over. Not only that, she'd lost about half her hairpins, and now her hair fell in a tumbled mess around her shoulders. This life of a Paratus would never do if one wanted to make a decent appearance. But her fit of pique ended as she rolled to one side and realized what it was that had caught her foot.

An arm.

Tibbets's arm to be exact.

And Tibbets? His eyes stared lifelessly at her.

Hermione opened her mouth to scream, but an icy cold hand clamped over her lips, and another hand caught her under her arm and hauled her up.

"What have we here?" said a cool, smooth voice.

Hermione twisted around to look at her assailant, her breath catching in her throat.

The fiend grinned. "Kitten! How lovely to see you again," Melaphor smoothed her tumbled hair back from her face before he leaned forward and whispered into her ear, "And such a timely arrival. I think you will come in quite handy in aiding me as I kill your beloved Paratus."

Rockhurst knew they could have killed him at any time, but the bastards were just toying with him, wearing him down, coming at him three at a time, then backing off to let the others have a go of it.

Teague had already proved himself half a dozen times over, showing he had the same wits and cunning as Rowan.

But the real battle was going on inside Rockhurst, as the darkness clamored to be set free, to fight these monsters with the aid of a black power that was sure to defeat any foe. Yet Rockhurst resisted. For if he unleashed it, how would he ever find his way out?

Without her . . .

He who had never wanted the help of another. The man who'd roamed London alone, fighting these demons unaided, now realized that being a Paratus was more than being just the sole avenging warrior.

That his forebears, even the infamous Thomas of Hurst, had missed the true meaning of being the Paratus.

That it wasn't enough to be at the ready, it was about being ready. And using every resource available to meet the danger of the dark realm beyond. Which included his Shadow's aid.

Rockhurst laughed, loud and hearty, as he sliced at the derga coming toward him, Carpio taking off the fiend's arm. *Of course, I come to this realization now. When I am about to meet my end.*

If anything, he could do one last thing that would give his death some honor.

He turned to Teague. "Go to her, boy. Go to her and protect her."

The dog stood his ground and barked.

"Go to her," he ordered. "Save her."

Then Rockhurst looked up and realized why Teague wasn't moving. Melaphor stood at the edge of his henchmen, his arm outstretched as if he held something in his grasp. . .no, rather make that *someone*.

And it didn't take eleven hundred years of Paratus wisdom to realize who it was that had Melaphor's smile tipped into such a triumphant curve.

"Let me go," Hermione said, struggling against Melaphor's grasp. There before her was Rockhurst, bleeding from an ugly slash on his arm, and he wavered slightly as he fought off the two derga currently trying to gain the upper hand.

"Why would I want to do that?" He tugged her closer. "You've changed, Kitten." He inhaled deeply. "You have his stench all over you."

Hermione ruffled. "I'll have you know that perfume is a very expensive blend from Floris—"

"Not that sad bit of spring," Melaphor chided. "But *him*."

Oh, this didn't bode well. She bit her lower lip and took a furtive glance at Rockhurst. Carpio no longer danced and sang through the air, and from her vantage point it looked like . . .

No, it couldn't be. He'd given up. And then she had her proof, for he turned to Teague.

"Go to her," he ordered. "Save her."

Most decidedly he was giving up. Sending Teague to her, before he began to fight to the bitter end. His end. But didn't he realize that if he gave up, then everything was lost.

She didn't know whether her heart was breaking or she was entirely furious. *If only he'd listened . . .*

Just then, Rockhurst looked up and over at where they stood, seeing his enemy for the first time, and she swore she saw something spark to life in his eyes.

"He knows I have you," Melaphor told her.

"He cares not for me—"

Melaphor's grip tightened. "I disagree. He's mated with you—whether he knows it or not—he's chosen you. Which means your fate is entwined with his."

"It is?" she asked, feeling for the first time a bit of hope—but then all too quickly realizing her hope was only going to feed whatever plans Melaphor had for the night.

Which meant there was only one thing left to do.

She glanced up at Melaphor. "He cannot care for me, for he's never seen me. He knows not who I am. So if you think to use me—"

"Not seen you?" The fiend laughed. "Well, let me enlighten him. Let him take the vision of your fair face to his grave."

"No, please," Hermione begged. "Not that!"

Melaphor swept his elegant hand over her, and she felt the veil of magic that had kept her concealed fade away.

This is it, she realized. The last moment she'd see nothing but love in his eyes.

For the shock was instantaneous. She could see it immediately.

Hermione Marlowe? How could I have been so deceived?

But there was more to the moment than just her heartbreak and the loss of his love.

There were no more secrets between them. Never again would she be his Shadow.

But she could save his life.

Hermione reached down and ever so slowly pulled the ring from her finger. And this time, it came off.

She didn't feel any different, but everything was.

Rockhurst gaped at her, as did the derga who until that moment had only seen their master standing there.

"Lady Hermione?" he said, taking a step closer.

"I am so sorry," she said, moving toward him as well.

"This is all quite touching," Melaphor said, yanking her back by her hair. "But she is mine now, Paratus." He pulled Hermione right up against his cold body. "And when I have Milton's Ring, all of this world will be mine as well."

"What ring?" Hermione asked. "Do you mean this one?" She held up the shiny bit she'd pulled from her finger.

"Milton's Ring?" came the muttering from the derga, and a light of suspicion rose in their eyes.

This was no longer about killing the Paratus as they'd been promised, for now a greater prize dangled within their grasp.

"Is this the ring you so covet?" she said. "If that is all you seek, have it!"

Then she threw it, as hard and as far as she could into the darkest reaches of the alley.

"No-o-o-o!" Melaphor screamed, releasing her and racing after his henchmen, "It is mine!"

But the derga were single-minded in their greed, and one of them swept Melaphor aside in his haste to seek the ring, leaving the fallen prince to scurry across the dirty cobbles like a rat to join the frenzy digging in the refuse.

Hermione rushed to Rockhurst and, to her shock and thrill, he caught her in his arms.

"What the devil are you doing here?" he demanded.

"Saving your demmed hide," she sputtered back. Then she caught up his hand and pressed the real ring into it. "This will close the hole, all of them. But you must not put it on, put it in the crack. Then I must repeat something in Gaelic. . .at least Mary and Mr. Cricks believe—"

He cut her off by towing her over to where Tibbets had slid his knife. He pulled it out and handed it to Hermione.

He looked down at it. "And here I thought you'd tossed it away—"

"'Tis Lord Hustings's engagement ring they are fighting over."

For it was true, she'd accepted Lord Hustings's offer not two days earlier in a fit of pique and regrets over Rockhurst.

"I don't think we want to be here when one of those derga finds out he is the future Lady Hustings."

Hermione laughed as Rockhurst slid the ring into the wall.

"Now what do I—" His words stopped short as suddenly he was pulled from behind. Melaphor caught him by the throat and began to cut off his air.

Carpio fell from Rockhurst's hand, and he gasped and fought as well as he could, but Melaphor's power was only intensified by his anger.

"Leave him be," Hermione said, tugging at the devil's arm. "Let him go."

Melaphor turned his red gaze on her. "When I am done with him, then it will be your turn, my little kitten."

Never, Hermione fumed.

"Come, Kitten," Melaphor cajoled. "Watch him die."

"I am not your kitten," she told him.

"Still have your claws, I see."

She glanced down and realized she still held Tibbets's knife. "Yes. Yes, I do," she told him, stabbing the blade between his ribs.

Melaphor's eyes widened with surprise, and but better still, he released Rockhurst.

The earl took a deep, wheezing breath and stumbled back.

Now they could close the hole, she thought, but

behind them one of the derga cried out he'd found the ring. His roars of triumph quickly changed to a menacing howl as her deception came to light, and they turned toward her with murder in their eyes.

"Now, Rockhurst, now," she said, pulling him to the wall and guiding his hand back to where the ring was lodged.

She took a deep breath and repeated the words that Mary had spent the entire ride over making her repeat.

"Saol amháin, grá amháin," she said in a strong, clear voice.

For a moment nothing happened, then a soft tremble vibrated through the air. A tiny ray of light pierced the darkness, but in an instant, it swelled to an explosion of power. Behind the derga the wall opened up, sucking them off their feet and back into their world.

Hermione slipped and lost her footing and found herself sliding across the alley toward the abyss, that is until a hand reached out and snagged her arm.

Yet to her dismay, it wasn't the earl who'd caught her, but Melaphor.

Melaphor, with Tibbets's knife still stuck in his ribs, and Hermione in his grasp, held his ground, fighting the power that would end all his meticulous plans.

Rockhurst caught up Carpio and stalked toward them, and Hermione knew a moment of true fear, for the devil's own darkness obliterated his vision.

He stuck the point into Melaphor's chest, and said, "Give her to me."

"No, my lord Paratus," Melaphor taunted. "Finish me if you can."

"Rockhurst, help me," she begged, then realized what a mistake she'd made.

For in that moment, the Paratus faded and the earl returned. He looked with horror at the choice he must make, and Carpio wavered in his grasp.

Hermione now saw the devilish nature of Melaphor's last-ditch effort. As long as he held her, he was anchored to this world, but if he were killed, she'd be swept along with him into his realm—and into a waiting mob of angry derga.

But the longer the void remained opened, the more powerful the vortex seemed to become, and soon it would sweep them all along into its hungry void.

"You are the Paratus," Hermione shouted at him. "Kill him, you ruthless bastard."

"No," he told her.

"But you must," she told him. "For if you do not, all will perish."

The blackness flooded his eyes again, and Hermione braced herself for what she was sure was the end.

He let out a loud, feral peal, an ancient war cry not heard in England since before the Romans. Then the Paratus pulled Carpio back, swung it high in the air, and drove it into Melaphor, even as Teague leapt from the shadows and caught hold of Hermione's skirt.

She hit the ground hard, her head slamming into the cobbles, and the last thing she saw before she lost consciousness was Rockhurst sagging to his knees and the entire alley exploding.

"There you are. I thought this is where I might find you."

Quince didn't even turn around. She just sat on the bench and stared at the Serpentine before her. The still water reflected the half-moon above them. "I'm surprised you're here, Milton."

"Why is that?" he asked, coming to sit beside her.

"I would have thought you would be with your ring. Or least doing your best to save it."

He leaned over and picked up a stone. After studying it for a moment, he tossed it into the artful pond that delighted so many who came to Hyde Park. The stone splashed into the still water, sending ripples out in all directions.

They sat side by side for a while, before Quince spoke again. "You do know what they intend to do with the ring."

"Yes."

"And you've come here to sit with me while it will most likely be destroyed?"

He shrugged. "I thought that was what you wanted. Finally to end all this. To end us."

"Harrumph," she sputtered, and crossed her arms over her chest, and again they sat in silence. A tiny part of her had hoped he would endeavor to do his best to stop Hermione. To recover his ring. To save them both.

Overhead, a shooting star fell, streaking across the sky, then disappearing.

Quince glanced over to see if Milton had seen it, and found him looking at her to see if she'd seen it. His eyes shone, like they had when she first met him, and she recalled what it had been like to be in love with him, when he had loved her.

"I certainly never wanted this," she whispered.

"I know. I regret my part in all this as well." He glanced toward the Dials. "There is no other choice. Melaphor has gotten too powerful of late. Too dangerous. He's stretched his claws too far into this realm, and he must be stopped. If he were to actually . . . could actually . . ."

"Kill the Paratus," Quince whispered. For as much as she feared the Earl of Rockhurst, a world without him would be a far less desirable place.

"Yes, if Melaphor was capable of killing him, ending his family's reign, then where would our Queen be? Our realm? Our kin? There would be no place for us to return to—that is, if we were ever granted such a pardon." Milton sighed. "No, there was nothing to do but to sacrifice our ring."

Our ring. Those words sent a shiver down Quince's spine. "'Twas a noble decision, my lord."

"Yours as well, my lady," he replied.

They sat for a time in the endless silence of the night.

"I will miss granting wishes," she confessed.

"I will miss being vexed with you for granting them." Then he leaned over and brushed a wayward curl back from her face. "You've looked younger of late."

"You noticed?"

He nodded. "I always notice you. Even when you are nattering on at me." Then he smiled, and Quince's heart skipped a beat.

"If the ring is destroyed, that will mean—"

"Aye, I know," he said, glancing away. "We haven't much time." Regret filled his words.

Quince glanced up at the ripples on the water. They were now spread out in wide circles, drifting apart and wavering. "I thought it was what you wanted."

"I thought it was as well, but now—" He looked at her again, and this time he reached out to cup her chin. "I'm not so sure. I fear I still love you, Quince. As aggravating and downright meddlesome as you are, I love you."

Quince's breath caught in her throat. She'd never thought she'd hear him say such a thing. But before she could tell him what was in her heart, a great blaze of light ignited in the distance.

The ring. The world around them trembled, and they knew what it meant. The ring had been used to close the holes, and with it all the magic inside it, the magic that bound them together was lost.

But suddenly they both knew they didn't want their marriage to end just like that, and Milton caught her in his arms. "I'll not lose you yet, my sweet Quince," he said, and then kissed her, sealing his vow.

Quince felt her toes curl up inside her slippers as his lips claimed hers, and once again she was young and full of dreams. He continued to kiss her, and she all but forgot that they were about to meet their end.

But that was just it—all things must end eventually, including a kiss, and when Milton finally pulled away from her, they looked each other in the eyes and realized two things.

They were still alive.

So the ring must have survived.

And there was also one other small problem.

Heavens! He still loves me, Quince realized, and she

let him prove it again with another kiss that lasted until the dawn.

Hermione wasn't the only Marlowe in Seven Dials that night. Near a gaming den frequented by those in the *ton* who were considered less than reputable, a group of young men were making their way down the street.

"I've got a notion I'll be in the pink tomorrow," Griffin Marlowe said.

Lord Delamere laughed. "You always say that!"

From nearby, a great explosion rocked the neighborhood, and all them stopped and gaped as a nearby alley lit up, then fell into darkness and silence.

"Devil of a place," Lord Percy Baker commented, having caught up with the pair.

"No, tonight is my night," Griffin told them. "My luck is about to change.

Then all of a sudden, he heard the clatter of something falling at his feet.

Griffin bent over and picked up the silver bit, then held it up to his friends. "Perhaps not pennies from heaven, but I daresay it might be worth something."

"Nothing that won't turn your finger green," Lord Percy teased as he leaned over to inspect Griffin's find.

"Well, I consider it a lucky token," he said, sliding the ring onto his pinky. "Now where was I?"

"Your lucky night?"

"Ah, yes. I do believe my fortunes are about to change for the better."

"Couldn't get much worse," Delamere said, nudging his friend in the ribs.

* * *

When Hermione awoke the next morning, it was by her mother's arriving uncharacteristically early and waking her up with a frantic cry. "Minny, dear, wake up!"

Hermione rolled over, for her head ached horribly. Then flashes from the night before brought her completely awake.

"Oh, demmit!"

"Hermione Marlowe!" her mother exclaimed. "Is this the sort of language you've been using around Lord Hustings? No wonder he and his mother are here."

"Here?" she asked, sitting up. She wasn't even sure how she'd gotten here. She'd been in the alley with Rockhurst, and she'd been sliding toward the abyss. "Oh, demmit!" she repeated, but this time under her breath. She tapped her fingers to her forehead trying to remember what had happened next . . . let alone, how she had gotten home.

Yet here she was, back in her bed. Not his bed. That didn't bode well! That is, until she peeked under the sheets and found she hadn't a stitch on. Naked? She certainly didn't remember that part. Oh, this was dreadful. She yanked the sheet up to her chin and managed a wan smile for her mother.

"Minny!" her mother exclaimed. "I fear there is something very amiss. And I think you should brace yourself. I suspect Hustings is here to cry off. Oh, this is a veritable disaster. If only your father were here, or even Sebastian." Her mother had gone into her closet and was plucking out one dress after another. "Oh, heavens, what does one wear for such an occasion?"

But Hermione wasn't really listening to her mother's dire prattle. She was still trying to recall how she'd gotten home . . . and if Rockhurst had survived.

"This is most vexing," she muttered. She glanced back under the sheet and considered that finding herself in her altogether must mean that Rockhurst had brought her home.

But he hadn't taken her to his bed, or kept her as he'd once vowed. No, now that he knew who she was, he'd brought her home and left her to her future.

Alone.

Her heart tore in two. "Wretched man."

"I'll say," her mother agreed, though her vehemence was directed toward Lord Hustings. "But we shall weather this disgrace, Minny, dear. And I am sure we will be able to find some nice baronet or some such who will overlook all this scandal and want to marry you."

If only that was the worst scandal she could manage. How would she ever live without Rockhurst? Without being his Shadow?

Hermione began to sob, and her mother came rushing to her side.

"Now, now, let us find something truly beautiful for you to wear, and you shall go down there and hear him out with your pride in place. You are a Marlowe after all, and a Pembly on my side. Who are these Hustings after all? Upstarts, I say."

Her mother smiled and helped her dress, and Hermione followed her downstairs.

"I suppose you'll have to give him back his ring,"

Lady Walbrook said, as she paused before the closed doorway to the morning room.

His ring! Hermione glanced down at her now-bare hand.

This was going to be difficult to explain. Not only to Lord Hustings, but to his mother as well.

"Bugger!" Hermione said under breath, and her mother shot a warning glance worthy of Nelson in her direction as she opened the door, a regal smile pasted on her strained features.

Lady Hustings, it seemed, was under no such polite constraints, for she sniffed disapprovingly as they entered.

"Welcome, Lord Hustings, Lady Hustings," the countess said, in a sunny voice. "How wonderful of you to call so early."

At the sound of Lady Walbrook's greeting, Lord Hustings turned in the wrong direction, only to find himself staring at a rather large fertility goddess Lord Walbrook had sent home from the South Pacific and the countess displayed quite proudly, despite the fact that the idol had four pendulous breasts and was completely unclothed. When he finally got oriented toward the door where Hermione and her mother stood waiting, he wore a pasty expression of shock.

Heavens! What was I thinking, accepting him? Hermione asked herself. She'd rather live the rest of her life on her memories of Rockhurst than spend one night with Hustings and his faint blushes.

And most likely that would be all that was left for her, memories, once the respectable and honorable Hustings cried off.

Hermione dashed away the tears that welled up at the very thought of him. *Oh, Thomas . . . I am so sorry I couldn't be the woman you desired.*

"It has come to our attention—" Lady Hustings began.

"Mother, I said I would do this," Lord Hustings told her.

The lady sniffed again. "Yes, but you needn't be involved in such a distasteful situation."

Hermione's mother, who'd never suffered fools gladly, stepped forward. "Lord Hustings, are you here to cry off?"

"Well, I mean to say, that is—" he blustered on.

"Yes!" Lady Hustings cried out, rising to her feet and nearly upsetting the tea table. "Of course he means to cry off."

"Mother!" The baron straightened his jacket and tried his best to look, well, commanding. "Please be seated. I will settle this." He took a deep breath and looked the countess in the eye. "Lady Walbrook, I would feel better if you and Lady Hermione were seated as well, as this news may be unsettling to you both."

Hermione noted he avoided glancing in her direction, but following her mother's lead, perched herself on a nearby chair.

"It has come to my attention of late that Lady Hermione is not in good health—"

"My lord," Lady Walbrook said. "'Tis only bridal nerves, I assure you. Most young ladies have megrims from time to time."

"Megrims, indeed!" Lady Hustings sputtered.

The baron shot his mother a censorious glance. "I think it best to say that on the subject of our former attachment—"

Hermione noted that he didn't use the word "engagement." Yet what ever could have Lord Hustings backing out of their betrothal in such due haste?

"—if anyone is so rude as to inquire, I will advise them that it was Lady Hermione's fragile health that was the reason for our mutual parting."

Lady Walbrook blew out an exasperated sigh. "Fragile health? No one will believe such nonsense. We Marlowes are always in excellent health." Her mother, faced with impending social disaster, leaned forward. "If you mean to end this engagement, you will tell me why, or I shall come to my own conclusions and share them freely about Town. Perhaps an inability to do your marital duties, partake in your conjugal visits—"

"That is high-handed, madam," Lord Hustings blustered. "I am trying to be fair when very soon the entire *ton* will know that your daughter has been—"

The door to the library opened, and Fenwick poked his nose inside. "My lady, there is a guest here to see you."

"I am not at home," Lady Walbrook told him in a sharp, panicked voice. "Not to anyone."

"Very good, my lady," Fenwick said.

Then to Hermione's shock, the stoic and possibly only normal member of their household shot her a wink.

A wink? From Fenwick? Had all of London turned upside down.

"Now, where were you, Lord Hustings?" Lady Walbrook asked in a tone that anyone of good sense would have known held a dangerous edge to it. The countess was often regarded as a flighty eccentric, but when it came to her children, there was nothing she took more seriously.

"Yes, as I was saying," Lord Hustings said, shifting uneasily in his seat and glancing one more time at his mother before he continued. "I cannot marry Lady Hermione because she was seen, madam."

Lady Walbrook shook her head. "Seen? What do you mean, seen?"

"She was seen early this morning," Lord Hustings said.

"I still don't understand—"

The dowager could stand it no longer and burst out, "She was seen just after sunrise by Lord Calkley in the company of a man—a very disreputable man—riding into Berkeley Square in this man's phaeton." Lady Hustings sniffed again. "Lord Calkley is my nephew and felt it imperative that Hustings know immediately what a lightskirt his cousin intended to marry."

Lady Walbrook's mouth fell open, then she turned to Hermione. "What do you say to this nonsense?"

"I have no memory of any such thing," she answered quite honestly.

The countess nodded. "See. It couldn't have been Hermione."

"She probably doesn't remember because the report was that she appeared highly intoxicated!" Lady Hustings rose to her feet. "I will not have some drunken strumpet darkening the halls of Hustings Manor!"

Hermione bounded to her feet. "I was not drunk," she declared, stopping short of denying the strumpet part because in truth, she'd walk across Hyde Park in her chemise to gain Rockhurst's favor just one more time.

"Harlot!" Lady Hustings cried out, pointing a finger at Hermione and clutching her handkerchief to her nose.

"Dear God, am I late?" Lord Rockhurst said from the doorway. "My apologies, Lady Walbrook, but I thought I was right on time for your rehearsal, but I can see you've begun without me. Lady Hustings, pray continue your scene."

Both women gaped at this very unexpected guest, while Hermione blinked back the tears that had sprung up in her eyes.

Rockhurst lived! And gloriously so. He strode into the room, resplendent in a dark jacket and crisp white shirt, a perfect cravat and his tall beaver hat at a jaunty, rakish angle. The sight of him quite took Hermione's breath away.

But what was he doing here?

Lady Walbrook appeared to regain her senses first. Never had someone come early to one of her practices, quite the contrary. And Hermione could see that her good mother was afraid to send the earl away lest he not return. But given the current tenor of the room, she could hardly include him. "I fear, Lord Rockhurst, the practice is not until four o'clock."

He glanced at the bracket clock on the mantel. "How convenient that I am early."

Lady Walbrook got up and tried to move him toward

the door. "I fear you've come at an inconvenient time, my lord. A family matter, if you will. If you wouldn't mind, perhaps coming back in a few hours—"

"Oh, I fear that won't work at all," he said, dodging around her and coming to Hermione's side. He held out his hand, his eyes shining with the light she'd come to love. She took his hand, and he pulled her up into his arms.

"I've come to practice now," he said, not to anyone but Hermione. "And I thought to start like this."

His head dipped down, and he kissed her. Not just any kiss, but one that plundered and devoured her.

Claimed her.

Hermione couldn't believe it and sighed so happily, so thoroughly lustily, that Lady Hustings fell back on the sofa in a dead faint.

When the kiss finally ended, he looked down into her eyes. "I am so glad they are green."

"What is green?"

"Your bonny eyes," he teased, kissing the tip of her nose.

"I told you they weren't very special."

"I disagree. They are splendid, as is the woman behind them. If I had a wish, it would be to awaken to their bright and splendid light every morning for the rest of my life."

"Truly?" she whispered.

"I wish it, so it must be so," he told her, before he kissed her again.

"Now see here, my lord," Lord Hustings sputtered. "That woman is not—"

"Any of your concern," Rockhurst told him, then

kissed Hermione again, claiming her with his usual undeniable flair. When he finished, which thankfully took some time, he grinned at her. "My apologies for arriving so late, but it was demmed hard to get the Archbishop to agree to a Special License when you've already had banns cried with another. Quite inconvenient." He shot a withering glance at Hustings, as if it was entirely his fault.

"I do believe Lord Hustings was here to cry off," Hermione said.

"Indeed I was," the fussy man said, as he began to wave the smelling salts Lady Walbrook had fetched under his mother's nose.

That was good enough for Rockhurst, for he was once again kissing his bride-to-be, and whispering his proposal as well as his promise for a wedding night she would never forget.

"Lord Rockhurst, what is the meaning of this?" Lady Walbrook said. "You happen to be kissing Caliban! Nowhere in Shakespeare did Prospero kiss his monster."

"This is my version," Rockhurst told her. "And I think you will find the ending quite diverting."

Hermione had to imagine even Mr. Shakespeare would approve of such a change.

Épilogue

May 1814

"Rockhurst!" came the cry through the town house on Hanover Square. "Rockhurst, where the devil are you!"

The servants who were within earshot of their mistress or anywhere near their master fled their posts, removing themselves to the kitchens.

When Lady Rockhurst had that note to her voice, they knew she was in a temper. Not that she was in a temper often, but she was possibly the only person in London who dared confront the earl and . . . well, it was often eventful.

"Oh, aye, and they'll be abed all day tomorrow," one of the maids said in a knowing aside to one of the newer maids as they hustled down the hall to the kitchens.

Best to wait out the storm over a plate of scones and play with the new pups that had been born recently.

"Rockhurst!" Hermione called out again, finally finding her husband in his armory. Though they had closed the holes in the Dials, and there hadn't been any problems in all of London for nearly four years now, Rockhurst still maintained his practice regime.

For he was still, by rights, the Paratus. And after some convincing, on Hermione's and Mary's parts, had begun a search of England for other families like his—protectors of the realm, though to date they had yet to find any clues as to the existence of others. But Hermione clung to the one line in Podmore, one he'd found in an ancient text that had her convinced that the Earls of Rockhurst weren't the only ones:

The four corners of England are protected by the most skilled and ancient of warriors, ordained and christened to fend off the reaches of evil.

"That is why," Hermione liked to argue, "it is called a 'League.' For you are not alone, Rockhurst. Never will be again."

But right this moment, he probably wished he wasn't so blessed with her help and love.

Hermione came in carrying their son in her arms. "Rockhurst!"

He turned from his practice, sword in hand, and smiled at his wife.

Hermione felt her pique take a direct hit, but she rallied her displeasure, for it was a matter most urgent.

"Rockhurst, my mother is coming over this afternoon, as well as your Aunt Routledge—"

"How thoughtful of you, my dear, to warn me." He came over and laid a kiss on her forehead, and then reached out and ruffled young Thomas's head. The toddler, just past his first year, was the spitting image of his father, same blue eyes and burnished hair. "I shall be at White's for the remainder of the day."

Hermione handed him Thomas and stuck her hands on her hips. "Oh no, you won't. For however will I explain this to them."

"Explain what?" he asked, smiling down at his son.

"This," she said. Then she leaned over to Thomas. "Say your word, darling. Say your word."

The boy looked at his mother, then his father, and said, "Carpio!" and clapped his hands together.

Rockhurst cringed, and Hermione glared at him.

"Whatever am I to say to them?"

"We could tell my aunt it is all your mother's doing," he offered.

"Harrumph!" She reached over and covered Thomas's ears. "You've been reading Podmore to this child, haven't you?"

"Well—"

Hermione cocked a brow at him.

"Not the scary parts," he demurred.

She groaned. "This is going to be impossible to explain."

He set Thomas down on the carpet and drew her into his arms. "Nothing is impossible when you set your mind to it. I know that with all my heart." Then he kissed her, thoroughly and expertly, chasing away every bit of her pique.

"You are a charming devil, Lord Rockhurst," she said, a little breathlessly. "But what about little Thomas? Whatever are we to do?"

Rockhurst glanced over her shoulder at the spot to which their son had toddled off. "I believe he has his own destiny in mind."

Hermione looked that way as well, only to find their son trying to pick up Carpio.

The boy got the hilt up off the floor and grinned triumphantly at them. "Paratus!"

"You knew what you were in for when you married me," Rockhurst said quickly, and before Hermione could protest, kissed her again until she trembled with desire. "Remember, this is what you wished for."

"Oh, it is. Ever so much so," Hermione said, glancing over at her son and trying not to be overly proud of the boy's accomplishments. For he was indeed, just like his father.

A man worthy of a thousand wishes.

Warm up the winter nights
with a sizzling hot read!
With four upcoming
Romance Superleaders
from bestsellers
Elizabeth Boyle, Laura Lee Guhrke,
Kerrelyn Sparks, and Kathryn Caskie,
you won't even feel the cold . . .

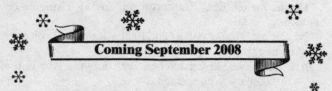

Coming September 2008

Tempted By the Night

**An exciting new paranormal romance
by *New York Times* bestselling author**

ELIZABETH BOYLE

*Lady Hermione Marlowe has loved the rakish Earl of
Rockhurst from afar forever, defending his scandalous ways
at every turn. One of her greatest desires is to follow after
him, completely unseen, so as to reveal his true noble nature
. . . and then, much to her shock, Hermione finds herself
fading from sight as the sun sets, until she is completely
invisible! Freed of the confines of Society, she recklessly
follows the earl into the temptations of the night and shockingly discovers that his disreputable veneer is merely a cover
for his real duty: safeguarding London as the Paratus, the
Protector of the Realm.*

Thomasin appeared in the same state of shock. "Oh. My.
Goodness," she managed to gasp, her eyes wide with
amazement as she gazed somewhere over Hermione's shoulder. "You are never going to believe this, Minny."

India blinked and tried again to speak, her mouth wavering open and shut as if she couldn't quite find the words to
describe the sight before her.

"What is it?" Hermione asked, glancing over her shoulder
and only seeing the narrow, tall figure of Lord Battersby
behind her. Certainly his arrival wouldn't have India looking like she'd swallowed her aunt's parrot.

"Oh, let me tell her," Thomasin was saying, rising up on her toes.

"No, let me," India said as she finally found her voice. "I saw *him* first."

Him. Hermione shivered. There was only one *him* in the *ton* as far as she was concerned.

Rockhurst.

Oh, but her friends had to be jesting, for the earl would never make an appearance at Almack's. She glanced at both their faces, fully expecting to find some telltale sign of mirth, some twitch of the lips that would give way to a full-blown giggle.

But there were none. Just the same, wide-eyed gaping expression that she now noticed several other guests wore.

Turning around slowly, Hermione's jaw dropped as well.

Nothing in all her years out could have prepared her for the sight of the Earl of Rockhurst arriving at Almack's.

"Jiminy!" she gasped, her hand going immediately to her quaking stomach. Oh, heavens, she shouldn't have had that extra helping of pudding at supper, for now she feared the worst.

And here she thought she'd be safe at Almack's.

"I didn't believe you," she whispered to India.

"I still don't believe it myself," India shot back. "Whatever is he doing here?"

"I don't know, and I don't care," Thomasin replied, "but I'm just glad Mother insisted we come tonight, if only for the crowing rights we will have tomorrow over everyone who isn't here."

"Oh, this is hardly the gown to catch his eye," Hermione groaned. "It is entirely the wrong shade of capucine," she declared, running her hands over the perfectly fashionable, perfectly pretty gown she'd chosen.

Thomasin laughed. "Minny, stop fussing. The three of us could be stark naked and posed like a trio of wood nymphs, and he wouldn't notice us."

"True enough," India agreed. "You have to see that you are too respectable to garner his fancy."

"He fancied Charlotte," Hermione shot back, trying to ignore the little bit of jealousy that niggled in her heart as she said it.

"Oh, I suppose he did for about an hour," India conceded, "but you have to admit, Charlotte was a bit odd the last few weeks. Not herself at all."

Hermione nodded in agreement. There had been something different about Charlotte. Ever since . . . ever since her Great-Aunt Ursula had died and she'd inherited . . . Hermione glanced down at her gloved hand. Inherited the very ring she'd found yesterday . . .

Beneath her glove, she swore the ring warmed, even quivered on her finger, like a trembling bell that foretold of something ominous just out of reach.

"Did you hear of his latest escapade?" Lady Thomasin was whispering. There was no one around them to hear, but some things just couldn't be spoken in anything less than the awed tone of a conspiratorial hush.

India nodded. "About his wager with Lord Kramer—"

"Oh, hardly that," Thomasin scoffed. "Everyone has heard about that. No, I am speaking of his renewed interest in Mrs. Fornett. Apparently she was seen with him at Tattersall's when everyone knows she is under Lord Saunderton's protection." The girl paused, then heaved a sigh. "Of course there will be a duel. There always is in these cases." Lady Thomasin's cousin had once fought a duel, and so she considered herself quite the expert on the subject.

"Pish posh," Hermione declared. "He isn't interested in her."

"I heard Mother telling Lady Gidding, that she'd heard it from Lady Owston, who'd had it directly from Lord Filton that he was at Tatt's with Mrs. Fornett." Thomasin rocked back on her heels, her brows arched and her mouth set as if that was the final word on the subject.

"That may be so, but I heard Lord Delamere tell my brother that he'd seen Rockhurst going into a truly dreadful house in Seven Dials. The sort of place no gentleman would even frequent. With truly awful women inside."

Hermione wrinkled her nose. "And what was Lord Delamere doing outside this sinful den?"

"I daresay driving past it to get to the nearest gaming hell. He's gone quite dice mad and nearly run through his inheritance. Or so my brother likes to say."

"And probably squiffed, I'd wager," Hermione declared, forgetting her admonishment to Viola about using such phrases. "I don't believe any of it. Whatever is the matter with Society these days when all they can get on with is making up gossip about a man who doesn't deserve it?"

"Not deserve it?" Lady Thomasin gaped. "The Earl of Rockhurst is a terrible bounder. Everyone knows it."

"Well, I think differently." Hermione crossed her arms over her chest and stood firm, even as her stomach continued to twist and turn.

"Why you continue to defend him, I know not," India said, glancing over where the earl stood with his cousin, Miss Mary Kendell. "He's wicked and unrepentant."

"I disagree." Hermione straightened and took a measured glance at the man. "I don't believe a word of any of it. The Earl of Rockhurst is a man of honor."

Lady Thomasin snorted. "Oh, next you'll be telling us he spends his nights, spooning broth to sickly orphans and bestowing food baskets to poor war widows."

India laughed. "Oh, no, I think he's like the mad earl in that book your mother told us not to read." She shivered and leaned in closer to whisper. "You know the one . . . about the dreadful man who kidnapped all sorts of ladies and kept them in his attic? I'd wager if you were to venture into the earl's attics, you'd find an entire harem!"

"Oh, of all the utter nonsense! How can you say such dreadful things about a man's reputation?" Hermione argued. "The earl is a decent man, I just know it. And I'll not let the Lord Delameres and the Lord Filtons of the world tell me differently."

"Well, the only way to prove such a thing would be to follow him around all night—for apparently only seeing the truth with your own eyes will end this infatuation of yours, Hermione."

She crossed her arms over her chest and set her shoulders. "I just might."

"Yes, and you'd be ruined in the process," Thomasin pointed out. "And don't think he'll marry you to save your reputation, when he cares nothing of his own."

India snapped her fingers, her eyes alight with inspiration. "Too bad you aren't cursed like the poor heroine in that book we borrowed from my cousin. Remember it? *Zoe's Dilemma* . . . No, that's not it. *Zoe's Awful* . . . Oh, I don't remember the rest of the title."

"I do," Lady Thomasin jumped in. "*Zoe or the Moral Loss of a Soul Cursed.*"

India sighed. "Yes, yes, that was it."

Hermione gazed up at the ceiling. Only Thomasin and India would recall such a tale at a time like this. She glanced over at the earl, and then down at her gown. Oh, she should never have settled on this dress. It was too pumpkin and not enough capucine. How would he ever discover her now?

Thomasin continued, "You remember the story, Minny. At sunset, Zoe faded from sight so no one could see her. What I would give to have a night thusly."

"Whatever for?" India asked. "You already know the earl is a bounder."

Their friend got a devilish twinkle in her eye. "If I were unseen for a night, I'd make sure that Miss Lavinia Burke had the worst evening of her life. Why, the next day, every gossip in London would be discussing what a bad case of wind she had, not to mention how clumsy she's become, for I fear I'd be standing on her train every time she took a step."

Hermione chuckled, while India burst out laughing.

"I do think you've considered this before," Hermione said.

Thomasin grinned. "I might have." Then she laughed as well. "If you were so cursed, Hermione, you could follow Rockhurst from sunset to sunrise, and then you'd see everyone is right about him."

India made a more relevant point. "Then you could end this disastrous *tendré* you have for him and discover a more eligible *parti* before the Season ends."

And your chances of a good marriage with them, her statement implied, but being the bosom bow that India was, she wouldn't say such a thing.

Still, Hermione wasn't about to concede so easily. "More likely you would both have to take back every terrible thing you've ever said about him."

"Or listen to your sorry laments over how wretchedly you've been deceived," Thomasin shot back.

Hermione turned toward the earl. Truly no man could be so terribly wicked or so awful.

Oh, if only . . .

Coming October 2008

Secret Desires of a Gentleman

The final book in the *Girl-Bachelor Chronicles* by *USA Today* bestselling author

LAURA LEE GUHRKE

Phillip Hawthorne, Marquess of Kayne, has his life mapped out before him. He is a responsible member of the peerage, and rumor has it he may become the next prime minister. And then he runs into Maria Martingale. Twelve years ago, Maria was the cook's daughter, and she fancied herself in love with Lawrence Hawthorne, the marquess's younger brother, but Phillip quickly put an end to that romance. Now Phillip, still as cold and ruthless as he had been all those years ago, is concerned Maria will ruin things for Lawrence and his impending marriage, so he does the only thing he can think of to distract her—seduction.

Maria started down the street, still looking over her shoulder at the shop. "Perfect," she breathed with reverent appreciation. "It's absolutely perfect."

The collision brought her out of her daydreams with painful force. She was knocked off her feet, her handbag went flying, and she stumbled backward, stepping on the hem of her skirt as she tried desperately to right herself. She would have fallen to the pavement, but a pair of strong hands caught her by the arms, and she was hauled upright, pulled hard against what was definitely a man's chest. "Steady on, my girl," a deep voice murmured, a voice that somehow seemed familiar. "Are you all right?"

She inhaled deeply, trying to catch her breath, and as she did, she caught the luscious scents of bay rum and fresh linen. She nodded, her cheek brushing the unmistakable silk of a fine necktie. "I think so, yes," she answered.

Her palms flattened against the soft, rich wool of a gentleman's coat and she pushed back, straightening away from him as she lifted her chin to look into his face. The moment she did, recognition hit her with more force than the collision had done.

Phillip Hawthorne. The Marquess of Kayne.

There was no mistaking those eyes, vivid cobalt blue framed by thick black lashes. Irish eyes, she'd always thought, though if any Irish blood tainted the purity of his oh-so-aristocratic British lineage, he'd never have acknowledged it. Phillip had always been such a dry stick, as unlike his brother, Lawrence, as chalk was from cheese.

Memories came over her like a flood, washing away twelve years in the space of a heartbeat. Suddenly, she was no longer standing on a sidewalk in Mayfair, but in the library at Kayne Hall, and Phillip was standing across the desk from her, holding out a bank draft and looking at her as if she were nothing.

She glanced down, half-expecting to see a slip of pale pink paper in his hand—the bribe to make her leave and never come back, the payment for her promise to keep away from his brother for the rest of her life. The marquess had only been nineteen then, but he'd already managed to put a price on love. It was worth five hundred pounds.

That should be enough, since my brother assures me there is no possibility of a child.

His voice, so cold, echoed back to her from ten years ago, and shaken, she tried to gather her wits. She'd always expected she'd run into Phillip again one day, but she had not expected it to happen so literally, and she felt rather at sixes and sevens. Lawrence she'd never thought to see again, for she'd read in some scandal sheet years ago that he'd gone off to America.

His older brother was a different matter. Phillip was a marquess, he came to London for the season every year, sat in the House of Lords, and mingled with the finest society. Given all the balls and parties where she'd served hors d'oeuvres to aristocrats while working for Andre, Maria had resigned herself long ago to the inevitable night she would look up while offering a plate of canapés or a tray of champagne glasses and find his cool, haughty gaze on her, but it had never happened. Ten years of beating the odds only to cannon into him on a street corner. Of all the rotten luck.

Her gaze slid downward. Phillip had always been tall, but standing before her was not the lanky youth she remembered. This man's shoulders were wider, his chest broader, his entire physique exuding such masculine strength and vitality that Maria felt quite aggrieved. If there was any fairness in the world at all, Phillip Hawthorne would have gone to fat and gotten the gout by now. Instead, the Marquess of Kayne was even stronger and more powerful at thirty-one than he'd been at nineteen. How nauseating.

Still, she thought as she returned her gaze to his face, ten years had left their mark. There were tiny lines at the corners of his eyes and two faint parallel creases across his forehead. The determination and discipline in the line of his jaw was even more pronounced than it had been a dozen years ago, and his mouth, a grave, unsmiling curve that had always been surprisingly beautiful, was harsher now. His entire countenance, in fact, was harder than she remembered it, as if all those notions of duty and responsibility he'd been stuffed with as a boy weighed heavy on him as a man. Maria found some satisfaction in that.

Even more satisfying was the fact that she had changed, too. She was no longer the desperate, forsaken seventeen-year-old girl who'd thought being bought off for five hundred pounds was her only choice. These days, she wasn't without means and she wasn't without friends. Never again would she be intimidated by the likes of Phillip Hawthorne.

"What are you doing here?" she demanded, then grimaced at her lack of eloquence. Over the years, she'd invented an entire repertoire of cutting, clever things to say to him should they ever meet again, and that blunt, stupid query was the best she could do? Maria wanted to kick herself.

"An odd question," he murmured in the well-bred accent she remembered so clearly. "I live here."

"Here?" A knot of dread began forming in the pit of her stomach as his words sank in. "But this is an empty shop."

"Not the shop." He let go of her arms and gestured to the front door of the first town house on Half Moon Street, an elegant red door out of which he must have just come from when they'd collided. "I live there."

She stared at the door in disbelief. *You can't live here*, she wanted to shout. *Not you, not Phillip Hawthorne, not in this house right beside the lovely, perfect shop where I'm going to live.*

She looked at him again. "But that's impossible. Your London house is in Park Lane."

He stiffened, dark brows drawing together in a puzzled frown. "My home in Park Lane is presently being remodeled, though I don't see what business it is of yours."

Before she could reply, he glanced at the ground and spoke again. "You've spilled your things."

"I didn't spill them," she corrected, bristling a bit. "You did."

To her disappointment, he didn't argue the point. "My apologies," he murmured, and knelt on the pavement. "Allow me to retrieve them for you."

She watched him, still irritated and rather bemused, as he righted her handbag and began to pick up her scattered belongings. She watched his bent head as he gathered her tortoiseshell comb, her gloves, her cotton handkerchief, and her money purse, then began placing them in her handbag with careful precision. So like Phillip, she thought. God forbid one should just toss it all inside and get on with things.

After all her things had been returned to her bag, he closed the brass clasp and reached for his hat, a fine gray felt Bromburg, which had also gone flying during the collision. He donned his hat and stood up, holding her bag out to her.

She took it from his outstretched hand. "Thank you, Phillip," she murmured. "How—" She broke off, not knowing if she should inquire after his brother, but then she decided it was only right to ask. "How is Lawrence?"

Something flashed in his eyes, but when he spoke, his voice was politely indifferent. "Forgive me, miss," he said with a cool, impersonal smile, "but your use of Christian names indicates a familiarity with me of which I am unaware."

Miss? She blinked, stunned. "Unaware?" she echoed and started to laugh, not from humor, but from disbelief. "But Phillip, you've known me since I was five years—"

"I don't believe so," he cut her off, his voice still polite and pleasant, his gaze hard and implacable. "We do not know each other, miss. We do not know each other at all. I hope that's clear?"

Her eyes narrowed. He knew precisely who she was and he was pretending not to, the arrogant, toplofty snob. How dare he snub her? She wanted to reply, but before she could think of something sufficiently cutting to say, he spoke again. "Good day, miss," he said, then bowed and stepped around her to go on his way.

She turned, watching his back as he walked away. Outrage seethed within her, but when she spoke, her voice was sweet as honey. "It was delightful to see you again, *Phillip*," she called after him. "Give Lawrence my best regards, will you?"

His steps did not falter as he walked away.

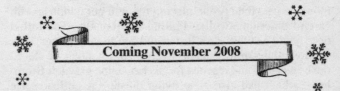

Coming November 2008

All I Want for Christmas Is a Vampire

The latest in the *Love at Stake* series
by *New York Times* bestselling author

KERRELYN SPARKS

Vampire Ian MacPhie is on a mission—he's on the lookout for true love. He claims that all he wants is another vampire. . . . until Toni Duncan comes along. Toni's best friend is locked up in a psycho ward, deemed insane when she confesses that vampires attacked her. The only way to get her out is for Toni to prove that vampires exist. So Toni comes up with a plan: make Ian lose control and beg him to make her one of his kind . . .

Ian felt ten degrees hotter in spite of the cold December air that drifted through the open window and over his white undershirt. The lamp between the two wingback chairs was turned on low, and it cast a golden glow across the room to outline her form with a shimmering aura.

She made a stunning cat burglar, dressed entirely in black spandex that molded to her waist and sweetly curved hips. Her golden hair hung in a ponytail down her back. The ends swished gently across her shoulder blades, as she moved her head from side to side, scanning the bookshelf.

She stepped to the side, silent in her black socks. She must have left her shoes outside the window, thinking she'd move more quietly without them. He noted her slim ankles, then let his gaze wander back up to golden hair. He would have to be careful capturing her. Like any Vamp, he had super strength, and she looked a bit fragile.

He moved silently past the wingback chairs to the window. It made a swooshing sound as he shut it.

With a gasp, she turned toward him. Her eyes widened.

Eyes green as the hills surrounding his home in Scotland. A surge of desire left him speechless for a moment. She seemed equally speechless. No doubt she was busily contemplating an escape route.

He moved slowly toward her. "Ye willna escape through the window. And ye canna reach the door before me."

She stepped back. "Who are you? Do you live here?"

"I'll be asking the questions, once I have ye restrained." He could hear her heart beating faster. Her face remained expressionless, except for her eyes. They flashed with defiance. They were beautiful.

She plucked a heavy book off a nearby shelf. "Did you come here to test my abilities?"

An odd question. Was he misinterpreting the situation? "Who—?" He dodged to the side when she suddenly hurled the book at his face. Bugger, he'd suffered too much to get his older, more manly face, and she'd nearly smacked it.

The book flew past him and knocked over the lamp. The light flickered and went out. With his superior vision, he could see her dark form running for the door.

He zoomed after her. Just before he could grab her, she spun and landed a kick against his chest. He stumbled back. Damn, she was stronger than he'd thought. And he'd suffered too much to get his broader, more manly chest.

She advanced with a series of punches and kicks, and he blocked them all. With a desperate move, she aimed a kick at his groin. Dammit, he'd suffered too much to get his bigger, more manly balls. He jumped back, but her toes caught the hem of his kilt. Without his sporran to weigh the kilt down, it flew up past his waist.

Her gaze flitted south and stuck. Her mouth fell open. Aye, those twelve years of growth had been kind. He lunged forward and slammed her onto the carpet. She punched at him, so he caught her wrists and pinned her to the floor.

She twisted, attempting to knee him. With a growl, he blocked her with his own knee. Then slowly, he lowered himself on top of her to keep her still. Her body was gloriously hot, flushed with blood and throbbing with a life force that made his body tremble with desire.

"Stop wiggling, lass." His bigger, more manly groin was reacting in an even bigger way. "Have mercy on me."

"Mercy?" She continued to wriggle beneath him. "I'm the one who's captured."

"Cease." He pressed more heavily on her.

Her eyes widened. He had no doubt she was feeling it.

Her gaze flickered down, then back to his face. "Get off. Now."

"I'm halfway there already," he muttered.

"Let me go!" She strained at his grip on her wrists.

"If I release you, ye'll knee me. And I'm rather fond of my balls."

"The feeling isn't mutual."

He smiled slowly. "Ye took a long look. Ye must have liked what ye saw."

"Ha! You made such a *small* impression on me, I can barely remember."

He chuckled. She was as quick mentally as she was physically.

She looked at him curiously. "You smell like beer."

"I've had a few." He noted her dubious expression. "Okay, more than a few, but I was still able to beat you."

"If you drink beer, then that means you're not . . ."

"No' what?"

She looked at him, her eyes wide. He had a sinking feeling that she thought he was mortal. She wanted him to be mortal. And that meant she knew about Vamps.

He studied her lovely face—the high cheekbones, delicate

jawline, and beguiling green eyes. Some Vamps claimed mortals had no power whatsoever. They were wrong.

Their eyes met, and he forgot to breathe. There was something hidden in those green depths. A loneliness. A wound that seemed too old for her tender age. For a moment, he felt like he was seeing a reflection of his own soul.

"Ye're no' a thief, are you?" he whispered.

She shook her head slightly, still trapped in his gaze. Or maybe it was he who was trapped in hers.

Coming December 2008

To Sin With a Stranger

**The first in the new *Seven Deadly Sins* series
by *USA Today* bestselling author**

KATHRYN CASKIE

*The Sinclairs are one of the oldest, wealthiest, and wildest
noble families in all of Scotland. The seven brothers and
sisters of the clan enjoy a good time, know no boundaries,
and have scandal follow in their wake. They are known
amongst the ton as The Seven Deadly Sins. But now their
father has declared they must become respectable married
members of proper Society . . . This is Sterling, Marquess
of Sinclair's, story of how greed and a young beauty, Miss
Isobel Carington, almost became his downfall.*

"As the Sinclair children grew older, they seemed to
embrace the sins Society had labeled them with.
Lord Sterling is cursed with greed." Christiana turned her
eyes toward the fighter and Isobel followed her gaze. "Lady
Susan epitomizes sloth, and Lady Ivy, the copper-haired
beauty, envy."

"This is nonsense."

"Is it?" Christiana continued. "Lord Lachlan is a wicked
rake. No wonder his weakness is lust. Lord Grant, the one
with the lace cuffs, is said to have a taste for luxury and
indulgence. His sin is gluttony. The twins are said to be
the worst of all." She raised her nose toward the Sinclair

with a sheath of hair so dark that it almost appeared a deep
blue. "Lord Killian's sin is wrath. Whispers suggest that he
is the true fighter in the family, but his anger is too quick
and fierce. Why, there is even one rumor that claims that he
actually killed a man who merely looked at his twin sister!
That's her, there. Lady Priscilla. Just look at her with her
haughty chin turned toward the chandelier—here, in a room
full of nobility! Her sin is, quite clearly, *pride*."

"Nonsense! I do not believe it," Isobel countered. "I do not
believe any of the story. The tale is not but idle gossip."

"I believe it." Christiana set one hand on her hip and
waved the other in the air as she spoke. "Why else would
they have come to London, if not to leave their sinful reputa-
tions behind in Scotland?"

"I am sure I do not know." Isobel saw Christiana's jaw
drop, then felt the presence of someone behind her.

"Perhaps I have come to London to ask you to dance with
me, lassie." His rich Scottish brogue resonated in her ears,
making her vibrate with his every word.

Isobel whirled around and stared up into none other than
Lord Sterling's grinning face.

"I apologize, I would address you by name, but alas, I
dinna know what it is. Only that you are easily the most
beautiful woman in this assembly room." Before she could
blink, he reached a hand, knuckles stitched with black
threads, and brushed his fingers across her cheek—just as
he'd done at the club. "English lasses dinna stir me the way
you do. You must be a wee bit Scottish."

Isobel gasped, drew back her hand, and gave his cheek
a stinging slap. "Sirrah, you humiliated me, made light of
my charity and my attempts to help widows and orphans of
war. Why would I ever agree to dance with an ill-mannered
rogue like you?"

"Because I asked, and I saw the way you were lookin' at
me." He lifted an eyebrow teasingly, bringing to the surface
a rage Isobel could not rein in. She slapped his face with

such force that his head wrenched to the left. He raised his hand to his cheek. "Not bad. Have you thought about pugilism as a profession?" He grinned at her again.

Isobel stepped around Sterling Sinclair and started for her father. But he was only two steps away. Staring at her. Aghast. She reached out for him, but he stepped back, out of her reach.

She glanced to her left, then her right. Everyone was staring. Everyone.

Isobel covered her face with her trembling hands and shoved her way through the crowd of amused onlookers. She dashed out the door and down the steps to the liveried footman who opened the outer door for her to the street.

She ran outside and rested her hands on her knees as she gasped for breath. Her father would cast her to the street for embarrassing him this night.

No matter what punishment he chose for her, Isobel was certain he would never allow her to show her face in Town again.

And Lord Sterling, the wicked Marquess of Sinclair, was wholly to blame.

At Avon Books, we know your passion for romance—once you finish one of our novels, you find yourself wanting more.

May we tempt you with . . .

- **Excerpts** from our upcoming releases.

- Entertaining **extras**, including authors' personal photo albums and book lists.

- Behind-the-scenes **scoop** on your favorite characters and series.

- **Sweepstakes** for the chance to win free books, romantic getaways, and other fun prizes.

- Writing **tips** from our authors and editors.

- **Blog** with our authors and find out why they love to write romance.

- **Exclusive content** that's not contained within the pages of our novels.

Join us at
www.avonbooks.com

An Imprint of HarperCollins*Publishers*
www.avonromance.com

Available wherever books are sold or please call 1-800-331-3761 to order.

FTH 0708